APOCRYPHA

APOCRYPHA ACT I

HENRY DOES

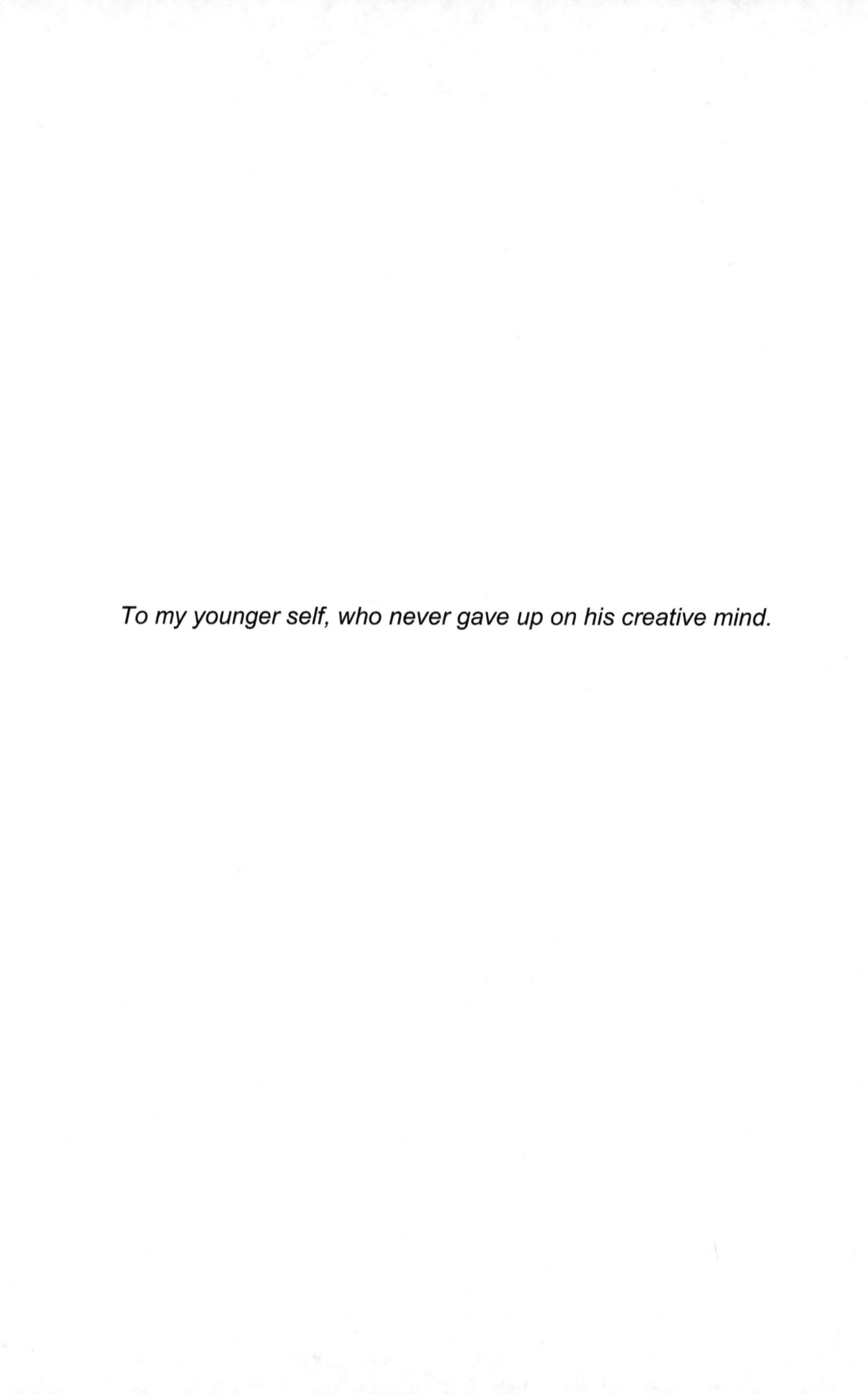

To my younger self, who never gave up on his creative mind.

TABLE OF CONTENTS

PROLOGUE

"We've been climbing through these mountains for two days. All I've seen so far is snow and more snow," Eliot complained.

The snowstorm began that morning, making the ascent challenging ever since. She wasn't surprised by Eliot's complaints; he was only fifteen years old and tended to grumble about everything back at camp. If he hadn't been so insistent, she wouldn't have allowed him to join. Nevertheless, having a companion on this journey seemed a wise decision, and she was grateful for any assistance available.

She saw that the terrain ahead levelled out once more.

Also, the sound of the snowstorm began to subside. "Just a few more steps, Eliot. I can see that the climb will be over soon. After that, we can take a break for a while," she said.

Once they finished climbing, they discovered a sheltered spot surrounded by trees where they could rest. She went to collect a few sticks while Eliot set out to hunt for food. He had a reputation as a skilled hunter.

She returned first with some sticks and rocks to prepare a fireplace. She didn't light too many sticks, preferring a dim light. It wasn't as if they were hiding, and there was little chance of someone seeing them in such a desolate place. However, she was always cautious, a trait she had learned since childhood from others.

"Marli, we're having rabbit for lunch," said Eliot as he returned, holding a rabbit.

She observed as Eliot began preparing the rabbit for cooking, skewering the meat on sticks and placing them near the fire.

They both settled around the fireplace, waiting for their food to cook.

"Don't gaze at the fire for too long, Eliot. Even looking at the flames can be dangerous," she warned playfully.

He grinned and said, "This little fire won't burn us. And if it did, I'm sure you could handle it."

She glanced at the fire again. "There was a time when even a modest fire like this would cause terror in people's eyes. I'm not so certain I would've survived those times," she reflected.

Noticing her piece of meat was ready, she grabbed a stick and started chewing on the flavourless meat. It wasn't gourmet, but having some food in her mouth was satisfying. Eliot had also started eating.

"You're referring to the War of Ashes?" Eliot inquired between bites.

"Yes, the war that occurred over six hundred years ago and supposedly lasted for fifty years. Did you know that during that time, we were in the Age of Ashes? After the War of Ashes, the surviving nations decided to rename it the Age of Reborn. Due to the devastation caused during the Age of Ashes, humanity rebuilt the Lower Lands—hence the name Reborn. Although, some lands were completely lost. Some books claim that two other continents existed, the Upper Lands and the Middle Lands, but they were lost beneath the ocean," Marli explained.

"I had no idea about the Age of Reborn. The old witch didn't mention that," Eliot remarked.

She realised she might have shared too much. "Don't worry, those perilous times are long gone. The deity of the Shabrani clan, Shabranibodoo, who started the War of Ashes, was defeated," she reassured.

"We all know that. But nobody knows how those witches brought their lord into the world. Do gods live among us, or do they come from a different realm?" he mused.

Meeting Eliot's curious gaze, she sensed she had indeed divulged too much. Once Eliot began his inquiries, it was challenging to dissuade him.

"Look, what we know is that the Shabrani Witches paid a terrible price for bringing their deity to this world. After the War of Ashes concluded, all the witches' councils unanimously agreed not to repeat the same mistake. For over five hundred years, we have lived in relative peace. There's no reason to think..." she trailed off, remembering the facade of peace among them could be a lie.

"Maybe we'll find more information in those manuscripts we're carrying. Perhaps they'll tell us if there were other gods before the War of Ashes," said Eliot, pointing to the bags they carried filled with manuscripts.

She glanced at the bags containing the manuscripts, wishing there was an alternative method of translation. "I hope so. Regardless, it's a task that was handed down to me. You're here simply because you won't leave me alone. Now, let's continue our journey; we've rested enough," she said.

The path ahead was less challenging than before, with no more mountains to climb. However, the persistent snow and cold wind were slowing them down. She wondered if they would ever reach their destination. It was known that others had ventured this way before and never returned. Before the Dragani clan was decimated, their Great Council sent groups of experienced witches in pairs or trios to find the translators. Now, with their numbers drastically reduced, only one witch was sent: her.

"So, the original transcripts are safer back at the Frostwild Towns?" Eliot inquired.

She signalled for Eliot to refrain from speaking while they walked, emphasising the need to conserve energy. However, the inquisitive Eliot paid little attention.

"The originals are well-secured. Since we don't understand the language, we've been trying to replicate the symbols on parchment and bring them to this part of the Lower Lands, searching for translators. A prophecy once said the translators could be found in the Glacier Crown," she explained, glancing at Eliot, who was listening intently.

"Whoa! I can't wait to find out what they say once we translate them," he exclaimed.

His enthusiasm struck her as a bit odd. "You do realise that if we don't find translators in these mountains, we might succumb to the cold or become bear food, right?" she warned.

Eliot responded with a big smile, "My life is more exciting than ever now. I wouldn't change it for anything, not even if there's a good chance of death."

"You are very peculiar, Eliot," she remarked.

They continued walking for some time. The night was approaching, and she contemplated stopping to find refuge. However, as foretold by the old witch, there was nowhere safe to seek refuge from the snow ahead. She decided to press on a bit more; she had no other choice.

After a while, the weather remained harsh. The cold wind stung her face, and night descended upon them. The moon hung in the sky, with some visible clouds.

Eliot stopped and went down on one knee. "I'm okay. I just, I just need to catch my breath," Eliot said weakly.

I should've left him back at camp, she thought. *This is too overwhelming for him.* She paused and glanced around. *Perhaps it's too much for me as well*, she reflected.

She pulled Eliot up and continued walking.

She didn't know how long she walked; it seemed to her it could have been only a few moments or years. Eliot finally gave up and lay on the snow, shivering from the cold. She still had energy to keep going. With her mission in mind, she understood the importance of pushing forward to find the translators, whether or not Eliot accompanied her. She considered abandoning him to his fate, yet found herself unable to do so.

A bit of magic won't hurt, she thought.

With the remaining energy she had, she made Eliot levitate and continued moving forward.

"Verily, thou art bold to weave enchantments in this place. Dost thou not fear the Great Conclave?" she heard a whisper in the wind.

The snowstorm suddenly stopped, and in front of her stood a man covered in black clothes. His face was the only body part uncovered. He was bald and painted in white.

"A witch hailing from a venerable lineage, nearly extinguished from the realms. Others akin to thee hath ventured into the Glacier Crown in quest of translators. The manuscripts thou dost carry, doth recount a tale of terror, blood, and fiery tumult," said the man, speaking in an ancient manner.

His voice grated on her ears, and the way he spoke made her nervous and scared. She sensed something else within the man—magic, which she knew was deemed impossible for men.

"I have been given the task to translate these manuscripts. I must find the translators. Are you one of them?" she asked.

The strange man approached her, causing her to slowly step backward. The man's presence and magic were overwhelming.

"Yes, I can lead thee unto them. Yet, thou must first undergo a trial, a test whereof none hath e'er prevailed. Wilt thou, my dear witch, accept this challenge?," he asked with a dreadful tone.

She took a look around; even though the storm had stopped, she could only see rock and ice. There was nowhere to go. Besides, she had committed to helping Eliot survive.

"Let's begin," she said.

DEMORIA

Year 600 after the War of Ashes.
The Age of Prosperity.

As she lay on her bed, trying to sleep, new and random thoughts invaded her mind, preventing any chance of drifting off. *These thoughts are going to be the end of me*, she complained. Tossing and turning, she attempted various tactics—counting, clearing her mind—but nothing seemed to work.

Unable to find sleep with her heart racing, Demoria contemplated the possibility of this being a sign, as others had suggested. She wished these signs would come at a more convenient hour. Giving in to her thoughts, she abandoned the idea of sleep and rose from the bed.

Peeking out of her tent, she hoped for a distraction—perhaps a passing animal. Yet, there was no movement. All she could see were the other tents belonging to fellow witches. She glanced up at the sky, noticing how dark it had become. The moon was barely visible through the thick clouds. She briefly considered stepping out for a walk but decided against it.

The darkness outside seems too thick to be walking around, she thought.

As she continued to peer outside, she noticed a shadow drawing near.

"I'm surprised you're awake, Demoria. You've been summoned by the Great Council. They expect you at the Crimson Castle," said the shadowy figure.

Now? I've only just returned from a mission. They usually call upon us after some breath from such tasks, she thought.

"I'll be there shortly. Thank you," Demoria replied.

Though she couldn't identify the shadowy figure, she knew it was a witch of rank one, often serving as messengers while completing their training.

She vividly recalled her days as a novice witch when she had to deliver messages at any hour, which was truly draining. There was nothing more demoralising than being scolded for rousing more powerful witches from their slumber. That's precisely why she didn't take it to heart when messengers brought news; after all, they were simply messengers. Some other witches tended to forget their own humble beginnings. *It's just the way the world operates*, she thought.

Demoria changed into a more suitable robe, opting for a red robe adorned with purple ornaments and flat shoes. Glancing in the mirror, she noticed her long, thick black hair was untidy, and she quickly ran a comb through it. She rinsed her mouth with lemon juice and spritzed a fragrance that carried hints of wood and lavender, her favourite scent. Over the years, she had learned to present herself well when facing the Great Council. *They scrutinise every detail*, she remembered.

The journey from her tent to the Crimson Castle wasn't a particularly long walk. Though she could have ridden, she opted for a stroll instead. The scenery was limited, mainly consisting of her sisters' tents. Occasionally, a rabbit or two would walk by.

The night sky was enveloped in a dense darkness, making it difficult to see far ahead. She pondered, *Has the volcano spewed smoke again?*

After walking for a while, she spotted distant lights emanating from torches positioned in front of the Crimson Castle. Even in the night, the silhouette of the Crimson Castle appeared imposingly large. As she drew nearer, she discerned more shadowy figures lurking in the darkness, likely more witches gathered near the castle.

She walked into an area where the tents stood larger and boasted superior quality. This particular section was designated for witches ranked three and four to reside in. Despite being a witch of rank three herself, Demoria chose to dwell among those of rank one. She found it quieter there, away from the more pretentious witches.

The rank one witches were typically gentler and more reserved, which suited her preference. There was hardly any drama in her life among the rank one witches, at least not while she was in camp.

She noticed the approach of morning as the sky gradually brightened. The emerging light also unveiled the massive figure looming behind the Crimson Castle: the volcano, Dukkah. Though now dormant, the volcano sporadically emitted dark smoke due to its nature, making it challenging for life to thrive in these lands and causing breathing difficulties for strangers. Shabrani Witches, on the other hand, were accustomed to the smoke.

For the witches of Shabrani, the volcano held historical significance. Since ancient times, it had been tied to their fiery magic specialties. Demoria, however, doubted the truth of this association, as she had never personally felt any such connection. Other witches described this link vividly, but she dismissed it as a ploy for favouritism from those in higher ranks. Even Demoria's own mentor believed that such a connection was non-existent.

Upon nearing the castle, she noticed a handful of other witches. Generally, the Shabrani Witches tended not to be very sociable, except when they desired something. Demoria wasn't an exception; she favoured solitude and keeping herself occupied. Since attaining her third rank, she had been scarcely present within the Shabrani clan. Her time was predominantly consumed by missions and travelling across different nations.

At last, she arrived at the black doors of the Crimson Castle, doors that remained perpetually open, whether day or night. The Shabrani Witches were known for their ceaseless dedication to their craft. As she approached, she noticed some of her sisters stationed at the entrance, all clad in black attire with hoods drawn over their heads.

If I ever become a member of the Great Council, I'll propose they remove those hoods, she contemplated. *I despise not being able to see the person I'm speaking to.*

The two witches at the entrance greeted her, "Please declare your name, rank, and reason for visiting the castle."

"I'm Demoria, rank three. I've been summoned by the Great Council," she responded.

The shorter witch on the left spoke, "Demoria, we've been instructed to grant you access. The Great Council awaits you in the Red Tower. If you possess teleportation skills, you may utilise them once inside the castle."

These rank ones think I don't know teleportation when I am rank three? she thought to herself. Demoria glanced at the witch, nodded in acknowledgement, and continued walking.

Within the confines of the Crimson Castle, she found herself in the main hall. Hundreds of candles illuminated the space, which was perpetually lit. Statues of witches adorned each corner, while the walls were adorned with pictures of landscapes from all over the Lower Lands. A prominent painting hung on the main wall—a close-up view of the Dukkah volcano from above. Demoria speculated, *who could have painted this from such a perspective? It must be a forgery.*

Mastering teleportation was an intricate skill for witches; its use was limited to short distances within visible range. However, a misstep could lead to dire consequences, such as being ensnared within the earth or confined within a wall. Incidents had occurred in the past—rank one witches disappearing and later discovered buried within the walls of the Crimson Castle after months, and sometimes even years. When eventually found, they were nothing but skeletons, a haunting testament to the dangers of mishandling this sort of magic.

She stretched out her arm towards the tallest tower and murmured, "To the Red Tower." A blue light enveloped her, and suddenly, the surroundings shifted. The main hall vanished, replaced by an old wooden door standing before her. It was a door she knew well, having visited it numerous times recently. *The entrance to the Great Council chamber*, she realised.

She turned the doorknob and stepped inside, discovering the members of the Great Council assembled within. They were all cloaked in hoods, concealing their faces, gathered around a substantial fire pit. The chamber had various tables with a modest spread of cheese, grapes, and cups of wine.

What a feast, she remarked silently to herself.

"Demoria, please come in. We've been expecting you, and there's much to discuss. Sisters, let us commence," spoke one of the witches, her voice heavy with age. In the context of Shabrani Witches, being *old* implied a minimum age of two hundred years.

One of the witches stepped forward and declared, "A raven has brought alarming news. The members of the Great Conclave have been killed."

Another witch, notably the shortest among them, stepped forward and added, "We lack details at the moment, but we anticipate receiving more information in the coming days."

The news was indeed distressing. The Great Conclave was an ancient order overseeing the behaviour of all witch clans. They preferred to remain hidden, always operating in the shadows. In fact, she had never encountered a member of this secretive group. Only the Great Council of her clan enjoyed that privilege. With their reported demise, she had two pressing questions: *Who would now prevent significant conflicts between witch clans, and who could be responsible for the conclave's demise?*

Another witch spoke, "We understand you must have questions, but for now, we request that you keep this news a secret. Following the reception of this distressing information, the Flame of Eldoria spoke to us, Demoria. A new quest awaits you, one with a time limit that we believe is connected to the assassination of the Great Conclave. Listen carefully," Demoria recognized the voice as her master, Lenithia.

"Go to Duskenwood and find the crying river. In twenty-one days, at sunset behind the tallest mountain, you'll encounter a man. Bring back his left arm," the witch instructed before falling silent. All eyes seemed to turn towards her, their gaze fixated, as if waiting for her reaction.

"Do you have any questions?" inquired another witch, her voice laden with age. "We understand this is a very odd quest. The flame has spoken, and we trust you shall fulfil this request."

She had several questions regarding the demise of the Great Conclave, but she knew they would not provide answers. She assumed the only reason for sharing the distressing news was to increase the pressure on her shoulders to fulfil her new quest.

"None. I shall depart at once," responded Demoria firmly.

As she prepared to take her leave, the familiar voice of her master resounded once more. "A word of advice. Duskenwood remains unknown even to us members of the Great Council. Be cautious, Demoria, for a mere man would not typically inhabit those lands."

Demoria nodded and replied, "Understood. With your permission, I shall leave now." The other witches granted her permission to depart, and thus she exited the Great Council room.

As she made her way out, she paused to survey the land from the vantage point of the Red Tower. Standing among the four tallest towers in the castle, the Red Tower afforded her a sweeping view of most of Gorgon's territory. With morning fast approaching, the landscape became clearer, revealing the numerous tents sprawled across the land, allocated for the Shabrani Witches' use.

Unlike other witch clans, none of the witches laid claim to a specific piece of land; they shared the territory. Consequently, they resided in tents, providing flexibility for missions or relocations. Upon returning from a mission, they'd find accommodation among their fellow sisters in the clan. The privilege of residing closer to the castle was granted to witches of ranks three and four, while those of rank one inhabited the outskirts of the land.

Demoria often viewed the rank one witches as shields; in the event of an invasion, they would likely face the initial impact. However, she doubted any other nation or witch clan would be foolish enough to attempt such an act. The reputation of the Shabrani Witches as formidable and not to be trifled with was well-known.

She reappeared in the main hall through teleportation.

To her surprise, faint rays of light filtered into the main hall, likely the extent of sunlight for the day. *The dense, dark clouds blanketing the land of Gorgon often deprives us of sunlight for days on end, but today seems to be an exception*, she thought.

"Wait!" Someone grabbed her arm. "Off on another adventure, sister?" asked a witch with short black hair, dressed in a black robe adorned with a red ribbon tied around her waist.

"Mila, is that you? It's been a while," replied Demoria. "Yes, duty calls. I just descended from the Red Tower. The Oracle and the Great Council have given their instructions."

"Oh, what a pity! I was hoping to catch up on our lives. It's been too long. There's so much to discuss. Tell me, are you still considered the finest witch in the Shabrani clan?"

Demoria chuckled. "Careful, sister. The older witches might overhear you and demote you back to rank one for spreading falsehoods." This was a reputation that often preceded Demoria. She had ascended to rank three swiftly, a feat that hadn't occurred in a century, as per the historian witch, Calcia. While Demoria was flattered by such assumptions, she never felt genuine pride about it. There was a hollow feeling within her, as if she didn't deserve the acclaim. She couldn't quite comprehend why.

"I don't have much time, but tell me about you, Mila. Where were you last?" inquired Demoria.

Mila intertwined her arm with Demoria's, guiding her out of the Crimson Castle. "I've been on a few journeys. A fat rich lord from Silverstone hired us to investigate one of the Frostwild Towns suspected of being under the influence of a Dragani witch, causing the town to halt tax payments," Mila narrated, taking a deep breath. "It took more than a week to reach that grim place—the terrain was rugged, and the harsh cold made it even more challenging. However, upon my arrival, I discovered it wasn't a Dragani witch's control but a town torn by internal strife. The people were in conflict, contending to overthrow the town's bailiff. The chaos led to their cessation of tax payments."

Demoria couldn't help but smile and let out a chuckle. "So, what did you do? Let me guess. Knowing you, you either joined the chaos or disposed of the fat lord."

"Sister! Anyone listening to you might take you seriously," Mila responded in a jesting tone. "I put the entire town into slumber and collected enough money to cover their taxes for the next three years. That appeased the lord, and our mission was accomplished."

"Good job, sister. Our Great Council might've been content," praised Demoria.

Mila chuckled. "You know them. They just said, 'Wait for the next mission.' I'm starting to think they view us as their weapons," she said sarcastically.

"You never change, sister. I'll be away for a few days. Hopefully, I'll see you upon my return," said Demoria.

"I hope so too, sister. I intend to stay put for a while. The last mission left me drained and exhausted. I've heard our sister Ophelia was dispatched south of the Golden Nation on a special quest. You know how she is with her unique abilities. Her magic is popular, thus we rarely see her," said Mila.

Demoria reflected on her friendship with Ophelia, recalling their strong bond since childhood. Mila's observation was accurate—Ophelia's unique talents often kept her distant, working in other locations. Ophelia possessed an unparalleled skill in transmogrification, the ability to transform into someone else. It was a gift beyond the reach of Shabrani Witches, but Ophelia had mastered it expertly.

"Ophelia, the hungry," she reminisced with a giggle. "That's what we used to call her back in our training days. She was never satisfied," she said

"I hope the three of us can catch up soon. I must go, sister," said Mila, bidding her farewell.

Demoria bid goodbye to Mila, parting ways.

"Demoria!!" echoed a voice, startling her. She turned to see a scroll hurtling toward her, which she dexterously caught. "I stumbled upon this during my last quest, purely by chance. I have no idea of its nature. I trust a skilled witch like you will discern its purpose. Best of luck, sister," said Mila before departing.

She examined the small scroll, bound with a thin black thread, and took it with her to her tent. She began making preparations to leave, deciding to inspect the scroll further. Once she was ready, she unfurled the scroll, and a sense of magic emanated from it. Inside was a mysterious glyph, unfamiliar to her. She hesitated briefly, wondering if it could be a trap. *What was Mila thinking? Nonetheless, it's intriguing. I'll take it along*, she thought.

As the day waned and the clouds veiled the sun more thoroughly, a sense of unease settled within her regarding her new mission. Despite her misgivings, she remained resolute. "Whatever it may be, I will succeed," she said.

THE BLOOD PRIEST

He found himself in a village recently ravaged by barbarians, who had left behind a trail of death and despair. The scent of death was strong, but he had grown accustomed to it. *Bodies littered the streets—children, adults—lives taken for what? A mere bit of coin,* the old man reflected. It was a recurring pattern throughout his travels.

This time, his journey had brought him to a small settlement south of the Rockshade Highlands, a region known for its scattered villages. The rugged mountains provided ideal cover but offered no refuge when raids struck. The Blood Witches he served often sent him to towns or villages devastated by natural disasters or attacks from thieves and barbarians, leaving dead bodies in their wake. How his masters knew of the towns' misfortunes remained a mystery to him. However, he had learned that the Blood Witches' instructions were always accurate, and this place was no exception.

The village had no survivors. He passed through several places—the inn, the stables, and the blacksmith's dwelling—where the overpowering stench of death hung thick in the air. Everywhere he turned, there was only devastation and ruin. As he walked among the village's remains, he recalled his assignment. "Find intact corpses, children or men, and load your cart with them," the Blood Witches had instructed him.

Looking around, scattered in every corner lay piles of human bodies, many charred beyond recognition. *These are unsuitable,* he thought. Among the ruins, he found bodies missing limbs—arms, legs, or even headless. *None would serve the witches' purposes,* he thought. He wandered, examining one lifeless body after another, only to discover that this time the barbarians had left no corpses unscathed.

He often wondered why the witches demanded the bodies be flawless; even the slightest imperfection rendered them useless for their purposes. Once, he had brought corpses missing eyes and tongues. "We asked for only one thing: flawless corpses. Our task is divine. You must not toy with us," the Blood Witches had reprimanded.

The witches ordered five lashes.

"Please, have mercy! I've never failed you before, I didn't realise, forgive me!" he pleaded.

Yet, five lashes were administered, scorching his back and searing it as though it were raw meat. Then, they cast him into a dungeon.

By the third day of his imprisonment—or so he believed—his health began to decline. His wounds festered, hunger and thirst gnawed at him, and the sole sustenance available was rats and rainwater. Suddenly, he beheld a white figure drawing near, radiant and luminous.

"As the figure approached, it revealed itself to be a woman—fair and tall, dressed entirely in white, seemingly hovering above the ground. As she came closer, her features grew clear: black eyes, as deep as the darkest night, long wavy blue hair, a black crown resting on her forehead, and a face that appeared no older than twenty. She also seemed taller than any human, with proportions far larger than anyone he had ever known."

"My Blood Priest, it doth grieve me to behold thy distress. Thou must forgive the others. Our duty is of divine origin; there is no space for errancy," she spoke to him in an archaic manner. Then, she extended her hand and unlocked the cell door. "Step forth anon, my Blood Priest. Accompany me, and resume thy task," the woman leaned in and kissed him on the mouth as he closed his eyes.

Her touch created a surge of energy that coursed through his entire being, miraculously healing his wounds and quelling his hunger and thirst. *This is witchery*, he mused. With that, she led him out of the dungeons. Beyond the dungeon walls, the world remained shrouded in darkness, yet her companion's radiance brought warmth, akin to a small sun.

"Who are you? Are you a goddess?" he inquired.

"I am hither in quest of one—or rather, one amongst many," the woman responded. His mind didn't fully grasp her words or their meaning.

After that encounter, he never saw her again. The Blood Witches' camp sprawled over a vast area. At its centre stood the core of the clan, surrounded by barriers made of human bones. He was forbidden from entering this sacred place, though he was certain it was where his saviour resided. The bodies he delivered were also taken to this forbidden area.

"Someday, I will uncover their purpose for the corpses. Someday, I will encounter her again," he vowed to himself.

Despite exhaustive searches, he found no usable bodies. Almost at the brink of despair, a sound emanated from one of the few houses yet standing. *Someone's alive*, he smiled. Slowly, he approached the house from where the noise originated.

"I know you're in there. There's no danger here. I'm a priest, and I've come to offer help. Come out, and I'll lead you to safety," he called out.

Silence lingered for a few moments. Then, a voice responded, "How we know you ain't with those savages?"

We? His smile broadened. "I am alone and I am no warrior. I'm here to aid as many survivors as possible."

"Who sent ya? We ain't comin' out 'til you show some proof," the unknown voice demanded.

"Here," he said, fibbing as he presented a golden medallion, supposedly a symbol from the Golden Nation. "They've dispatched me," he lied.

As soon as he spoke, an elderly man and two children emerged from the house. The old man wore a tattered brown shirt and weathered leather pants, along with boots so decrepit they were peeling all over. His face was smeared with blood, perhaps from a skirmish or an injury. The two children, covered in dirt and mud, appeared no older than ten—one a boy and the other a girl.

He retrieved a piece of bread from his bag, extending it to the children who seized and devoured it hungrily—evidently famished from days without a proper meal. The elderly man also had a small piece of bread.

"The Golden Nation sent folks to help us—the ones who ain't got much. Did they come with an army?" the elderly man asked.

"I haven't received any information about an army's arrival in this region. Do not fear—I'm certain His Majesty, the King, is resolute in eliminating the barbarian threat from these lands," he lied again.

"Hallelujah for the Golden King and Queen! I'm Truinan, and these youngsters here—the boy is Searc, and she is Caitrin—I saved them when the savages attacked our village. What do folks call you, mister?" Truinan inquired.

He paused momentarily. Encountering survivors during his travels was uncommon; he'd never had reason to divulge his true name. Yet, seeing no harm, he disclosed his real name. "My name is Alabaster. I've come to escort you to the Golden Nation, where you'll find refuge under His Majesty's protection," he lied once more.

Alabaster—I had nearly forgotten that name, he thought. A pang of nostalgia swept over him, reminding him of his former life as a Balor priest in Duran, the capital city of Silverstone. He had been beloved in Duran, a trusted confidant to all who sought solace, serving as a priest for the deity Trobalor.

Balor priests were known as men who sought spiritual guidance and protection from the god Trobalor, a deity revered by many, especially in Silverstone. Witch clans didn't have direct involvement with priests, as men couldn't wield magic. However, it was known that some priests were appointed by witch clans to spread the teachings of their lords. Such was the case for Alabaster; in his early thirties, he had ventured into the Dark Forest to join the Balor clan for employment. Initially relegated to menial tasks such as cleaning and kitchen duties, after persistent efforts, he ascended into the ranks of the Order of Balor Priests—a cohort of men within the Balor witch clan trained to spread the teachings of Trobalor across villages, towns, and nations.

Balor Priests' teaching tool was the Book of Trobalor which contained primarily revelations, recitations, and songs. Alabaster, for a time, ardently believed in Trobalor's words. Its message spoke of salvation and love—a sentiment he desired. At the same time, he recognized the witches' ambition to expand their influence, which is why they trained priests to spread their message to all corners of the Lower Lands.

Upon his investiture as a Balor priest, he was sent to the northern outskirts of Silverstone, to the capital city of Duran. Situated near the Sea of Casda, Duran, though modest, was known for its beauty and abundant fish and wildlife. The Balor clan capitalised on these resources for trade and even erected a church for him. He lived contentedly there for several years, during which many significant events unfolded.

He fell in love and welcomed a son. The three of them found happiness residing within the church until that terrible night when his family was ripped away from him. Alabaster, not a warrior, could do nothing to defend his newfound family. He didn't know how but he promised to seek revenge on his family's assassin. The assassins, cloaked in black animal fur—possibly wolf or bear—had sharp objects attached to their wrists. It was too dark to distinguish what, or even who, they were. That dark night altered Alabaster irreversibly; he ceased preaching Trobalor's words to the people of Duran, embittered by their inaction in aiding his family's defence.

At the same time, another coven of witches arrived in Duran, pledging to locate the perpetrators behind the murders of his wife and son. This marked his entry into service for the Blood Witches. He forged a contract with them, bound by blood and not easily severed by conventional means. For ten years, he was obligated to serve them. After fulfilling his tenure, in exchange, the witches promised to disclose the assassin's whereabouts. His determination had been strong at the start, even though the tasks commanded by the Blood Witches were unconventional. Over time, however, he struggled to comply with their demands. At times, he regretted the day he accepted the witches' pact, feeling his humanity slowly slip away.

"Now, it's time we depart. These lands are perilous; the barbarians could return anytime. We must leave swiftly," urged Alabaster.

"We can't leave yet. We need to find Aliune," said young Searc.

"We ain't got time for this nonsense, lad! Ain't you listenin' to the priest? Those savages who took your kin will be comin' back for you if we don't leave now," Truinan angrily interjected.

"Who is this Aliune? Could it be another survivor?" he inquired.

"Aliune is my cat, but not just any cat. She's the goddess of the moon, she once told me. We have to save her, sir, please. Searc and I won't leave until we find her," Caitrin pleaded, nearly in tears, tugging at his hand.

Though he was tempted to dismiss the childish plea, a part of him wanted to help the children. Perhaps they reminded him of his own son. "Look at that tall pike to the south," he said, pointing. "Once the sun touches it, that's all the time we have to find your pet. After that, we must leave. Understood?" he added calmly, a smile crossing his face.

Both children nodded. They scoured their surroundings, searching under stones, amidst rubble, and even near the heap of human corpses. He learned that Searc was twelve years old and Caitrin was eight. Truinan, the elderly man, had been a close friend of their parents. During the barbarian attack, the children's father had entrusted Truinan with their safety while he joined the village men to confront the invaders.

The villagers couldn't resist the barbarians for long, enduring mere minutes against the barbarian might. The barbarians ravaged the village, killing and assaulting the women they encountered. Truinan sheltered the children and their mother in his house.

When the barbarians arrived, the wife sacrificed herself, succumbing to a sword's blow. Truinan, witnessing the grisly scene, hid himself while the barbarians committed their atrocities, shielding the children from the full horror. He refrained from telling them their parents' fate, though they harboured suspicions. Searc, showing courage, urged his sister not to cry, though both mourned for hours after the barbarians had left. Alabaster reflected on this tragic event. Knowing that more suffering awaited the elderly man and the children, he felt he had no choice but to comply with the Blood Witches' demands.

"I found her! She's here, please help me!" Searc said out loud. Listening carefully, he noticed the cat cries coming from beneath a pile of stones that had collapsed from one of the ruined houses. The cat sounded injured. Together, they unearthed her and found a wound on her left hind leg. He pulled a piece of cloth from his satchel and carefully bandaged the injury.

"This will help heal the wound," he said, as he bandaged the cat's injury and provided some bread and water for the animal.

"Time to get going," said Truinan.

"Thank you, sir. You are a true hero," Caitrin said tearfully to Alabaster, who smiled back at the little girl.

"I'm so happy we found you. You and Caitrin are the only family we have now. I'll protect you with my life," Searc said to the cat, then urged his sister to take charge of the feline.

The children and Truinan gathered a few useful items they found among the village ruins: satchels, water bags, hard cheese salvaged from the remnants of a communal kitchen, pieces of clothing, and a few daggers.

"These will work," said Truinan, distributing a dagger to each kid.

"In case of an emergency, use it if you must. Use the sharp end," Truinan advised. Searc accepted the dagger, but his sister, Caitrin, was frightened by it.

"I'll take Caitrin's dagger. Two are better than one, right, friend?" Searc said to him. As he glanced at the boy, he couldn't shake the feeling of guilt for what the future held for the children and Truinan.

There's no turning back. If I don't deliver the three of you to the witches, they'll never help me find my family's assassins, he thought.

"Yes, of course. You'll be a brave warrior when you grow up. The Golden King will surely make a fine captain out of you," he assured the boy, who smiled proudly.

The trio followed him to his wagon, which was parked at the village's entrance. The wagon, robustly constructed from steel and wood, was drawn by a mature brown horse.

"This is Brave Legs. He's accompanied me on many adventures. Though aged, he's still swift. That's how he earned his name," he explained, hiding the fact that he had named the horse after it aided his escape from a town north of the Golden Nation. The townspeople had turned hostile toward him after he searched for bodies in their graveyard.

The wagon was laden with various supplies, with a designated space left for corpses—a detail he also chose not to disclose.

"There's space at the back for the three of you. I'll walk alongside Brave Legs," he said.

They complied without complaint, except for the cat, who hissed at him whenever possible. *Animals sense intent, they say. No surprise there—the cat knows I'm sending them to their demise*, he thought.

"The Golden Nation camp lies to the east. It'll take at least five days of riding to reach it. Please make yourselves comfortable and let me know if you need anything," he said.

Their expressions radiated euphoria, as if they'd won a fortune. *It's only natural—they think I've saved them. If hell exists, there's surely a special place reserved for me, he mused.*

BASON

Since childhood, he had lived a life of privilege. Growing up as a member of the royal family in the Golden Nation, he was accustomed to having anything he desired at his beck and call. All he needed to do was utter a request, and servants would promptly fulfil it. The Golden Nation had fostered a culture where serving the royal family was a deeply ingrained tradition, and this unwavering loyalty was one of the reasons why the nation was successful in many aspects. In addition, poverty was virtually nonexistent. Even those responsible for menial tasks such as cleaning the privy were generously compensated for their work. The populace adored living in this prosperous land, which attributed to its reputation as the most influential and beloved nation among all.

Things were not always as they were now. During the War of Ashes, the Golden Nation was known as the Last Nation. It was a city constructed to act as the final bastion in defence of the world against Shabranibodoo, a deity whose presence in the Lower Lands wrought widespread devastation and death six hundred years ago. In a united effort, the remaining witches from all clans and the dwindling forces of men rallied together to vanquish Shabranibodoo. Following the deity's defeat, the city of Solaris was hastily erected. Many courageous individuals chose to remain in the city, while others ventured forth to reconstruct the cities they had lost.

Among all the clans of witches, only the Starr Witches remained in the nation after the war. This alliance marked the only known pact in the world between witches and men. They renamed the land as the Golden Nation, ambitiously expanding its borders to new limits. Their pledge was to honour and safeguard the less privileged by providing substantial wages to all who remained loyal to the nation. And thus, the Golden Nation was established.

"It's time for my morning training routine, Recaro, Valecio!" Bason's voice reverberated through the lavish estate as he called out.

"My lord, we have brought your armour and prepared your first meal before training: poached eggs, bacon, and bread, along with a serving of orange juice," Recaro said respectfully.

"Would you prefer to have your breakfast here, or would you rather enjoy it outside on the balcony?" Valecio inquired courteously.

Bason's room was spacious enough to accommodate twenty beds. Most of his furniture, including the plates and cups, boasted a lavish gold finish. Opening onto a sizable balcony adorned with flowers of various colours, his room offered a picturesque view of the capital city of Solaris. In a shaded corner of the balcony, a small, elegant table accompanied by a chair faced the morning sun. It was his routine to have breakfast in this serene spot most mornings.

"Set up my breakfast on the balcony. Afterward, I'll need assistance donning my armour," he said to his two servants.

His servants acknowledged his instructions and promptly began preparing his breakfast. Draping a white silk robe over his bare brown skin, Bason strolled out to the balcony. At twenty-four, he had smooth skin and shoulder-length blond, curly hair, with a fit build and average stature.

Recaro, twenty-one, with brown skin, dark hair, and a skinny build, and Valecio, twenty-eight, with olive skin, blonde hair, and a muscular build, had been his servants since childhood. They shared an intimate bond with him that, on occasion, extended to sharing beds.. Bason had always been self-assured about his preferences. From a young age, he leaned more toward an affinity for boys than girls, though his inclinations shifted at times. In the Golden Nation, the freedom to choose one's affections, regardless of gender, was celebrated.

Occasionally, Bason indulged in mind games with his two servants. He would take one on outings to the capital for days, leaving the other behind at Solaris Castle, intentionally creating tension between them, which sometimes escalated into quarrels. Once, Valecio's jealousy led him to confine Recaro in his quarters, seeking exclusive time with Bason. This infuriated Recaro, who responded with death threats against Valecio.

Feigning anger, Bason threatened to dismiss them both if their squabbles continued. Instead, he resolved the conflict by reconciling them through an intimate moment.

What a tumultuous relationship I've created here, he thought.

"Shall we play a little game? If either of you can provide an answer that satisfies my curiosity, I'll treat you to a day out," he said to his servants, noting their blushing yet eager expressions.

"Surely you've heard various stories about why the Fire Lord, Shabranibodoo, arrived in our world. What's your take on it?" he inquired, noticing his servants exchange confused glances.

"Oh, don't be shy. I understand these tales have been circulating for generations, blurring the actual truth," he said, emphasising how loosely these stories had been told.

"My lord, this is a tale I heard from my mother's uncle," said Valecio, closing his eyes briefly before continuing. "The story goes that Shabranibodoo, the deity of the Shabrani Witches, descended to our world in search of a powerful object hidden within these lands. In his quest, he destroyed the two continents that existed before the Age of Reborn—the Upper Lands and the Middle Lands—searching for this object. Legend has it that this object would grant him and his witches limitless power, enabling them to conquer both our world and hell itself."

"A familiar theory, one that isn't as far-fetched as some others I've come across. What do you think, Recaro?" he inquired, expressing interest in Recaro's opinion.

Recaro made a mocking sound that almost sounded endearing. "My lord, this is a belief held by common folk from other nations. The Golden Nation, however, holds different insights."

He raised an eyebrow. "Go on," he said.

"The bond between witches and men was formidable. Shabranibodoo, feeling threatened, emerged from hell to eradicate them. However, he underestimated the strength of the Golden

Nation during the Age of Ashes," explained Recaro, detailing the historical events.

During the Age of Ages? he thought. He was about to have a taste of fun with Recaro.

"I hope you're not suggesting that the Golden Nation has lost its worth, are you? I doubt my father, the king, would appreciate a servant in the castle harbouring such thoughts," he said, subtly hinting at the potential repercussions of such sentiments.

"Forgive me, my lord. I didn't mean to imply that. It was a regrettable choice of words on my part," expressed Recaro, displaying a sense of remorse for his statement.

He sighed deeply. "I shall forget your disrespect, dear Recaro."

He paused, sighing again. "The truth remains elusive. Neither the Golden nation nor the Starr Witches possess it. The War of Ashes is shrouded in time. The real truth perished with Shabranibodoo; I presume."

Continuing, he added, "My best conjecture is that the gods harbour animosity toward our world." Rising from his seat, he continued, "But mark my words: one day, I will unveil the real reason behind the War of Ashes. There are numerous unexplored ruins and caves in distant lands such as Artoria or Celen. Even beyond the azure sea, the answers lie waiting. I'm certain of it."

Recaro and Valecio knelt before him. "We are at your service, my lord. We will fulfil your request and accompany you wherever you go," they pledged earnestly.

He sat and began eating.

"Did the librarians bring more books from Echo?" he asked, fixing his gaze on Valecio.

Valecio brought a stack of new books and placed them on the table where he was enjoying his meal.

"Yes, my lord. Here are the latest books brought by the librarians.

They have already departed for the Castle of Whispers to gather more books for you," Valecio replied.

Bason had numerous obsessions, among them beauty and knowledge. He was particularly fixated on uncovering the true motive behind the War of Ashes.

His attention shifted to the books, and he began picking them up one by one. They were all quite old. He hoped to discover something intriguing about the War of Ashes. It was widely known that the Castle of Whispers housed the largest library in all of the Lower Lands. He had never had the chance to visit such a magnificent library, but he aspired to witness it himself one day. *The Castle of Whispers in Echo isn't too far away; perhaps I could take my two servants on a little adventure*, he thought.

"Knock, knock." There was a visitor at his door.

Before he could respond, the door swung open, revealing an unexpected intruder.

"Who dares trespass into my chambers without permission?" he exclaimed, his voice filled with indignation.

"Forgive the intrusion, Prince Bason, but I bring urgent news," spoke a woman's voice.

He recognized the figure that entered his chamber—it was the woman wedded to his father.

"Queen Elise, what an unexpected visit. This might be the first occasion you've personally knocked on my door. How may I assist you?" Bason attempted to maintain a veneer of politeness.

When he was thirteen, he lost his mother. After her passing, his father, King Delray, married Queen Elise, the daughter of the king of a neighbouring nation in Echo. The new queen did not fill the void left by his mother. There was no warmth or affection from Queen Elise; she was never maternal. Instead, she remained a distant stepmother, and their conversations revolved solely around governmental affairs whenever they spoke.

"Bason, your presence is needed. Come with me to the Heavenly Tower immediately," said the queen with a sense of urgency.

He glanced at his stepmother. "The Heavenly Tower, you say? What mischief are the Starr Witches stirring up this time?" he inquired.

The Queen ignored his question and simply stared at him.

"Your Majesty, I comprehend the urgency regarding the witches, but elegance cannot be hurried. Allow me to finish my meal, take a hot shower, and then I'll make my way to the witches' tower," he said calmly.

The Queen glared at him with a hint of anger before quickly masking her expression. "Prince, the King has summoned the entire royal family to gather at the Heavenly Tower immediately. I trust the news from the witches will appease your thirst for knowledge," she informed him.

Suddenly, at the mention of the word "knowledge," a surge of adrenaline coursed through him.

"Should have mentioned it earlier, stepmother," he said with a smile. "I'll accompany you right away."

"Valecio, assist Queen Elise while I dress. Recaro, aid me in getting dressed," he commanded his servants.

He wore a white shirt adorned with golden accents and selected blue leather pants. "Fetch the boots, Recaro. Bring me the purple leather boots with golden embellishments—the ones my dear aunt Amina gifted me last year," he instructed, and Recaro promptly obeyed.

Turning to his servants, he continued, "Ensure my armour is readied as planned. I'll delay my training for a while. Meet me at the training arena," he ordered, and they nodded in acknowledgment.

"May I escort you to the Heavenly Tower, my Queen? Allow me to take your arm," he offered courteously.

"Indeed, Prince Bason. I would be honoured," responded the Queen graciously.

He was keenly aware of the queen's evident aversion to their exchanges, a fact that only fuelled his desire to test her patience further. He took a sort of delight in pushing her to her limits.

As they strolled toward their destination, he engaged her in conversation. "It's known that Echo was once the domain of the Dragani clan—a group of witches believed to have been decimated to a mere few," he remarked to his stepmother. "I often ponder, why weren't you dispatched to the Dragani clan for initiation? A witch princess could prove quite useful, wouldn't you agree?" he teased the Queen.

The queen closed her eyes, took a deep breath, and responded, "You are well acquainted with my story, Bason. Must I repeat it for your entertainment?" her words conveyed a sense of knowing that he was mocking her.

When she was a child, Queen Elise indeed attempted several tests conducted by the witches of the Dragani clan which at that time were residents in the Castle of Whispers. Young Princess Elise aspired to master the arts of gravital magic, the specialty of the Dragani clan. Despite her attempts at various tests administered by the Dragani Witches, she faced failure. Her endeavours revealed that she lacked any inherent magical ability.

The transmission of magical abilities occurred through generations, yet its patterns remained unpredictable. Curiously, no man was known to possess magic, prompting numerous theories to explain this phenomenon. Among these, the Starr Witches believed that ancient gods had cursed men. In contrast, Bason inclined towards the belief held by other witch clans, suggesting that magic came from another realm into this world. According to this belief, only women, who are capable of creating life, held the key to accessing this mystical power. However, not every woman possessed the ability to wield magic, leaving this theory with more questions than answers.

"There's no shame in it, my Queen. Men lack the ability to wield magic, so I empathise with your situation," he said, enjoying teasing her. However, the queen chose not to continue the conversation.

The Heavenly Tower stood tall and wide beside Solaris Castle, its construction attributed to the witches' efforts during the War of Ashes to combat the Fire Lord. Ensuring sturdy support was a priority, thus explaining the tower's considerable width. Within its expanse, the Golden Nation had established the Library of Sol, a space meticulously designed to house an array of books and scrolls. Furthermore, it served as the dwelling place of the Starr clan. The tower's rooms were countless, concealing secrets even from the royal family, granting the witches absolute freedom within its walls.

During his childhood, he found solace in the residence of the Starr clan—a favourite haunt. Enjoying the privileges bestowed upon him as part of the royal family, he frequented the tower, revelling in the pleasure of exploring the library's contents. However, certain sacred rooms remained off-limits to him. Nevertheless, the witches held a fondness for the young prince, often engaging him in playful activities. They would create glowing lights for him to chase, fostering a bond that persisted through his youth. It wasn't until his teenage years that Bason began to grasp the true extent of the witches' powers, which instilled in him a sense of apprehension toward the Starr Witches.

"Your Majesty, Prince, welcome to the Heavenly Tower. I'm Serisa, and we've been anticipating your arrival. The King and other members of the royal family are currently gathered in the Crystal Room," greeted a young witch stationed at the tower's entrance. He noticed her blonde hair was tied in a ponytail, and she was wearing a silver robe, white slippers, and a black belt.

"If you would kindly follow me, I shall transport you there using a teleportation spell," said Serisa.

He was well aware of the Starr Witches' ability to teleport short distances within their domains. He harboured a deep curiosity about this particular type of spell; whenever it was cast upon him, he felt as though he could almost feel its magic.

"Are you new around here? You seem unfamiliar to me," he lied, trying to gather information about the witch. In reality, he could not remember the face of any Starr witch except for their leaders.

"Yes, Prince. I'm newly appointed to this role. Previously, I resided within the tower, delving into the study of Starr magic. I've recently been granted one star," said Serisa.

Over the years, he had gathered information about the hierarchy within the Starr clan. Stars were granted based on a witch's readiness for greater responsibilities or when their powers grew stronger. Witches with one or two stars were assigned smaller tasks, managing affairs within the Heavenly Tower or the Golden Nation. Those with three or four stars undertook missions beyond the nation's borders. However, he remained unaware of the roles of five and six-star witches, though he knew they could be part of the ten-member Great Witch Council within the Starr clan.

As a child he was told stories of Starr Witches travelling outside the Lower Lands. Valecio and Recaro had once shared tales of these enigmatic figures being sent to the stars themselves to watch over them. He, no longer a child, didn't place much belief in such notions anymore.

Serisa guided them into an inner chamber where they observed other witches teleporting in and out.

"This chamber is one of our new additions, designed for teleportation within the tower. Please, take my hand," Serisa instructed them respectfully.

They complied with Serisa's request, and suddenly, a bright blue light began to envelop them in a serpentine motion. In just three rapid blinks, their surroundings transformed. They found themselves in a different chamber with expansive windows and silver walls. He approached one of the windows and gazed out, seeing the entire Solaris capital city spread out below. It became evident that they were now situated atop the Heavenly Tower.

"Such magnificence. All of this will be mine one day," he said proudly.

"We must hurry; they are waiting for us," the Queen exclaimed urgently.

Serisa led them out of the chamber and along a narrow passageway, exposed to the open air, that led to another circular chamber with a sturdy silver door. As they stepped outside, they were greeted by a strong wind. Serisa quickly conjured a spell to calm the wind, ensuring a smoother walk. Ahead lay the Crystal Room—a venue reserved for the gatherings of the Great Council of the Starr clan. He knew that, on occasion, the council extended invitations to the royal family for important meetings. He recognized this room well, having visited it several times in the past.

"I must take my leave now. It's not permitted for me to approach this sacred room. Only the royal family and the Great Council are allowed entry. It was my pleasure to serve," Serisa announced before departing, retracing her steps back to the previous chamber, leaving them at the silver door.

The Queen and Prince stepped into the magnificent Crystal Room. Its grandeur was unmistakable, even for Bason, who had visited before. The walls and furnishings were made of crystal and diamond, with silver and gold-adorned vases, plates, cutlery, and decorative pieces. At the apex of the room sat a colossal crystal sphere—a vital tool used by the Great Council of the Starr Witches to observe the world outside and receive news from other witches within their clan. They called it the Eye of Meteora. Bason often likened the enormous sphere to a colossal eye, a seer of sorts. Yet, it had its limitations, unable to view other clans or nations beyond the Golden Nation and the Starr clan.

The Great Council of the Starr clan consisted of ten witches, but only one of them interacted directly with the royal family—her name was Velaska. Some referred to her as Queen Velaska, though never in the presence of the royal family, especially Queen Elise. Velaska usually wore a silver dress, often concealing most of her head beneath a silver hood. However, on this particular occasion, she had foregone the hood out of respect for the royal family. She had a fair complexion, blonde hair, a petite pointed nose, feline-like features, and striking green eyes. To him, she didn't look more than thirty years old, though he knew that witches often appeared much younger than they actually were.

Velaska approached to greet them. "Good day, Your Majesty, and Prince," she reverently addressed them.

"We have significant news this morning that will please the royal family. Please, come with me," she urged, leading them closer to the Eye of Meteora where the other members of the royal family and the Great Council were gathered.

The other nine witches of the Great Council stood around the Eye of Meteora, while King Delray Artois, his elder brother Terrence, and his younger sister Beatrice sat patiently in front of the gathered witches. His father, the king, aged sixty-five, wore a leather shirt paired with pants, boots, and the regal golden crown. His brother Terrence, twenty-eight, and sister Beatrice, eleven, were dressed in resplendent golden royal attire beside the king. He noticed the absence of his aunt, Amina Fitzroy.

"Good day, Father. It seems we're missing one member of the royal family—Aunt Amina. We should wait for her," he said.

"Bason, always demanding and arriving late to royal meetings. You ought to know that Amina left the capital this morning. She received a letter from Borraral—your grandfather has fallen ill," said the king.

Bason was visibly taken aback by the news. He had developed a strong attachment to his grandfather, King Hendrik Fitzroy of Borraral. From a very young age, he struggled to connect with his own father, but the King of Borraral had always been warm and welcoming toward him. He reminisced about the time spent in Barral, the capital city of Borraral, known for its expansive forests and towering trees. As a child, his grandfather often told him fantastical stories of how these trees could reach the sky and touch other worlds.

During his time at the castle in Barral, he had learned to ride horses and was taught the fundamentals of sword fighting alongside his two servants. Despite his grandfather's important duties as king, he always made time for him—whether for play or horse riding lessons. However, in recent years, Bason hadn't seen his grandfather often, as the king had been largely confined within the castle walls.

"I do hope he can recover soon, I would like to see him again", he said.

The king appeared indifferent to his concern. "We shall see. The old man seems to have fallen from his horse and broken several bones. However, the matter of the old man can wait; it is time for more important news," remarked the king.

He was disappointed by his father's lack of concern regarding his grandfather.

"Velaska, with all members present, please do not delay this news any longer. What is it that you wanted to tell us with such urgency?" the king inquired, attempting to maintain a respectful tone despite the urgency in his voice.

Velaska cleared her throat. To him, it seemed she wore the triumphant smile of someone who had just won a war.

"King, esteemed members of the royal family. We have both good and bad news. The bad news is that the members of the Great Conclave have been assassinated in cold blood. The good news is that we now know who the killers are. The seeds we planted in the Shabrani Witches many years ago have finally borne fruit. It has been confirmed: our informants have reported that the Shabrani Witches are responsible for the demise of the Great Conclave," said Velaska.

ALABASTER

"We'll reach nightfall shortly. We must find a place to camp," he said to his companions. While journeying through the Rockshade Highlands, they encountered some greenery, predominantly consisting of small flowers. Occasional trees and grass sprouted, but not as plentiful as in other lands. The towering mountains surrounding the area were staggeringly impressive, with some even breaching the clouds. It was rumoured they rivalled the height of the Heavenly Tower in the Golden Nation.

"Hey friend, what do ya think those mountains are? Some people have some crazy ideas 'bout 'em!" shouted the elderly man, Truinan, from the rear of the wagon.

Some said the towering mountains were ancient technology, crafted by the Primes to battle the hellish legions. Over time, these mountains had been buried under stone, mud, and greenery, blending seamlessly into nature. Naturally, there was no proof of this theory, he thought. *Even in all my studies with the Balor clan, no record ever mentioned such claims from the Age of the Primes. Most of that age remains lost to history anyway. All we have are rumours whispered by inebriated storytellers.*

"Yes, numerous theories exist. I typically favour the most credible explanation—the mountains are natural formations, likely shaped by elevational factors and environmental alterations over time," he said, trying to sound convincing.

"What are the locals saying around here?" he inquired.

"It's hard to say, ya know? Folks from the Rockshade Highlands are scarce all around. We chat and trade with other villages, but there's so many folks comin' and goin' that it's hard to keep track. The tale I like the most is that this land was special, found by the Primes. They built those mountains to point to where hell was—as in, hell's above the sky or somethin'. Those mountains stored some kinda keys to the gates of hell itself, lettin' hell demons come and go as they pleased. But the Primes destroyed the keys and sealed the gates to hell forever. Ain't nobody got a clue how to open the gates again," replied Truinan.

This is nonsense, he thought.

They were deep in conversation, discussing various topics, when the sun began to set in the distance.

"We should stop here. Nightfall is approaching. It would be wise to rest now and continue our journey in the morning," he said to the others.

After agreeing on the plan, his companions helped him pitch a small tent and set up a fire pit. Though modest in size, the tent accommodated all of them with some squeezing. The nighttime temperature in the Rockshade Highlands wasn't too low, though an occasional chill lingered in the air. They lit the fire cautiously, keeping it subdued to avoid attracting unwanted attention. Despite the seeming isolation—barbarians had massacred everyone in the vicinity—they doubted they would return.

Inside the tent, Alabaster retrieved bread and cheese from his provisions, dividing it evenly among his companions. *Let them eat heartily while they can*, he thought to himself.

"Sss!" Aliune, the cat they had rescued, hissed at him every time he came near. *It seems the cat is well aware of my true intentions toward these three poor souls*, he thought.

"Thanks, mister! You're our hero," exclaimed little Caitrin who seemed grateful for the food provided.

"Seems like your pet isn't too fond of me. Does she act this way with everyone she meets?" he asked, curious about the cat's behaviour.

"I'm not sure. In our village, we rarely encountered travellers, especially priests. I believe she just needs a bit more time to get used to you," replied Caitrin.

Alabaster smiled and attempted to pet the cat, but it hissed aggressively back at him and swiftly exited the tent. Caitrin hurried after the cat into the darkness.

"I'll watch over them. You two stay here," he instructed Searc and Truinan.

He stepped outside the tent to follow Caitrin, noticing Searc and Truinan trailing behind. *These ignorant people—they never listened, did they?* he wondered.

In the distance, he spotted two shadowy figures. At first, he mistook them for trees, but trees don't move.

Suddenly, Caitrin screamed, "Barbarians!"

The next thing they all heard was Caitrin's scream as the barbarians rushed toward her, seizing her by the left arm and pressing a knife against her chest. She died instantly.

The barbarians left Caitrin's dead body on the ground and charged at him.

We're doomed. I know I deserve this, he thought, resigned to his penance arriving sooner than expected.

He covered his eyes with his hands, bracing for the fatal blow. Instead, warmth enveloped him. When he uncovered his eyes, he saw Aliune—the cat that despised him—radiating a vibrant blue light. The barbarians stood frozen, staring in shock at the strange spectacle.

With the aid of the blue light radiating from the cat, he could make out the features of the barbarians—two burly men in rugged leather attire. Their muscular arms and legs stood out, and their long black hair only added to their intimidating presence. His attention quickly shifted to Aliune, who, still bathed in blue light, had begun an unnatural transformation.

The cat began to grow larger, shifting into a human form while still emitting that same comforting blue glow.

A young girl materialised in front of him. The mysterious girl appeared scarcely older than twelve, with long, semi-curly blue hair flowing down her back. Suddenly, a silky blue dress materialised out of thin air, covering her as the blue light continued to radiate from her. For a moment, he wondered if she might be connected to the woman who had once saved his life at the Blood Witches' camp, given her similar blue hair and fair skin.

Looking up at the sky, the moon seemed to shine more brilliantly than ever. The girl raised her hands toward the moon, murmuring words he couldn't quite make out as she began to levitate. Her blue hair started to grow longer and longer. Then, one of the barbarian's bodies twisted in all directions, making him scream in excruciating pain. Blue light burst from the barbarian's eyes, nose, and ears. The last thing Alabaster heard was the barbarian's agonised screams, as though he were exploding from within.

The barbarian's body collapsed to the floor, lifeless. Blood poured from his eyes. The other barbarian, looking furious, prepared to attack the mysterious girl, gripping his axe tightly. "You pay. Life is finished," he growled.

Suddenly, a long, gleaming blue sword appeared in the mysterious girl's right hand. Before the barbarian could even touch her, she sliced the barbarian's arms and legs off. Her attacks were so fast that he struggled to follow her movements. The barbarian's scream resembled that of a dying animal, yet he was still not dead.

As she stopped levitating, her hair returned to its original length, and the blue glow dimmed. The girl's magical sword vanished as well. She then walked towards the limbless barbarian body. Grabbing him by the hair, she dragged the barbarian towards him.

He was impressed by the events unfolding before him. *How can such a little girl carry such a beast with just one hand?* he wondered.

"Begone! Thou obstruct'st my path," the girl ordered him.

He stepped aside as she continued walking, dragging the barbarian's body by the hair and leaving a trail of blood on the way. She stopped in front of Searc. The boy stood frozen, his eyes wide with fear, tears streaming down his cheeks as he trembled.

"He hath slain thy sister before thine eyes. What dost thou intend to do?" the mysterious girl said to Searc.

The boy glanced down at the barbarian, who was still screaming in agony. He noticed that the boy hesitated for a moment, but then his expression shifted to one of determination. Searc swiftly grabbed the two knives Truinan had given him from his belt and struck on the barbarian's eyes.

Now, the louder screaming came from Searc, who was stabbing in and out as fast as he could with his daggers. The barbarian had long been dead by the time the boy finally stopped.

"Thou hast performed admirably, lad", the mysterious girl said.

Then the mysterious girl, striding with purpose, approached him.

"I have been in quest of thee, Blood Priest. Lead me hence to thy blood masters with all haste," the mysterious girl commanded.

ELLA

She removed her sandals to experience the sensation of the crystal-like stones scattered across the ground. She walked barefoot, craving the sensation of the soil and crystals. They appeared to dim beneath her feet. The Dark Forest, the place she called home, held stunning tiny stone fragments, smaller than the tiniest pebbles. Tales said that in the past they energised anyone who touched them.

Some elder Balor Witches often spoke of Silverstone as a land where magic crystals the size of humans once thrived ages ago. Legends claim these crystals were long since destroyed, and the small stones found today are their remnants. It is from tales such as these that the land earned its name, Silverstone. The first time she laid eyes on these small, crystal-like stones, she was mesmerised. Their appearance was a spectacle, especially at night when they gleamed brightly. However, during the day, within the confines of the Dark Forest, these stones remained dim. The dense canopy of dark leaves prevented the sunlight from reaching them. Nonetheless, they retained a captivating beauty. The darkness of the forest enveloped everything, rendering it nearly impossible for anyone to see inside. Only the Balor Witches possessed the secrets to navigate the paths of the Dark Forest in complete darkness.

She has spent her entire life dwelling within the Dark Forest, a land where the Balor clan of witches had built its primary city. Surrounded mostly by trees, foliage, branches, and an array of plants, the city, constructed by the Balor clan, consisted of numerous buildings crafted from wood and stone. Concealed within the shadows, the city remained a realm unknown to most outsiders.

In ancient times, the Balor Witches summoned protective barriers, known only to them, that shielded the pathways into their domain. Unauthorised attempts to breach these barriers led to certain death. Despite warnings, barbarians often tried to bypass these defences. Whether they were lost or simply curious remained a mystery to the witches. The barriers manifested as fields of poison and decay, proving lethal to any unfortunate soul who dared to challenge them. The corpses of those who failed were often found scattered across the dark expanse of the forest.

Only select groups of men and a few allied witch clans held the knowledge required to navigate these protective barriers. These individuals were chosen for specific roles, often travelling through the forest as traders. Furthermore, some witches from the Dragani clan possessed this knowledge, thanks to their friendly relations with the Balor Witches—though this was before their near annihilation.

"It's time," a witch informed her.

"Just a little longer, please. I won't have another chance to see this place. Just a few more moments," she pleaded. The other Balor witch granted her a few more moments alone.

To Ella, the dark forest and the Balor Witches' citadel were her entire world; she couldn't imagine anything beyond them. From her earliest memories as a child, she remembered nothing but the dark trees and the gleaming stones beneath her feet. Her childhood was brimming with joy, dashing through the terrain and revelling in the sensation of dust and crystals. However, adulthood wasn't as kind to her. She soon realised she wasn't the brightest or most skilled witch, but this realisation only fuelled her determination further. Despite being mocked by other witches for her efforts to improve, she refused to give up.

During a poisons class, a critical final test required students to concoct two potions. The first was a venom, a sinister toxin undetectable to any tongue but capable of swiftly closing the throat, resulting in a dreadful death by suffocation. The second potion was the antidote designed to counteract the venom's effects. Every witch was obligated to ingest both the venom and the antidote. Survival determined acceptance into the Balor witch clan. Aware of the tales of many others perishing in the final test due to either an excessively potent venom or an inadequately prepared antidote, she was terrified. Yet, her determination to succeed outweighed her fear.

She was the last witch left to create both the venom and antidote. Amidst the chaos, she witnessed fifty percent of her peers succumbing right in front of her. Desperately trying to maintain her focus, she repeated to herself not to look at them, not to lose control.

When she finished, she braced herself and swallowed the venom. In seconds, her throat began to constrict, and she prayed that her antidote would work as intended. With trembling hands, she administered the antidote, hoping to escape the fate that had befallen so many others. *Please work, please work, I don't want to die, I don't want to die*, she repeated in meditation.

The antidote failed to counter the venom's effects. Panic seized her as her lungs struggled for air, and an intense pressure built within her head. Darkness crept into her vision as consciousness slipped away. In her final moments, all she could perceive were the faces of the peers who had tormented her, their mocking laughter echoing hauntingly in her mind. *I lost and they won*, she concluded.

One week after the gruelling final test, Ella regained consciousness to find herself in the nursery.

"You're alive! It's a mystery how," a voice exclaimed. "Your venom was too potent, and the antidote was too weak. The venom should have taken your life, yet here you are, with only a few injuries in your throat that will heal over time."

She attempted to speak, but no words emerged.

"Don't strain your voice; your throat is injured. I advise you to rest for some time. Nonetheless, be proud. Despite your failed final test, our Great Council has bestowed upon you the title of Balor witch. It appears your body has a natural resilience to powerful venoms. You're a rare witch, one in whom the old witches have taken keen interest," explained the nurse witch.

That day, she cried tears of happiness until nightfall.

At that time, she didn't grasp the full meaning of "keen interest" or understand the intentions of the old witches toward her.

Some time after, Ella was summoned by the Great Council of the Balor Witches. They held their sessions underground, accessed through a tunnel hidden deep within the city. The tunnel stretched far into the depths, enveloped in darkness, with only sporadic fires casting faint light along the corridor. Eventually, she reached her destination.

Inside the Great Council chamber, eight figures donned in brown and green robes stood before her, their faces concealed beneath large hoods. The only body parts she could see were their hands, some of which had turned yellow, while others appeared greener. They were the witches of the Great Council who awaited her arrival.

"You have been chosen," one of them said.

"Selected to join a secret group within our order," added another.

"A group known only to a few among us," continued another witch.

"If you wish to join, you must take the vows," they collectively announced.

"Eat the seed of knowledge."

"It will reveal your true self," another added.

"We shall monitor your interactions and movements," concluded another.

They're speaking in turns, almost as if they're a singular entity rather than multiple individuals, she thought to herself.

"You must have questions, ask away", said one of the witches.

She hesitated, unsure of where to begin.

This was her first encounter with the Great Council, and the experience felt entirely overwhelming. She struggled with the sudden flood of thoughts racing through her mind. What came to her first was the time she spent confined to the nursery, a time that seemed an eternity. They extracted blood from her every day, studying not just her blood but also small pieces of her flesh. Though the cuts were small and almost painless, her body bore the marks of continuous bruising and scars. Whenever she asked why they needed her blood and flesh, the witches remained silent. A single response she once received stated they were studying her anatomy. *But why?* That remained a mystery to her.

Summoning her courage, she found the nerve to ask questions.

"What... What did you do with my blood and flesh? What is this se... secret group? What does... it do?" she stammered, her voice trembling. Despite her fear, she managed to voice the questions that had been haunting her.

"No need to be frightened," one witch assured her.

"We had to ensure your potential for this secret group, so your blood and flesh were studied," another witch explained.

"The secret group of the Balor Witches was established many years ago, before any of you were here," the council spoke in turns again.

"It's very old, indeed."

"We are inherently peaceful, but the threat is escalating every day."

"It's time to counter the forces of evil that pose a threat to our clan."

"This secret group is formidable. Fortified with immense power."

"The most potent among us, wielding magic unlike any other witch of Balor."

"You will be sent away on a mission."

"To eliminate our enemies from the shadows."

"You won't return to the Dark Forest."

"No one must discover your true identity."

"You must eliminate them all. None can escape."

"Power, beyond your wildest dreams, will be yours."

"Now, decide, child. We need you to fill the final seat among the most powerful. There's only one spot left, and it's for you."

Silence enveloped the room, and she found it hard to think clearly. *A secret group of Balor Witches operating in the shadows, their existence stretching over many years*, she reflected. Furthermore, only one seat remained, and she had been chosen to take it. *What was this seed of knowledge they spoke of? Could it be possible for me to become more powerful than the witches who had always mocked me?* she asked herself.

"I accept," she heard herself saying. *Is this truly what I want?*

"So be it," the witches all spoke in unison.

The next thing she saw was a shadowy figure approaching from the darkened corner of the room.

It is walking towards me, she realised.

She glanced at the strange creature as it approached one of the torches positioned around the chamber. Its height matched hers, and its body was made up of vines instead of limbs, with numerous branches extending across it. What struck her as most terrifying and peculiar was its face, resembling a large flower-like plant adorned with green and yellow petals. In the centre of its face, she noticed a hole that she deduced to be its mouth, given the sharp, tooth-like structures surrounding it.

"S...he... mu..s...t ta...k....e i...t," the strange creature spoke in a non-human manner, its speech faltering.

The creature walked awkwardly, resembling a baby taking its first steps. Suddenly, it stopped its movement towards her and began convulsing, as if experiencing a panic attack.

In an instant, a long vine shot out from its mouth, swiftly heading towards her and entering her mouth. The events happened so quickly she didn't have time to react. She noticed that a small object, no bigger than a stone, passed into her from the vine, causing a searing sensation within her stomach and organs. After leaving her mouth, the vine returned to the strange creature. Ella fell to her knees, experiencing an excruciating pain unlike anything she had ever felt. Nausea and a relentless burning sensation surged through her, making her fear for her life. Then, she lost consciousness.

When she regained consciousness, she found herself in a cold, unfamiliar room. Slowly opening her eyes, she realised she was confined within a cell. Her back ached as she noticed she was lying on a hard bed made of stone and wood. Nearby, a bucket of water sat waiting. Looking around, she noticed that the cell was small and desolate, lacking any other furnishings.

She approached the cell door, surveying her surroundings. The cavernous area housed numerous cells similar to hers. Abruptly, her head began to spin as a wave of illness overtook her—her body ached with fever, and her skin felt unbearably itchy.

She felt an irresistible urge to scratch her skin to ease the discomfort. As she examined her hands, she noticed a change in her skin tone—now tinted with a yellowish colour. Her mind immediately flashed back to the object she ingested during the encounter with the strange flower-like creature in the Great Council chamber.

This must be the seed of knowledge they mentioned, she realised, connecting the dots. *That thing is causing all this pain.*

Amidst the pain, she noticed something peculiar—her senses had sharpened. She could now distinctly perceive traces of magic emanating from various directions. Even more remarkably, she could sense the presence of numerous seeds and growing plants beneath her in the ground.

"You're recovering well. Many witches in your condition haven't made it this far. You've undoubtedly one of us," remarked a witch who had come to check on her.

"I'm Ceca, the leader of our secret group. We're known as the Dark Thorns. The bad news is it'll take some time before you can feel normal again. The good news is, you'll wield vega magic beyond any other Balor witch. Do you have any questions?" inquired Ceca.

"Am I still human?" she asked.

"If I were to simplify it, you're somewhere between an immortal magic plant and a human. You might have noticed your increased power, like a flow of boundless energy. This will only continue to grow. You'll have so much energy that sleep won't be necessary. But, there's a small price: your skin and hair will likely change colours, as you may have already noticed. Mine turned green, while others changed to red or yellow. Who knows, you might even like it. Another benefit is that killing you is now more difficult. You'll soon discover you can recover from wounds and even regrow lost limbs. You've become a lethal, undying weapon. Be grateful to Lord Trobalor and the seed of knowledge," explained Ceca.

If this is true, Lord Trobalor has heard my prayers. I won't be a weakling anymore, and the others won't laugh at me. I will be stronger than those bully witches, she said to herself with newfound confidence.

"I pray to Lord Trobalor to grant me the strength to overcome whatever he desires from me. I am his," she said with pride.

"Lord Trobalor chose wisely to grant you such resilience," said Ceca before leaving her.

The months that followed were the hardest. The pain she felt throughout her entire body became a constant companion. Gradually, Ella managed to overcome the physical torment, acclimating herself to the persistent ache. Upon leaving her cell, she encountered others similar to her. Some members of the Dark Thorns appeared very young, while others were much older. A witch named Arela revealed she was almost two hundred years old.

"The pain never goes away, but you will get used to it. Everyone experiences it differently," Arela shared with her.

Indeed, the discomfort persisted, yet with time, it became more bearable. In addition to her increased magical abilities, she decided to embark on learning weaponry—a skill not typically taught to ordinary Balor Witches.

"Our mission is dangerous; we need to strengthen not just our spirits, but also our bodies. We must master the use of any weapon,"

Ceca stressed.

The Dark Thorns consisted of forty-nine witches, each adorned with distinct features. Some witches were completely green, from head to toe, even including their hair. Others displayed patches of various colours on their skin, while a few had eyes entirely yellow or red. Some witches had ears resembling leaves, with a pointed shape. Ella's skin had turned yellow, and her hair had taken on a light green hue. However, the physical changes didn't bother her much. What amazed her the most was the transformation in her magical abilities.

She sensed an endless surge of vega energy within her. Putting this newfound power to the test, she discovered her remarkable ability to manipulate the growth of trees and vines with extraordinary precision, surpassing even the most skilled Balor Witches. Overtime, controlling vines and trees became instinctual for her. Her fellow Dark Thorns sisters advised her to keep an assortment of seeds in her pockets at all times. Tossing these seeds to the ground allowed her to command their growth and movement, enabling her to craft poison vines, miasma, tree traps, and projectile branches, among other useful techniques.

In addition to mastering vega magic, Ella dedicated herself to refining her abilities in wielding knives and swords. She engaged in daily training sessions with her peers and found particular enjoyment in sparring with Matena, a witch of similar age who had joined the Dark Thorns shortly before her. They also spent time together outside of training, occasionally sharing beds and keeping each other company. Matena played a crucial role in helping Ella understand certain aspects of her new body.

Her new body also brought some disadvantages. She found it increasingly difficult to sleep and had completely stopped eating meat. Her sustenance came solely from vegetables, and she drank significant amounts of water, vital for maintaining her energy flow. Matena shared stories about their peers losing control due to dehydration, which prompted Ella to ensure she always had a steady supply of water in her quarters.

She hadn't seen any other Balor Witches outside of the Dark Thorns group for a while now, so it seemed to her that they were secluded in a distant area, far from the rest of their kind.

"There's no need to interact with other witches. We're all part of a grand plan that has been unfolding for years. Be grateful for this. Now that our group is assembled, we'll soon receive orders for our next steps," declared her leader, Ceca. Being one of the eldest and most knowledgeable among them, Ceca was the only one in their group who could communicate with the Great Council directly.

One morning, Ceca gathered all the witches from the Dark Thorns.

"The time has come. I've been tasked by the Great Council to fulfil our destiny, the very purpose for which we embraced the seed of knowledge and became a weapon for our clan's sake. We owe gratitude to Lord Trobalor," Ceca informed the witches.

"We're set to depart in seven moons. Our destination is the Blue Bell Mountains in Lakefields, where we'll receive whatever awaits us," explained Ceca.

Seven moons swiftly passed. Ella gazed one last time at the breathtaking scenery of Silverstone and the Dark Forest.

I may never return here again, but I must believe in my ability to survive whatever lies ahead for me, she resolved.

She looked up at the towering green trees, cherishing the beauty of her home. "Goodbye, home," she whispered softly.

Ella set out on her journey towards the meeting point of the other witches, carrying only a few essentials: some clothing, a small rug for bedding, a couple of saddles filled with vegetables for sustenance, a waterskin, and an assortment of powders and seeds. Secured beneath her dark garments on her right thigh was a knife wrapped in a leather belt, while a small sword, her preferred weapon, was fastened to her waist.

When she arrived, all forty-nine witches were united and ready to depart from their homeland.

Ceca addressed the group. "We are to depart from the Dark

Forest and reach the Blue Bell Mountains within seven days. The witches of the Great Council have foreseen days of rain, which will allow us to travel day and night."

Being among the most skilled of the Balor Witches, Ella and her companions could stay awake for days without rest if they had enough water. She had tested this method before, lasting almost twenty days without rest while staying hydrated. *Unlimited power*, they had told her, and it had proven true.

"Before we depart, you must wear these hoods. They will completely conceal your face and body. In case we encounter any other company en route to the Blue Bell Mountains, we are to present ourselves as ordinary witches of Balor journeying to Lakefields under orders of our Great Council and King Larus Rickers. I possess a letter sealed by the king himself to serve as evidence," Ceca explained to the group.

If Ceca's words are true, does it mean that the King of Lakefields is aware of the existence of the Dark Thorns? Is this a part of our mission that must remain a secret? she thought silently.

Ella observed the other witches exchanging uncertain glances, perhaps pondering the same idea.

"I must remind you, sisters, we are not to question the decisions of our superiors. We are nothing but weapons now. We do as we're told, nothing more," Ceca asserted firmly, noticing the confusion among the witches.

Ceca then distributed the hoods among the group. Ella put hers on. "I can't see who you are. These hoods seem to work well," Matena said with a smile. Ella appreciated Matena's presence on this journey; she had been a supportive companion.

"One last thing," Ceca interjected suddenly.

"If we encounter unknown adversaries during our journey, we are to fight and eliminate them."

Ella and the rest nodded in agreement and chanted in unison, "For Lord Trobalor."

HALLARD

It was another warm season in the region of Lakefields. Historically, this land lacked the traditional seasons. Cold winds were absent even during the evenings, or overcast skies. It was often described as a realm of eternal spring, a beloved characteristic attracting travellers from distant lands. The favourable climate greatly benefited farmers and fishermen, making it an ideal place for year-round crop cultivation. Surrounded by numerous intersecting rivers that flowed into lakes, the area provided an abundance of fish, thus earning it the name Lakefields. Among these lands, the city of Springrest stood out as the most prosperous, serving as the capital of the region and the residence of the royal family, founded by the earliest settlers long ago.

This was Hallard Rikers's birthplace. Hallard's father, Hollard Rikers, happened to be the brother of King Larus Rikers. From his earliest years, Hallard held a fervent passion for combat. He consistently engaged in tournaments, enlisting himself in quests against the barbarian threat.

The barbarian clans posed the biggest threat to the region of Lakefields. When Hallard Rikers reached the age of fifteen, he experienced his first taste of battle against the barbarians. Despite his parents' strong disapproval and prohibition against his enlistment, Hallard's determination to engage in actual combat remained firm. His father's disapproval caused a strain in their relationship, leading to a noticeable change in their interactions. His mother, however, endeavoured to support his decisions. She procured the finest armour and weapons for him, along with various talismans for good fortune among which was a necklace embellished with a golden leaf, believed to bring luck in the Rikers family.

Upon his enlistment, Hallard had no choice but to comply with the king's decree. Despite his lack of battle experience, his royal lineage ensured protection by numerous valiant warriors, all under the orders of Lord Hollard and his brother, King Larus. The surname

"Rikers" commanded great respect among Lakefields people. His inaugural battle proved challenging. Hallard didn't aim to display bravery; merely surviving was a significant accomplishment for him. He continued to join numerous battles against the barbarians, and by the age of twenty-four, he had earned a distinguished reputation as a skilled warrior.

Hallard evolved into a highly accomplished warrior, displaying exceptional proficiency across various weapons in the armoury. He was particularly skilled wielding the long two-handed sword. With remarkable agility, he manoeuvred the heavy sword swiftly and with unparalleled speed, rivalling that of other weapons. In due course, Hallard ascended to the rank of captain, emerging as a respected leader among the Lakemen. Recognizing his prowess, the king entrusted Hallard with the finest men, granting him command over five hundred Lakemen. Despite his youth, Hallard was revered by many for his remarkable achievements. However, a faction resented his swift rise to favouritism within a short span, breeding a small but hostile group. The antagonistic group propagated falsehoods regarding Hallard's accomplishments, yet their fabrications were swiftly debunked by the public following Hallard's most significant triumph to date. Engaged in a battle against a barbarian clan, Hallard faced the clan's leader in a fierce hand-to-hand combat. The barbarian leader, known as Black Teeth due to his lengthy black canine teeth, resembled more of a dog than a man. The clash between the two captains was relentless, exchanging punch after punch. Though Hallard faced a formidable adversary, his final strike defeated his opponent. Despite receiving multiple injuries during the confrontation, Hallard remained resolute, solely focused on securing victory.

Lord Hollard, Hallard's father, held strong objections to his son's path toward warfare. Nonetheless, his dissenting opinion wielded little influence as Hallard's decision now had the king's endorsement. This choice served as a catalyst for a growing divide between the king and his brother eventually leading to their estrangement.

"He is my son, just a boy, and upon my death, he will inherit my lands as the lord of Rivercrash. You never should have allowed him to engage in battle without my consent," Hollard expressed to the king.

"Brother, it's time you cease worrying over this trivial matter. I have no inclination to discuss this further. Hallard is no longer a boy; he's a man, committed to his family and the throne. As one of royal lineage, it's only fitting that I provide him my backing. When the time comes, ensure Hallard remains at Rivercrash and assumes lordship. I trust you'll be able to persuade him of that, at the very least," King Larus retorted to his brother.

Unfortunately, at the age of twenty-eight, Hallard received devastating news. Lord Hollard Rikers had a dreadful accident two days before while hunting wild boars in a nearby forest close to his homeland.

"Wild boars? In Rivercrash?" Hallard exclaimed, unaware of such animals in his homeland.

"The letter says Lord Hollard was ambushed by the animal. He didn't stand a chance; the lion pierced through his ribs, damaging many organs. He is now in the care of the healing sisters," said a Lakeman who was reading the letter to Hallard. At the time of his father's accident, Hallard was out near the southern border of Springrest.

"It cannot be. He would not have been so careless as to be killed by a single wild boar," exclaimed Hallard. "Prepare my horse. I shall leave at once for Rivercrash," he ordered one of his squires.

"Sir, if you permit me, there is also a letter from the king. Should I read it to you?" said the squire.

Hallard allowed his subordinates to read letters to him while he was preparing or occupied with other tasks. "Please proceed," he said.

"Captain, I understand your desire to travel to Rivercrash in light of your father's misfortune. However, our kingdom's priorities must take precedence. Complete your current task first. We will await your return," the message conveyed.

He knew I would be inclined to travel to Rivercrash immediately. Furthermore, 'We will be waiting for you'—does this mean the king himself is journeying to Rivercrash? Hallard was taken aback. He retrieved the parchment from the squire's hand, noting the broken seal bearing the king's insignia.

"He expects me to stay here while my father is dying slowly?" he said, still fixated on the small letter.

He left the parchment with the squire and stepped outside his tent. Throughout the encampment, numerous tents had been set up where his men were resting. It was early morning; the sky displayed a serene blue colour while the weather remained warm. Nearby, several small rivers ran across the encampment, where some soldiers preoccupied themselves by washing up or hunting fish for breakfast.

"Sir, a group of barbarians has been spotted north of the Blue Bell Mountains," reported one of the soldiers to him.

"Excellent. Ready three hundred men and keep the rest here for support. We march in an hour," Hallard ordered decisively in response to the soldier's report.

Horns blasted through the encampment, a signal for the soldiers to ready themselves for battle. Hallard and his company received orders from the king to eliminate a new group of barbarians congregating near the Blue Bell Mountains, south of Springrest. To him, the barbarians were a dangerous enemy, adept at hiding within the mountains and secret caves across the land—a relentless nuisance. While he had faced numerous barbarian clans, only the tribe led by the notorious barbarian, Black Teeth, had truly posed a significant threat to him and the Lands of Rivers.

Hallard returned to his tent, finding his squires had completed his travel arrangements. Supplies including food, water, a dagger and his two handed sword were neatly laid out beside his horse, ready for his departure.

"We'll be back before sundown. Prepare the encampment for our return," he instructed one of his men.

"Wren, you're coming with me. It's time you witnessed a battle firsthand," he directed towards one of his squires.

"Yes... Yes, sir," replied Wren in a shaky voice. Hallard noticed Wren's uncertainty. *Despite being only fourteen years old, war does not discriminate between a boy and a man*, he thought to himself.

Three hundred men departed, Hallard leading at the front with his squire Wren Presleye and a few others he chose to keep close by. They rode south toward the Blue Bell Mountains, the furthest point in the Lakefields region. In this region, the rivers were narrow and often dwindled into small lakes. The vegetation here wasn't as lush, and water wasn't as abundant. Contrary to their name, these mountains weren't blue, but the occasional sight of blue lakes nearby led to the name. The mountains had an unusual shape resembling that of a bell, broad at the bottom and top with a distinctive curve in the middle. To Hallard, they resembled a group of robust women.

Beyond the Blue Bell Mountains, the rivers faded away. Vegetation became scarce and water was a rarity unless it rained. Wild animals were barely spotted, but that was the extent of life there. On the opposite side lay Gorgon, the domain of the Dukkah Volcano—a realm where the Shabrani clan of witches resided.

Witches living at the base of a volcano must be either very brave or very foolish, he thought while riding. He had roamed through Gorgon territory previously. It was a barren region mainly frequented by merchants; the Shabrani clan paid generously for clothing, food, and water. In the past, he had encounters and exchanges with a few witches from the Shabrani clan, mostly concerning trade or information on barbarians.

Religiously, the Lakefields region took pride in its commitment to religious freedom, allowing individuals the autonomy to practise any faith or worship any deity of their choosing. Minority groups were known to offer prayers to the fire god Shabranibodoo and various other deities. However, the majority of Lakemen revered the god Trobalor for his profound connection to nature. The Balor Witches, who were devoted to Trobalor, had, with the king's approval, erected churches across the region.

At court, there were rumours circulating about the king's possible intentions to incorporate a group of Balor Witches into the Lakemen army. Though unconfirmed, Hallard was ready to express his opinion if this rumour came true. He recalled his uncle's words: *The kingdom comes first.*

"Spread the word: When we reach the base of the nearest mountain, we'll halt and send groups to all the other mountains. Divide the men into squads of fifty and await further orders," commanded Hallard to his men as they rode. Following his instructions, as they reached the foot of the closest mountain, they swiftly divided into groups of fifty.

"Lakemen!" He addressed his company.

"The moment has arrived. Barbarians have been spotted among these mountains, likely establishing a new encampment. We will exterminate them in the name of his majesty, the king. Each squad will be equipped with a war horn. If you see barbarians, sound the horn once. If they attack first, sound it twice. For any other threat besides barbarians, sound it thrice."

"Yes sir!" echoed his men.

The squads dispersed in various directions within the Blue Bell Mountains. The silence in the surroundings would amplify the war horns, making it easier to pinpoint their source, he thought.

Hallard's group curved toward the right, moving between two mountains. For a while, their path showed only scattered trees and occasional bodies of water. They encountered rabbits and small wildlife but found no trace of barbarians. At times, they crossed paths with other groups of his men. "Nothing in that direction, sir," reported a knight named Brooke Easome.

"Let's join our groups; it'll help us cover more ground," he said.

"Rwar!!!," The war horn sounded from the east. He and his company swiftly rode in that direction, passing a couple of smaller mountains. This area had more water and trees, providing ample cover for the barbarians. He caught sight of his men clashing with the barbarians.

"Attack!" He roared.

There were no more than twenty barbarians gathered together. The first Lakemen squad who encountered them were already engaged in battle. By the time Hallard and his company arrived, the Lakemen numbered one hundred and fifty. The barbarians posed no threat and were rapidly defeated.

"Seems you've taken all the excitement, Wybert Townere," he jested.

"My apologies, sir. But speed was essential. Do you suspect there might be more barbarians hidden on other sides of these mountains?" Wybert inquired.

"It's possible. Let's gather whatever could be useful for the realm from these savages and ride ahead," he replied.

With one hundred and fifty men, they rode off to join the others. However, they encountered no further adversaries for a while, prompting Hallard to feel a sense of unease.

"Wybert, we'll split again to cover more ground. Take 40 men with you and—" his words were cut short by the blast of a war horn.

"Rwar!" The horn's blare echoed in his ears. *More barbarians*, he realised.

"Rwar!" A second war horn sounded. "They're attacking our men, damn it!" he said. Then, a jolt of apprehension shot through him.

"Rwar!" The distant echo of a third war horn emanated from the west of the Blue Bell Mountains indicating an unknown threat different from barbarians. Hallard and his company spurred their horses, racing as fast as possible. Suddenly, the air thickened around them; a strange mist had enveloped the land. *When did this mist descend upon us?* he wondered.

"Sir, look over there!" One of his men, clearly distressed, pointed towards a mist-obscured area.

Once the mist became clearer, Hallard witnessed a grim sight: his men hung from strange trees. Upon closer inspection, he found them deceased, impaled by dark green trees in the shape of crosses.

"Witchery! Arm yourselves, we are under attack by witches!" Hallard commanded his men.

As his men readied their weapons, barbarians emerged from the mist, charging towards them. Though Hallard couldn't discern their exact numbers, he could see many advancing relentlessly. Equipped with his two handed sword, he started hacking at the barbarians from horseback. Some of his comrades fell beside him, succumbing to the barbarian onslaught. He fought to protect as many as possible, particularly keeping a watchful eye on his squire, young Wren Presleye.

This isn't how it ends. I have to save them, he resolved.

Hallard battled fiercely, drenched in the blood of his enemies. The heat of combat made him feel more alive than ever. Yet, defending his men while launching attacks was an overwhelming challenge.

After a time, the barbarians ceased their advance from the mist. The Lakemen had been decimated, their numbers dwindled to less than half of what they were before the attack. Under Hallard's orders, they formed a defensive circle, bracing for further confrontation. It was their best recourse given the dire situation. However, as time passed, the atmosphere grew increasingly oppressive. Hallard sensed something amiss—his vision began to blur, his movements felt sluggish. There was something malevolent in the mist.

"Poison! It's poison! Fall back, away from the mist, now!" Hallard urgently commanded.

But it was too late. From behind, a new threat emerged. They weren't barbarians. Clad in dark garments from head to toe, these figures resembled shadows, their faces hidden beneath hoods. There were at least forty or fifty of them, advancing ominously.

Hallard quickly assessed the situation. *We can take them*, he thought confidently.

But the earth began to tremble, causing his horse to startle and throw him off. Vines, strong as serpents, suddenly burst from the ground, ensnaring some of his men who were caught off guard. The vines twisted around their limbs and their thorns caused severe bleeding, making them vulnerable targets.

"Retreat!" Hallard urged, never having faced such a threat before.

Desperate and enraged, he witnessed the vines that had killed his men morphing into crosses, piercing the fallen lakemen's bodies, ensuring their death. It was a sinister magic that infuriated him.

He tried to fight back while fleeing; however, the shadowy figures proved too swift, and the poison from the mist began to impede his movements. He kept a watchful eye on his squire, relieved to see he was still unharmed.

Suddenly, one of the vines snared Hallard's foot, causing him to stumble and fall to the ground.

In that moment, he felt the proximity of his impending demise.

Yet, in an unexpected turn, something slipped out from around his neck—an item he had nearly forgotten: the necklace gifted by his mother on the day he first ventured into battle as a young recruit.

Recollections of his mother's words flooded back to him, clear and vivid: "This necklace has been handed down through generations in our family. It's believed to bring luck in moments of courage."

The necklace, adorned with a small golden leaf, had always appeared to be made of copper, though he had never confirmed this through expert examination. Something extraordinary occurred then—the leaf's colour changed dramatically, shifting from its previous colour to a dark crimson colour, resembling the colour of blood.

The vines suddenly reacted and released his leg. He didn't pause to contemplate the reason for their retreat. He hastily got to his feet and continued to flee. However, one of the shadowy figures, wielding a sword, charged toward him aggressively. Summoning the last of his strength, Hallard hurled his two handed sword, directly at the assailant. The blade struck the figure forcefully, knocking them to the ground and uncovering its hood.

At that moment, Hallard recognized the attacker—a woman with light green hair and a face adorned in yellow colours.

These aren't warriors; they're Balor Witches. But why? What could drive them to this?

His thoughts raced for a short moment before he promptly turned and fled.

THE HATEFUL SIX

He sat on the cold, hard stone floor, shivering as a fresh storm brought back the chill. His ragged clothes offered little warmth.

"Ugh, another storm! If we have to deal with more rain for a whole month, I might as well chop my own head off," he complained to his cellmate.

"Quiet, boy, the guards might hear you complaining. We don't need more trouble," said his cellmate.

He stood and looked out of the only window in the jail cell as the rain began to pour heavily. Thankfully, their cell was at the top of the pyramid. *At least we won't drown*, he thought.

"Anyway, what's your name, old man?" he inquired.

"I am Hagar, and you must know I'm not as old as you think, boy, I am fifty five," said Hagar.

An uncomfortable silence followed, which he detested.

"Well, thanks for asking," he said sarcastically. "My name is Silas, and I'm fourteen."

Hagar didn't pay attention to him.

Silas sat back on the floor. Glancing around, the cell held two beds made of wood and stone, accompanied by a bucket for the prisoners' necessities, only to be swapped out once a day. Reflecting on his life, he had been in other jails before, though never in the Pyramid of Dum. This structure was reserved for dangerous criminals such as murderers or rapists, known for its inescapable design and the dreadful treatment of prisoners. The Pyramid of Dum was exceptionally cold, particularly in winter, reaching freezing temperatures. Some inmates would die due to the low temperatures, while others perished from death sentences. Legend claimed the Primes intentionally built the massive prison within the Hateful Six. The Hateful Six comprised six islands: Pater, with its main city as Mater; the Twins, Patmos and Samos; and the Three Daughters, Esther, Ruth, and Maria. The islands were designated solely for criminals during the Age of the Primes.

A bell sounded in the distance, signalling that the only meal of the day was about to be served.

Hagar remained seated on his bed, completely still.

After a while, footsteps approached. It was one of the guards, carrying some bread and a bucket of water.

The guard tossed two pieces of bread and placed a bucket of water near the steel bars, then departed. To drink water, they would need to cup the water in their hands through the bars from inside the cell.

Silas observed as Hagar took a piece of bread and began eating it.

"How did a simple thief like you end up in the greatest jail in the Lower Lands?" inquired Hagar.

Seems like all it took was a bit of food to loosen the mute's tongue, he thought.

"I stole a ring from a wealthy family. I planned to sell it and buy food for me and my mates," he said, grabbing his piece of bread. He noticed it was as tough as a rock and covered in green and black spots. *If I don't freeze to death, I might just die of food poisoning*, he thought grimly.

"A ring from a rich family, huh? I've lived on the streets of Samos, Patmos, and Mater. I've never heard of anyone ending up in the Pyramid of Dum for stealing. You must have seriously angered someone important—perhaps one of the leaders of the Hateful Six," remarked Hagar, also struggling to eat his portion of bread.

He glanced at his companion, wondering why the sudden interest in his life. Suspicion flickered within him. Truth be told, he harboured doubts about everyone. He never knew his parents. As an infant, he was discovered at the doors of an Astorr Cathedral in Esther, one of the Three Sisters islands. The cathedral was home to two Starr Witches who took him in. However, at the age of six, the witches deemed him old enough to leave, and he was cast out onto the streets. From that point on, he lived primarily on the streets, forming a bond with a group of other homeless children who called themselves the Forgotten Ones.

He journeyed alongside the Forgotten Ones for a considerable time, sailing between islands, resorting to thievery to purchase food and secure shelter. They constantly had to remain on the move to evade capture by the guards.

However, at the age of twelve, an event occurred that led Silas to sever ties with the Forgotten Ones. Since then, he travelled solo, assisting other homeless children whenever he could.

Reflecting on his life's journey thus far, he couldn't have imagined ending up at the Pyramid of Dum. It was common knowledge that once imprisoned within its walls, there was no hope of escape.

"Hey, boy! Hey!" Hagar yelled. "What are you thinking? I asked about that strange scar on your neck."

He realised he had been daydreaming, as he couldn't recall Hagar's question. He traced his fingers along the scar on his neck, recalling what the Starr Witches had told him—that he was born with it. To him, it resembled a snake, though some said it appeared more akin to a slingshot or a whip.

"I was born with it. I don't think it's anything. Didn't carve it myself with a knife, if that's what you're thinking," he said to Hagar.

"How come you're all chatty now?" he asked.

Hagar was still chewing his bread. "If my stomach is empty, I don't function. Outside, they called me Hagar the Hungry."

Silas wanted to laugh, but he held it in. He knew better than to mock a prisoner of the Pyramid of Dum. For all he knew, Hagar could be a skilled assassin, although he couldn't see how. Hagar was skinny, lacking muscle in his body.

"Looks like it's going to rain for a while. Better eat slowly to keep your insides warm. The cold kills, boy. Remember that," said Hagar.

"I've lived in the streets all my life. I'm no stranger to this cold," said Silas, which was only half true. He knew about the cold, but on the outside, he could find covers, seek refuge or a warm beverage in a tavern. In here, he had neither covers nor warm drinks.

He didn't engage in further conversation with Hagar that day. Night fell, and he struggled to sleep due to the heavy rain and low temperatures. *The cold has become unbearable*, he contemplated.

Silas managed only a few hours of sleep when Hagar woke him up.

"Hey boy, you want to see this," Hagar said, pointing to something outside the cell.

He realised it wasn't morning yet; but amidst the storm, distinguishing between day and night became a challenge. Faint screams echoed from a distance, growing louder as they drew nearer. Silas edged closer to the bars of his cell, curious about the source of the commotion.

The guards were dragging a woman by her hair. She was a mature woman with wounds and bruises all over her body wearing only an old rag. Silas recoiled in horror at the sight of her injured body; it seemed evident to him that she had been subjected to punishment by the guards. The woman glanced at Silas for a quick moment before the guards pulled her away, her agonising screams fading gradually.

"This fate awaits all of us here, boy," said Hagar. "Once our sentence is passed, we receive whippings before decapitation. It's better you know now than later."

He had known about the decapitations but not the whippings. A sense of defeat washed over him. He wasn't ready to die, not yet. He'd endured a difficult life, holding onto hopes of someday escaping the Hateful Six islands for a better future.

"It's alright to feel despair, boy. You can cry if you want. You're only fourteen; it's natural. You'd be foolish if—" He cut off Hagar.

An unexpected surge of determination coursed through Silas. He didn't want to entertain thoughts of perishing. "I refuse to die here. I'll find us a way out," he declared firmly to Hagar.

"I was going to say you're not stupid, but you really are if you think there's a way out of this," said Hagar, reclining on his bed.

He scoured every corner of the cell, tapping on walls and ground, searching for any vulnerable spots.

"What are you up to now?" inquired Hagar.

He contemplated dodging the question but then decided to share his thoughts with his cellmate hoping for assistance.

"I picked up a few tricks from others—to check walls and floors. Sometimes, you stumble upon a weak point or a hollow space where you can start digging," he explained.

"You won't find any of that here, boy. Rumour has it the stones used to construct the walls and floors of the Pyramid of Dum were sourced from the Upper Lands, a territory lost during the War of Ashes. They're said to be harder than any other material in the world, perhaps even tougher than diamonds. You won't break them or find a weak spot," Hagar said.

He soon realised Hagar wasn't lying. He scrutinised every inch of the cell, but there was no vulnerable point.

"There must be something we can do," he exclaimed determinedly.

Hagar rose from his bed. Silas watched as a red light emanated from within his cellmate, illuminating his entire body. Silas's eyes widened in disbelief, struggling to comprehend the transformation unfolding before him. Hagar's form began to shift, transforming into something else entirely. His tattered rags morphed into a dark robe, his stature changed, seemingly shrinking, and his face took on more refined features. His short black hair lengthened, weaving into long black braids.

"Silas, I've been following you for quite some time," spoke a woman who now stood before him. "It's a pleasure to finally meet you."

"Who are you?" he queried, though he realised he should've asked more precise questions: *What are you? Are you a witch? Are you here to help me escape?*

"My name is Ophelia. I am a Shabrani Witch sent to watch over you. You are a special boy, Silas," explained the witch.

He remained bewildered by the sudden transformation that had taken place before his eyes. Hagar, a middle-aged man, had turned into a witch—a Shabrani witch, no less. He had heard stories about the various witch clans scattered throughout the Lower Lands: the Starr, Shabrani, and Balor clans, with rumours circulating about the Dragani clan, supposedly dismantled. Among them, he knew from the tales that the Shabrani clan was the most feared, with their formidable control over fire.

"Long ago, the Shabrani Witches ruled the world with their deity, Shabranibodoo. Those who dared oppose the Shabrani clan met death by fire—the most dreaded for the agonising pain it inflicts," he recalled from a conversation with a woman at a tavern in Patmos.

"Let me clarify. You're a Shabrani witch who's here to save me? How did you find me?" he inquired.

Ophelia regarded him with a perplexed expression. "You're asking the wrong questions, boy," she said before stepping towards the cell bars and peering outside. "It seems the guards are absent. We must seize this chance and escape immediately."

"Go? Where? How?" he continued enquiring.

The witch shook her head. "You're still asking the wrong questions," she remarked, offering a faint smile.

Then, he observed as the witch closed her eyes and murmured some words while raising her right arm towards the cell's entrance. The steel bars began to glow red and emit heat. For a moment, he relished the warmth in such a frigid place. After a few moments, the bars started to melt.

He was awestruck. "I'm free! How did you do that?" he asked.

The witch chuckled this time. "You really need to refine your questions. I'm a Shabrani witch. I control fire. I used my power to melt these steel bars. It wasn't a difficult spell, but the steel was very old. I ended up using more energy than I intended," she explained, still giggling.

"Wait, how do I know this isn't a trap?" he said.

Ophelia nodded. "Finally, a good question. I guess you'll have to trust me, won't you?" She extended her arm toward him.

He didn't know what to think at this point. He had no choice but to follow his new companion if he wanted to escape.

"I trust you," he said.

Ophelia smiled. "Well, grab my hand now, quickly. I'll cloak us from the naked eye. Let's hope no one notices our escape until we're out of the Pyramid of Dum," said the witch.

He wanted to ask more questions. He still didn't know why a witch was rescuing him and he wanted to know where they were going.

"I'll explain everything once we are in a safe place, I promise," said Ophelia, as if she was reading his mind.

He took her hand, and suddenly, he felt a surge of energy emanating from his palm. It wasn't painful, just a bit tingling.

"Sorry, I forget normal folks aren't used to magic. Try to get used to this sensation; I promise it'll fade away," Ophelia said, sounding apologetic.

They both left the jail cell, and it seemed to Silas that the witch knew exactly where to go.

"This way," she whispered.

Outside the jail cell, the passage was very narrow. He and his new companion had difficulties walking side by side. "Don't make any noises. Others could still hear us," whispered the witch.

He saw other jail cells along the way. Most of the other prisoners were sleeping or shivering from the cold weather. After a while, they reached some stairs that descended to lower levels. They started going down the stairs for a few levels when, unfortunately, they heard voices in the distance below. *Probably guards heading up the stairs*, he thought.

"Let's stop here," said Ophelia.

They stopped three levels below where they were before, waiting for the guards to pass. He noticed the guards also stopped at the same level where Silas and Ophelia were now waiting.

Two imposing figures, clad in steel armour, started to walk towards them. At their waists, they carried a whip on one side and a sword on the other. The passage on this level was as narrow as the one they had just left, making it difficult for them to hide from the guards.

"Quick, go backwards," Ophelia whispered urgently, grasping his arm.

He complied, manoeuvring backward to avoid being seen by the guards.

"As soon as they stop at their destination on this level, we'll continue our journey," said Ophelia, speaking softly to avoid drawing attention.

When the guards finally stopped and entered a cell, they seized the opportunity to proceed forward. Passing by the cell where the guards had stopped, Silas caught sight of the prisoner inside—an elderly woman dressed in worn grey rags with short grey hair.

"Mirta?" he uttered in surprise.

"Quiet, boy! We can't afford to draw the guards' attention," the witch warned.

He couldn't believe it. Mirta, one of the Starr Witches who had cared for him as a baby, was now a prisoner in the Pyramid of Dum. After being cast out from the Astorr Cathedral, he had lost track of her. What could have happened to her to end up in this place? he wondered.

"We can't leave her here," Silas insisted. "We need to rescue her too."

Ophelia shot him an angry look. "Listen, boy, whatever connection you have with that woman, it's over. You have a chance to live if we go now. Let's go!" she whispered, her tone sharp and insistent.

Memories flooded Silas's mind, memories of a time when Mirta was the only one who cared for him, almost as a mother would. He recalled the day it was decided he needed to leave the cathedral, and how Mirta had opposed that decision. "Please, don't hate me. I didn't do this," her words echoed in his memory.

"If you want to go, then go. I'll help Mirta," he declared.

Releasing Ophelia's hand, he dashed toward the cell. As he entered, the two guards noticed his presence.

"Who are you?" questioned one of the guards.

"How did you get here?" the other guard shouted, readying his sword for attack.

"You, it can't be," Mirta exclaimed, lying on the ground with shackles binding her hands and feet.

Then, Silas felt the guard's sword coming closer to his face. Bracing for the inevitable, he shut his eyes tight.

Suddenly, he heard the sound of the guard's sword hitting the ground. He cautiously opened his eyes to find the sword lying on the ground, emitting an intense heat. The metal armour worn by the guards began to heat rapidly, scorching and consuming them. Their screams soon fell silent, leaving behind corpses, burned by the blazing metal.

Behind him, he noticed Ophelia was casting a spell. Silas turned around to express gratitude, but before he could, he received a sharp slap from the witch.

"Silas, do you have any idea how much effort it took to rescue you? I could kill you right here and now, but I've chosen to go along with your plan. For some reason I still don't understand, the Flame of Eldoria needs you," said Ophelia, her voice tense with anger. "Now, who is..." Ophelia's mouth hung open.

"That old woman is a witch. Though I don't sense much power from her," Ophelia completed her sentence.

The sound of the bell ringing echoed. *They know we've escaped*, Silas thought.

"Silas, it's really you," Mirta weakly exclaimed.

"We can't talk now, we need to leave. Ophelia, please help me carry her," he urged.

Ophelia hesitated for a moment before replying, "Alright, but we'll settle all of this once we're out of the pyramid."

Silas spotted the keys to Mirta's shackles lying on the ground, likely dropped by the guard. Using them, he freed Mirta and helped her to her feet. The trio hurried as fast as they could, reaching the stairs and descending through various levels. Along the way, they encountered a few guards heading up.

Ophelia took a small snake from her robes and tossed it down the stairs. In a remarkable transformation, the snake expanded into a colossal, flaming serpent that consumed everything in its path.

"Careful, don't touch those flames," warned the witch.

The narrow staircase posed a challenge, but eventually, they reached the base of the pyramid and found the exit.

"Wait!" Ophelia interrupted just before they left the pyramid.

Silas grasped Mirta's arm and halted.

"Guards are approaching this way. I'll create a disguise," Ophelia declared.

Ophelia took a dust-like substance from her robes and scattered it toward the exit. "Now's our chance," she said.

Ophelia took hold of both Mirta's and Silas's arms, urging them to hasten their exit from the pyramid. Outside, rain continued to pour relentlessly, mingling with a dense mist conjured by Ophelia that obscured their vision. Despite the challenging conditions, he couldn't help but notice that the Shabrani witch seemed to navigate effortlessly through the mist.

Suddenly, something whizzed past his ear.

"Arrows!" Mirta cried out.

"Keep moving," Ophelia said. Suddenly, the arrows ignited and turned to ashes before they reached them; Ophelia was conjuring a spell. He marvelled at her skill, still unable to see anything through the heavy mist.

"There are too many guards. This mist won't shield us much longer," Ophelia warned, continuing to burn the incoming arrows.

"I know someone in the city of Mater who can help us," Mirta suggested, sounding weak.

"We should follow Mirta's suggestion. If we don't, we'll die," he pleaded with Ophelia.

The Shabrani witch didn't respond for a few moments, and then she commanded, "Agreed. Look down at the ground, now."

She raised both arms toward the sky, conjuring a massive fireball from her hands that exploded after a few seconds in the air. The blast emitted a blinding light that could have dazzled him if he'd looked directly at it. Additionally, the explosion dispersed the mist conjured by the witch.

"It is safe to look up again. Where should we go next?" Ophelia asked Mirta.

Mirta gestured towards the city. As they advanced, he noticed the guards who had been attacking them. He counted at least twenty of them on their knees, hands shielding their eyes, unable to move.

The capital city of Pater, Mater, wasn't far from the Pyramid of Dum. Upon entering, to his surprise, the city was deserted, possibly due to the constant rain. Seeking cover, Silas and the others ducked into a side street.

"How much farther do we have to go, old woman?" Ophelia inquired, with an assertive tone.

"Her name is Mirta!" he interjected.

"It's okay, Silas. We need to get to the markets and then follow the track to the bay. A friend of mine lives in a house along that path," said Mirta calmly.

Ophelia reached into her robe and pulled out three stones, which she magically transformed into leather clothing. The garments included shirts, capes, pants, gloves, hats, and boots. Ophelia handed them to him and Mirta, and they quickly changed into the new clothes.

He noticed that his attire was small, but he refrained from complaining. He realised that these new clothes would help them blend in with the locals, making it harder for the guards to spot them.

"We might just be the first to successfully escape from the most heavily guarded prison in the world," he said, feeling a surge of hope as the realisation sank in.

"Let's keep moving. The armies of the Hateful Six will be searching for us any second now," urged Ophelia.

DEMORIA

It had been two days since she received her new mission. In the night sky, the moon shone brightly above her. She had distanced herself considerably from the Dukkah volcano and the Shabrani clan. There were scarcely any signs of smoke, dust, or ashes left; although the land retained its yellow-brown colour.

Looking at the landscape, she noticed a few dead trees forming eerie shapes. In the distance, two ravens circled, hunting a small rabbit that appeared lost from its family. *Such is the nature of life*, she thought.

On the fourth day of her journey, her thoughts were consumed by her mission. "Bring us his arm!" The voices of the great council echoed constantly in her mind. That particular side of her mission troubled her deeply. *What significance could a single man's arm hold for them?* she meditated. In addition, the urgency of the time limit and the potential connection between her mission and the assassination of the Great Conclave weighed heavily on her. With no other choice, she had to push ahead as quickly as possible.

Travelling from the lands of Gorgon to Duskenwood at a steady pace usually took about nineteen days on horseback. Any unforeseen delay might render her incapable of fulfilling her mission. She thought about barbarian activity reported across Duskenwood. Encountering hostile barbarians could potentially lead to conflict, further impeding her progress and complicating her mission, she worried.

"I will not fail," she resolved, determined to banish those lingering doubts from her mind.

She urged her mount forward, a sleipnir, pushing its pace throughout the day and resting only briefly at night. Sleipnirs were a specific breed from the region of Gorgon, specially bred by the witches of the Shabrani clan. These mounts were renowned for their unique traits—a smaller, robust build and dual horns. Stories say that during the Age of the Primes, the Shabrani Witches experimented with crossbreeding bovines and horses. Their goal was to create an animal capable of both fast travel and strength. The sleipnir proved to be swifter than most horses. Its distinctive attribute, the horns, and its sturdy frame were the only features inherited from bovines. Over time, sleipnirs became the preferred mounts for the Shabrani Witches due to their exceptional speed and ability to carry heavy loads. Other clans and nations attempted to breed similar mounts, but they were unsuccessful outside of the Shabrani clan.

She remembered the day she chose her sleipnir. The stables in the Shabrani clan offered many options, however, she settled on a striking white and black sleipnir with curly dark horns that caught her eye.

"You'll do just fine," she said.

"This one is a daughter of the fastest we have at our disposal. It doesn't have a name, but some witches call it Darkhorn because of the blackness of its horns. No witch has complained about it thus far. If your mission has a time limit, this is the best we can offer," explained the witch in charge of the stables at the Shabrani clan. As soon as Demoria mounted the sleipnir, she could tell this was no ordinary animal.

On the eighth day of her trip, she turned her head around and could no longer see the Dukkah volcano on the horizon. Only faint signs of ashes were visible in the distance. *If I keep going this way, I will get to my destination earlier than expected*, she realised.

Even the land was changing, from a yellow-brown earth to grey and green colours; she would soon reach the edge of Gorgon. There, she could stop at the Grey Skull, a very old tavern on the border between Gorgon and Duskenwood. Many travellers would stop there to sleep and recover from their voyages.

Night fell as she finally glimpsed the Grey Skull in the distance. During her training as a witch, she learnt that the tavern was built in the ruins of an ancient castle, possibly dating back to the Age of the Primes. The grey stone that once belonged to the castle could still be seen till this day. From afar, the tavern resembled a human skull.

For a while, she had trouble seeing this until another witch showed her the correct angle to perceive the skull.

"There it is," she murmured to herself as she drew closer. As Demoria approached, she could discern voices and flickering candlelight emanating from the tavern. The establishment consisted of several towers, repurposed to function as rentable rooms. She led her sleipnir into the stable attached to the tavern.

"Stay here for now, I'll return for you in the morning," she said softly to the animal, gently caressing its head. The creature simply regarded her with its gaze.

She concentrated, trying to detect any traces of magic inside the tavern, but she couldn't sense anything. This meant there were no witches present this time. The establishment was owned by Celen people, known for their friendly and peaceful nature. Their appearance differed slightly from others; they had slender waists, arms, and legs, making them quite swift. They were said to be distant descendants of the Primes, as Demoria remembered a witch mentioning in the past.

"Ah, there you are, my friend! It's been a while. You still look as young as ever. Will you stay and share stories with us?" greeted the Celen man who managed the tavern.

"My friend," Demoria greeted him. Though she had met him a long time ago, she couldn't remember his name.

"I'm glad to see you well. I need a room for the night. I'm exhausted and would like to rest as soon as possible. The storytelling will have to wait for another time, I promise. Also, could I have some food and a table, please? I'd like to have a quick meal before resting," she requested from the Celen man.

Taking a seat at a corner table near the window, Demoria was served eggs, bacon, and bread. She also requested ale to accompany her meal.

Demoria surveyed the tavern's interior; among the guests were men and women, likely merchants resting before their next journey. Everyone knew this was a neutral ground; no one wished to disrupt its peace, especially at such an isolated tavern that aided travellers. However, despite the prevailing calm, Demoria sensed the subtle glances directed her way. As a Shabrani witch, she knew her kind wasn't well-regarded, mainly due to the War of Ashes. Though their past sins were forgiven, their reputation lingered, imprinted in the memories of others who would never forget.

Mid-meal, the sound of approaching horses caught her attention. Her initial thought was an attack from barbarians. Peering out the window, she observed a group of horsemen riding towards the tavern.

Demoria recognized the flag they bore—they were from the region of Lakefields. She found the Lakemen' presence unusual; a company of Lakemen approaching a tavern at night wasn't their standard practice. She felt something was amiss. Her experiences taught her about neighbouring customs, and Lakemen typically preferred setting up quick posts and tents when travelling together.

As the Lakemen arrived, Demoria watched the tavern owner, the Celen man, step outside to welcome the new guests. She noticed the man at the forefront of the Lakemen dismount from his horse and engage in conversation with the Celen man. He seemed to be their captain, she presumed.

After a few moments, Demoria observed the Lakemen setting up their tents in front of the tavern, while their leader accompanied the Celen man inside. As they entered, she had a clearer view of him. He was tall, around thirty years old, with fair skin and a muscular build, indicating his long-standing warrior status. His short black hair framed a square face with a prominent nose. His demeanour and features hinted at noble lineage. Suddenly, the tavern owner gestured toward her, drawing both of their gazes. *Fantastic! Now it seems I'm getting involved*, she thought to herself. Then, the leader of the Lakemen began walking in her direction.

"Apologies for interrupting your meal, my lady. I am Hallard, son of Hollard Rikers from the region of Lakefields. I am seeking someone with expertise in magic. I presume, by your attire, that you are a witch. Can you assist me? I have coin if that is what you require," the man attempted to sound formal, though there was a hint of pain in his voice that Demoria noticed.

If her memory served her well, Demoria remembered that the Rikers family held sway over the Lakefields region, with Larus Rikers as the current ruler. *This man belongs to high royal blood,* she thought.

"Indeed, you have interrupted me, sir," she said to him. "I am Demoria, a witch of the Shabrani clan. We don't often receive requests for aid from the Salt Lakes Region, especially not from a member of the royal family. This must be my lucky day," she replied with a dry smile and a touch of sarcasm. "But, I can't assist you until I know the nature of your troubles."

Hallard knelt down, clearly in pain. She stood up and tried to offer assistance.

"Thank you, my lady, but I'll manage. It's my men who need help," Hallard said, his expression twisted in pain. "We were ambushed by witches on our way to eliminate a barbarian threat in the Blue Bell Mountains. It seems Balor Witches were working with them, catching us completely off guard. Many of my men fell victim to their magic. Those cursed by the witches have developed yellow spots on their skin, slowly weakening them. We've been riding for the last two days. We're too afraid to return to Lakefields in our current state, which is why we came to this tavern, our only refuge until we regain strength to confront the witches and barbarians once more," Hallard explained.

It looks like he's been masking his pain for two days to avoid showing weakness in front of his men. How intriguing, Demoria reflected.

What piqued Demoria's interest most was Hallard's claim that Balor Witches were collaborating with barbarians—an unprecedented occurrence, if true.

"You mentioned Balor Witches cooperating with barbarians. How are you so sure?" Demoria inquired, seeking further details. She knew that falsehoods came as naturally to men as breathing.

"I'm almost certain they were Balor Witches. They could control vines and poison. You're likely more knowledgeable about these matters than I am; forgive my ignorance, my lady," Hallard explained humbly.

Since when am I a lady? Demoria mused.

"Balor Witches are hardly considered fighters; they're more inclined towards farming, brewing potions, and healing," she remarked, pausing to catch her breath. "If what you say is true and the Balor Witches have fighters within their clan, they would want to keep it a secret. The ambush's purpose was likely to wipe you out to prevent spreading the news of fighter Balor Witches. Your escape was fortunate; however, it is likely they are trailing you as we speak, Hallard, son of Hollard Rikers," she said firmly.

Hallard appeared increasingly unwell as she finished speaking.

"I need to see these yellow spots you mentioned. Show me," she requested.

Hallard removed his armour and leather clothing, revealing a robust physique marked with yellow spots. She refrained from touching them, recognizing the severity of the illness. She knew that various poisons could inflict ghastly effects on the body—some caused flesh to rot, altered skin colour, or targeted vital organs and the nervous system. She identified the yellow spots as poison magic, an innate skill of the Balor Witches.

"It's poisonous; the skin appears inflamed, resulting in the change of colour. From what I observe, the poison seems to be targeting your senses, gradually progressing to inflict harm on your internal organs which will deteriorate over time. In my clan, it's often referred to as the Yellow Decay," Demoria explained, examining the yellow spots on Hallard's chest and back.

"Can you help my men? We have suffered too much loss already. We had to leave half of us on our way here. We didn't have time to properly bury them," Hallard implored.

Demoria paused, realising Hallard's plea wasn't for his own healing but for the well-being of his men. *Is he some sort of hero?* she pondered silently.

"Let me be frank," she said firmly, meeting his eyes. "You're brave, Hallard, but bravery alone won't save you in this situation. I lack the necessary tools to properly heal you or your men. I could attempt to use fire magic to purge the disease from within, but it will be excruciating for all of you. If any organs are already affected by the poison, my fire magic will only intensify the pain by burning them. Some might survive, but others may not."

Hallard's expression shifted to one of devastation upon hearing her words.

"I can tell your organs haven't been harmed by the poison yet. That means I can assist you if we act promptly. Afterward, I can assess your men and save those who can be saved. It's your call, but this service won't come cheap. It'll require every coin you possess, plus a debt to me, a Shabrani witch." she stated calmly, though the situation was far from easy.

What am I doing, aiding these men? I have my own mission to complete, she reflected.

Hallard turned and sat beside her, contemplating his options, visibly troubled.

"If my men are doomed either way, which death would be quicker? Your fire or the poison?" Hallard questioned.

"My fire will be faster. The fire will bring pure agony, but it will only last a few moments. You must decide swiftly, Hallard," she urged him.

Why am I helping them? Is it for the money? Is it for the debt he would owe me? Or is it something else?

"Do it, start with me. I want to experience what they will feel," Hallard said, almost pleading.

"Kneel, sir," she requested.

Hallard complied with her request.

She stood up and placed a hand on top of Hallard's head.

"This might hurt. Be brave, Hallard." She closed her eyes, focusing and channelling her energy, sending it to Hallard. Her energy tracked the poison inside him, guiding her to pinpoint where to use her magic. She could sense vega magic inside Hallard. *This was the work of Balor Witches. But, why did the Balor Witches attack these men?* She wondered.

Once she finished locating the position of the poison inside Hallard's body, she initiated her fire magic. Sending another wave of energy through him, Hallard grunted slightly as her fire began burning away the poison. It lasted only mere moments; the fire eliminated all traces of the poison within Hallard.

"You can open your eyes now, Hallard. You are healed," she said, trying to sound reassuring.

Hallard opened his eyes. The yellow spots on his skin had turned brown.

"They will vanish in a few days, I promise," she assured him.

"Thank you, Demoria. I already feel much better," Hallard's face looked relieved, no longer in agony.

"Demoria? That's a bit personal, don't you think? I prefer 'm'lady,' Hallard," she said with a teasing tone.

Hallard laughed, appearing almost endearing to her.

"Rwar!!!" a horn sounded somewhere outside.

"We're late, the enemy is here," Hallard said.

THE QUEEN OF THE BLUE MOON

A full blue moon hung brightly in the sky, radiating a strength akin to the yellow sun during the day. Lunara stood as the only land in the Lower Lands where nights extended longer than days.

She looked at the moon in the sky. The brilliance of the moon was overwhelming, yet she noticed a faint shadow obscuring a portion of its glow.

The dark moon, a prophetic omen. It doth appear solely when a deity is poised to descend unto the world anew, Astra meditated.

She stood in the throne room, which opened to the night sky, offering an unobstructed view of the celestial wonder above. Around her, fellow witches from the moon clan gathered. They wore flowing blue and white dresses, some adorned with towering, pointed hats while others allowed their blue hair to cascade freely. Astra herself wore a delicate blue gown, complemented by white slippers adorning her feet and gold ornaments on her wrists and arms. Her white skin resembled the colour of milk, and her long, straight blue hair cascaded over her shoulders and down her back.

A soft breeze blew her dress and gently ruffled her hair. Raising her hand, she revealed a small key-like item in her palm, exquisitely adorned with a miniature crescent blue moon.

"Mother, grace me with thy divine power. Selene, goddess of the moon, hear my plea," she murmured in a hushed tone.

As the words left her lips, the key began to shimmer and tremble. Rays of light surged forth, causing the key to expand gradually until it transformed into a long white staff. At its apex rested a sizable crescent moon, embellished with intricate patterns of gold and silver. Grasping the staff firmly with her right hand, Astra extended it skyward and murmured a series of incantations. A radiant blue aura emanated from her staff, altering the atmosphere as a veil of blue mist materialised before her.

Within the mist, a vision took shape—a young girl, unmistakably a Moon Witch.

"Selene, art thou present?" she inquired.

Accompanying the young girl were a boy, an elderly man in rugged clothes, and a man in dark robes. *He must be the Blood Priest for whom Selene was sent to seek*, she thought.

Abruptly, the atmosphere shifted once more, transforming into intense heat that made her and the gathered witches uneasy. They collectively observed the astonishing and unpredictable changes in the air around them.

The blue mist had transformed into an ominous dark red colour mist. The figures of the young girl, the boy, and the man had vanished, replaced by six figures who were decapitated by a sword. The vision changed again to a lone woman within the mist. She appeared to be singing or perhaps chanting, holding a fruit resembling an apple. As the woman from the mist continued her chanting, a colossal tree materialised before her—an arboreal giant similar to the size of a castle. The tree produced a distressing cry, piercing through Astra's mind and causing profound discomfort.

Suddenly, the tree split apart, unveiling a being—a creature so unfamiliar and sinister. It exuded a fiery red and dark aura, clutching a cup and fixing its abyssal gaze upon Astra. The creature began advancing towards her with deliberate intent.

"Nay! Thy hour hath not yet come. Begone!" she pleaded urgently, imploring her staff for aid. A burst of energy erupted from the staff, aiding in dispelling the unsettling vision, causing it to dissipate entirely.

The force of the energy left her weakened, compelling her to kneel. Using her staff for support, she steadied herself and rose to her feet.

Might the lady holding the fruit serve as the catalyst of a new apocrypha, an event that reshapes our destiny? she speculated, casting her gaze upon the gathering of witches who had come to witness her.

"'Tis time to converse with my sisters," she resolved quietly.

As she glanced at the full blue moon, she again noticed the dark moon in front of it. *This doth be a sign of trouble ahead*, she reflected. Turning her attention to the gathered witches, she began to speak.

"Nine ventured upon a vital quest, yet solely one hath prevailed. The vision was lucid, mine own daughter, Selene, hight after our goddess, hath discovered the Blood Priest we pursued for years." Pausing briefly, she continued, "'Tis now the hour for us to aid her. Without our assistance, I am assured Selene shall not vanquish our adversary with ease. I shall not impose this burden. Instead, I do solicit volunteers—valiant witches devoted to serving our goddess without a moment's hesitation."

Astra couldn't ignore the pressing issue—they lacked numbers. Currently, the Moon clan consists of only thirty-eight witches. In the Age of the Primes, the Blue Moon Goddess, Selene, would send babies to Lunara in response to prayers from the queen. Although she had frequently prayed to the goddess, her prayers had gone unanswered. The other option was procreation, a gift granted only to the queen of the Blue Moon, currently Astra.

Moon Witches could not procreate on their own. In return, they did not age or face natural death. It took approximately five hundred years for them to reach maturity, after which they ceased ageing.

In her eight hundred years of existence, she had been granted only one child. Nearly three hundred years ago, she gave birth to Selene, her first and only child. The day of Selene's birth was etched into her memory—celebrated for seven days and seven nights throughout the Millennium Kingdom. It was the only occasion during her reign when the other two cities of Primes in Lunara were invited to the Moon Castle.

Terra and Ganimed were established by the Primes. Over time, they lost their territories in the mortal realm and begged Queen Astra to allot a portion of Lunara to them in exchange for loyalty and service. This pact was mutually agreed upon by the Primes and Moon Witches. She granted them the north and south lands of Lunara, and only a select few were given the opportunity to enter the Millennium Kingdom.

"My Queen," a moon witch addressed her, "Grant leave for the Primes to return to their homelands and lend aid unto our princess. They have faithfully served us; permit them to join the fray as they once did in days of yore."

Astra regarded the witch and responded, "Hetica, my sister, I have summoned the King of Ganimed to offer support in this pressing hour. They have an army ready at our behest. Whilst the Primes shall lend their aid, I cannot solely lean upon them for such a weighty undertaking. Though they may possess vigor, we hold greater expertise and prowess. Hetica, I beseech thee, extend thy aid unto the princess."

"I shall stand beside the princess and serve the Goddess of the Blue Moon. My life is thine, my Queen," Hetica said as she knelt.

She expressed her gratitude to Hetica with a smile, feeling reassured knowing Hetica was going; among her sisters, she was the most trusted. Soon after, ten other Moon Witches also expressed their willingness to accompany them. More witches volunteered, but she intervened, "I am thankful, sisters, yet we must also attend to our community here. I cannot allow all of you to depart," she explained.

Astra addressed the group once more, "'Tis settled thus. Eleven of us shall traverse the Silk of Remembrance and venture to the realm of mortals to aid Princess Selene in her quest." She paused, her expression tinged with sorrow, as she glanced at her staff.

"There is one final matter. I have dreamt that the Moon Staff hath selected a new bearer. Following these visions, the staff hath not responded to me as afore," she paused briefly, then continued, "I dread an imminent coronation. My daughter, Selene, shall inherit the Moon Staff and ascend to the throne. The coronation must proceed without delay. You, my eleven valiant sisters, shall convey the Moon Staff unto Selene, and the coronation shall commence.

Pray that you reach the princess ere it be too late."

She saw her sisters surprised by the sudden news. After some moments, they all nodded and agreed to follow Astra's plan.

After the assembly concluded, she remained in the throne room to address another guest.

"King Hildebrant Adler from the land of Ganimed hath arrived," informed one of the throne room guards.

"Grant him entry," commanded the queen.

King Hildebrant stepped into the throne room, wearing a suit of silver-plated armour adorned with grey embellishments. The armour enveloped his entire body, leaving his head uncovered, save for the silver crown—the emblem of the King of Ganimed.

Hildebrant knelt before the queen. "Thy Majesty, as commanded, we have convened," he said in a subdued voice.

The king was a direct descendant of the Primes. When the Primes sought refuge in Lunara, they were allowed to procreate naturally, ensuring the preservation of their original lineage. They were born warriors, their martial prowess innate and deeply ingrained in their very beings.

Seated upon her throne, she acknowledged him, "I am grateful for thy compliance with my summons. Thou mayest stand."

"A force of five hundred of my stoutest men await beyond the walls of the millennium kingdom, ready to heed thy command. We are here to uphold the pact forged by my forebears with thee, Queen Astra," said Hildebrant.

She rose from her throne and offered her hand to Hildebrant, which he accepted. "Hildebrant, accompany me."

They exited the throne room and strolled through a corridor overlooking the castle grounds. Astra marvelled at the beauty of Lunara. The blooming trees seemed akin to a divine blessing from the Goddess of the Moon. The blue moon continued to cast its ethereal light over the entire land.

"Eleven of my sisters shall journey with thee. Thou art acquainted with Hetica; she shall be my voice amidst thy company. Obey her directives as though they emanate from mine own lips," she said calmly to the king.

"Our task is to aid Princess Selene, who hath encountered a Blood Priest we deem may summon forth another dark entity into this world. Selene shall need all available aid to forestall another War of Ashes," she explained further.

The king halted and released the queen's hand gently. "My queen, my men stand ready to serve at thy command. Yet, following this venture, shall they be allowed to return to Lunara?" inquired the king.

She gazed into his eyes, as if searching for the true significance behind his words. "I comprehend thy apprehension," she said.

Hildebrant was about to speak again when she gently placed a finger on his lips, offering a warm smile. She closed her eyes briefly, then said, "I created the Silk of Remembrance after the War of Ashes ended. It doth stand as our protection 'gainst the malice of mortals and sundry entities. This staff I doth bear in my grasp," she pointed at the Moon Staff, "I can forge an opening to traverse. Yet, the Moon Staff must be conveyed unto my daughter in the realm of mortals. Thereafter, mine ability to unseal the portal, to return thy men to Lunara, shall wane."

The king clasped her hands delicately. "Thy words doth honour me, my queen. Thy men shall settle once more in the mortal realm," said Hildebrant.

Astra felt satisfied that her conversation with the king had gone smoothly.

"Be mindful, for I purpose to dispatch my son, Emmerich, to command the army of the Primes," revealed the king.

"The prince?" she asked. "Dost thou speak of thine own son, the very heir fated to inherit thy throne upon thy death?" her tone grew more assertive. "Pray tell, is there aught thou art withholding, Hildebrant?" she asked.

The king's expression shifted to one of concern. "Nay, my gracious Queen, there is no concealment intended. 'Tis solely to ensure the success of our army. As Hetica stands as thy voice, so shall my son stand for me."

Astra had encountered Emmerich before: a young, courageous man whose courtly manners were always impeccable.

She took a deep breath. "The affairs of the Primes lie within thy dominion, Hildebrant. I place my trust in thy discernment. Thou art dismissed," she said.

The king respectfully bowed before her and then left her presence.

"What aim doth he harbour in dispatching his lone progeny? This scheme appears bereft of sense. Nonetheless, 'tis naught to be concerned. They shall honour their vow to render service unto us," she murmured softly to herself.

Three days had passed since she cast the vision that would lead eleven of her sisters and an army of five hundred Primes to the mortal realm in order to aid Princess Selene on her quest.

She stood before the coast of the Millennium Kingdom, gazing out at the waves and the expanse of the blue ocean. The rhythmic sound of the waves always brought her solace. Spread before her were fifty battleships, set and prepared. At the back of the Primes' fleet was a smaller vessel, its figurehead depicting a crescent moon crafted from wood and metal—the Traveller, they named it. It was the ship designated to carry the eleven Moon Witches.

"My Queen, all stands ready for our departure. We await but thy command," Hetica informed, standing by her side.

"I thank thee, sister. May thou and thy companions find joy in the mortal realm," she said, knowing that Hetica and the others would not be able to return to Lunara. She hoped they would establish a Moon clan in the Lower Lands, perhaps creating a new citadel in honour of their goddess.

Astra raised the Moon Staff toward the blue moon. "Mother, grant the Moon Staff the power to forge an opening within the Silk of Remembrance," she prayed to the moon.

Blue light emanated from the Moon Staff, the air grew dense, and the silk materialised before her eyes as a white veil that covered the land of Lunara. She watched as the veil split from the middle, creating an opening.

"The opening shall endure until thou hast traversed it, Hetica. I bestow upon thee the Moon Staff. Deliver it unto Selene at the precise moment we have deliberated. Timing is of utmost import," she said.

"Now, fare forth, seize the Moon Staff, and fulfil the desires of our goddess," she concluded.

Hetica accepted the staff and signalled her readiness. "So shall it be, my Queen. We shall not falter," Hetica said confidently. Then, she boarded the Traveller.

Astra lingered until the entire fleet departed from the coast, the ships eventually disappearing into the distance.

As the ships vanished from sight, she sensed a wave of weakness wash over her. "It must needs be, for I hold not the Moon Staff anymore. Henceforth, I didst become the Queen Regent," she murmured.

"What hast thou wrought, Astra?" a whisper carried through the air with a sinister tone.

She startled, spinning around and searching for the source of the mysterious voice. Despite her efforts, there was no one in sight. The blue moon continued to shine brightly in the sky, its radiance contrasting with the lingering shadow of the dark moon.

Perchance 'tis but a trick of the mind, she thought.

DEMORIA

Demoria was seeking some peace in her room at the Grey Skull when a series of knocks interrupted her tranquillity.

"Who is it?!" she shouted.

"It's Wren Presleye. Lady... witch… ma'am, the Balor Witches are back. They're attacking the barrier," a voice responded from the other side of the door.

I can't have a moment to rest, can I? she thought.

Rising swiftly, Demoria rushed along to the door. She flung it open and found Wren, the squire of Hallard, standing there. Wren couldn't have been more than fifteen, she estimated.

"Ma'am... your…" Wren stuttered.

Demoria noticed that the boy's face had reddened, and his gaze was fixed upon her chest. She then realised she was naked from the waist up.

"Oh, damn it, have you never seen a woman's body before? Don't you have a mother or sisters?" Demoria inquired.

"My mother's aren't as pretty," said the embarrassed boy.

Demoria blushed slightly at the unexpected comment.

"That's... a compliment, I guess. Boy, turn around while I change. Tell me, what's happening downstairs?" replied Demoria with a brusque tone.

Wren obeyed, facing away. "The Balor wi-witches, they're attacking the barrier. They're thro- throwing what seemed to be explosives, that—that are weakening your ba-barrier, ma'am. Sir Hallard has requested your presence downstairs, if it pleases you."

"It does not please me the slightest, Wren," she said

sarcastically.

Demoria noticed that Wren seemed to struggle with speaking after seeing her half-dressed. *I'm a bad influence for boys*, she thought. She was also growing tired of being caught between the Balor Witches and the men from Lakefields.

She descended the stairs to the main area of the Grey Skull. On her way down, she recalled recent events in the tavern. Last night, she received confirmation that the Balor Witches, disguised as ordinary thieves dressed in black, had attacked the Lakemen who were investigating a barbarian insurrection in the Blue Bell Mountains. Despite the Lakemen' valiant fight, most of them succumbed to the witches' power. Only a few escaped and rode towards the Grey Skull. Following their path, the Balor Witches have come to the tavern, under the cover of the night, intending to exterminate what remained of Hallard's army. Hallard implored Demoria for help to rid his men of a terrible poison called the Yellow Decay that had infected them. Left with no choice, she reluctantly agreed to help Hallard and his men. She erected a fire totem of protection using stakes and a skull found inside the tavern, hoping it would grant them some time to shield themselves from the Balor Witches' menace.

The totem formed a circular barrier around the tavern. The Balor Witches, unaware of Demoria's presence in the tavern, crossed her barrier and ignited from the inside out, dying on the spot. She sensed that at least eight witches had crossed her barrier, while the rest remained outside of it.

"What is it?! Hallard, I've already provided all the help I can for now," she said upon entering the main hall, where Hallard, his men, the owner of the tavern and some other travellers were gathered. Glancing quickly at her fire totem, she noticed it was beginning to crack.

"I'm so sorry," Hallard apologised earnestly. "You're our only hope right now. If those witches destroy your barrier, they'll kill us all."

She then walked towards a window and peered outside. She realised Wren was right; the Balor Witches had set up some sort of explosive object which was slowly dismantling her barrier. She hadn't anticipated the Balor Witches breaking her barrier so soon. *They must have found a weakness in the barrier*, she thought.

"I erected the protective totem rapidly; it's no wonder they've found a weakness. The way it goes, it will last a few more moments. You should pray to your favourite god or demon, arm yourselves, and prepare for battle," she said feeling uneasy under the realisation she would have to fight the Balor Witches.

Hallard knelt before her, grasping her hand. "Demoria, our lives are in your hands. We're few, but we'll do as you say. There must be a way out of this. Please, help us."

Be careful what you ask of a Shabrani witch, she thought.

It was a grim truth: even if she fought, she couldn't possibly end up victorious towards a group of witches. Moreover, the witches outside the tavern were not ordinary Balor Witches; it appeared they had been augmented to wield even greater power. *They might take me as a prisoner*, she reflected, *and perhaps torture me, or worse.* She had to act.

But she also had her own mission to complete, and time was slipping away. *I've already lost too much time. If I'm going to die here, I'll try to take those Balor Witches with me*, she mused.

Demoria took Hallard's hand. "Hallard, magic isn't always the solution. Sometimes, it causes more harm than good," she said.

Releasing Hallard's hand, she moved toward the fire totem, touching it gently with her right hand. She sensed the totem's energy decreasing rapidly. *Soon, it would be nothing more than an inert object*, she realised.

"There's a way we could vanquish our enemy tonight," she said, turning around to see the faces of Hallard and his men, transitioning from despair to hope.

"Don't think it'll be easy, because it won't be. I need all of you to gather on the right side of this room," she commanded Hallard's men.

They exchanged confused glances, Hallard then backed her orders and the Lakemen moved as they were instructed. Then, she quickly assessed each one of them, selecting a few of them and guiding them to the left side of the room.

The Lakemen appeared puzzled. "Tell us, Demoria, what is your plan?" inquired a man of an athletic build, muscular yet not overly bulky, with a well-defined physique that suggested strength and agility. His dark brown hair was cut short, neatly framing his face. She learnt that his name was Wybert Townere, a renowned warrior in whom Hallard placed great trust.

These men lack patience, she thought, *but it's understandable given the circumstances. They're facing imminent death.*

"When I healed you from the poison of the Balor Witches, I said it was impossible to know if you would completely recover," she took a deep breath, "The men I've placed to the left side of the room won't survive more than a few days due to the lingering poison within their bodies. Your lives should not go in vain. If you allow me, I plan to cast a spell on you," she said, studying their faces carefully. "In simple terms, this spell involves channelling some of my fire energy into you. For some time, you'll be able to control fire at your will. We Shabrani Witches call this magic Fire Specters. But after my magic wears off, you will lose your lives."

A heavy silence settled in the room. Suddenly, a massive explosion outside rocked the tavern, sending dust and fragments of wood raining down from the roof.

Hallard was the first to break the silence. "I can't let my men die this way."

Another man interjected, "They're facing death either way. Let them face it with honour in battle rather than doing nothing."

Another one who looked older than the rest spoke up, "I'll willingly give my life to protect the younger among us. I've lived a full life, I have no regrets. Captain, let me sacrifice myself to defend you."

Several others from both sides voiced their thoughts. She noticed that most of the men she selected to be sacrificed seemed willing to take on the task. *Men sacrificing for other men—perhaps this world isn't as broken as I believed*, she contemplated.

Hallard paced the room, lost in thought. Suddenly, another explosion violently shook the tavern, causing part of the wooden roof to splinter and break.

"I don't like this plan. But it's our only option, and time is against us. As a captain, I've already failed by allowing so many of us to die," Hallard paused, his voice wavering slightly. "Your names will be sung in the songs of Lakefields for centuries to come. Your lives will not be in vain. I'll make sure your families know of your sacrifice."

Hallard called for his steward, Wren, but he was nowhere to be found. It took some time for him to come running.

The steward hurried, "Sorry, sir, I was in the restroom."

Hallard instructed Wren to fetch parchment and distribute them to the men willing to sacrifice themselves. They each wrote their full names on the parchment. She observed that Hallard appreciated being organised and keeping records, a quality not many men possessed.

"I never knew a man so organised. If I had met you before, I might have asked you to organise my bedroom," she tried to joke. Hallard smiled but didn't respond.

Another explosion, stronger than the previous, shattered mirrors and lanterns.

"Please, my lady, do something before they destroy my tavern. I'll give you all the gold I have if that's what you want," pleaded the desperate tavern owner.

"We'll begin shortly. I don't need gold, but I will take some food and water once this is over. My travels are long," she said to him.

Sensing the fire totem's energy declining rapidly, she addressed the Lakemen. "We should start now. Those not chosen, arm yourselves and be prepared to attack. Once the barrier falls, we'll fight the Balor Witches."

They acted swiftly. Even the steward was ready to join the fight.

"Hallard, I have another task for Wren if you allow me to. It will serve to distract the Balor Witches," she said. Hallard took a good look at her; he was scanning her eyes.

"Are you serious? Do you really doubt me?" Demoria questioned, a mixture of anger and amusement playing across her face.

"By nature, it's difficult for me to trust someone I've just met. Forgive me, you can make use of my steward as long as he comes to no harm. He's a good lad, and his parents are friends of mine. If something happened to him, I wouldn't know how to explain it to his father and mother," Hallard said.

She studied Hallard attentively. *He looks quite endearing*, she thought to herself.

"I promise to take care of Wren," she assured him.

"Hey, Wren, come here," she called the steward over.

Reaching into her robes, she retrieved a small bag and emptied its contents into her hand. Wren startled as soon as he saw the contents.

"Don't be frightened. This is an eye, a bull's eye to be precise. It's enchanted by me to create a distraction. I won't give you too many details; you'll know what to do with it when it's activated," Wren nodded in understanding. "On my signal, take this eye in front of your right eye, and you'll see what I'm talking about," she instructed.

The boy took the eye but paused before placing it over his right eye.

"No, not now. Wait until I tell you," she ordered Wren.

All the men were ready, including the men she was going to turn into fire spectres.

"Does it hurt?" inquired a young man, seemingly no more than twenty-five.

"What's your name, brave soldier?" inquired Demoria.

He seemed nervous as he responded, "My name is Dane, my lady."

"Dane, I won't deceive you. From what I know, there will be pain. Your body isn't accustomed to this type of energy. It'll affect your nervous system, so it might sting. But don't panic; I'll guide you through it. Just remember to breathe. Inhale and exhale. Hopefully, your body will acclimate to my energy soon, and then the pain will feel like a small prick on the back of your toes. Not something to worry about too much after that."

Another man asked, "How would we know how to use fire magic? We are not witches, is it even possible?"

Demoria smiled reassuringly, "Oh yes, once my energy is in you, you will have a sense of handling fire magic. You will know what to do, believe me."

Hallard explained the plan to everyone in the room. The strategy was for the volunteers to act as a surprise. While the Balor Witches were focused on them, the rest of the Lakemen would swiftly follow to take the witches down. Demoria believed the plan was sound.

"Hallard, a word with you," she said.

They both moved to a corner of the main area in the tavern.

"Once my energy is within your men, I will be very fatigued. I will need to rest for a while in my room. I won't be able to contribute much after that".

"You have my thanks…" Hallard was expressing gratitude when she interrupted him.

"Don't thank me yet, we could all be dead by morning. I've created Fire Spectres before but never more than one at the time. In any case, keep yourself alive Hallard, the Lower Lands need more brave men like you," she attempted to sound optimistic.

She approached Hallard and whispered in his ear, "Besides, it would be unfavourable if someone like me died in a place like this. It is not fitting for a Shabrani witch." She noticed Hallard was blushing.

"I'll keep my promise, I will see you in the morrow." Hallard then took her hand and kissed it.

If the room was observing the scene, she didn't care. No one had ever made her feel as though she were a proper lady before, and she intended to savour the moment.

She was ready to start. Approaching the volunteers, she saw some looked scared while others seemed determined.

"This may sting a little," she warned them.

She closed her eyes and extended her hands, murmuring a few incantations. She felt the energy emanating from within her and flowing through the air. Her energy manifested as red and yellow flares, edging closer to Hallard's men, almost touching them. As the flares began covering them, the room was filled with screams. Some of them were resisting her magic.

"Do not resist the fire energy. Embrace it, let the pain pass through you. Resisting will only make it worse," she urged them.

One of the men collapsed to the ground immediately, unable to withstand the energy; his heart couldn't endure the pain. Panic began to grip the other men.

"Lakemen, remember our training, recall who you are and what you protect," Hallard's voice echoed across the room. "You protect your families and lands. If this evil threat wins, they'll destroy the lives of those we swore to protect. Give your life for them, think of them in this time of peril!"

The captain's words seemed to strengthen the men. They stopped resisting her fiery energy and the screams stopped.

The men's eyes began changing to a dark colour. Simultaneously, their veins became clearly visible on their faces and necks, turning into a deep crimson red colour.

"The Fire Spectres are ready," she announced.

She suddenly recalled what a witch taught her during her training days. *They are one of the greatest weapons created by the Shabrani clan since the Age of the Primes. A few spectres can eliminate an entire army.*

For just a moment, she forgot about the perilous situation she was in. She knew that creating Fire Spectres was a triumph, something to be celebrated. She felt a surge of accomplishment as she saw them poised for battle.

ELLA

The night is unusually bright, she thought. There were no clouds in the sky, allowing a clear view of the stars above. In the Dark Forest, such clarity in the sky was a rarity, with the black trees and dense vegetation obscuring much of the sky. As a child, she had heard stories about the sky outside the Dark Forest and had always been intrigued by it. However, as an adult witch, her focus had been solely on becoming the best witch she could be. Despite her relentless efforts, there were always witches more skilled than her, and regrettably, some of them took pleasure in bullying her.

But things are different now, she contemplated. *I possess power—power beyond any other Balor witch. Even if they told me I won't be back, I wish someday I can return to the Dark Forest and show those bullies the true extent of my new strength*, she vowed to herself.

Her current power proved formidable, allowing her to survive a mortal wound inflicted by a man's attack at the Blue Bell Mountains just two days ago. The attacker had wielded a two handed sword, a heavy weapon that landed directly on her chest, tearing it open and causing significant damage to organs and bones. Any ordinary mortal would have died instantly, but she endured.

After the attack, she remained unconscious for a while. Upon waking, she learned from her fellow Balor Witches that the group of Lakemen had managed to escape their ambush.

"They needed to die. We could have killed them," angrily declared one of her sisters named Fila, a proud witch who only spoke about how powerful she was and her accomplishments in the Balor clan.

"We were all afraid of the unfamiliar magic emanating from that lakeman, which allowed them ample time to slip from our grasp. It was a force unlike any I've seen before—ancient magic, I believe. I was afraid he could have annihilated us all with his mysterious power," replied Ceca, the leader of the Dark Thorns.

Ella witnessed the mysterious power first hand, just a brief moment. With her small sword in hand, ready to strike the man, she suddenly felt an unusual energy emanating from him that nullified her magic. The shock made her flinch. That momentary hesitation was all the time the man needed to land a decisive blow on her.

The impact made her lose consciousness as her body instinctively initiated the healing process. Upon awakening, to her surprise, there was no lingering pain even though her stomach was still wide open trying to heal itself. The open wound revealed her flesh and bones entwined with red and yellow vines.

This is the state of my body now. I am half plant, half human, she reflected.

"We've waited long enough, great leader. Have you pondered the mysterious power, or should we bring it before the Great Council? I can almost smell the banquet they'll prepare upon our return. They might even grant you a seat on the council—just as you desired." Fila spoke in a sarcastic tone to Ceca.

Ceca's expression turned to anger, and in one swift motion, she sliced Fila's right arm with her sword. Fila screamed, dropping to one knee and glaring at Ceca furiously.

"This serves as a warning to anyone challenging my authority. Fila, consider this a mercy. Cross me again, and you'll lose more than an arm." Ceca sounded menacing. "Sisters, we depart immediately. The Yellow Decay infesting the Lakemen' bodies leaves a trail of magic we can follow."

Turning away, Ceca walked towards the group of barbarians. Ella had almost forgotten about them.

A few days before the confrontation in the Blue Bell Mountains, Ceca had informed the Dark Thorns about an acquaintance they would encounter on their journey. Despite inquiries, Ceca refused to disclose any details.

"It's all part of the Great Council's plan," said Ceca.

On their journey, they crossed a small forest near the intersection between Gorgon and the Lakefields region. She didn't know the name of the forest, but the trees were a yellow-green colour, much like her own skin.

In the deep areas of the forest, they found an encampment that seemed hastily built. Tents were half-assembled, using animal pelts as roofs and walls. The horses were not properly taken care of, running rampant throughout the camp. She noticed the absence of sentry guards to warn of incoming enemies. *They must be reckless barbarians*, she thought.

A group of barbarian men and women readied their weapons at the sight of the Dark Thorns.

"Stop! They are our guests. Keep doing your chores!" ordered a barbarian who seemed to be their leader, judging by the way he commanded.

"Apologies, witches. We rarely distinguish between foe and friend. My name is Amaru, and I am, as you would call it, one of the leaders in this clan."

The barbarian leader looked older; however, he exuded fierceness, evident in the deep scars marking his body. He carried small axes on each side of his waist, clad mainly in leather with metal plates covering vital organs.

"My name is Ceca, and I am in charge of this group of Balor Witches. Tell me, I've always been confused by how the barbarians organise their leadership hierarchy. No one really knows how many clans exist in these lands and how many leaders. What do you call your clan, Amaru?" asked Ceca.

Amaru laughed, "You are amusing. Yes, there are many clans of barbarians. I have lived among them since I was born and do not know all of them. Some say if you kill a barbarian clan, two more come up from underground. Our clan is called Runakuna, which in your language means 'those who fight'." While speaking, Amaru walked, circling and studying them from head to toe.

"But, you are just a few fragile women. The old witches claimed you are worth more than five hundred men. Is that true?" the barbarian leader jested.

Ceca smiled back at the barbarian. "I assure you, we are worth that and more," she replied in a confrontational yet respectful tone. "Tell me, Amaru, how many barbarians will be riding with us?"

"All of us. We are two hundred in total, and I can assure you, we are worth more than a thousand of those common men from the region of Lakefields," said Amaru defiantly.

Ceca took a good look at the barbarians, and Ella knew exactly what she was thinking. *These barbarians look young, like they've never fought before. They must not be the most experienced of the clan. The rest of the clan are probably located elsewhere, and these barbarians are just part of an exercise to gain experience or gather intel*, she thought.

Ceca approached the barbarian leader and offered her right hand. "This will do," she said. Then, they shook hands.

After sealing the agreement, Amaru returned to his clan and initiated preparations. Ella watched as they disassembled the half-built tents and gathered the horses for departure. She pondered whether they would indeed journey alongside the barbarians. To her knowledge, an alliance between a witch clan and barbarians was unprecedented.

Maybe the Great Council didn't trust the Dark Thorns completely, which is why they forged a pact with the barbarians, she thought.

She felt the urge to ask questions about the unusual alliance, but she held back. Asking questions was never her role; it was a task for someone bolder, such as Fila.

The barbarians took some time to prepare. Eventually, Amaru and another, who appeared to be no more than thirty years old, approached them. They addressed Ceca directly. "We are prepared, witch. This is Atoc; he will lead the group of barbarians accompanying you. Though young, he is strong and a respected leader among our clan."

"You are not joining us, Amaru?" asked Ceca.

Amaru laughed again, "You ask too many questions, witch. I am an old man; I will only slow you down. My bowels move several times during the day, you see." Ceca tried to hide her disapproval.

"I am needed elsewhere. Safe travels, witches. We of the Runakuna clan hold faith in the sun god. May its blessings be upon you all." With those words, he rode off to the north.

Atoc, the newly appointed leader of the barbarians, was not much of a talker. As they journeyed towards the Blue Bell Mountains, the witches grew concerned, noticing Atoc's struggles with the common language.

Reflecting on the battle alongside the barbarians in the Blue Bell Mountains, Atoc and his warriors proved to be a valuable distraction during the assault on the Lakemen. The plan was for the barbarians to initiate the attack, allowing the Balor Witches to swoop in later as a surprise ambush. The strategy proved successful; the element of surprise, combined with the poisonous mist, resulted in heavy casualties among the Lakemen. *If it weren't for that man's strange magic*, she muttered to herself, *we could have vanquished them all.*

Following the battle, the barbarians appeared defeated and grew distrustful of Ceca and the Dark Thorns.

"Pact done, pact done," said Atoc.

She saw how Ceca attempted to remain patient. "Hold on. We hold the advantage here. The Lakemen' forces have been diminished considerably. If we pursue them at full speed now, we'll catch up to them soon. Remember, they are infected by our poison; they won't be able to travel far."

Despite their advantageous position, Atoc refused to act. He insisted it was too late to pursue their enemies. "They are now fleeing into Gorgon, which falls under the territory of the Shabrani Witches," explained Jacqui, a female barbarian warrior who could speak the common language and served as Atoc's translator at times. "The Shabrani Witches are too powerful. We are not allowed to engage with them."

After some time, the discussion ended. Ceca couldn't persuade Atoc and his barbarians, even when she offered him gold, which he promptly refused. Ella remembered another witch once telling her that barbarians were usually more attracted to gold than anything else. It seemed Atoc was different.

Furious, Ceca ordered the Dark Thorns to pursue the Lakemen, leaving the barbarians behind in the Blue Bell Mountains.

They rode through the desolate land of Gorgon, tracking the poisonous trail left by their infected enemies. The landscape was arid, with most trees either dead or dying. Ella saw no signs of wild animals, only a few crows and sparrows scavenging for food.

From an early age, she had learned about the Shabrani clan in Gorgon, witches proficient in fire magic. This magic was so formidable that other witch clans feared it. Due to their power, the Shabrani Witches had contracts with most nations, except the Golden Nation, which was already occupied by Starr Witches. It was widely known that Shabrani Witches were not to be taken lightly; they could be formidable adversaries.

They rode for a day and a half, yet their enemies remained out of reach. Inspecting the wound inflicted by the man's large sword, she felt a tingle on her stomach. Though it didn't cause intense pain, it produced a ticklish sensation.

She was riding next to Matena, whom she trusted. Ella knew she could speak freely with her companion. "How is it that our enemies have covered so much ground already? They should be dying."

"Lakemen are direct descendants of the Primes, who were said to be the strongest and most resilient creatures that walked these lands more than six hundred years ago. They likely inherited some of these attributes. Despite their strength, they won't survive for long, sister. No mortal being can escape our lethal poison," explained Matena.

Fila joined them, riding alongside. "Our great leader is scared," she said.

Here she goes, Ella thought as Fila launched into her narrative. Ella and Matena exchanged confused glances.

"You two are clueless as always," Fila remarked, punctuating her statement with a sarcastic gesture. "I'm talking about Ceca's altercation with the Shabrani clan in the past. Our leader is very old, probably one of oldest among us in the Dark Thorns. The gossip says that in the past, she fell in love with a man from a nearby town in the Dark Forest. However, the man was deeply infatuated with a Shabrani witch. When Ceca discovered this, she attempted to kill the Shabrani witch while she was on her way to visit the man. Ceca stood no chance against the Shabrani witch and survived only because the fire witch spared her. When Ceca returned to the Dark Forest, she bore many wounds and was on the brink of death. Want to guess what saved her?" asked Fila.

Matena and Ella exchanged confused glances once more.

"The Great Council gave her the Balor seed," Fila said.

She understood. The Balor seed had cured Ceca from her injuries, granting her a second life among the Dark Thorns.

"Ceca survived after absorbing the Balor seed," Matena confirmed.

Fila nodded. "It's common for the Shabrani Witches to ride in this territory. There's a high chance we could encounter them. I wonder if our leader, Ceca, has considered this possibility." Fila's face betrayed a hint of excitement.

She had only heard tales of Shabrani Witches, never encountering one herself. If a confrontation occurred, she knew blood would be spilled.

Curious, she asked, "What is it that you dislike about our leader? Despite being tough, she has guided us well."

Fila responded angrily, "You're really naive, Ella. Ceca isn't interested in leading us; she'd lead us straight to hell if she could. All Ceca wants is a seat in the Great Council. Everyone knows that.

The only reason she hasn't killed us one by one is the Balor seed. The Great Council can hear everything we say."

She disliked being called names. "You should be aware that the Great Council is listening to this conversation too," she shot back at Fila in anger. While Ella got along with everyone in the Dark Thorns, she never felt comfortable around Fila, whom she saw as somewhat of a bully.

"Ella's right. I hope you understand that there's a Balor seed within you as well," Matena remarked to Fila.

Fila touched her stomach and asked, "Are you sure about that?" then urged her horse to quicken its pace, putting distance between herself, Matena, and Ella.

I really dislike her; something should be done about her, she thought to herself.

Confused by Fila's words, she turned to Matena and asked, "What do you think she meant? I thought we all went through the same process, she should have a Balor seed inside too." Matena was just as puzzled.

After a lengthy ride, they spotted a tavern in the distance. Matena informed her that the tavern, named the Grey Skull, belonged to a Celen man. In this part of the Lower Lands, taverns were precious and considered neutral territories, serving as the only places where one could find refuge.

Ceca halted the group. "The poison trail leads to the Grey Skull. Our enemy must be inside," she said.

"If that's true, we cannot attack it. We must wait until they leave the tavern," advised Avera, a witch as old as Ceca and second in leadership.

Ceca, however, disregarded Avera's caution. "Sisters, our task is in a dire situation. We cannot allow ourselves to wait any longer. Our enemy is right in front of us. We shall destroy them no matter where they are," Ceca said, walking with her hands behind her back.

Fila stepped forward defiantly.

"If we do that, we will be destroying a valuable asset in these lands. That tavern is not just used by Shabrani Witches or Lakemen. It's also used by our people. If we destroy the tavern, Balor Witches will be in danger if they seek refuge in the future," Fila argued.

Ignoring Fila, Ceca insisted, "We will leave our horses here. Hurry up, sisters; there is no time to lose."

Ella noticed that Fila was ready to continue arguing with Ceca. Before Fila could say another word, an explosion erupted right where she was standing. When the dust settled, Fila's lifeless, headless body lay on the ground.

"Does anyone else have anything they'd like to say?" asked Ceca defiantly.

Afterwards, no one dared to defy Ceca's orders. The Dark Thorns started walking toward the Grey Skull in silence. Outside the tavern, they found the remaining Lakemen.

"Attack!" Ceca ordered.

She thought they had the advantage and could eliminate their enemies swiftly. However, before the attack commenced, Ella sensed another presence inside the tavern—a presence emanating a raging energy she had never felt before.

How did we not notice this before? she wondered.

She noticed how the energy was growing bigger and bigger.

Then she heard Ceca screaming, "Sisters, stay back, now!"

Ella, positioned at the back of the group, had enough time to react, but some of her sisters were not as fortunate. A barrier materialised before her eyes. The Balor Witches caught within the barrier erupted in flames, screaming and desperately trying to escape it by throwing themselves on the ground. Yet, the flames refused to dissipate.

After a few agonising seconds, the flames swelled, culminating in a violent explosion. Blood stained the ground, leaving nothing of her sisters, not even a trace of flesh.

Plants cannot withstand fire, she thought. She had a hard time seeing her sisters die the way they did.

Regrouping, she counted less than half the Dark Thorns among them. Between them, Matena survived, and her leader Ceca also managed to escape the barrier as well, although she was injured by one of the explosions.

"What was that? Our sisters—half of us are dead," Avera panicked, demanding answers from her leader.

She noticed that her leader bore wounds on half her face and left arm, which were already healing. Ceca didn't react to Avera's question.

"Speak, leader. What are your orders?" Avera screamed, shaking her leader by the arms.

Ceca's eyes, initially vacant, shifted from Avera to the remaining Dark Thorns.

"Let go of me!" Ceca yelled back, pushing Avera to the ground. She started walking toward the barrier but stopped just before crossing it.

Ceca's hands were shaking. Ella then realised her leader was afraid.

"It is a Shabrani witch, no doubt about it. Start preparing rot bombs; they should be enough to destroy this barrier," said Ceca angrily.

Ella had never witnessed Ceca in such a state; her typically brave and confident leader now appeared profoundly afraid. In a flash, she remembered Fila's earlier tale of Ceca's encounter with a Shabrani witch, realising how this might have intensified her leader's fear.

"Ella, quick, give me the rot powder you brought; I will help you make some bombs," said Matena, who also appeared nervous.

Why am I not nervous? wondered Ella.

Rot bombs were a mixture of rot powder and various other elements gathered by the Balor Witches. To create the bombs, they had to combine all the ingredients inside an empty satchel. Once mixed, the reaction would commence shortly. After the reaction, the satchel would explode, generating a shockwave followed by a rot cloud infecting everything nearby with rot. Timing was crucial; if they threw it too late, the explosion could reach them. Rot was one of the many poisons in the Lower Lands, infecting skin and organs with irreversible effects.

Ella attempted to assist in making the bombs, but she lacked the skill in the science of mixing ingredients. A miscalculation could lead to a backfire, and without instruments to measure, only experienced Balor Witches could create the bomb safely.

Observing the fear in Matena and the other witches, Ella realised she had to take action.

She took Matena's hands, looking into her eyes. "Everything is going to be okay. I will protect you, my friend."

Glancing at her leader, she found Ceca on the ground near the barrier, hands covering her face, muttering unintelligibly.

She's lost all control; someone needs to step up, thought Ella.

"Focus on making those bombs," she heard someone saying.

Ella took a moment to identify the voice's source. There was no mistaking it. Fila was the one speaking as she walked toward Ceca.

"It can't be; we saw you die. I killed you myself," said Ceca.

"Well, it seems it's not so easy to kill one of us, even if our heads are severed". Fila then pointed to her head, "Look, my head is still healing," Fila's head had a tender appearance, her flesh had turned green and she had lost her hair.

Fila took Ceca by the arm, pushing her to the side. "Our great leader, you are useless. Stay out of our way," Fila declared.

"Even if our heads are cut from our bodies, we can still live. That is remarkable," Matena said to Ella.

Then, Fila stood before the Dark Thorns. "Sisters, I will now assume command. Our leader, Ceca, has relinquished her position," Fila announced, locking eyes with each of them defiantly.

"Is there anyone who disagrees?" Fila challenged the group, though her gaze was fixed squarely on Avera. As the second in command, Avera should technically take over after Ceca.

Avera remained silent.

"I thought as much," Fila said, her smile brimming with satisfaction. "Now, those bombs that are ready, start throwing them!" Fila commanded.

Ella began hurling the bombs that were ready, and the other Balor Witches followed. They watched as the barrier slowly weakened. The shockwaves from the bombs were so powerful that the tavern inside the barrier visibly shook. To her surprise, despite the strength of the explosions, the barrier diminished very slowly.

The Shabrani witch must be something else to conjure such a strong barrier that even our rot bombs are struggling to break, she meditated.

The rot bombs left a vast trail of poison; any other human who made contact with it would be infected and die painfully. However, for the Balor Witches, it posed no threat, as they were immune to rot affliction.

Fila approached Matena and Ella. She could see that Fila's face was still in the process of healing, looking somewhat puffy and tender.

"It seems it will take us some time to destroy this bloody barrier," exclaimed Fila.

"It will take a while. The rot bombs were made hastily; they're not as powerful as the ones made in the laboratories in the Dark Forest," Matena said firmly.

Fila's eyes remained fixed on the barrier, as if studying it. Then she lifted her right hand and pointed with her finger to a specific area in the barrier.

"Look, again, it is starting to shatter," said Fila.

She observed the spot Fila indicated. It was cracking akin to the shell of a boiled egg, a clear sign that the barrier was coming down.

"The barrier will be destroyed. Look for the weak spots and throw the bombs at them!" Fila shouted to all the remaining witches.

She saw everyone doing their best. *Perhaps Fila is a better leader than Ceca*, she considered.

On the other hand, Ceca was still on the ground, her arms now wrapped around her body. Avera was beside her, seemingly trying to bring their former leader back to reality.

Suddenly, the barrier came down completely, making a loud noise like shattering glass. Small red fragments scattered across the ground, resembling red snowflakes that vanished slowly into thin air.

She saw shadows approaching from the tavern. As they came closer, she recognized them as Lakemen. Some were riding horses, while others ran on foot behind them. Their numbers seemed diminished, indicating most had already perished by the Yellow Decay.

Some of her sisters prepared to launch an attack against the Lakemen. She was also ready to fight.

"Something is wrong; stay put!" screamed Fila.

The unexpected twist unfolded before them. The Lakemen on horses stopped halfway, while those on foot continued approaching. As they neared, she saw a difference in their appearance, their veins were pronounced and crimson. She could also feel fire energy within them.

Suddenly, the energy within them intensified. Light emanated from their eyes and mouths, followed by agonising screams as though they were being torn apart from the inside. In an instant, their bodies transformed into living fire, their faces and forms consumed by flames. Over their heads, fire crowns materialised over their heads, making them even more threatening.

"Do not fear, sisters! Get ready for their attack. We will not be surprised this time," Fila tried to lift their spirits, but she knew it was too late. Their sisters looked astonished at the presence of the fire monsters.

Another unexpected event happened; she witnessed black smoke rising from the Grey Skull in the distance. The smoke took shape into a horrific figure—a humanoid with huge black horns, red eyes, and pointy teeth. She recognized it as the embodiment of the Fire Lord, Shabranibodoo, a creature from the tales of the War of Ashes.

The figure was horrifying to behold, unsettling her sisters, who began to scream in fear. Ella herself felt a surge of fear. Every Balor witch had learned about the War of Ashes and the time when Shabranibodoo had walked the Lower Lands. She vividly recalled her lessons about the war and how her teachers had described the appearance of the Fire Lord. Now, that exact description stood before her, a chilling reality.

She looked at her new leader, Fila, who was desperately shouting orders that went unheard amidst the chaos. The fire monsters charged at them. She quickly discovered that vega magic was useless against this new enemy, who retaliated with intense fireballs, engulfing everything in flames.

The agonising screams of her sisters pierced the air, causing her distress. She tried to locate Matena but could only see fire and smoke. *This can't be happening. We are the best of our clan; we cannot be defeated like this*, she thought desperately as the inferno raged around them.

A fireball struck her right shoulder; one of the fire monsters was attacking her. The fire didn't dissipate, instead, it began spreading along her right arm. Without hesitation, she took immediate action. Drawing her small sword, she cut her right arm. She bit her tongue to hide a scream, the pain lasting only a few seconds. Several more fireballs were directed at her, but she managed to dodge them all.

Then, she heard a disconcerting noise—a voice and screams she recognized all too well. Matena was in agony.

She ran, following the screams, until she found two of the fire monsters cornering Matena, relentlessly hurling fire at her. Matena struggled to dodge the relentless assault.

Ella rushed to aid her sister, but her attacker was still targeting her. Placing her hand on the ground, she channelled all her vega magic into the earth. Hundreds of vines emerged from the ground beneath her enemy, ensnaring it as much as possible. *This won't kill it, but it should buy some time to help Matena*, she thought.

With her adversary momentarily restrained, she sprinted towards Matena. Memories flooded back as she ran. Recollections of their early days with the Dark Thorns flooded her mind, when Matena was her only friend. Nights when they shared the same bed for comfort. Moments when Matena offered solace during times of pain. She realised Matena was everything to her.

When she reached the spot where Matena should have been, there were only ashes. She had arrived too late.

For the first time since receiving her new life, she realised tears were still within her capacity. Clutching the ashes with her sole remaining hand, she carefully placed them in a pocket inside her black robes. Anguish and emptiness welled up inside her. She fought to contain her pain, but sorrow overcame her as she wailed for her lost friend.

Then, a strange sensation swept over her. She felt somehow taller, almost as if her body was growing in height. Glancing to her right side, she noticed her missing arm had already returned.

Surveying her surroundings, she noticed three fire monsters closing in on her. She tried to locate her other sisters, but the enveloping fire and smoke obscured everything.

Anger surged within her once more. "The Shabrani witch inside the tavern is to blame. She has taken Matena from me, my beautiful Matena", she exclaimed angrily. Fury ignited in her as she vowed vengeance.

Ella was startled by an abrupt explosion. She realised the blast originated from within her. It obliterated everything in its vicinity, including the fire monsters.

The echo of the explosion lingered as she heard a voice calling her name. "Wake up, Ella. We need to leave," Fila said.

Though the events that followed were unclear, she became aware that she couldn't run or move, even if she desired to. Glancing down at her body, she discovered the absence of her limbs.

Rather than panicking, a serene smile graced her face.

HALLARD

The battle with the Balor Witches unfolded with a few unexpected changes. The plan started just as they had intended. Once Demoria's barrier got dismantled, Hallard's men would charge at the Balor Witches. When in close proximity, the selected Lakemen would transform into Fire Spectres and attack first.

"The plan is good; it will catch the Balor Witches off guard," Demoria remarked. Following that, they planned to let the spectres engage the Balor Witches, with the remaining men intervening only if absolutely necessary.

The other part of the plan fell to his squire, Wren. Gifted with an item from Demoria, Wren would project a vision resembling a humanoid-demon figure. Hallard had heard that this was the commonly believed appearance of Shabranibodoo, the lord of the Shabrani Witches.

"The Balor Witches have bought into the same tales, Hallard. They'll be terrified before realising it's just an illusion," said Demoria.

Everything had proceeded according to plan, except for an unforeseeable twist. The Fire Spectres, whose strength surpassed expectations, were eliminated in a massive explosion caused by a Balor witch. Before triggering the explosion, the witch underwent a transformation that was beyond description.

"It was a huge beast with countless arms," recounted one of Hallard's men, who escaped the explosion.

"Not quite, more like a tall tree with a human face," said another.

Whatever it was, it obliterated everything in its vicinity—the Fire Spectres and the remaining Balor Witches.

The explosion left behind a toxic cloud, which made it impossible to look for potential survivors. After some time, Hallard ventured to survey the area's safety. He realised it was suitable for exploration; however, he found no survivors, only ashes and scorched patches on the ground, likely remnants of the fight with the Fire Spectres.

Yet, in the heart of the battleground, he discovered a small area covered with grass and yellow flowers, an unexpected sight amid the destruction. There, among the grass and flowers, he located the two handed sword he lost in the Blue Bell Mountains. While relieved to see his weapon again, it dawned on him that the Balor witch he had struck at the Blue Bell Mountains must have survived and made her way to the Grey Skull. *She's probably dead now*, he thought.

After Demoria examined the strange patch of grass and flowers, she commented, "This is the result of vega magic, I can feel it. This area could have been the epicentre of the explosion that ended the Fire Spectres and the Balor Witches." Demoria also assured him that she could sense neither vega magic nor the presence of Balor Witches nearby.

Back in the tavern, the owner was very grateful for having his life saved. "Here, take this; you've earned it," he said. Hallard and his companions enjoyed complimentary food and drinks, along with a few days of free accommodation. The generous offer was extended to Demoria as well, but she declined.

"Since I'm no longer needed here, I must leave right away. I have other tasks to take care of," Demoria announced as she made her way upstairs to her room, likely to pack. Hallard understood that she must be on a time-sensitive mission to be in such a rush to depart.

He couldn't allow Demoria to leave without expressing his gratitude. After all, it was thanks to her that they were still alive, and he felt compelled to express his gratitude and offer his services. As he made his way to Demoria's room, thoughts of the Shabrani witch crossed his mind. He had been struck by her eyes the first time he saw her—full of confidence and defiance, he recalled. Amidst the chaos of battling Balor Witches, he hadn't considered Demoria in any other light. Now that the battle was over, his feelings towards her became clear.

He reminisced about his youth when he was popular among the ladies at court in Rivercrash and Springrest. Before he joined the

Lakefields army, he enjoyed the freedom to interact with any woman he pleased. While he wasn't a regular at brothels, his travels to various cities provided opportunities to connect with women in taverns and outposts. Curiously, he had never been with a witch, and he wondered if the experience would be any different.

Standing before Demoria's room, he knocked on the door.

"If that's you again, Wren, I swear I'll turn you into a frog," came Demoria's voice from the other side of the door.

As the door opened, he noticed Demoria was surprised by his presence. A faint flush coloured her cheeks.

"Hallard, it's you. You startled me. I wasn't expecting anyone. What can I do for you?" said Demoria, her surprise evident in her voice.

He then knelt down on one knee. "I'm here to thank you again and to assure you that you'll always be welcome in the Lakefields region. I can't speak for the king, but my father's castle, Rivercrash, will always have its doors open to you."

"There's no need for this, Hallard. I—" he interrupted her.

"Also, I would like to offer my services from now on. I want to travel with you, to be your shield and sword whenever you need me. It's the least I can do for all you've done for us," he said, remaining on one knee.

Demoria took him by the hands and helped him stand up. Up close, he noted her delicate appearance, realising she barely reached his shoulders in height. It was hard to believe the immense power she held within. He couldn't help but steal glances at her partially covered breasts beneath her black dress.

"Thank you for the offer, but I doubt I will be well received in the Lakefields region," Demoria closed her eyes, pausing. Then she continued, "As for coming with me, that's not possible. My next destination is the unknown Duskenwood. I'll need all my wits to survive such a desolate place. I'm afraid you'd only be an annoyance in my way," said Demoria.

She then unbuttoned her dress, letting it fall to the ground. Naked, Demoria's dark skin looked stunning against the candlelight.

"I believe there's another way you can repay me," Demoria said, and then she kissed him.

He didn't know when it happened, but at some point they were both naked and kissing each other in Demoria's bed. Hallard kissed her in every single spot of her body. *She is exquisite*, he thought. While he was inside of her, Hallard noticed her long black hair was now moving on its own. Demoria's hair wrapped him around the waist and started thrusting harder and harder.

"Is this how witches make love?" Hallard inquired.

She placed a finger on his lips as they continued throughout the night.

Hallard awoke with the first rays of the sun streaming through the window. He stretched his arm looking for Demoria but she was no longer beside him. Yet, her essence lingered, impregnating the bed.

Dressing quickly, he descended the stairs, hoping to find Demoria still in the tavern. Considering her earlier mention of being in a rush, he speculated she might have already departed.

The atmosphere in the tavern felt different that morning compared to the previous night. Just moments ago, they were all in peril, but now, the travellers were enjoying their meals and drinks without a care. A traveller played a lively tune on a small guitar, contributing to the serene atmosphere. Hallard scanned the tavern spotting Demoria seated in a corner, quietly enjoying a meal and a drink by herself.

"Good morning. I am glad you haven't left yet," he greeted her.

Demoria smiled as she greeted him and pulled out a chair for him to join her. "Hallard, I didn't expect you to be up so early after last night," she said.

She sounds enchanting, Hallard thought, which brought a smile to his face. "I was hoping you changed your mind about taking me with you," he added.

Before she could respond, Wybert Townere, one of Hallard's men, interrupted their conversation.

"Sir, sorry to interrupt, but our men are wondering this morning if you have decided on our next move," Wybert asked.

Hallard glanced at Wybert, silently wishing he hadn't brought up that question at this moment.

Demoria chuckled softly.

Hallard hadn't yet formulated a plan for the next steps. Waiting seemed the prudent choice, but if the Balor Witches intended to instigate a conflict with the Lakefields region, informing King Larus was imperative. However, the thought of alerting the king about the Balor Witches made him uneasy. There was also the matter of the remaining half of his army near the Blue Bell Mountains, potentially facing threats, and the concern for his ailing father.

"You'll have my answer after I finish my talk with Lady Demoria," Hallard informed Wybert.

Wybert nodded respectfully and left the room.

"Your men are honest and brave; you've got good company with you," Demoria noted. "I couldn't help but notice your pause before responding to your man. Is there something bothering you?" Demoria asked him.

Hallard considered it wise to share his doubts with Demoria. As an experienced witch, perhaps she could help him decide on the best course of action.

"Ever since the ambush by the Balor Witches and barbarians in the Blue Bell Mountains, something has troubled me. It's evident they were aware of our presence, almost as if they anticipated our every move. How could they have known?" he questioned.

He observed Demoria taking another spoonful from her porridge.

"You're right. Additionally, the alliance between the barbarians and Balor Witches is concerning. Barbarians typically prioritise gold and can be swayed by any clan or nation offering it. However, for the Balor Witches to stoop to such an arrangement, there must be something more they're seeking," she explained, taking another spoonful. "As for your other concern, there is a traitor among your ranks, and from what I can tell, it must be in one of the highest ranks," said Demoria.

Hallard's suspicions were confirmed by Demoria's words, and he had an inkling of who the traitor might be. *I hope I'm wrong*, he reflected.

"If you'll hear me out, Hallard," Demoria leaned in closer, her voice low and confident. "There's a larger game at play here. You'll require allies, beyond just the man in your employ. Consider forging an alliance with a witch clan or nation," she suggested in a whisper.

Hallard noticed she had finished her meal. As she stood up, he delicately took her arm.

"The Shabrani Witches—they're the nearest clan to the Lakefields region. If you could vouch for us, your clan's support could be invaluable," he proposed.

Demoria gazed into his eyes. "Our clan typically avoids such big affairs," she said. "However, there might be a way. You'll need to sway the Great Council of our clan; they are a group of witches who decide our tasks. The old witches will demand something in return. Yet, even if they are satisfied with your offering, you're essentially proposing to start a conflict with the Balor Witches and barbarians— a monumental task. I can't recall a time when we've been tasked with something of this magnitude," Demoria explained.

He knew that what he was asking was almost impossible, but he had to try. The war could escalate quickly, and Demoria was right— he needed allies.

"I could offer part of Lakefields to the Shabrani Witches. As I told you, I am Hallard Rikers, the heir of one of the biggest cities in the Lakefields region, Rivercrash. Once the land passes to my name, the Shabrani Witches will be welcome to enter whenever they like," Hallard proposed.

Demoria let out a laugh. "The Great Council might like that. Gorgon is not precisely the richest land. However, they might still deny the petition," she said. "You will also need to speak to the Great Council in person, which means you need to be granted permission to enter the Crimson Castle. There is only one way to…"

Suddenly, they were interrupted.

"Sorry to interrupt," Wren, his steward, said.

Wrong time to interrupt, Wren, Hallard thought.

"The owner of the tavern, Grey Skull, tavern has found something outside. Please come; he is asking for both your presences," Wren seemed worried.

He didn't like the way Wren was looking at him; something was wrong. Following Wren's steps, Demoria and he walked outside the tavern.

"The Celen man thinks he found the remains of a Balor witch," said Wren.

He felt uneasy. *If this is another attack, we will be vulnerable*, he thought.

Arriving at the area Wren mentioned earlier, they found the Celen man on his knees, examining something on the ground. It was the same grassy spot where Hallard had found his two handed sword. As he approached, he could see a green and yellow thing among the grass, resembling a small putrid fruit. It seemed to pulsate, mimicking the beats of a heart. *Whatever it was, it was alive*, he realised.

"Demoria, what is it?" he asked, hoping the Shabrani witch knew more about it.

Demoria examined it for a few moments. At the same time, the Celen man extended his finger to touch it.

"Stop! Do not touch it," Demoria ordered.

Surprised by the witch's voice, the Celen man stumbled backward, nearly falling.

"Interesting, I can sense vega magic from it. I think this creature is the remains of one of the Balor Witches we fought yesterday. It appears to be focusing on recovering, but it doesn't have enough energy to do so. If you touch it, it is possible it will try to assimilate your flesh and steal your energy. We don't want that to happen, do we?" explained Demoria, looking at the Celen man.

The Celen man nodded.

"It wasn't here before when I surveyed the area," said Hallard.

Demoria placed a hand on her chin, deep in thought. "It's possible it was hidden underground. If my theory is correct, this thing is more intelligent than I initially believed. This is concerning," she said.

"What do we do with it, Demoria? We can't leave it here," he asked.

Demoria continued to gaze at the thing on the ground. "No, we can't. We must take it somewhere else," she said.

"We must bring this to my clan, to the Dukka volcano. The Great Council will know what to do with it," Demoria said, touching his chest almost affectionately. "Captain of the Lakemen, you wanted a way to get into the Shabrani clan and speak to our Great Council. This is your chance."

She was right. It feels as if fate has placed that thing deliberately, giving me the perfect opportunity to seek an alliance with the Shabrani Witches, he thought.

"Hallard, a word with you, in private," asked Demoria.

They walked away from Wren and the Celen man. Hallard noticed that Demoria made sure they were a good distance from the others.

Taking a small piece of parchment from inside her robes, Demoria pricked her finger tip and began writing. Once finished, she handed the parchment to him. "You must deliver this glyph to a Shabrani witch named Mila in our clan. The last time I spoke with her, she mentioned she would be staying within the clan for a while. As soon as she sees this glyph, she will help you," explained Demoria.

He couldn't imagine how or where to find Mila once he was inside the Shabrani Witches' clan. "How would I recognize Mila? And why her?" he asked.

Demoria placed a hand on her chest. "Use your heart to find Mila. I am sure you will succeed. Why Mila? Well, let's just say she has a strong dislike for Balor Witches. She can explain more when you meet her. Mila will ensure the great council examines the thing you're bringing," said Demoria.

He had a good feeling about Demoria's plan. It gave him a sense of hope.

Afterward, they both returned to where Wren and the Celen man were standing. Demoria used her magic to make the thing levitate and placed it in a small leather bag she took from her robes. She spoke a few words, turning the small bag red.

"I have sealed this bag with magic so it won't open from the inside in case this thing tries to escape. It's important that you don't open it, Hallard. Only open it when you reach your destination," Demoria explained.

He knelt before Demoria and said, "On my honour as a member of the house of Rikers, it shall be done," looking directly into her eyes.

Demoria smiled at him. "Do it for yourself, Hallard. It won't be an easy task, but I wish you the best of luck. I must leave now."

Before Demoria departed, almost instinctively, he reached out and took her hand. Initially uncertain of why he did so, he soon realised he simply didn't want to let her go yet.

Getting close to him, she whispered, "We'll see each other again soon." She smiled at him one last time, and with that, she left.

Hallard felt conflicted; one part of him yearned to pursue her, but the other part knew he had a crucial role to play. He needed to travel to Gorgon and the Shabrani clan, for the future of Lakefields..

Then, placing the bag in a secure spot within his armour made his way back to the tavern. On the way, he spoke to his squire. "Wren, please tell our men to prepare to leave the tavern. We will depart as soon as everyone is ready," he requested.

He suddenly remembered something that was in his head since he woke up, and he ran as fast as he could towards the stables. By the time he arrived, Demoria was about to leave on her mount, a sleipnir, nonetheless. He had seen sleipnirs before but had never ridden one himself. They were a peculiar breed, a cross between a bovine and a horse—smaller than horses but reputedly faster.

"Well, it seems we're seeing each other sooner than anticipated," Demoria remarked, her surprise evident in her expression.

He grabbed the necklace he had around his neck. The necklace was an heirloom cherished through generations in his family. Its pendant bore the shape of a golden leaf. With resolve, he tossed it to Demoria.

"Catch!" he said.

"The necklace belongs to the Rikers family, said to protect the bearer from any mortal wound. It saved me in the Blue Bell Mountains, although I don't entirely understand how it works," he explained to Demoria.

Demoria gave the golden leaf a good look. "Thank... you? I mean, we Shabrani Witches don't wear a lot of jewellery."

Without saying another word, he ran away from Demoria making his way back to the tavern. Though he heard her calling out to him, he resisted the urge to glance back. He understood it was time to bid her farewell and follow ahead on his own path.

Back at the tavern Hallard and his men prepared to depart.

They bid farewell to the owner of the tavern, who was already busy attending to more travellers who had arrived that morning.

"We owe you, my friend, thank you for your generous hospitality," Hallard tried to recall the name of the Grey Skull's owner, however they were not properly introduced. "Excuse me, sir. What is your name? I've been calling you Celen man all this time," asked Hallard.

"Rem, sir. My name is Rem. There is no need to thank me. I built this tavern to help anybody who needs it. It just happened this time it was you," said Rem very calmly.

He then extended an open invitation to Rivercrash, assuring Rem that he would be welcomed with the utmost hospitality, treated as royally as he deserved for his invaluable assistance.

He walked out of the tavern to find his men ready to go. Back at the Blue Bell Mountains, they were two hundred and fifty. Now, the numbers had dwindled to only twenty-two.

"Wybert Townere, you will be in charge of the company from now on. You are to reach the rest of our army waiting near the Blue Bell Mountains. Once you find them, regroup with them and ride as fast as you can to Rivercrash. I will meet you there," he said.

Wybert, Wren, and the rest didn't react well to Hallard's news.

"I fear there is a great threat coming to our nation. I need to find allies as soon as possible," he explained.

Then, he had a few private words with Wybert.

"If for some reason I don't reach Rivercrash in time, you must tell my father and mother about our fight with the Balor Witches and the barbarians." *If father is still alive*, he thought.

"Though I would prefer to deliver the news to my family in person, it's imperative that our nation prepares for battle as swiftly as possible," he declared.

Wybert nodded.

His squire had red eyes and was trying not to cry when Hallard bid farewell.

"Follow Wybert's orders to the letter, Wren. You are a good lad and a great warrior. Do not doubt your skills," Hallard tried to lift Wren's morale.

After that, he rode west alone.

THE BLUE PRINCE

Looking at the entire fleet, he was bothered by how slow they were moving. *At this rate, we shall arrive at our destination in a thousand years' time*, he thought sarcastically. They had to move at the pace of the Traveller, a small ship carrying Moon Witches, which was much slower than the Ganimed battleships. He couldn't shake a feeling of unease about their journey with the Moon Witches, as it marked the first time in a long time that they were working together.

He recalled the last time someone had departed Lunara, nine Moon Witches crossed the Silk of Remembrance to find a Blood Priest in the Lower Lands. *A Blood Priest*, he reflected. He learnt that the priest played a crucial role in the Moon Witches' visions, foretelling a prophecy of death and despair. According to the prophecy, the Blood Priest was destined to bring a new Age of Ashes to the world. Emmerich had accepted to go with the Moon Witches as it was his duty; however, he had doubts that the witches' visions were true. *If thou dost ponder upon the Moon Witches being misled, then mayhap their visions were not always infallible*, he contemplated discussing these concerns with his father, the King of Ganimed, although at the last minute, he decided to keep his doubts to himself. He knew the king had to obey the Moon Witches, no matter what.

Emmerich sailed aboard the Leviathan, the largest and most powerful battleship in the Ganimed fleet. Designed specifically for warfare, it was equipped with numerous cannons and harpoons strategically placed at the front and back. The vessel was a formidable force, and its immense size allowed it to withstand any weather conditions, no matter how turbulent.

Positioned at the forefront of the fleet was the Leviathan, while at the very rear sailed the Traveller. Despite its delicate appearance, the Traveller stood out as the brightest in the fleet, shining brightly under the light of the blue moon. Emmerich knew the witches carried a very important item with them: the all-powerful Moon Staff. He had learned that the queen had entrusted Hetica, the moon witch leading the company, with the task of delivering the Moon Staff to her daughter in the mortal land. According to moon witch traditions, this symbolic act signified the queen stepping down and passing the baton to the young princess, who would become the new queen upon making contact with the Moon Staff.

"Verily, 'tis a curious custom," he said aloud once safely back inside his cabin. "In most realms, titles are inherited by the next heir upon the demise of the sovereign. Moon Witches, indeed, possess a peculiar custom."

A knock echoed on the door. "Prince, 'tis Harrik. Didst thou summon me?"

He welcomed him in. Harrik, the general of the Ganimed army and second in command after Emmerich, was a few years older than him and therefore more experienced in battle.

"We must converse in private," he declared.

Since he had been tasked with travelling alongside the Moon Witches, the king often stood between him and Harrik, preventing any private conversations. He had been eager to speak frankly with Harrik for some time.

"I have known thee for many a year, and I am aware that we hold akin beliefs. We both harbour a profound love for the realm of Ganimed, prepared to undertake all in service of our king and our folk. Nevertheless," he paused, taking a breath, "Grant me pardon! Art we truly destined to follow the Moon Witches and meet our demise for their cause?" he observed Harrik nodding in agreement.

"Speak thy mind freely, Harrik," the prince remarked.

"Thy words ring true, prince. Though they bring me no joy to utter, it appears our king hath bestowed excessive authority upon the Moon Witches over our kin. I comprehend the oaths our forebears swore, yet this accord shall not yield contentment among them. The multitude accompanying us on this journey doth raise concerns. Furthermore, the recent hostility of the men of Terra towards our realm cannot be ignored. Were Terra to attack us, Ganimed would find itself vulnerable and undefended," Harrik explained.

He agreed. He had raised the Terra threat with his father multiple times in recent years, but the king had paid no attention to the warnings.

"Enough! The folk of Terra are akin to us, Primes of pure blood. I am acquainted with the monarchs of Terra; they harbour no ill intent towards us. Despite occasional discord between our nations, the Moon Witches intercede to mitigate any perilous circumstances. I am confident all shall be well," Emmerich recalled a conversation he had with the king.

'Tis fruitless to dwell upon the past. We are embarked upon our journey, and there exists naught we can alter therein, Emmerich reflected in silence.

"This is wherefore I sought privacy in our discourse, Harrik," his tone grew more serious. "Swear to me, that irrespective of the circumstances, we shall prioritise the welfare of our people. Swear to me in the name of our folk, the Primes of Ganimed." he requested.

Harrik didn't respond immediately; he began to pace slowly around the room. *Should he betray me, I can kill him this very moment, and none shall take note*, he thought.

After a moment, Harrik kneeled, saying, "My allegiance is yours, prince. It shall be done." Harrik swore his allegiance.

"Prince!" someone yelled from outside his cabin.

Emmerich grabbed his sword and hurried out with Harrik. There stood Harper, a member of his royal guard— a formidable warrior who had won several tournaments back in Ganimed.

"Pardon me, sir, thou must see this," Harper pointed to the east.

On the east side of the fleet, the water was raging. It appeared as though the area were boiling, with countless bubbles disrupting the surface. Emmerich had never seen anything akin to it before.

After a while, a bright blue light started to shine from the turbulent water.

"Bring me the enchanted glass!" he shouted, urgently.

The Moon Witches had provided him with various artefacts, each serving a different purpose. Among them was an enchanted glass, daggers, swords and helms. The enchanted glass allowed communication with the Moon Witches inside the Traveller.

Emmerich took the enchanted glass in his right hand and uttered the words taught by the witches, "I call you, Hetica."

The object glowed with a pale blue light.

A voice came from the enchanted glass. "Prince, we see the strange behaviour of the waters. We don't know what it is, if perchance thou dost ponder upon it. Beneath these waters lie mysteries, even beyond the ken of us Moon Witches. I suggest we swiftly sail away from this place with all haste," Hetica advised.

"Hetica, at this present hour, we traverse the silk. Should some unknown force assail us, we must procure safeguard. I beseech thee, or one amongst thy sisters, to hasten unto the Leviathan. 'Tis but a matter of safeguarding our security," he asked politely.

There was a moment of silence before Hetica spoke again.

"As thou hast requested, I shall dispatch two of my sisters to the ships stationed upon the east and west flanks of our fleet. Another amongst our kin shall make haste to the forefront, to the Leviathan, with all speed. My own presence, however, shall remain here at the Traveller, bearing the Moon Staff whilst we traverse the silk."

Before he could respond, a shockwave jolted Leviathan. The force was so intense that he feared the mighty battleship might snap in half.

Chaos ensued on the Leviathan; screams filled the air. Initially, he struggled to comprehend what was happening before his eyes. The sheer size of the Leviathan made it difficult for him to believe it could shake so violently. His crew rushed from top to bottom, left to right, attempting to repair parts of the ship that had broken during the shockwave. He witnessed his men grabbing ropes and pieces of wood.

A second shockwave struck the fleet.

"Ahhh!" he screamed. He managed to grab onto one of the support bases of the ship, preventing himself from being thrown overboard. On the other hand, some of his men were thrown into the sea.

In the midst of the chaos and madness, Emmerich turned around and saw a colossal figure emerging from the turbulent waters he had noticed earlier. This gigantic entity seemed to be lifting itself from the ocean, appearing as if it was made of light. Its head was covered by a silver helmet of monumental size. He found it challenging to take in the giant of light with his eyes.

Amid the clamour surrounding him, some of his men worked feverishly to repair the Leviathan before it sustained more damage, while others stood, stunned by the sight of the giant of light.

He held the enchanted glass once more.

"Hetica, prithee, what sorcery is this? What doth unfold ere our very eyes?" he screamed at the glass. The glass remained silent; there was no response from the Moon Witches.

What do they now? This giant of light shall rend us asunder if it continueth its ascent! he thought anxiously.

He moved as swiftly as possible, navigating through the tumultuous movements of the ship to climb one of the towers on the Leviathan. The ascent was challenging with the ship's constant motion. Reaching a high vantage point, he surveyed the damage inflicted upon the entire fleet by the shockwaves. Some ships had already been destroyed, and men who were thrown into the ocean were swimming desperately away from the giant of light.

Emmerich spotted Harrik nearby.

"General! Proclaim far and wide! Command the captains of the Swifter, Blue Feather, Strong Wind, Skinny, and any other swift-sailing ships to hastily assemble the men stranded by the loss of their ships. Bid them to gather them forthwith unto the Leviathan; ample space doth await their arrival," he shouted to the general.

Harrik nodded and immediately began communicating the orders to his crew.

Suddenly, a piercing sound emanated from the giant of light. The high-pitched noise left him astonished. He observed the water moving ominously and saw the giant lifting something from below the surface.

A third wave slammed into the fleet. He had no time to react, and the shockwave threw him down from the tower. Landing on his back, the impact was so forceful that he bit his tongue, tasting his own blood. It took him a while to stand up; his head was dizzy, and blood ran down his forehead. Fortunately, his heavy armour protected him from further harm.

"Prince, art thou well? I prithee, take thy seat and rest," said Harrik.

"Aye, I am well. Pray, what be the damage wrought by the latest shockwave?" Emmerich asked.

"Prince, we hath suffered the loss of a third part of our fleet. Our men do journey to other ships by means of swimming, yet the tempestuous billows doth thwart their efforts; the greater part of them are engulfed by this accursed sorcery," said Harrik, who looked nervous.

"The Moon Witches! Curse them, one and all! They must hath been known to the presence of the giant of light. They dispatched us foremost in the fleet as their defence shield. 'Tis the reason their ship, the Traveller, doth linger at the rear of the fleet," he said, agitated and angry.

He looked at the giant of light, wielding a huge blue sword with both hands, pointing it down towards his fleet.

This doth appear to be our final hour, he thought, a sense of impending doom setted over him.

Suddenly, a bright blue light coming from the south seized his attention, momentarily blinding him. As his vision cleared, he witnessed the Traveller, the Moon Witches' ship, flying at full speed towards the giant of light. In any other circumstance, he might have deemed it a beautiful sight, but the dire situation overshadowed any appreciation. The Traveller was enveloped in a blue light, leaving a silver trail behind it in the air, resembling something out of a dream.

The giant of light began swinging its massive sword down towards the fleet. He observed his men covering their faces with their hands, as if that would shield them from imminent death. However, the Traveller positioned itself in front of the impending blow. The clash between the small ship and the giant's sword produced a high-pitched sound. It left a tingling noise in his ears. The last thing he saw of the Traveller, it turned into a cloud of blue dust descending from the sky. The blue dust covered the entire fleet, transforming everything into blue—from the ships to the armour they wore, even their hair.

To Emmerich's and everyone's surprise, the giant of light began to melt, dissipating from their sight.

I did curse them; I owe an apology unto them. The Moon Witches hath rescued us all, he thought in astonishment.

"Prince, behold!" one of his men shouted. He glanced to the sky, and there it was—the opening created by the Moon Witches in the Silk of Remembrance was closing down.

If we don't hurry, the silk shall soon close upon us, he realised.

In desperation, he issued new orders.

"Spread the word! There is no time to spare for the rescue of our men. Let every ship exert its utmost power to move forward. This instant!" He commanded whoever remained alive.

ALABASTER

"Stop that at once!" he shouted.

He felt another rock strike his forehead, catching him off guard. The blow opened a fresh wound, adding to the three he already bore. *This gives the Blood Priest's name new meaning*, he thought.

"I said, stop!" he shouted again.

For the past several days, Searc had been throwing stones at him, blaming him for Caitrin's death. A part of him felt sympathy for the boy; he understood his grief.

Following the events in the Rockshade Highlands, the mysterious girl—who had once been known as Aliune when she was a cat—forced him to reveal the location of the Blood Witches' clan in Duskenwood. Although tempted to lie, Alabaster knew it would only delay his own mission. Despite the perilous situation, he carried three living bodies with him, hoping the Blood Witches could still make use of them.

The journey had been long and slow, further hindered by the extra passengers in the wagon: Searc and the old man Truinan, who had decided to accompany the mysterious girl. To Alabaster's surprise, she didn't oppose their company.

Since the encounter with the barbarians in the Rockshade Highlands, the mysterious girl had grown notably silent. She rode at the front of the wagon with Truinan by her side, while Searc and he travelled at the back. They travelled all day and rested briefly at night. Thanks to the girl's protective magic, they remained invisible to other travellers. *She doesn't want to deal with more barbarians*, he thought.

After a failed escape attempt, the mysterious girl bound him with magical ropes, impossible to untie by conventional means. He was her prisoner, something he was beginning to grow accustomed to. *First, I was a prisoner of the Blood Witches, now I am her prisoner. Nothing ever changes for me*, he thought.

The mysterious girl and Truinan guided the horse on their journey. Truinan seemed well-acquainted with the Rockshade Highlands, even leading them through what he claimed was a shortcut. However, in Duskenwood, the old man proved helpless.

Duskenwood was a vast swamp, covered in a heavy mist that rendered seeing into the distance nearly impossible. Even the sun struggled to penetrate the dense fog. Rumours circulated of strange creatures and animals inhabiting the region. With no roads to follow, their journey became exceptionally challenging, requiring frequent stops during the day. At times, they felt lost, and at others, they were certain they were moving in circles. The only person capable of guiding them through this daunting terrain was him—he had traversed the region before.

They brought the wagon to a halt. As the mysterious girl and Truinan approached, he couldn't help but wonder if they would ask for his assistance.

He took another good look at the mysterious girl, noticing her long, semi-curly blue hair flowing gracefully down her back. She was still wearing the same silky blue dress and was barefoot. Surprisingly, her feet were clean, as if freshly washed. After witnessing her use of magic, Alabaster had no doubts she was a witch, though he wasn't certain what kind. He had encountered witches before, including Starr, Balor, and Shabrani Witches. If he had to compare, the mysterious girl most resembled a Starr witch. However, there was something undeniably unique about her. Beyond her archaic dialect, her presence felt different—almost godly.

"I was waiting for you to ask for my help. We've been going in circles for days. It's wise of you to seek my assistance. Now, untie me, and I'll gladly help," he said.

"Verily, rejoice not overmuch, thou butcher. Thou shalt indeed aid us; yet, I harbor no intention to unbind thee," said the mysterious girl.

"Stupid little girl. I won't help you then. These lands are very difficult to traverse; you'll go in circles forever without my help," he said angrily.

He saw Searc drawing his daggers, ready to attack. Bracing for the imminent assault, he was caught off guard when Truinan stepped between them, intervening.

"Easy, Searc. This dude's gonna bite the dust soon. Let's stick to the little miss's plan for now," said Truinan, trying to calm the enraged boy.

Searc, seething with anger, protested, "He should be dead! We should've killed him at Rockshade Highlands. Aliune told us all about his evil plan. He was all set to bump us off and offer us up to his crazy god. No Golden Nation or army was riding to our rescue. That shiny medallion he flashed was just a fake!" Searc shouted.

Alabaster felt a twinge of remorse for the boy, a sign that some humanity still remained within him. He wished they could understand his situation—he was bound to serve the Blood Witches and honour their pact.

The mysterious girl placed a hand on Searc's shoulder. "I doth swear by mine honour, I shall deliver this man unto thee upon our arrival at our appointed haven. Grant me but a modicum more of time," she assured calmly.

Afterward, he noticed the mysterious girl drawing closer to him.

"Stay away from me. I won't help you," he said.

The mysterious girl placed a hand on his forehead. Instantly, it felt as though his head might explode. The pain was overwhelming, drowning out even his own screams. Past recollections flooded his mind, and suddenly, he understood what was happening—she was delving into his memories. He realised she was searching for a path through Duskenwood by examining his past. His memories unfolded like the pages of a book, revealing moments from his time with the Balor Witches, before he assumed the title of Blood Priest. Then, he glimpsed his lost family—his wife and infant son.

"No, not this. I don't want to remember this!" he cried out.

Once again, he relived the tragic day when assassins invaded his home, ruthlessly murdering his wife and child before his very eyes. Then the memories shifted. He saw himself journeying through Duskenwood, engaging with the Blood Witches. The scene changed once more, and now he found himself speaking with the woman who had once aided him during his captivity by the Blood Witches. Suddenly, the memories stopped.

He opened his eyes slowly looking at the mysterious girl's face. Her expression betrayed a sense of shock.

"Did you find what you were looking for?" he asked, still agitated. He noticed blood dripped from his eyes, ears, and nose, which he wiped away with his robes.

"Verily, the sole cause for thy continued existence rests upon our requirement of thy presence to enter the Blood Witches' encampment," said the mysterious girl.

The mysterious girl shot him a resentful look before returning to the front of the wagon, with Truinan following behind her.

Recalling his memories left him deeply troubled. For a time, he couldn't stop thinking about his past life in Duran with his wife and son. *Those dreadful memories had resurfaced—no!* He began to cry. For years, he had tried to bury the pain of the past. At first, it felt as though his chest would explode. Over time, the anguish became a part of him, and then, eventually, it seemed to fade.

Reliving those memories brought back all the guilt and emptiness. He wasn't sure how he could endure them again.

"Curse you, curse you, girl!" he yelled and cried.

A stone struck his nose, and he feared it had broken as blood began to trickle down, touching his lips. He could taste the metallic tang of his own blood.

"If you don't stop yelling, I'll just keep chucking rocks," said Searc.

Alabaster fell silent, fearing for his life. In the stillness, he cursed everything—his life and everyone he had ever known. He cursed the day he was born, his parents, and the gods, if they even existed. He cursed falling in love, becoming a priest, the Blood Witches, and the woman who had saved his life. Despair consumed him as never before.

He tried to hold back his tears. *This is not the time to feel defeated*, he realised. *Things can still turn in my favour. If the Blood Witches rescue me, they'll have three bodies for their work. Then I can ask for my reward*, he thought.

This newfound resolve made him feel slightly better. *After this last job, the Blood Witches would reveal the location of the assassins who had killed my family. I just needed to endure a little longer*, he contemplated.

Their journey continued, and it became clear to him that they were now following a different path. *It seems she knows the way*, he realised. The mysterious girl had found the right path to the Blood Witches' camp by delving into his memories.

Searc had stopped throwing stones as well, but the boy remained ever vigilant.

Alabaster recognized the route they were travelling. In the past, he had chosen this same path to enter and exit Duskenwood. It was the safest route, far from swamps and filth, known to only a select few. The only people he had ever encountered here were merchants—peaceful individuals who preferred avoiding confrontation to safeguard their supplies.

Considering playing mind games with the boy, he asked, "Tell me, boy, what do you know of the mysterious girl—the one you called Aliune?"

He observed as Searc clenched a stone in his hand. "She's gotta be a witch; that's all me and the old man can figure," replied Searc.

He's not throwing the stone at me? Perhaps I've piqued his curiosity, he thought.

"Indeed, she can use magic, and she is a witch. You know what all witches secretly search for in this world, don't you?" he said, attempting to capture the boy's attention.

The boy gazed at the sky, lost in thought, and began tossing stones one by one outside the wagon.

"It appears you don't know. I can imagine what it's like living in a place such as the Rockshade Highlands—you rarely receive any education there," he said.

Searc shot an angry look at him again.

I better not provoke him, unless I want another stone thrown at me, he thought.

He continued, "The books say that witches obtain their power from their masters. These masters are believed to be gods, deities, or lords of hell. You see, they go by many names. In exchange for their granted magic, witches promise to bring their master into this world through a ritual known only to them."

He locked eyes with the boy. Searc was paying full attention. *I've captured his interest*, he thought.

"What I'm saying is that the little witch over there is secretly trying to bring whatever god she serves to this world to destroy the Lower Lands. The last time one of these deities walked these lands, many men, women, and children were killed. They call it the War of Ashes," he explained.

"Lies!" the boy shouted, holding a stone in his right hand, threatening to throw it at him. "Your lies ain't foolin' me; Aliune warned that you'd spin tales to turn me against my own." said Searc.

He's not as naive as he looks, Alabaster thought.

"Say what you like, boy, but if you ask any scholar in the Lower Lands, they'll tell you the same." He paused, glancing around before leaning in closer to Searc. "Even though what I said is written in the history books, no one truly knows what's behind the witches' schemes and their magic," he said.

"Shut up!" Searc yelled, hurling a stone at him. This time, it struck his stomach.

They travelled all day until late into the night. When it became too dark, they stopped to make camp. They used his old tent and set up a small fire with sticks and stones. Not only did they use his tent, but they also took his utensils—a small pot and a few wooden bowls. The aroma of cooked rabbit filled the air.

As on other nights, they provided him with little food—this time, just a rabbit leg with almost no meat. He hadn't realised how hungry he was until he found himself gnawing on the bones, searching for any remaining scraps.

Soon after, the others put away the cooking utensils and prepared to sleep inside the tent. As usual, they placed him at the back of the wagon. He didn't mind sleeping on a hard surface—it was the cold of the night that unsettled him. *Perhaps this is punishment for all the times I carried dead bodies in this very wagon. The bodies were cold, and soon I will be too*, he reflected.

"Disliking thy new bed, Blood Priest?" The mysterious girl's voice came from the shadows, startling him.

"Witch? Why are you here? I've already told you everything I know about these lands," he said.

A dim blue light appeared in front of him, revealing the mysterious girl's face. She had conjured the light, illuminating the space between them.

"Whilst I was looking at thy memories, mine eye saw something that seized mine interest. Who is that woman with blue hair from thy memories? She is not a Blood witch," asked the mysterious girl.

At first, he didn't know what to say. The only woman with blue hair from his past with any connection to the Blood Witches was the one who had freed him from their dungeon. He still remembered the warm energy that radiated from her.

"You had no right to see those memories," he said angrily. "All you saw is all I know. She helped me once, when I was a prisoner of the Blood Witches. I know nothing else."

The mysterious girl approached him and leaned in close to his left ear.

"Verily, I perceive thou art concealing something. I could peruse thy memories anew and delve deeper therein. Yea, I couldst be led astray and venture backward through time to revisit the hour when thy kin were beset by misfortune. Dost thou desire such a thing?" the mysterious girl whispered in his ear, her voice soft and eerie.

Alabaster's eyes widened as he tempered his anger with the realisation that refusing to cooperate with the mysterious girl would only provoke her fury. The mere thought of her delving into his memories again was enough to deter him; he didn't want to endure that painful process once more.

"No, please, not that. I can't endure any more," he pleaded, tears streaming down his face.

"Then, impart unto me! What else dost thou know regarding the woman with blue hair?" commanded the mysterious girl.

Wiping his tears with his hand, he spoke. "From what I could gather, she's a witch, though different from the Blood Witches. The Blood Witches I'm familiar with are always cloaked in dark robes, their faces completely concealed. To tell you the truth, I've never actually seen their faces. But the woman with blue hair, as you call her, wore white garments and exuded a gentle energy. She even healed me when I was in need, so she must possess some control over magic. What kind, I can't say."

The mysterious girl listened intently, occasionally nodding her head as if fully engrossed in what he was saying.

"I witnessed thou didst converse with her. What prithee didst thou say unto her? And be not deceitful in thy response unto me," said the mysterious girl with a menacing tone.

"She mentioned seeking someone; beyond that, I don't know," he responded.

The mysterious girl paused, seeming to meditate on what she

had just heard.

"Didst thou behold her again after thy first encounter?" she inquired.

He cast a hateful glare at her, knowing it was prudent to speak.

"I did not. She vanished after freeing me from the dungeon. I haven't seen her since. My suspicion is that she resides in a place beyond my reach." He abruptly stopped speaking, sensing he had revealed too much.

The mysterious girl looked at him with curiosity. "Proceed," she demanded.

"There's a section within the Blood Witches' camp where none may enter but the Blood Witches themselves. I believe that's the place where they lay the corpses I deliver to them. It could also be where the woman with blue hair lives," he realised he had crossed the point of no return by divulging this knowledge, thus betraying the Blood Witches irreversibly.

"She must needs be the leader of the Blood Witches," said the mysterious girl.

"It's known that witch clans have their own governing bodies—the Great Council. I imagine the Blood Witches operate under a similar structure," he remarked, unafraid to speak his mind.

When the witches find out I have freely shared their secrets, they will probably kill me anyway, he thought.

"Thou art mistaken. Blood Witches were not amongst the earliest witches nor partook in the convocation of the Great Conclave. They are renegade witches, newly spawned in these latter days," said the mysterious girl.

Alabaster made a quirky gesture with his mouth. "Who are you? You know too much for your age. Or is that small body of yours deceiving me?" he asked.

The mysterious girl looked at him with disdain. "We are done here," she said.

The blue light disappeared and the darkness of the night returned. He could no longer see anything.

"One piece of advice, no matter what you do, the Blood Witches shall not aid thee in finding the assassins who did slay thy kin," He heard the mysterious girl's voice coming from the darkness of the night.

"What do you mean? How do you know?" he shouted, but there was no response.

For the next few hours, he pondered the girl's words. *Could it be possible that the assassins of my family will never be revealed to me? But the Blood Witches promised!* He thought about it over and over until his body hit the hard wood of the wagon, and he fell asleep.

The sound of an arrow striking the wagon near his face startled him awake. He opened his eyes, shaken by the sudden impact. They were under attack. He glanced at the attackers—horsemen in black armour, closely following the wagon, which was moving at full speed. Two of them wielded bows and fired arrows as quickly as they could. In total, there were six riders.

Despite his past training as a priest, familiar with the sigils, flags, and armour of various countries, these attackers were unknown to him. He couldn't discern their identities, the armour they wore, or even their appearance. *They are not from these lands,* he thought.

He didn't see Searc around in the back of the wagon, which made him think that the boy was in front of the wagon with the others. Contemplating escape, he found no viable method as the ties around his hands and legs were sealed with magic.

After a few moments, one of the riders drew closer to the wagon, which was gradually slowing down. *Damn, they'll kill my horse, Brave Legs, if they keep pushing him!* he fumed, his anger mounting.

The unknown attacker leapt from his horse and climbed into the back of the wagon. He quickly noticed the attacker was wielding a sword.

"Please, don't hurt me! I am a prisoner. They put me in magic ties; please free me, and I will help you with whatever business you have against my captors," he begged.

The attacker extended one hand and grabbed him by the neck. He felt the pressure on his neck and struggled to breathe.

"We are after you, Blood Priest!" said the attacker.

Before the attacker could finish him, the wagon came to an abrupt stop, violently throwing both him and the attacker out. His head struck the ground, and blood began to flow. It took him a few moments to open his eyes and make sense of the scene before him. The attackers were advancing together, weapons in hand, ready to strike the mysterious girl, who stood alone in front of him. He scanned the surroundings but saw neither Truinan nor Searc.

Four of the attackers ran towards the mysterious girl. Before they could strike with their swords, a blue light emanated from the girl's hands. Simultaneously, her blue hair grew longer and began to sway in the night sky. Then, two small blue swords materialised in her hands, crafted of the same magic as the greatsword she wielded to vanquish the barbarians in the Rockshade Highlands

Before he could blink, the mysterious girl had already decapitated the attackers. The remaining attackers, positioned at a distance, unleashed a barrage of arrows at her. With graceful movements, she skilfully evaded the incoming attack. Extending her right arm, she projected a beam of blue light that pierced through the chest of one of the archers. His lifeless body hit the ground with a heavy thud.

The remaining archer appeared frozen, stunned by the shocking demise of their comrades. Seizing the opportunity, the mysterious girl aimed another beam at the archer, who narrowly evaded the attack.

"We doth seek only the Blood Priest, hence, stand aside!" said the archer. He couldn't help but notice that the archer spoke in the same archaic manner as the mysterious girl.

The archer removed his helmet. Alabaster observed that the attacker was a man, bald with his face completely covered by strange white glyphs. He had never seen anyone like him before.

"He is my prisoner. Thou hast no right to take him at this moment," said the mysterious girl.

Alabaster saw the girl poised for an attack with her swords as he observed the man removing the armour from his left arm. Beneath the armour, he struggled to comprehend what he was seeing at first. The man's hand was entirely black with red nails, and six white wings were attached to the sides of his arm.

Immediately after removing the armour from his arm, an immense heat wave hit him in the face, compelling him to shut his eyes. Then, he witnessed the mysterious girl, for the first time, threatened by the entity before them.

The man pointed his strange arm to the night sky, gesturing toward the moon.

"Behold! The preparations art complete for a new Apocrypha, O Moon Witch. The six elder witches hast met their doom. The dark moon doth rise once more," the man said.

He gazed at the moon in the sky; at first, he discerned nothing, but soon he noticed a faint dark shape in front of the moon.

He turned his gaze toward the mysterious girl, who was also beholding the moon. She seemed astonished. Alabaster noticed her long hair returning to its normal length and her enchanted swords vanishing into thin air. *Apocrypha*, he reflected. *I think I read that somewhere when I was studying as a Balor priest. And... she is a Moon Witch? Such a clan is unknown to me.*

The moment he averted his gaze from the mysterious girl, he was blinded by a white light emanating from the man's strange arm. Everything around him vanished, including the ground beneath him.

He screamed as he descended into what appeared to be an

endless white abyss.

BASON

In other parts of the Lower Lands, a royal entourage typically consists of just a few horses and men accompanying a member of the royal lineage. However, in the Golden Nation, royal entourages were a unique spectacle, especially when commanded by the prince himself. Bason convinced his father, King Delray Artois, to organise the most extensive royal entourage the nation had ever seen. Under the king's command, a formidable delegation was assembled, comprising thirty thousand warriors from the renowned Golden Army, along with horses, battle elephants, and battle lions.

This grand entourage was being prepared for Bason's upcoming visit to his grandfather, King Hendrik Fitzroy, at his castle in Barral, capital of Borraral. It had been quite some time since Bason last visited, and he was determined to make a memorable entrance.

At the centre of the royal entourage, Bason's golden royal coach shone bright in the sunlight. It was adorned with intricate gold engravings and equipped with a spacious bed, tables, chairs, and all the necessities fit for a prince. Accompanying him were his devoted servants, Recaro and Valecio, who shared a large bed during the journey. The majestic coach was being carried by two imposing battle elephants.

Riding in the royal entourage alongside her brother, Princess Beatrice Artois had a smaller coach, but the opulence typical of the royal family was evident. She travelled in the company of several ladies attending to her needs and a Starr witch named Velaska, whose presence Bason did not particularly favour.

In the middle of the day, after several days of travel, Bason remained in bed, attended by his two servants. Valecio was meticulously combing his blonde hair, while Recaro busied himself with serving grapes, cheese, and bread.

"Do you know what the best part of riding in such a huge company like this is, Valecio?" he asked.

Valecio set the comb aside and teasingly pinched Bason's nipple. "This?" he said with a cheeky tone.

He delicately grabbed Valecio's hand. "I need you to focus on my hair for the meantime," he said to Valecio, who took up the comb again.

He continued his previous statement. "I don't have to attend to every single need. I have a general, and he has commanders who handle the simple things. That gives me time to enjoy the ride and sleep as much as I want," said Bason.

His thoughts then turned to his little sister and how insistent she had been about joining this trip. She claimed she wanted to see their grandfather, whom she hadn't visited since she was very young. However, he knew the true reason for Beatrice's journey. Velaska was part of the royal entourage, and Beatrice idolised the Starr witch. He understood that his sister aspired to become a more powerful Starr witch herself. *Perhaps, by being in close proximity to a Starr witch like Velaska, she hoped to accelerate her magical training*, he thought.

"Velaska…" he reflected.

Bason still recalled Velaska's words from their meeting with the royal family in the Heavenly Tower several days earlier.

"A long time ago, the royal family of Artois and the Starr clan reached an agreement to infiltrate a Starr witch into the Shabrani clan. This decision stemmed from growing concerns that the Shabrani Witches intended to resurrect their lord in the Lower Lands once more. After realizing that the Great Conclave did not share our concerns, we felt the need for a contingency plan to halt such actions if they were ever initiated. A few years ago, the infiltrated witch, now part of the Shabrani Great Council, established contact with another Shabrani witch in their council who supported our plans and kept our intentions a secret. Since that day, we've been monitoring the Eye of Meteora for updates from our spies. It wasn't until last night that we received shocking news: the Shabrani Witches have slaughtered all members of the Great Conclave," he recalled Velaska's words.

Suddenly, the royal entourage came to a halt.

"Recaro, go check the reason for this pause," he ordered.

His servant set a bowl of fruit and bread on a side bench and swiftly exited the royal coach.

Bason's thoughts once again drifted back to the day he met with the Starr Witches and the royal family. After hearing about the news regarding the Great Conclave, he had requested the king's permission to visit his grandfather before anything unfavourable occurred to him. Before the king could respond, his older brother, Terrence Artois, interjected. "Brother, stop! There's nothing we can do for our grandfather; he is too old and ill. On the other hand, the Starr Witches should be honoured for their impressive findings. Father, we should start celebrations immediately if you ask me," Terrence's authoritative tone rang out as usual.

King Delray cast a grim gaze at Terrence and said, "Do not attempt to tell me what to do, boy. I am still king, and I say it's prudent to keep this news hidden for the time being. We shall not make our schemes public; isn't that obvious?" The disappointment in the king's voice was evident.

You get what you deserved, older brother, Bason thought.

This had been their dynamic as long as he could remember. Terrence, as the elder son, often bore the weight of the crown as if it were his own. On numerous occasions, he tried to assert himself above the king, a behaviour the king disapproved of. Bason couldn't decipher whether Terrence sought to please the king or if he had intentions of seizing the crown. His older brother remained an enigma.

Turning his attention back to the matter at hand, the king addressed Velaska, "I congratulate you, and all the Starr Witches involved. We shall act before the Shabrani Witches' plans come to fruition." Bason noticed the complacent expression on Velaska's face as she received the king's praise.

Seizing the moment, Bason decided it was the right time to ask a favour of the king. "Father, with your permission, I would like to travel to Barral with the largest royal entourage to visit Grandfather and ensure his recovery from his injury," he said respectfully.

Initially looking displeased, the king's gaze shifted to Queen Elise, who nodded in approval. "You may; however, you will also take part of our Golden Army with you," the king decreed. At that time, he didn't understand why his father insisted he travel with the Golden Army, but she chose to ignore the matter.

Beatrice then emitted a high-pitched sound, seeking attention.

"You will also take your sister. She is eleven years old now, and it's time for her to get involved in royal matters. Take care of her," the king instructed. He had no other choice but to accept.

Turning to Velaska, the king added, "I hope you can guide my son and daughter as well," to which the witch nodded approvingly.

Beatrice had displayed magical prowess since birth. By the time she turned eight, she had already earned the title of witch, holding a one-star rank. Despite being a witch, she was the only exception among the clan allowed to leave the Heavenly Tower freely, as she needed to fulfil her role as the princess of the Golden Nation. The common folk often spoke of the princess's ability to wield magic and the belief that she would never be able to conceive children—a trait shared by all witches. Even within the palace, he heard whispers that if anything were to happen to the princes, the royal family line would end, as the princess could not bear children.

The fact that Velaska was also coming in the royal entourage made Bason wonder about hidden motives. It seemed strange to him that Velaska had to accompany them to Borraral. *What other schemes were the witches and the king planning?* he wondered.

Recaro finally returned.

"What took so long, Recaro?" he reprimanded.

Recaro, looking agitated as if he had been running, replied, "Prince, there is a messenger coming from Barral. They have a message for you."

"A message from Barral? What are you saying? How do they know we were coming?" he questioned.

Recaro remained silent, clearly unaware of the details. *He's just a servant*, he thought. Bason instructed Recaro to allow the messenger to enter.

Recaro left briefly and soon returned, accompanied by a woman whom Bason estimated to be no more than twenty-five years old. She had olive skin, wore leather with a cape, and bore the sigil of Borraral on her left shoulder.

"Prince, my name is Caffia Titus. I have been sent by your aunt, Amina Fitzroy. She asked me to deliver this letter to you in person," explained the messenger.

He took the letter and examined it, noting the seal of Borraral.

"Caffia, you said. I don't recall seeing you around my aunt. Do you live in Barral?" he inquired, setting the sealed letter on a nearby bench.

"Indeed, I live in Barral, but I have travelled with your aunt before, both within and beyond the Golden Nation. We actually met about a year ago—your aunt introduced us," Caffia explained.

Bason was taken aback by this revelation. He couldn't recall Caffia at all. In fact, aside from Recaro and Valecio, he couldn't remember anyone from the servitude who resided at Solaris Castle.

"I see," he replied. He then turned to Recaro and instructed, "Recaro, tell the general not to continue the journey until I give the word."

Recaro nodded and left the royal coach once more.

He then addressed Caffia, "So, would you like a drink? What was it, Cacia? Valecio will be pleased to attend to your needs. We have the finest wine in all the Golden Nation and the most succulent mangos and grapes," he said.

He noticed that the Barral messenger seemed visibly displeased.

"My name is Caffia. Prince, I must insist you read the letter sent by your aunt. She said it was of importance and needed to be dealt with as soon as possible. I have ridden for four days non-stop to deliver it to you. I beg of you to read it," Caffia urged.

He stretched her arms and legs, then began walking toward Valecio.

"What is her problem? I offered her the best of the wines and fruit we have to offer in the Golden Nation. Why won't she take it?" he asked his servant.

Valecio looked back at him with confusion. "Prince, it seems there is an urgent matter regarding this letter. Wine and fruit can wait until you read it," Valecio said respectfully.

He was still puzzled. *What could be so crucial that it needed to be opened immediately?* he wondered.

"Okay, okay! Caffia, you are very convincing. I now know why my aunt chose you for this task," he said, smiling.

Taking the letter, he opened it up. The moment he saw the content, he recognized his aunt Amina's distinctive handwriting. Growing up, Amina had been a mother to him in contrast to his stepmother, Queen Elise. She taught him to write and sing, guided him in dressing and speaking, and took care of him when he was sick.

"Bason, I've been informed by a raven that you are coming to Borraral with thirty thousand warriors. You may believe your father allowed you to travel to visit your sick grandfather, but I suspect he is sending you to persuade him into battling the Shabrani clan. I'm unsure how he plans to achieve this, but perhaps that's why Velaska is accompanying you. Consider this: the thousands of warriors you bring, combined with those in Borraral, would create one of the largest armies in the Lower Lands. I must urge you to remain where you are until your grandfather recovers, and I can discuss these matters with him privately.

P.S. I trust Caffia with my life; she is no mere messenger but one

*of the most skilled strategists and warriors I've encountered. You
can trust her too.*

*Your dear aunt,
Amina"*

As he finished reading the letter, he swiftly located the nearest
candle and began burning the piece of paper. The realisation struck
him: his aunt must have had someone infiltrate the Starr clan to
possess such detailed information about the royal entourage. *Who
could this insider be?* Bason struggled to recall the faces or names
of the Starr Witches, finding it challenging to remember details.

Frustration and anger surged within him. While he had indeed
sought his father's approval to assemble the largest royal entourage
ever seen in the Golden Nation, the scale of his father's
endorsement and the unexpected inclusion of the Golden Army
caught him off guard. The king's hidden motives were now apparent,
leaving Bason feeling deceived.

"Looks like I've been played the fool by my father," he said
angrily.

Strolling about, he contemplated his next move. Should he defy
his father, it could jeopardise his reputation. However, if he
disregarded his aunt's advice, he risked disrespecting the person he
trusted the most in all the world. He continued pacing, weighed
down by the gravity of his decision.

Suddenly, an unexpected visitor entered his coach—Velaska,
the Starr witch. She wore a silver robe adorned with black
ornaments, long, pointy earrings, and a beautiful silver necklace, her
blonde hair neatly tied up in a bun. Velaska bowed before Bason,
while Recaro reappeared, retracing her steps.

"Prince, Princess Beatrice is worried. She would like to know why
we suddenly stopped. Did something of importance happen?"
Velaska inquired. He noticed Velaska's eyes scanning the room,
with a particular focus on Caffia.

He understood that Beatrice's concern was likely a façade and
that Velaska was attempting to delve into his affairs. "Velaska, it's

good to see you. You look unwell. Have you been sleeping well?" he asked, attempting to deflect her probing questions.

"I'm sleeping well, thank you for your concern, Prince," Velaska replied, her expression unchanged.

An awkward silence followed, as Velaska maintained unyielding eye contact with him.

"Oh, yes. You must meet Caffia—she's from Barral. I wanted to catch up with her, and I can't have the royal entourage moving while I extend my hospitality to her. I'm sure my sister will understand," he explained.

Velaska greeted Caffia with a smile, which was warmly returned.

"Well, that is very considerate of you, Prince," Velaska said.

After a lengthy pause, Velaska continued, "As the guide appointed by the king himself for you and your sister, I must ask you to conclude this reunion as soon as possible. We have important matters to attend to in Borraral, and we must not delay any further," Velaska said calmly.

He detested Velaska's attempts to assert her importance in his presence. If it weren't for his father's decision, he would never have willingly travelled with the Starr witch. *The witch is a nuisance*, he thought to himself.

"Of course, my dear Velaska," he replied sarcastically. "Now, if you'll excuse us, I'll finish the reunion with…" He struggled to recall the messenger's name.

"Caffia," Recaro interjected.

"Oh, yes! Caffia! You have a strange name that is difficult to remember, my friend," he said to Caffia in an amicable manner.

Then, Velaska's calm expression quickly shifted to one of worry. She began walking toward the candles on a nearby table, where Bason had burned the letter from his aunt. He wondered what the witch intended to do. He observed Velaska moving her hand over the candles as if she were trying to glean information from the ashes of the burned letter. He grew nervous; he was uncertain about the extent of Velaska's powers. If she could reconstruct the letter from the ashes, it would be detrimental to him and his aunt.

"Strange," Velaska commented, then turned her attention to Caffia, as if attempting to read her mind.

"Well, Velaska, I think you are leaving," he urged.

Velaska gave a final look around the room before exiting and closing the door behind her. Bason felt as if he was a child once again, trying to avoid reprimand for a misdeed.

"Caffia, tell my aunt I will delay here for as long as possible. We are close to Junction City; perhaps I can extend our stay there a bit longer. It's imperative that you leave now. Starr Witches have peculiar ways of finding what they seek, and I suspect Velaska already knows we're up to something," he said.

Caffia nodded, preparing to leave. Meanwhile, he called to Valecio, "Prepare my bath. All this talking and decision-making have made me tired."

"It won't open!" Caffia exclaimed.

He glanced at Caffia, who, alongside Recaro, was struggling to open the door of the royal coach.

"Velaska! She did this. This is treason, and she will pay for it," he shouted, seething with anger. He knew it was Velaska's magic that had sealed the door shut.

He approached a chest near his bed that contained his armour and weapons, extracting a sword adorned with golden ornaments.

"Stay aside!" he shouted.

With a powerful blow, he swung the sword at the door. However, the sword bounced back so fiercely that Bason fell backward to the ground.

"Arghh," he complained. "That bloody Starr witch! She will pay for this!" his anger intensified.

"Apologies, prince. This is necessary for the well-being of the Golden Nation," a voice emanated from the door itself—Velaska's voice.

"Why are you doing this?" Caffia asked.

There was a moment of silence, then Velaska's voice emerged again, "I know what Amina's plans are. I must ensure that the royal entourage reaches the King of Borraral as soon as possible. As the guide appointed by the king himself, I will prevent any insurrections, even if they come from the prince himself."

Insurrection? he thought.

Beyond angry at this point, he no longer cared about his words. "Don't lecture me about insurrections. May I remind you that the Starr Witches broke the rules when they decided to infiltrate one of their own into the Shabrani clan? Isn't that against the rules of the Great Conclave?"

"Prince, you should not speak of such matters before others. Your father will hear of this, and..." Velaska's words were abruptly cut off as he interrupted her.

"How can we be certain that the Starr Witches aren't plotting to summon their own deity to the Lower Lands? I've never trusted you, Velaska—least of all, now," he said.

Aware that the Starr clan had pledged not to bring their god, Astorr, into these lands, he continued, "It seems your kind enjoys lying through their teeth." Recent events had made it clear to him that caution was needed when dealing with the Starr Witches. *Why hadn't Father considered this?* he wondered.

Velaska remained silent for a moment before replying, "Our lord, Astorr, among all the entities we witches serve, is the most benevolent and kind. He would never seek to endanger humankind. Astorr grants us magic so that we may do good in the Lower Lands; that is his only purpose. This has been known since the creation of the Starr clan. You have nothing to fear, prince. My sisters and I seek only to protect everyone with the power of our lord."

She is a fraud, he thought to himself.

"Enough, Velaska! This is nonsense. You will free us at once. This is an order," he exclaimed.

Velaska did not respond. Instead, Bason and the others noticed that the royal coach was moving again. *The royal entourage must have resumed the journey*, he thought.

"She got us. We cannot do anything," said Recaro, tearfully.

"That's not going to help us, Recaro!" reprimanded Valecio.

"Stop, the two of you!" he ordered. "There is nothing we can do. It is widely known that the Starr magic used by Velaska is strong; we won't be able to break her magic so easily. I suggest we stay here until we reach Barral. Once there, I will make sure she pays for this. My aunt and grandfather will know of her actions," he said, attempting to calm down his servants.

Caffia walked up to Bason and kneeled. "Prince, with your permission, I believe there is a way to escape this prison. Hear me out," she said.

He looked at her with arrogance, initially contemplating dismissing her. However, something about Caffia's determination made him change his mind.

"Go on," he said.

DEMORIA

Twenty days had passed since she departed the Shabrani clan. She knew she had only one more day to find the man from her quest and somehow obtain his arm. She considered her approach: *should I politely request to sever his arm? I hope he proves cooperative*, she joked to herself.

Guided by the instructions of the Shabrani Great Council—"Go to Duskenwood and find the crying river. In twenty-one days, at sunset behind the tallest mountain, you'll encounter a man. Bring back his left arm"—she reached Duskenwood two days ago. However, her quest to locate tall mountains became a challenge, as the landscape resembled a vast swamp covered in heavy mist. Furthermore, Duskenwood offered only dirty lakes, bushes, marshes, unwelcome encounters with crocodiles and, her least favourite, mosquitoes.

Navigating through the difficult terrain proved challenging, leaving her with the unsettling feeling that she might be going in circles. To test her theory, she inscribed incantations on stones. The absence of recurring incantations provided some reassurance, suggesting she wasn't hopelessly lost.

Additionally, there were no known maps of Duskenwood. Even the scholars of the esteemed library in the Castle of Whispers, renowned for their wisdom, had no records of such a map.

As dusk approached, she decided to set up her tent as soon as she found a suitable spot.

"We'll rest soon," she assured her sleipnir, whom she had recently named Lucy. Giving her mount a name for a more personal touch, Demoria found solace in conversing with Lucy, who never complained. The last meaningful conversation she recalled was with Hallard Rikers from the Lakefields. She shook her head, attempting to divert her thoughts.

Before sunset, she found a dry spot to set her tent. Afterwards, she gathered stones and sticks to start a fire. While setting up her tent, she observed Lucy peacefully grazing nearby. She envied the apparent ease of Lucy's life. "At least you don't have to go around looking for men you don't know," she said to the animal in a sarcastic tone.

After the fire was ready, she ventured out to search for some meat to eat. In Duskenwood, edible animals were scarce, unlike in other lands where wild rabbits were more abundant. She looked around for some time, but could not find any wild animals. Realising she had to make do with whatever vegetables she had in store, she checked her bags. Except for a few rotten potatoes and beans, she discovered she was out of vegetables. She had brought leeks, lettuce, and tomatoes from the Grey Skull, but had consumed them all. Understanding the need to replenish her supply, she set out once again in search of nearby vegetables.

"Great! Now I'll spend days searching Duskenwood for vegetables," she remarked sarcastically to Lucy, who continued munching on grass without a care.

Surveying the area in search of vegetables, she had no luck. She considered the possibility of finding mushrooms instead. After a while, she realised there was nothing suitable, except for dead vegetables and poisonous mushrooms. She decided to venture a little further without straying too far to avoid getting lost in the marsh.

Despite her efforts, she found nothing and reluctantly began her way back. However, on her return, a distant lake caught her attention. She speculated that it could be a potential mushroom-growing spot. The verdant colour of the lake hinted at flourishing plant life nearby. Drawing closer, she uncovered small, white mushrooms dotting the shoreline. Realising they were indeed edible, she swiftly gathered as many as her satchel could hold. She prepared to depart when another sight captivated her eye.

Across the lake, she saw a figure. Initially dismissing it as a trick of light, the form solidified into that of a white woman wearing white clothes who stared back at her. Blinking, Demoria found the mysterious woman vanished.

Approaching the spot where the woman had been standing, she found it deserted. "How odd. Maybe I imagined her," she mused, puzzled.

Back at her tent, she prepared a meal for both herself and Lucy, who she discovered could eat anything. Using beans and the mushrooms she had gathered by the lake, along with a handful of spices from her provisions, she cooked up a dinner that, while not her finest culinary creation, would do for the night and the following morning.

The next day marked the twenty-first day since she departed from the Shabrani clan. The pressure weighed heavily on her as she faced the final day of her mission. Rising early, she embarked on the last leg of her journey, aiming to locate the tallest mountain and the crying river from her mission before sunset.

Contemplating the term "crying river," she realised she had yet to come across any rivers. So far, she's only found small swamps and the lake she discovered the previous night. The word "river" triggered thoughts of Hallard Rikers and the Lakefields region once again.

"Oh!" she exclaimed so loudly that even Lucy turned her head to look at her.

"Why didn't I see it sooner? Lakefields lie north of Duskenwood. If there are rivers to be found, they must be north of our current location," she remarked while gently petting Lucy, who seemed to enjoy the attention.

She gathered the last of her belongings scattered on the ground, mounted her sleipnir, and set off in a northern direction.

Initially, the landscape appeared much as it had before—marshy, dirty, with grass, trees, and mist—making her doubt if she was truly heading north. However, as she encountered more and more bodies of water, she grew confident that she was on the right track.

After some time, she finally spotted small, narrow rivers. This brought her joy, as she knew she was nearing her goal. After riding for a while longer, she noticed mountains in the distance. Though relatively small and uniform in height, rivers flowed around them. Recalling her mission, she got closer to identify the tallest one.

Looking at all the rivers around her, Hallard's image intruded into her thoughts. She hoped he was safe and likely nearing the Shabrani clan by now.

As she approached, she realised that most of the rivers ran at the base of the mountains, not quite fitting her image of "crying rivers," which were also part of her mission. Nonetheless, she couldn't be certain how such rivers should appear. Continuing north, she encountered a dense fog that obstructed her view, making it challenging to navigate. Frustrated, she thought, *I can't even see where the sun is now*. However, after some time, the fog dissipated, revealing a large river. *This looks promising*, she thought.

To her surprise, in the distance, she saw two small caves perched on top of a tall mountain that had come into view, with two rivers flowing from them.

"Yes, the tall mountain and the crying river!" she exclaimed, triumphant. Now, the challenge was to locate the mysterious man from her mission.

Suddenly, something struck near her on the head, and she found herself blinded by her own blood. The hit had opened a wound above her right eye. To avoid another blow, she quickly jumped off Lucy, leaving her sleipnir to flee into the nearby bushes.

"Come face me, you coward!" she screamed defiantly.

Abruptly, her attacker materialised in front of her—a bald man with a peculiar face inscribed with white glyphs, clad in armour except for his left arm. His left arm had a strange appearance: it was black with red nails, and several wings moved gracefully along its side. She sensed magic emanating from it, leading her to believe that this was the arm she needed to complete her mission.

Also, she recalled seeing the glyphs on the man's face somewhere before. *Where have I seen those glyphs?* she wondered.

She didn't have time to remember, as her attacker was already preparing to strike again.

"That arm of yours, I need it! Will you give it to me willingly, or shall I rip it from your corpse?" she said menacingly.

The man remained silent in response.

"Fire, it is!" Demoria yelled.

Taking charge, she unleashed instant explosions at her foe's location. Although her enemy adeptly dodged the initial explosions, she, as a skilled Shabrani witch, had a surprise under her sleeve. The explosions she left behind transformed into small fire missiles that relentlessly pursued her foe. He used his magic arm to defend against the missiles. Noticing this, Demoria conjured projectiles more potent and designed to strike anywhere despite the enemy's location. She pressed on until dust, smoke, and blood obscured her vision, signalling a direct hit on her enemy.

Once the smoke dissipated, she saw her foe kneeling on the ground, injured and with most of his armour gone. She noticed his body was covered with the same white glyphs he had on his face, which she thought were magic, although she could not discern their meaning.

"What are you?" Demoria inquired.

Those glyphs? They look like the ones inscribed on the scroll Mila gave me at the Shabrani Citadel before I departed, she finally recalled. *Mila had said she found it during her last mission, which was in the Frostwild Towns near the Glacier Crown. Could my enemy be from those cold lands?*

She was distracted by feeling magic increasing from her enemy. The wings attached to her enemy's strange left arm began to move rapidly. He extended the arm, murmured unintelligible words, and two white halos materialised around it while the wings continued to flap vigorously. Before Demoria could react, a sudden electric blast caught her off guard, slamming her into the ground. Although she felt the impact on her stomach, there seemed to be no major damage—only a bruise.

Moreover, the attack she received was of electric waves, an art believed to have been lost during the Age of the Primes. *His left arm doesn't belong to this age*, she realised.

"How? That blast was meant to kill thee! No mere mortal could endure such. Who art thou, witch?" her foe said in an ancient tone.

The man's voice hurt her ears somehow; it was a sound she had never heard before. Moreover, the way he spoke made it seem as if he belonged to a different time, confirming her suspicion that he had probably lived during the Age of the Primes.

"The best witch in the Lower Lands, you bastard," she replied defiantly.

Looking at the bruise caused by the last attack, she realised the man was right—the last attack was supposed to kill her. Then, she felt something warm on her chest and discovered the necklace with the golden leaf that Hallard had given her in the Grey Skull. The leaf had changed to a red colour, reminiscent of blood.

A sudden heat struck her face as the man in front of her uttered unintelligible words once again. More halos appeared around his left arm, and the wings on it began to flap even faster.

She realised the only way to defeat her foe was by using all her power in a single attack.

"Burn in hell!" she screamed.

Using most of her energy, she conjured the fires of Volcano Dukkah itself. A small eruption erupted beneath her enemy, enveloping him in searing flames. She could hear his cries and screams as his flesh began to catch fire. Rushing in, she drew a knife hidden beneath her robes and swiftly severed his left arm.

With her foe reduced to ashes, Demoria held his left arm high, signalling her triumph and completing her mission. She had questions about the strange man's identity and the magic that emanated from his arm; however, she decided to save them for the Great Council. It was time for her to return to the Shabrani clan.

As she moved away from the battle scene, a beam of light

emerged from where her enemy was defeated. The beam transformed into a large white cross and then shaped into a human figure.

"Thou art a powerful witch, yet no common mortal can kill me with such ease. Behold, the glyphs upon mine body can restore and regenerate mine flesh. I shall require that arm returned. Give it to me!" declared her foe, who had regained his form again, though he was missing his left arm.

She then took the scroll given to her by Mila from under her robe and showed it to him. "This scroll has the same glyphs inscribed on your skin. It was found near the Glacier Crown. Who are you?" she asked, attempting to gather more information about her enemy.

"That scroll," said the man, looking perplexed. "Fate hath freely bestowed it upon thee, only for thee to return it unto me, its former master. This can only mean thou must be slain at all costs. I shall take thy life anon. Yield me that arm, and thou shalt have a painless death," he spoke angrily.

"I'm afraid I cannot give you this arm. It's mine now, and you'll have to kill me to get it back. Let's see what you can do without it," she said.

"Foolish witch," the man sneered.

Suddenly, the man charged towards her. She responded by launching fire projectiles, but he skilfully dodged them. She observed that her opponent had grown quicker than before. Moreover, she lacked the energy to muster another powerful spell. Driven by desperation, she contemplated switching tactics and attacking with her knife instead of relying on magic.

As the man closed in, she tried to stab him with her knife, but he effortlessly dodged her once more. Channelling all her remaining power, she imbued her knife with magic. Her next slash conjured a formidable wall of blue fire through which the man crossed.

Then she saw the man stop moving. He closed his eyes for a moment, then threw a punch using his right arm from a considerable distance. At first, she didn't react, thinking the punch would never reach her. However, he struck the air with such force that the impact hit her, catching her off guard. She tried to dodge, but it was too late—the blow grazed her belly, sending her to the ground.

Simultaneously, the man, having crossed through the blue fire wall spell, began to ignite with blue flames.

"These blue flames, I cannot dispel them!" he screamed in pain.

"The fire I conjured will not turn you to ashes, but it will burn you for a very long time. Suffer, you bastard!" she said through agonising pain.

Summoning her mount with a whistle, she called out to Lucy. The sleipnir emerged from the bushes, galloping towards her with urgency. Despite the intense pain in her side, Demoria moved as swiftly as possible and mounted Lucy.

"Nay! Thou can't take that arm with thee. Thou knowest not what thou are doing!" the man screamed in agony.

In the distance, she casted a final glance at her enemy. His screams of pain echoed through the air. Lucy ran towards the north, or it could be the south. She wasn't sure what direction the sleipnir was going. The wound on her belly stung too much and she felt she was losing consciousness. The worst part was that she had used all her energy; she could not conjure more fire magic, not even to cauterise her wound.

She tore a piece of cloth from her robes and pressed hard into the wound. *This should stop the bleeding*, she hoped.

They had been travelling for a while, and Demoria thought it wise to stop and let Lucy rest for a few moments. She herself needed to rest and perhaps eat something to regain her energy. She pictured a flat area surrounded by rocks, with the ground lightly covered in grass. She could also hear the sound of running water, suggesting there might be a river nearby.

"A river; we must be in Lakefields. Looks like you rode north, Lucy," she said to her sleipnir.

Lucy made a noise and started eating grass while she dismounted and sat on a rock. The pain from her wound intensified. The cloth covering it was soaked through with blood and no longer effective. Dizziness overwhelmed her, and her vision blurred.

Don't sleep, don't sleep. You might not wake up, she said to herself.

She brought her hands closer together and attempted to conjure fire magic through her fingers. Nothing happened; she couldn't feel magic. It dawned on her that she hadn't felt this powerless in a long time, maybe not since her early days as a rank one. A tear welled up in her left eye and rolled down her cheek.

"That wound needs special treatment," said an unfamiliar voice.

From behind a large rock emerged a female figure clad in leather and metal armour. She recognized the attire immediately; her visitor was a barbarian.

Suddenly, she remembered Hallard mentioning his previous encounter with barbarians in the Blue Bell Mountains and speculated that they might have ventured as far west as this place.

She struggled to think clearly as the pain from her wound intensified, making her feel increasingly unsettled. The female barbarian approached slowly. Just before losing consciousness, she glimpsed the barbarian's hand reaching out towards her.

SILAS

A few days had passed since he escaped from the Pyramid of Dum. The rain outside continued, and although it was lighter than it had been earlier, he still found it bothersome. After their miraculous escape, Mirta led them to the home of a friend she trusted. The fisherman, Finnegan Tridecast, welcomed them warmly.

The fisherman couldn't have been more than fifty years old, with a robust physique and a weathered face that bore the marks of a well-lived life. He consistently wore shorts and a loose-fitting shirt, typical attire for his occupation. Despite his efforts to stay clean, the scent of fish always lingered on him. Finnegan, as it turned out, had a cheerful disposition and was easy to talk to. He lived with his wife, Livia, who was always busy attending to their newborn twins. Their home was located north of the city of Mater, near the shore.

To their surprise, Finnegan refrained from asking any questions about why they were in hiding.

"He's very trustworthy. We share a history, but I won't disclose it now. We can trust him. He knows we're hiding from the guards," Mirta reassured both him and Ophelia.

Every day, Finnegan would depart early in the morning to catch fish and return later in the day. In addition to his catch, he would bring news from around town. The guards from the Pyramid of Dum were still on the lookout for fugitives, offering a reward of five hundred gold coins, according to the latest news.

"The guards, they're desperate, ya know? Ain't nobody escaped from the Pyramid of Dum that I've heard of. You lot really made the great leaders in Pater pretty darn mad," said Finnegan.

He couldn't believe it—five hundred gold coins for his head. With that much money, he could envision a great life anywhere in the Lower Lands just as he had always wanted.

"We can't stay in your house any longer. The guards will soon be searching every house in Mater. We don't want to cause trouble for you and your family, Finnegan," said Ophelia, the Shabrani witch.

Mirta and Finnegan exchanged glances and then broke into smiles.

"Don't you worry 'bout me, I've been hankerin' for an adventure like this for a good while now. The thought of bein' smack in the middle of one of the grandest events the Hateful Six has seen in years warms my heart. As for my family, they know where to head if things go awry," said Finnegan.

Silas couldn't understand Finnegan's motives. *Why was he so willing to help them?* he wondered.

On the other side, Ophelia grew increasingly anxious each day. Every morning, she concocted a new escape plan to lead them safely out of the Hateful Six islands. However, as island experts, Mirta and Finnegan swiftly shot down Ophelia's plans.

"The guards won't be looking for us everywhere; there must be streets or alleys even they don't know about. If we make a move early, before dawn, we could navigate those hidden spots until we hit the bay. Once there, Finnegan, you could lend a hand getting us a boat to run off this island," suggested Ophelia. She was munching on a hefty fish with some potatoes. In fact, he noticed she was always eating. *They call me 'Hagar the hungry'*, she had once said, recalling a chat they had back at the Pyramid of Dum before she revealed herself as a Shabrani witch.

Finnegan shook his head, signalling his disapproval.

"Uh-uh, that ain't gonna work. It ain't just them guards sniffin' around, folks in town are keepin' an eye out too. Don't forget, there's a fat bounty of five hundred gold coins sittin' on top of your heads. And them boat guards got the whole dang bay on lockdown, makin' it a real tough to getaway, ya know?" explained Finnegan.

Silas then pondered, *Even if we leave this island, where is Ophelia taking me?*

After Finnegan departed for his typical day, Silas sought out Ophelia. He found her in the main room engrossed in studying maps of Pater while sipping goat milk and indulging in bread and cheese. He suspected she was likely plotting another scheme for Mirta and Finnegan, one they would most likely disapprove of again. Mirta was also in the main room, gazing at the fireplace which provided warmth during the current cold weather.

"What's on your mind, Silas?" Ophelia inquired.

He had come to trust the Shabrani witch to a degree. She had helped him escape from the Pyramid of Dum, and her strong determination to keep him safe gave him plenty of reasons to rely on her. However, talking with her still made him uneasy, given her reputation as a Shabrani witch, known as one of the most fearless in the world. He worried that saying something wrong could lead to a fate akin to the one she had effortlessly dealt to the guards back in the Pyramid of Dum.

"I've been wondering, if we do manage to leave this island, where are you taking me?" he cautiously asked.

Ophelia scrutinised him. "Haven't we already discussed this?" she seemed perplexed.

He tried to remember their conversations once more. The only opportunity they had to properly talk was at the Pyramid of Dum. Since then, Ophelia seemed so busy that he didn't want to interrupt her with trivial questions.

"I don't think we have," he replied.

Ophelia widened her eyes and gently covered her mouth. "Goodness me, you must be dying to know. Come with me," she said.

The witch led him to the fireplace, where Mirta still sat nearby.

"Please, look into the fire," Ophelia said.

He nodded, curious as to why they were fixating on the flames.

"There is an ancient device controlled by us, the Shabrani Witches. It's called the Oracle of Eldoria. It manifests as an inextinguishable red flame that occasionally gives insights into our future. You can think of it like this fireplace. The witches in our Great Council interpret these insights and turn them into missions. One of these missions was assigned to me. In essence, it involved rescuing you from the Pyramid of Dum and guiding you to the Golden Nation," explained Ophelia.

He was left speechless by the revelation. A flame capable of predicting the future was indeed a marvel. However, the idea of travelling to the Golden Nation wasn't particularly appealing to him.

"Sorry if this information is overwhelming," said the Shabrani witch. "Feel free to ask any questions you have."

He didn't realise she could read his face so easily. *I should hide my emotions more often*, he thought.

"Is your oracle always right? And why are we going to the Golden Nation?" he inquired.

Ophelia gathered her long braids, which rested on her shoulders, and moved them behind her back. "The Oracle of Eldoria can be somewhat ambiguous. Don't misunderstand; its predictions are always accurate. However, our missions usually bring the Shabrani clan some form of advantage, whether it's a new alliance or additional wealth. I won't know what my mission with you will bring to our clan until I successfully complete it. As for why we are going to the Golden Nation," she paused.

Ophelia slipped her hand inside her robes and retrieved a dagger. The dagger was silver in colour and appeared worn, perhaps due to age. Its blade was curved, and strange characters were etched into the handle.

"This is a kris, a type of special dagger. Do you recognize it?" she inquired.

He took hold of the dagger. The weapon didn't appear particularly sharp, and it bore the signs of ageing. He noticed unfamiliar characters on the handle.

"I do not," he replied.

Ophelia took the dagger back and cut her arm with it. Silas instinctively stepped back, puzzled by her actions.

Why did she do that? he wondered.

With a smile, the witch presented her unharmed arm to him. There was no cut, no wound, and no blood.

"Now, give me your finger," she requested.

Silas complied. Ophelia pricked the tip of his finger with the dagger, causing a small drop of blood to emerge.

He was confused by the events. The dagger hadn't cut Ophelia, even though she had used it to cut herself earlier, yet it had cut him.

"How is that possible?" he asked, bewildered.

Ophelia pointed to the scar on Silas's neck.

"The scar you showed me back in the Pyramid of Dum isn't from birth. Everything suggests it was made by this dagger," she explained.

He became even more perplexed.

"This is a magical dagger, designed to recognize important individuals. During the War of Ashes, many people would impersonate royal family members. It was convenient because those of significance received priority treatment for rations and healthcare. The Starr clan," she paused, casting a glance at Mirta, "crafted these special daggers to distinguish between the important and the unimportant. Most of these daggers were lost long ago. The one in my possession must be the last."

He was about to speak when he was interrupted by Mirta, whom he had forgotten was in the same room.

"Where did you get this kris?" Mirta inquired.

Ophelia didn't even glance at the Starr witch. "I took this dagger from a wealthy merchant in Samos. I extracted all the information I could from him, but he was unaware of the original owner," she explained.

He remained silent as he absorbed the information.

"There's something else you should know," Ophelia said. "My mission didn't specifically instruct me to rescue a boy named Silas. The Oracle of Eldoria tasked me with obtaining this kris and uncovering its story. Once I had it in my possession, I found that the characters on the handle were written in an old language used in the Hateful Six many years ago, even before the War of Ashes. I travelled around the islands for some time looking for a translator, and eventually found a few librarians in Xaderfos who could translate it. The message spoke of a boy born in the Golden Nation who was left at the Astorr Cathedral on the island of Esther. This boy could be recognized by a scar on his neck, made by this very dagger," Ophelia explained

"Since then, I've been trying to follow your steps, using magic and seeking information about you," she added.

"If what you say is true, Silas is part of a royal family," said Mirta.

He struggled to piece together the unfolding revelation until Mirta vocalised it. *Does it mean I come from a royal lineage?* he realised, feeling even more perplexed than before.

"So, who am I? Are my parents some sort of rich people? Do they live in the Golden Nation? Is that why you're taking me there?" he asked.

"Woah, woah, calm down, young man. I do not know. All I know is that we will find the answers to those questions in the Golden Nation. This dagger will hopefully guide us on our journey," said Ophelia.

Mirta took Silas by the hands and hugged him tightly. "I had a feeling you were meant for grand things."

"Thanks," he replied awkwardly.

Mirta released him and turned to Ophelia, "You should have said this earlier. We must hurry and find a way out of this island as soon as possible," the elderly woman insisted.

Ophelia regarded Mirta with indifference, "I was just following orders. I don't get attached to missions," she replied. She then shifted her gaze to him, "However, I must apologise to you, Silas. I should have spoken sooner," she said calmly.

He observed the rivalry between Ophelia and Mirta, realising that witches from different clans don't get along very well.

"Silas, do you understand now why we can't take Mirta with us in our escape?" said Ophelia. "I won't be able to take care of you two. I will only be able to safeguard your well-being, young man."

He understood the practicality of Ophelia's statement. Taking Mirta along could only impede their escape, but the thought of leaving her behind weighed heavily on him.

"What the Shabrani witch says is correct. I don't possess the power I once had; my magic has almost left me. I'll be fine, my boy. I'll stay with my friend Finnigan until my last days," Mirta reassured.

He nodded in agreement, feeling reassured knowing Mirta would stay with Finnigan, whom he had learnt to trust.

Mirta then shared the story of how she came to be in the Pyramid of Dum.

She explained that prior to her imprisonment, the master of the island of Esther had closed the Cathedral of Astorr, forcing Mirta and the other Starr Witches to move away. The Starr Witches, who disagreed with the master's decision, decided to go against his decree by reopening the cathedral. The master of Esther, displeased with this act of rebellion, dispatched guards to remove the witches from the cathedral. Despite the witches' resistance, the guards proved overwhelming. In the end, Mirta was the only survivor and was imprisoned in the Pyramid of Dum for opposing the master—an act deemed a crime in the Hateful Six islands.

"Since then, I heard the masters of the islands have been closing all our cathedrals one by one in all the Hateful Six islands. Our clan and the Golden Nation won't be happy about these events. The masters are playing a dangerous game," said Mirta.

He observed Ophelia paying keen attention to Mirta's words; it seemed the news intrigued her. "Were you aware of these events?" he asked Ophelia.

Ophelia looked at him while taking another bite of bread. "When I was following your steps, the first thing I did was inquire about the abandoned Cathedrals of Astorr. All I could gather from nearby locals is that the Starr Witches were no longer in charge of the cathedrals," she said, giving a meaningful look at Mirta.

"After they took me in, I was sentenced to die in the Pyramid of Dum. I lost all hopes of living. I'll be forever grateful to you, Silas, and Ophelia for rescuing me," said Mirta with tears in her eyes.

Ophelia seemed to disregard Mirta's grateful words. The Shabrani witch didn't acknowledge Mirta as he had hoped. After all, it was his idea to rescue Mirta, and Ophelia was compelled to go along with his plan.

For the following days, Ophelia continued to focus on studying maps and old books. The matter of their departure from the island of Pater presented a challenge; none of Ophelia's plans garnered support from the others. He wondered if they would ever successfully leave the island.

On a very rainy day, Finnigan came back from fishing earlier than usual.

"Friends, ya' moment is here, it's now or never," Finnigan exclaimed, clearly agitated, his breath indicating he had been running.

"Sit, sit here, Finnegan," Mirta extended a chair for the fisherman to rest.

"Ain't no time to sit. Them guards leaving the bay, headin' up south-west to Three Sisters. Rumour has it that the Golden Nation's sent a small army to kill them Hateful Six masters for shuttin' down all them Starr cathedrals. Looks like they'll be tied up for a bit," Finnegan said, still agitated.

Ophelia discarded the maps she was studying, "That means it is safe to leave. However, we still need to find a ship willing to take us to the Golden Nation. If the rumours you brought are true, no ship captain will be willing to take us across the sea," the Shabrani witch pointed out.

Finnegan finally sat and gazed at the roof and said, "Ya got a point there".

"Echo, the ships would still leave for Echo," said a voice he was not familiar with. It was Livia, Finnegan's wife.

Finnegan stood up from his chair and took Livia by the arm. "Woman, it's prob'ly best if you stick to your rooms with them twins. This ain't a spot for ya, ya hear?" said the fisherman angrily.

Up until now, Silas believed Finnegan was a good man who treated people with kindness. However, the way the fisherman spoke to his own wife made him think otherwise. He was surprised by Finnegan's misogynistic behaviour. This discriminatory behaviour was common in the islanders, but it never aligned with Sila's own values. *What an asshole*, he thought.

Ophelia's face turned to anger, reminiscent of when she killed the guards at the Pyramid of Dum. "Let her speak!" she exclaimed. Silas was glad Ophelia defended Livia. An act that made him trust her even more.

Finnigan, looking nervous, released his wife's arm.

Livia spoke in a shy tone, "There are ships that go to Echo from the bay. From Echo, it will take you a couple of days horse riding to get to the Golden Nation".

Ophelia fiddled with her braids as she looked around, deep in thought. "Echo, the land of forgotten Dragrani witches. It is known their clan was banished long ago. It seems dangerous, but it could be our only choice. I'd rather not linger on this island any longer," she said, looking at Finnigan, who still appeared very nervous.

"The boy must decide," said Mirta. Everyone in the room turned to Silas.

"Silas, I've neglected to give you all the information regarding your escape before. Everything I've done so far has been to fulfil my mission, but at the end of the day, it is your life. I will let you decide our next steps. Do we go to Echo, or do we find another way into the Golden Nation?" asked Ophelia.

He felt a sense of companionship unlike anything he had experienced before. Even when he was part of the band of the Forgotten Ones, his decisions and thoughts were never valued.

"We'll go to Echo," he said.

After a while, Ophelia and he were ready to leave. They gathered as much food as they could from Finnegan's house, mainly for Ophelia, who was always hungry.

Saying goodbye to Mirta for a second time wasn't easy, especially now that he had witnessed Finnegan's behaviour towards his wife. *Is Mirta truly safe here?* he wondered. He wanted to ask Mirta, but he didn't find the chance to do it, as the fisherman was constantly in their presence.

"Farewell, my boy. I will pray to our Lord Astorr for your well-being," said Mirta. Her eyes were watery, seemingly holding back tears. He noticed the Starr witch looked fragile and powerless, revealing her age under her teary eyes.

They didn't have a chance to say goodbye to Livia. Finnegan excused his wife, who had been caring for their twins. He thought the fisherman was lying, probably hiding his wife. He disliked him even more.

When they left, he noticed something peculiar. Two slim women the same age as Livia were waiting outside Finnegan's house. He wondered what they could be doing there.

Outside, it was raining lightly. He was relieved to be finally out in the open. They both wore hoods, just in case they were recognized by the citizens of Pater, which would jeopardise their only chance to leave the island.

"What do you think about Finnegan now?" asked Ophelia while walking next to him along a narrow street.

Did my face give away my feelings towards the fisherman? he mediated.

"I am grateful for everything he's done for us, but I didn't like how he treats his wife. That's all," he replied. He noticed there were all sorts of locals around, from merchants and vendors to homeless people asking for coins.

"He is under some sort of spell. Mirta's work, I presume," she said while looking around.

He stopped walking, "What do you mean?"

Ophelia took him by the hand and pulled him to resume walking.

"Please, don't stop all of a sudden. We must not attract any attention. I do not recognize the spell, but it seems to me that Mirta cast it before being thrown into the Pyramid of Dum. Again, I am not sure. What you last witnessed the other day was the spell starting to dissipate. Finnegan was beginning to revert to his original self, treating his wife poorly again," she explained.

He didn't expect to receive this news. "Are you saying the spell makes Finnegan somehow docile?" he asked.

Ophelia looked at him in surprise. "Finally, you are asking the right questions. You are growing up quickly, Silas," Ophelia said with a giggle.

"Yes, the spell somehow makes Finnegan compelled to do anything. Perhaps without it, he would have never agreed to help us. And then there's the matter of the twins and those women waiting outside the house when we left," said Ophelia.

He turned to the Shabrani witch, looking confused.

"Oh, perhaps I should explain. The twins have magic powers. I believe the spell on Finnegan caused the twins to be born with magic. As for the women outside the house, I suspect Mirta is planning to have them get pregnant by the fisherman to procreate more gifted children," Ophelia explained.

Silas was left more confused than before. "Are you saying Mirta is raising an army of magical babies?" he asked.

Ophelia laughed loudly, drawing the attention of a few onlookers. Quickly, she grabbed Silas by the hand and pulled him into a small corner where they could talk more privately.

"Well, those babies will grow up at some point, Silas," Ophelia said, still giggling. "Mirta is creating magical beings with starr magic. Forcing magic into newborn humans is forbidden by the Great Conclave. I will report her actions to my clan when I get the chance. But right now, my priority is you and completing my mission," she said with determination.

He understood the situation better, although he did not understand why Mirta would do such a thing.

"Do not worry about it. We have a bigger challenge ahead. Focus on staying alive, Silas," Ophelia said firmly.

As they continued walking, the smell of dead fish and saltwater was unmistakable. They both entered the bay. Once there, it wasn't difficult to find the ship to Echo. Among merchants selling all kinds of fish and oysters, others were yelling the names of various locations.

"Trip to Patmos leavin' soon," yelled one man who appeared as though he had never had a shower in his life.

"The ship to Samos is leavin', board now!!" screamed a woman who didn't have teeth.

After some time walking along the bay, Ophelia said, "There is our ship."

At the end of the bay, there was a child holding a sign that said

Echo. Behind him, a medium-sized ship was ready to depart.

They both ran towards the ship, gave some coins to the child for passage, and boarded the ship.

Inside, they learned that the ship was called the Serene Horizon. They were given cabins for sleeping. They noticed the ship was full of merchants, all offering things at a low price, possibly trying to sell the last of their goods.

He separated from Ophelia, who decided to stay in her cabin. He walked up to the deck for a clearer view of the ocean. As the ship started moving, he realised that the rain was finally stopping. Although the sun was still hidden by the clouds.

The wind blew strongly, propelling the ship swiftly across the water. Before long, he could spot the shores of Pater in the distance, with the sun breaking through the heavy clouds. A smile showed across his face as he realised he was leaving his old life behind.

Change is coming, he thought.

ALABASTER

The last thing he heard was his own screams as he fell into an endless void. At some point, without realising, consciousness slipped away. Upon awakening, he discovered himself in an unfamiliar land, completely alone.

The unfamiliar terrain was enveloped in sand dunes. As he regained consciousness he felt an intense thirst and hunger, realising he hadn't had proper food or water in a very long time. On top of that, he had numerous wounds across his body that required attention.

Everywhere he saw there was only sand and heat due to the scorching sun. He walked aimlessly for a while, realising his worn-out sandals showed signs of use which could break any moment. He hoped they would endure the journey ahead.

His immediate priorities were to locate assistance, water, and food. After walking for some time, he felt exhausted. *Perhaps if I was twenty years younger, I could survive this journey*, he thought. The necessity to rest forced him to stop frequently; however, he knew that his breaks couldn't be prolonged for too long. The absence of shade and the relentless strength of the sun could kill him at any moment.

He wondered about the whereabouts of his former companions—the mysterious girl, who had revealed herself to be a Moon witch, and Truinan and Searc, locals from the Rockshade Highlands. He had planned to sacrifice them to the Blood Witches, but recent events had completely changed his plans.

Desperation surged within him as he reminded himself, *I must not fail the Blood Witches.*

He acknowledged the possibility of returning to the Blood Witches empty-handed. He knew he would have to find a new sacrifice to offer them. *They will never aid me in avenging my family's assassins unless I provide a final sacrifice,* he reflected anxiously. Also, the fear of facing punishment weighed heavily on him.

His thoughts turned to the strange man who had attacked him and his former companions. *Who was he?* he thought. *I've never encountered anyone like him in my life.* It occurred to him that the strange man's last attack might have somehow teleported him away from Duskenwood. *A man who can wield magic. That's quite a tale to tell. In all of the Lower Lands, it's widely known that only women can wield magic*, he contemplated.

A more intriguing thought crossed his mind: *Why was the strange man after me?* His best guess was that it paralleled the reason the Moon witch desired to keep him alive. They all seemed to share a common goal, him, the key to unlock the Blood Witches whereabouts.

Being a Blood Priest, his presence held a vital role in gaining access to the Blood Witches' camp. This was the sole reason the mysterious girl, the Moon Witch, had refrained from killing him in the past.

He couldn't recall when the sun had set, but now the moon adorned the night sky. As he gazed at the moon, he noticed a small, peculiar dark celestial body in front of it, easily overlooked.

"The arrangements are all in place for a new Apocrypha," he recalled the strange man saying. *Apocrypha, if only I could remember where I read about it*, he thought.

Suddenly, his knees gave up, and he could no longer walk. All around him, there was nothing but sand, with only the sound of the wind breaking the silence. The last remnants of his energy deserted his body, leaving it unresponsive. Collapsing to the ground, he tasted the grit of the sand. In despair, he cried out and cursed his life, reflecting on the recent events that had led him to this perilous situation.

The next morning, he was abruptly awakened by water dripping onto his parched lips. At first, he thought it was a dream.

"More, more!" he said.

With his eyes closed, he drank all the water he could.

"Can you get up, old man?" someone asked him.

He tried to move his body but it didn't seem to react. Slowly, he opened his eyes, realising that he wasn't dreaming. In front of him stood a soldier clad in light brown armour. Beside him, there were two other soldiers mounted on horses. He quickly glanced at the sigil on their armour. On the chest plate, the soldiers bore a sigil he recognized.

Echo, they are Echo soldiers, he thought. That meant he might be in the Silent Dunes, which bordered the lands of Echo.

He attempted to move again, but his body still wouldn't respond. Additionally, his stomach ached from hunger.

"Food, please, I need food," he begged the soldiers.

One of the soldiers retrieved a piece of bread and an apple from a satchel hanging from his horse.

Alabaster's body, upon seeing the food, automatically started moving. He sat up, received the food, and began eating as quickly as he could.

"Feeling any better, old man?" the soldier asked.

He took some time to respond, then extended his hand to the soldier for help to stand up. The soldier took him by the arm and assisted him in standing.

"Yes, I thought I would die in this desert. You have my eternal gratitude, soldier..." he replied, waiting for the soldier's name in return.

"I am Lotar," he said, then gestured to the other two soldiers, "These are Carion and Barraco."

"Should you say our names out loud? What if he is allied with our enemies?" questioned the soldier named Carion.

Lotar's face turned slightly angry, "Look at him, he is old and skinny as a homeless beggar outside the Castle of Whispers. This man is in no condition to be a threat to anybody," said Lotar.

Lotar then turned his gaze to him, "Who are you, old man? How is it that you are all alone in these sand dunes?"

Alabaster contemplated saying his real name, but he opted to adopt a more fitting name from these lands. In the past, he read about Echo customs and folklore while studying to be a Balor priest which came in handy in this situation.

"I am Decar, I am a librarian. I usually work at the library in the Castle of Whispers. I was drunk a couple of nights ago. Some bandits captured me and stole all my belongings. They rode northwest from Echo. I overheard them saying they were taking me to a barbarian clan hidden in the sand dunes to exchange me for gold coins. They starved me for two days," he lied.

He was aware of the librarians in Echo, established to keep records of the history of the world. Rumours suggested that the library inside the Castle of Whispers contained an extensive collection of books, unrivalled by any other library in the Lower Lands.

By lying to the soldiers, he hoped they could take him to Echo, giving him time to contemplate his next move.

"Barbarians!" yelled the other soldier named Barraco.

The sudden scream startled him as he began anxiously scanning the surroundings for signs of barbarians.

"Do not worry, Decar. Barraco is quite a prankster," said Lotar.

Indeed, Barraco and Carion were laughing uncontrollably at his startled expression.

He paid them no mind.

"Apologies, Decar. My companions tend to make jokes about serious matters. Echo has received reports of a barbarian group riding along the sand dunes. We have been commanded to find the savages."

He was surprised by how accurate his lie turned out to be. *There's a real barbarian camp around? The odds must be with me*, he thought.

"Are you the only company looking for the barbarians?" he asked.

He noticed Carion drew his sword and pointed it at him. An act that made him crawl backwards.

"Are you saying we are not enough?" Carion said to him angrily.

Lotar also drew his sword and met Carion's sword.

"You must control your impulsive behaviour, Carion. How on earth did you get a position in Echo's army?" Lotar said in a menacing tone.

"Echo's soldiers have grown weak after pledging allegiance to the Golden Nation. Perhaps they want someone more like me in their lines and less soft like you," responded Carion, clearly teasing Lotar.

Alabaster decided to intervene.

"Please, it was not my intention to cause this disagreement. We, as Echo citizens, should remain on the same side," he pleaded with the two soldiers.

Carion put his weapon aside and walked away.

"Apologies again, Decar. That one should be in the fighting pits and not in recon missions. To answer your question, No, we are not the only group of soldiers looking for the barbarians. There are others searching for them as well. We left Echo three days ago. Our food rations are now depleted, so we are returning. We will take you with us," said Lotar.

He was pleased to hear these words. After their conversation, he felt better physically and in spirit. He rode with Lotar on his horse.

The soldier also mentioned that they were not far from Echo's borders.

On the way, Alabaster meditated about his former companions. *It is possible that they have also been teleported to the Silent Dunes. Maybe they are as lost as I was. I hope they are dead, especially that little witch*, he thought.

The night descended swiftly that day, or at least, that was his perception. They had long surpassed the desert, and the landscape welcomed them with a more fertile terrain. He observed a scattering of trees and palms, indicating that he had entered Echo territory.

"We'll drop you off as near as possible to the Castle of Whispers. From there, you can proceed on your own," said Lotar.

"Yes, indeed. Thank you, Lotar," he said.

He observed that the streets of Echo were spookily empty. He recalled that most of Echo's residents had either fled or resettled in the Golden Nation. This mass exodus occurred some time ago when the Golden Nation invaded Echo. King Roland sought to prevent another War of Ashes after learning that the Dragani clan was attempting to bring their god, Dragan, to the Lower Lands.

Recalling details from a history book, he learned that the battle was remarkably brief. The Golden Nation, with its formidable forces, including the Starr Witches, quickly overpowered the Dragani Witches, the protectors of Echo. The Dragani Witches were nearly wiped out in the conflict, and the surviving few sought refuge in the north near the cold Glacier Crown—at least, according to gossip. The Golden Nation withdrew from Echo only after installing their own ruler in the Castle of Whispers. Since then, Echo has remained subservient to the Golden Nation.

As they arrived at the Castle of Whispers, Lotar inquired, "Will you be alright from here on, Decar?"

Alabaster dismounted and expressed his gratitude to Lotar once more for the journey.

"You've been a saviour. I foresee a bright future for you, young man," he said appreciatively.

He saw that Barraco and Carion were trailing behind Lotar. "Until next time, old man," Carion said with a smile, mirrored by Barraco's cheeky grin.

He wasn't fond of those two.

Once the soldiers departed, he found himself contemplating his next moves. Alone in a city unfamiliar to him, the Castle of Whispers loomed before him, not as imposing as he had envisioned. He recalled that the castle earned its name following the battle with the Golden Nation. The new lord of the castle detested noise above all else, it was said he would kill anyone who dared to sneeze in his presence. Observing the scene, it became evident to him. Even from the outside, there was an eerie absence of sound emanating from within the castle. Two guards stood sentinel at the main doors, but to his surprise, they made no inquiries about his reasons for being there. Taking advantage of the opportunity, he resolved to try and enter the castle, aiming to find the library. Perhaps he could persuade someone inside that he was a genuine librarian.

Once inside, he noticed many candles and fireplaces adorning the corridors, yet he encountered no one he could talk to. Pressing on, he traversed the corridors until reaching an expansive area. Tall stands filled with books surrounded him, confirming that he had indeed found the library.

"Hey! You! Are you lost?" a voice called out.

Turning around, he spotted an old man cloaked in robes addressing him.

A librarian, he realised.

"Friend, I am new to this castle…" he began introducing himself when he was interrupted.

"Are you the one the golden boy sent for more books?" the old man inquired.

Alabaster paused for a moment. *The golden boy?* He speculated whether it referred to Prince Bason or Prince Terrence from the Golden Nation.

Opting to play along, he replied, "Yes, yes, I was sent here for more..." before he could finish, he was interrupted once again.

"Well, there's not much reading to do at this hour. I can see you're nearly as old as I am; your eyes will need more than these candles to see," remarked the old man. "Come with me; I'll take you to your dormitory. It's best if you change those robes as well. You must have been on a very dirty road. You look homeless," the old man added.

Alabaster complied, following the man to a room in one of the corridors.

"You can stay here. Food and beverages were prepared for you. I've also asked the servitude to prepare a bath for you as well. You'll find clean clothes on the bed. One last thing, do not linger outside on your own. The Castle of Whispers might not be kind to new visitors at night. Rest well," the old man advised as he closed the door.

For once, Alabaster couldn't believe the luck he had since waking up in the Silent Dunes.

It seems that the gods are with me, he remarked to himself. Although which god, he didn't know.

As he undressed, he noted the transformation his body had undergone. Once carrying extra weight around his belly and legs, he now found himself reduced to bone and skin. Scars, still healing, marked the spots where Searc, the boy who had thrown stones at him, had wounded him. He cursed the boy, harbouring a wish for his demise.

A cold plate of potatoes and steak awaited him on the side table next to his bed. He devoured it without concern for its temperature. After finishing, he immersed in the warm bath, having a moment of respite. Even the haunting memories of his past seemed to start fading away.

"If gods are real, this must be a message; I must stay here before finding a new sacrifice for the Blood Witches," he contemplated.

Exiting the bath, he changed into fresh clothes and prepared for sleep. The bed was comfortable enough, it couldn't compare to the cold back of a wagon where he had spent the past days.

Then, it struck him—he hadn't thought of his horse, Brave Legs. *The poor creature must be dead*, a realisation that brought a tinge of sadness.

The following morning, he awoke to the sun's warmth and the sweet melody of singing birds coming from outside the castle. Looking for new clothes to wear, he found blue and white robes, along with new sandals and a blue square hat. He recognized them as the colours and attire of Echo's librarians.

As he stepped into the corridor, he tried to recall the location of the library. He also saw a few people walking by in silence. Contemplating asking for directions, he was interrupted by a familiar voice.

"Hey, you! Up early, I brought milk, bread, and fruits for you to eat."

Recognizing the voice, he realised it was the same old man he had encountered at the library the previous night.

"That's very kind of you. How about we go inside my chambers to enjoy this meal?" he suggested, mimicking the same whispery tone.

The old man nodded in agreement.

The food appeared delicious, a luxury breakfast he hadn't experienced in a long time. He intended to savour every bite, though a nagging thought crossed his mind—why were they treating him so well? The comfortable chambers and now a generous meal delivered to him raised suspicions.

"My name is Olar. I am one of the oldest librarians around here. What is your name, friend?" inquired the old man, taking a bite of an apple.

Recalling the false name he had provided to the soldiers the day before, Alabaster decided to stick with it during his time in Echo.

"I am Decar. I work at the library in the Golden Nation. I may not be the oldest, but I am certainly the wisest," he said in a playful manner.

Olar chuckled, "I like you; you have a good sense of humour. The others were not very talkative. 'Give me the oldest book, is that all you got, go find me more'—they just kept ordering. You see, the books here are plentiful, and most haven't even been read yet. You should be aware that most of the librarians are young and inexperienced; they don't know much yet. You see, it takes time to find things. Maybe if the bloody Golden Nation hadn't killed us when they invaded this castle, we could be of more help..." Olar's hand covered his mouth abruptly.

"Don't worry. You are among friends," he reassured him calmly.

"I'll refrain from making such comments; someone could hear us. The lord of this castle won't like a librarian talking ill about his precious Golden Nation," Olar expressed with resentment.

Alabaster noted the lingering animosity towards the Golden Nation.

"Anyway, I'll let you finish this meal. I need to go to the library now; let me show you where it is," Olar said, providing him with directions.

After finishing his meal, he followed Olar's directions and headed to the library. Along the way, he encountered a diverse array of individuals, from soldiers to servants and cooks. The Castle of Whispers buzzed with activity this morning. Although, he realised how everyone tried to keep quiet. He also couldn't help but wonder where the lord of the castle resided.

After some time, he finally reached the library. Despite having been there the night before, the library appeared even more expansive in the daylight, perhaps revealing additional hidden spaces.

Spotting Olar engaged in conversation with other librarians, Alabaster approached them.

"Decar, come! I have gathered all these librarians. Please tell us the instructions from Prince Bason; we will do our best to follow them," Olar said with a respectful tone.

Prince Bason? Alabaster found this revelation surprising, as rumours depicted him as a lazy prince with a preference for lustful activities with men and women.

Taking a moment to reflect, he considered the opportunity at hand. With access to the oldest books, he could inquire about the Blood Witches, potentially uncovering information not widely known. However, he dismissed the idea to avoid appearing suspicious. Another thought crossed his mind—books about routes and the best way to reach Duskenwood, though he was aware that there was no direct road from Echo.

He sensed the librarians scrutinising him with curiosity, prompting the need to say something.

"Apocrypha," he said.

The librarians gathered around him, and one with a smooth face, likely one of the youngest among them, asked him to repeat it.

"The prince has asked about any references to the word Apocrypha," he clarified to the librarian.

Recalling that this was the same word mentioned by the strange man in Duskenwood, he felt an urgency to learn more about it, especially if it was connected to his enemies.

"I must admit I've never heard that word before, and I am the oldest here," said Olar.

"Prince Bason's orders were clear," he insisted, attempting to sound convincing.

"Yes, yes, yes. We know all about the prince's requests," Olar replied impatiently.

Olar snapped his fingers, and the other librarians swiftly moved into action, engaging in conversation and poring over books. He observed them coming in and out from hidden passages within the library.

Approaching Olar, he inquired, "I see the librarians have already started the search. How long do you think they will take?"

Olar patted his shoulders, "We've never heard that word before. It's going to take a while. You better go around the castle or explore other books here. Just don't go to the left wing of the castle; that is where the lord of Echo, his court and the Starr Witches live. Let's just say they are not fond of us."

In the following three days, Alabaster enjoyed the privileges of his stay in the castle. He relished a variety of meals and was treated as an honoured guest. He discovered that at least three Starr Witches resided in the castle's left wing. When he spotted one in the corridors, he kept his distance, having had his fill of encounters with witches after meeting the girl named Aliune in cat form, later called a Moon witch by the mysterious man in Duskenwood. Considering the potential danger if the Starr Witches learned of his presence, he chose to avoid them, wary of their ability to discern lies.

As two more days passed, Alabaster grew increasingly anxious. The urgency to leave and find a new sacrifice for the Blood Witches weighed heavily on him. *The Blood Witches won't be happy if I don't bring a sacrifice soon*, he thought.

Having secured a horse and some coins for his departure, he was ready to leave at a moment's notice. Olar's constant presence was the only thing preventing him from departing sooner. Also, there lingered a slim hope that the librarians might uncover something about the word Apocrypha, but as time passed, his expectations dwindled.

Another day unfolded. At night, the moon casted its glow upon the night, creating an unusually bright atmosphere. It was nearing the time when the librarians would start winding down their activities.

Another day had passed, and they still hadn't found any information about the mysterious word, he reflected.

"Well, looks like this will be a big challenge. So far, the librarians have gone through many books, from new to old, but there is no mention of Apocrypha anywhere," Olar conveyed, sounding defeated.

He attempted to conceal his disappointment, but after days of waiting, it became increasingly challenging to maintain a facade.

"Do not worry, Decar. We will for sure find something for the prince," Olar reassured, attempting to project a positive note, possibly sensing his disappointment.

As Olar was about to leave for his dormitory, a sound caught their attention.

"Miau..." said a cat that had entered the library through one of the windows. Alabaster was startled, his thoughts immediately drifting to his former companion, the Moon witch.

"Are you okay, Decar? That is just a cat; there are actually lots of them around Echo. Look there, more are coming in. They must be looking for mice inside the castle. This happens every now and then," Olar explained.

Indeed, more cats entered through the window, numbering at least ten. Alabaster couldn't help but sweat as he scrutinised them, trying to discern whether the Moon witch was among them.

Alabaster tried to recall the Moon witch's appearance in her cat form: *She was a black cat, No, she was black with white spots. No, she had a strange brown spot on her tail.* But the details eluded him. His memory, altered by recent events, failed to provide a clear image.

Amidst his realisation, a young librarian named Copernio said, "I found something!" He learned that Copernio was a relatively new librarian, having worked in the library for less than a year.

Showing a flat piece of stone to him, the young librarian

explained, "I started looking at the section where unknown items are located. Most of them are old furniture, art, and plates, among other items. I found this stele, and on it, look at this."

The stele was in a bad state, showing signs of breakage. Looking closely, he noted it bore strange characters. Copernio pointed with his finger to one character that read *Apocrypha*. The rest of the characters were indecipherable to him.

"Wonderful job, boy!" said Olar, admiring the stone. "This is why we never heard of it."

Examining the stele, Olar continued, "This is the oldest thing you can imagine. I cannot know how old. And these characters, they are as old as the Primes. We could only guess that it is a language lost in time. Your mysterious word doesn't belong to the common language; it belongs to a language that I can assure you no one in the world speaks."

He took the stele, touching the carved characters with his fingers. Despite the important discovery, his thoughts were consumed by the impending matter with the Blood Witches. *I need a sacrifice for them*, he thought.

Suddenly, a blue light emanated from inside the library. Alabaster recognized the light, having seen it in the past. Before him, one of the cats transformed into a little girl with blue hair. Alabaster's body trembled with disbelief.

"No. Impossible! Why are you here?" he screamed.

"Magic! What is happening here, Decar? Do you know this girl?" asked Olar.

As the witch approached, a distant bell rang loudly. Olar quickly took him by the hand, pulling him towards a wall of books inside the library.

"The Starr Witches are coming; they must have sensed magic from within the castle. We must stay away from their wrath!" Olar shouted.

True to Olar's warning, three women dressed in silver robes with their faces concealed beneath silver hoods made their entrance. They were Starr Witches. Pointing at the Moon witch, they recited something incomprehensible to him.

Chains emerged from all corners of the library, hurtling toward the Moon witch. Some coiled around her hands, feet, and neck, while others, with pointed ends, pierced her left shoulder, stomach, and right leg. The chains hoisted her into the air, suspending her above the ground. The Starr Witches remained focused on the Moon witch, who screamed in agony.

"Yes!" he exclaimed. A surge of happiness coursing through him for the first time in a long while. He harboured a desire to see the Moon witch suffer even more.

"She is an enemy of the Golden Nation; you must kill her now!" he yelled at the three Starr Witches.

"This girl needs to be interrogated by the lord of the castle. We will take her to him. He will decide the girl's fate," stated one of the Starr Witches.

"No!" he screamed. "You don't know her; she is too powerful. Kill her now while you can."

Frantically searching for anything he could use to pierce the girl's heart; Alabaster's desperation reached a fever pitch.

But it was too late for him. The Moon witch's blue hair began to grow and danced towards the moonlight streaming in through a large window. He recognized the unfolding events—similar to the moments when the girl had mercilessly killed men in Duskenwood and barbarians in the Rockshade Highlands.

"Star witches, ye be mine own offspring. Naught can ye do to hinder me," declared the Moon witch, her words echoing with an undeniable power that seemed to pierce through his ears.

A brilliant blue light enveloped the chains that restrained the girl. She emitted a scream, and the chains disintegrated, leaving only remnants of the radiant blue glow. Waving her hands towards the

Starr Witches, most of the residual blue light in the air surged across the room at incredible speed, slicing through everything in its path. Columns, furniture, candles—everything was severed into numerous pieces. Even the Starr Witches were not exempt from the destructive force. Their vital limbs were cut and they died instantly.

The Moon witch, still suspended above the ground, turned her gaze towards him and the group of librarians who had gathered together.

With another scream from the witch, the remaining blue lights shot towards them. Alabaster reacted swiftly, pushing Olar to the side while narrowly avoiding one of the streaking blue lights. The violent scene continued, with the librarians caught in the crossfire of the Moon witch's powerful magic.

As the blue lights struck the librarians, they fell to the ground dead. The force of the magical onslaught had wreaked havoc in the library, cutting through furniture and leaving books strewn across the floor, many of them damaged or sliced in many pieces. The once serene atmosphere of the library had transformed into a chaotic destruction.

Thinking he had successfully dodged the attack, Alabaster realised blood was trickling down the right side of his face. Panicking, he reached up to touch his right ear, only to find that his ear was gone, severed by the last assault.

Despite the pain and the desire to cry, he knew he had no time for emotions. He needed to escape while he still could.

Chains suddenly entwined his body from toe to head, causing him to lose balance and collapse to the ground. The impact was so forceful that he suspected he might have broken some ribs.

"Thou wert hiding here, within a library, of all places, O Blood Priest," said the Moon witch.

Chains also covered his mouth, rendering him unable to speak. Instead, he moaned in response to the Moon witch.

"Think not thou wert fortunate; had I desired, I could have slain thee. The sole reason thou livest is for that I need thee to unlock the entrance to the Blood Witches' camp," said the girl.

Captured once again by the Moon witch, Alabaster couldn't believe his misfortune. Just when things seemed to be going his way, he found himself imprisoned. Anger and pain clouded his thoughts, and though he yearned to inquire about Searc and Truinan, the overwhelming desire to end the Moon witch's life took precedence. He then realised her captor had to be the sacrifice for the Blood Witches.

The Moon witch threw a blue beam at one of the walls, creating a big hole in it. Parts of the library's roof began to descend slowly, indicating the significant damage inflicted on the structure.

She then whistled, summoning a horse that galloped through the hole. Using her magic to levitate him, the witch tossed him onto the back of the horse before mounting it herself. As they exited the castle's borders, the distant sound of ringing bells and echoing screams reached his ears. *The Echo soldiers must be searching for us*, he suspected.

Suddenly, soldiers emerged in front of them, forcing the witch to bring the horse to an abrupt halt. He almost tumbled from the saddle. Before them stood at least fifty Echo soldiers armed with swords and bows.

"For the order of the lord of Echo, you have been accused of killing Echo citizens and destroying public property. You are to come with us immediately. You will be put in jail and then wait for your execution by sword," said one of the soldiers positioned at the forefront.

He recognized the soldier's voice; it was Lotar, the Echo soldier who had aided him a few days ago. Inwardly, he pleaded with Lotar to leave, but the chains covering his mouth allowed only moans to escape.

"Wouldst thou plead for these men?" the Moon witch inquired to him calmly. "I shall reveal unto thee the depth of mine earnestness."

He saw that the witch's hair began to glow blue, growing long and dancing towards the bright moon in the night sky. Levitating above the horse, she extended her arms, and numerous blue spheres materialised around her.

"Attack!" Lotar's scream echoed in the distance.

He couldn't witness the soldiers' assault, as all he could see were the blue spheres hovering around the witch, hurtling swiftly towards the men. Next, the air was filled with screams of pain and agony from the soldiers. He noticed that the attack not only reached the intended targets but also extended to nearby houses, destroying them and potentially causing harm to innocent citizens. All of a sudden the atmosphere changed; he could smell blood around him.

The Moon witch ceased floating and landed back on the horse, resuming their journey. They passed through the area where the soldiers lay dead. Alabaster, unable to distinguish the soldiers, only saw lifeless bodies strewn across the ground, some still twitching.

Despite being accustomed to the stench of death, he felt a sting of sorrow for the fallen soldiers, especially Lotar. His tragic demise left him in tears.

As they crossed the Echo border, the landscape transformed into the Silent Dunes. Uncertain of the witch's destination, he assumed they were heading northwest, potentially back to Duskenwood. If his estimate was accurate, they could reach the Blood Witches' camp in approximately fifteen days.

They rode through the night, the radiant moon still dominating the sky without a single cloud to obscure it. Then, he saw it again—a small black celestial body in front of the moon. *The dark moon stands once more*, he recalled the strange man saying back in Duskenwood.

As the sun began to rise, the girl halted the horse in the midst of the sandy expanse. Alabaster, surrounded by the desolation of the Silent Dunes, wondered about the witch's intentions. With no visible signs of water or sustenance in the barren landscape, he questioned what the witch would do.

He observed the Moon witch dismounting and walking across the sand as if searching for something.

"Herein, it may yet be opened," he heard the witch say.

Upon touching the sand, a radiant blue light emanated from it. Though he couldn't clearly discern from the distance, the ground beneath the witch seemed to warp and distort.

Returning to the horse, the Moon witch grasped the saddle and pulled it toward the altered ground. Upon closer inspection, He saw that the once sandy terrain had transformed into a crystalline wall, akin to a mirror but lacking any reflection. Through the transparent crystal, he glimpsed dirt and green leaves—a clear contrast to the Silent Dunes.

Duskenwood? It can't be, he thought, his eyes widening in disbelief.

"Judging by thy reaction, I assume thou comprehendest. This portal shall convey us directly to where we encountered that creature in Duskenwood. Thy end approacheth, O Blood Priest," the witch said ominously.

HALLARD

"For the last time, entering our clan without a proper invitation is strictly prohibited," said a witch positioned in front of the main gate.

Hallard attempted to persuade the witch that he carried an important message for the Shabrani witch named Mila. However, it seemed that only those with a formal invitation could access the Shabrani Witches' citadel.

"What about them? They don't appear to be witches. How come they're allowed in?" he questioned, gesturing towards a group of men loaded with bags and supplies.

The sentinel witch glared at him.

"They are merchants. We are acquainted with them, and they possess special authorization to enter our clan," said the witch who grew increasingly more impatient.

He took a deep breath and surveyed his surroundings. The citadel of the Shabrani Witches was encircled by a formidable tall wall made of stone, adorned with intricate writings that resembled glyphs. The main gate, larger than anything he had encountered before, was of dark red colour and stood slightly ajar. Positioned in front of the entrance was a group of Shabrani Witches serving as sentinels, with whom he had been engaged in an argument.

Redirecting his attention to the witch he was arguing with, he struggled to discern her face which was concealed beneath a dark hood. Garmented entirely in black robes, he couldn't help but notice her diminutive stature, realising she may not be a full adult yet.

"Don't even think about it. A word of advice: do not attempt to climb the walls. You won't last a second," warned the sentinel witch.

Hallard couldn't help but smile. *Does she assume all men are that foolish?* he pondered.

With time slipping away, he found himself running out of ideas on how to enter the citadel. He needed a way to enter promptly, especially since his men were expected to arrive in Rivercrash in a few days. It was crucial for him to finish his business with the Shabrani clan and then reach Rivercrash at the same time as his men.

He then decided to show the piece of parchment given by Demoria. Retrieving it from his belongings, he unfolded it and presented its contents to the sentinel witch.

"Is this enough?" he asked.

The sentinel witch accepted the parchment, closely inspecting the glyph written on it.

"Where did you get this?" the sentinel witch asked, sounding surprised.

"As I mentioned earlier, a Shabrani witch named Demoria sent me a message for Mila. She requested that I deliver this parchment to her," he explained.

The sentinel witch tucked the parchment into her robes.

"Hey! That's not for you. It's for..." he was cut off by the sentinel witch.

"Put this man in a cell. Somehow, he managed to kill one of ours and brought this parchment stained with our sister's blood," she shouted to the other sentinel witches nearby.

He considered defending himself by force, but he decided it would be wiser to maintain a low profile and comply. Perhaps, as a prisoner, he could still find a way to reach Mila within the citadel.

"Sisters, stop! You're making a mistake," intervened another witch who entered through the main gate.

He observed that the unknown witch was notably tall compared to the other witches he had met. She wore black and red robes with her hood down, revealing a face with strong cheekbones and short black hair.

"Let me see that parchment," the unknown witch ordered. He sensed that she held a higher rank based on her commanding tone.

The unknown witch placed a finger on top of the glyph.

"Do you know Demoria?" she asked in a hushed voice.

Hallard was surprised that she gathered that information just by touching the glyph. *Must be some sort of magic*, he thought.

"She sent me here with a message for a witch named Mila," he said.

The unknown witch then addressed the sentinel, "This man has my permission to enter our citadel. Let him in."

"I must inform our superiors of any new visitors, Mila. You know the rules," said the sentinel witch.

Mila. How did she know I was here looking for her? Was it a coincidence? he contemplated.

"Do as you must," Mila responded, almost disregarding the sentinel witch.

After that, Hallard had to provide his name and reasons for entering the Shabrani clan once more. This time, the sentinel witch recorded the information in a book she had with her.

I never thought witches were so well-organised, he thought.

"Well, come with me, lakeman," said Mila.

He followed Mila through the main gate of the citadel.

"I gather it's your first time in our citadel. Aren't they impressive? the door and the walls, I mean. It is believed that the Primes built them when the volcano Dukkah was still active. If it wasn't for the imposing walls, the lava expelled by the volcano would have spread beyond the lands of Gorgon. You can still see remnants of the burning imprinted on the walls," said Mila while examining him from head to toe.

He examined the walls from inside the citadel. Mila was correct; at the base of the walls, there were black spots that resembled old burns.

"The volcano. Is it dormant these days?" he inquired.

She smiled at him, saying, "I hope you're not scared by it."

Are all Shabrani Witches sarcastic? he wondered, recalling Demoria's sense of humour.

The volcano Dukkah became increasingly visible as they ventured deeper into the citadel. Even from a distance, its imposing presence was formidable, resembling a colossal titan that seemed out of place in the world.

"The volcano has been dormant for hundreds of years, or so our historians say. It emits dust and smoke every now and then, but that's the extent of the danger you'll encounter," said Mila.

They walked in silence for a few minutes. The Shabrani clan unfolded into a vast space with small tents scattered throughout. Various other structures, such as stables, taverns, and some unidentifiable buildings, dotted the landscape. Near the volcano, he caught sight of the renowned Crimson Castle—a place he had heard about as a child from other members of the Lakefields royal court.

"Is that where your Great Council congregates?" he asked, pointing towards the Crimson Castle.

Mila looked at him, almost as if scanning his thoughts. "Is that why you came here? To seek an audience with our Great Council?" she inquired.

He was surprised by her precise guess. "Yes, I have matters to discuss with them. Demoria thought you could..." Mila interrupted him.

"Not here, Hallard. It is not safe," she cautioned.

Walking by other witches, he noticed how they all shared the same attire, dark robes and hoods concealing their faces. They walked past several tents until reaching Mila's own tent.

Upon entering the tent, he took a moment to survey the surroundings. Despite its modest size, it was well-equipped with a bed, bath, table, and chair, along with some furniture, presumably for clothes and personal items. The most striking feature was the multitude of candles. It seemed Mila had a particular fondness for them, with at least a hundred small candles arranged around the tent.

"I know, I know. I've been told many times I shouldn't have so many candles in such a small space. I just can't help it. There's something dark yet mysterious about candles. Plus, I don't mind the smell of smoke," she said, smiling.

He returned the smile and proceeded to leave his weapon and bag on the floor.

"First of all, I would like to thank you for letting me in. I was getting very worried. If you hadn't come, they would have taken me as a prisoner," he said. "On that note, how did you know I was coming to find you?"

Mila held up the piece of paper with Demoria's glyph. "This isn't just any glyph. It's a signal only I and another witch, friends with Demoria, can sense when it's in close proximity. You see, Demoria and I grew up together, we're very good friends. We used to play, drawing these glyphs when we were just rank one witches. These blood glyphs were quite useful back in the day. I didn't know they could still be useful," explained Mila.

Magic, he thought. He was starting to feel comfortable in front of Mila. She seemed to be telling the truth. She mentioned another witch who knew about those glyphs too, and he wondered who the other witch was.

"By touching the glyph with my finger, I could tell the blood belonged to Demoria. For her to be giving you such a message, it means she trusts you, which I will do as well. Tell me, what is the message, and why do you need to speak to our Great Council?" asked Mila.

He began recounting his encounter with the barbarians and the Balor Witches in the Blue Bell Mountains. Mila's expression grew more serious at the mention of the Balor Witches. He continued by describing his meeting with Demoria and the battle they had in the Grey Skull.

"And this is the only thing that was left of the Balor Witches; according to Demoria, it is one of them but reduced to almost nothing," he explained, taking out the bag containing the small Balor creature they found near the Grey Skull.

Mila accepted the small bag. "I recognize this spell. It is enchanted, stopping any magic inside it. A very difficult spell, but if cast in such a small space, it can be done easily."

"You must keep this for now," said Mila, handing the bag back to him. "I will not open it, not here and not by myself. I trust what you told me; the Balor Witches must have found a way to live even when their bodies have been destroyed. This thing in the bag, it could attack us if we let it free, I am afraid."

He understood and took the bag back.

"I must speak to your Great Council. I must tell them what I've seen and experienced. It is my belief that the Balor Witches are planning an attack on Lakefields. I also suspect there is a traitor informant in our higher ranks; otherwise, the witches would never know of our move into the Blue Bell Mountains," he said firmly.

He kneeled in front of Mila. "Please, Mila, I've lost too many brave men. I've seen what these Balor Witches can do. We, in Lakefields, won't stand a chance against them," implored Hallard.

Mila had her mouth open.

"You Lakemen are really something. I understand why Demoria likes you," she winked at him.

He blushed a little.

"I do what I can. Killing Balor Witches is my favourite hobby," said Mila.

He recalled Demoria mentioning that Mila disliked Balor Witches. He did not inquire further about it, considering it a private matter.

"But first, I must summon my master, a witch greater than me in knowledge and power. She will know what to do with that thing you brought. Please make yourself comfortable in this humble... tent," Mila gathered a few belongings and prepared to depart.

"I might take some time. You must stay inside the tent, don't let anyone else see you. The bath is still warm; you must shower. My master does not like... dirt," she said, sounding displeased by his appearance.

Then, Mila left the tent, leaving him all by himself.

He sniffed his armpits, and noticed the smell of sweat and dirt. *I haven't showered in days*, he contemplated.

Putting his armour aside, along with his leather clothes and underclothes, he stepped into the bath.

The bath carried a distinct scent, perhaps lavender or lemon— he wasn't adept at identifying aromas. After a few moments under the water, he began to feel better. His muscles, long sore, were finally getting some respite. Even his mind, preoccupied with thoughts of impending wars, started to drift and shut down. Suddenly, his thoughts shifted to his family in Rivercrash. He didn't know if his father was still alive or if the healers couldn't save him. If his father couldn't make it, he would be the lord of Rivercrash as the next in line. The prospect of courtly responsibilities, tedious meetings, constant demands from his people, and diplomatic travels made him feel anxious.

Then, the matter of marriage surfaced. He would need to marry to uphold tradition and secure an heir. Demoria, the memory of the night they spent together, lingered in his mind. If he had to choose someone, it would be her. However, she could reject him. *A Shabrani witch as the lady of Rivercrash—now that would be something*, he thought.

"Hallard, I need you to dress! My master is here with me!" came Mila's urgent call, jolting him out of his own thoughts.

"Give me a few moments," he responded to Mila who was standing outside the tent.

Hallard stepped out of the bath, feeling rejuvenated. He dressed in his clothes and armour, ready to talk to the witches.

"I am ready," he said.

Mila entered the tent with another witch wearing red robes and black slippers. Her uncovered face revealed a mature black woman with black and grey hair.

"I introduce you to my master. This is Lenithia, a Shabrani witch of rank four and a member of the Great Council of our clan," said Mila.

He was surprised by those words; Mila's master was a member of the Great Council. *She could be of great help*, he realised.

"I am Hallard Rikers from Lakefields; I am at your service," he kneeled before Lenithia.

"You can stand, Hallard. Mila has told me of your perilous situation. It is so unfortunate we have to meet in such circumstances. Before we talk, you must know that I trust everything you have said," she then walked to one of the corners of the tent where there were many candles. "My dear Demoria, for her to help you during a quest. She probably didn't have any other option," said Lenithia.

"Demoria mentioned she was in a hurry to complete a quest, but the Balor witch's attack left her no choice but to stay and fight. Are you Demoria's master as well?" he asked.

Lenithia smiled. "Yes, indeed. I am a master of many. Among them, Demoria is a particular witch. She was very special and skilled in our arts from a very early age."

"Ahem," interrupted Mila.

"Of course, Mila. You three were very special," said Lenithia.

Three, it must be the other witch to whom Mila was referring earlier, he thought.

She then looked at Hallard seriously.

"Show me the creature," Lenithia commanded.

He handed over the bag where the Balor creature had been sealed. Lenithia then proceeded to examine it.

"I can feel vega magic inside this bag, though it's only a small amount. It seems almost dormant, waiting to be awakened.," explained Lenithia.

Afterward, she traced a pentagram on the ground with her finger. Placing the bag at the centre of the pentagram, she spoke a few words he could not comprehend, and the pentagram glowed red. A red light began to flicker in front of him emanating from the pentagram. Lenithia murmured a few more words, and then, "Boom!" A small explosion came from the bag.

The smoke that had triggered the explosion began to change. At first, its form was indistinct, but soon it took on the shape of a woman.

"Tell me, who are you?" Lenithia inquired.

"A Balor witch, a member of... No, I cannot reveal it; it's a secret," a voice emanated from the smoky figure.

"What is your purpose?"

"To serve our Great Council."

"Why can't you be destroyed?"

"We are different; we possess boundless energy, we... we..." the voice started to falter.

He interrupted the interrogation.

"What do you want with Lakefields?" he asked.

The figure turned to Hallard. "You... You!" It screamed. "It is all your fault; your ancient magic made us fail in our mission. I hate you, I hate you!" It screamed louder and louder.

Lenithia spoke a few words, and then the smoky figure and the pentagram disappeared into thin air. The bag remained on the ground as if nothing had happened.

"That was uncalled for," said Mila.

"It's okay, Mila. That thing was programmed not to say anything," she paused for a moment and then approached Hallard.

"The ancient magic it spoke of. What is it, Hallard?" Lenithia asked him.

He tried to remember; perhaps it was the golden leaf he was carrying.

"It was an heirloom in the shape of a golden leaf. It passed from generation to generation in my family. Somehow, it protected me from a deadly attack by a Balor witch in the Blue Bell Mountains. I don't really know how it works. I decided to give it to Demoria the last time I saw her," he said.

Lenithia and Mila exchanged glances. It seemed to him that they were unfamiliar with this sort of magic.

"Do you know what ancient magic means, Hallard?" asked Mila.

In fact, this was the first time he had paused to consider it. His understanding of magic was very basic. He knew that witches across the Lower Lands could wield various types of magic. It was a known fact that only women possessed the ability to manipulate magic, though the reason for this remained a mystery, despite some intriguing theories. As for ancient magic, he was entirely in the dark.

"It's okay, not even we witches know much about it," said Lenithia. "Ancient magic is an art that existed before our own. It is said that when the gods walked these lands—if you believe those tales—they could manipulate every natural element, not just fire, plants, or light. At some point in the past, certain aspects of ancient magic were lost, and what remained was divided into the types of magic that we witch clans wield today. Ancient magic is, to put it simply, the origin of our powers. This is why our magic is nullified in the presence of ancient magic. Again, these are all just speculations; the artefacts that can channel ancient magic have mostly been lost. You must have held something truly unique—or I should say, had," Lenithia added.

He was taken aback by Lenithia's words.

"I thought Demoria would need it more than I did. Now that I say it aloud, I realise I had a feeling it might protect her from some future danger—almost like a premonition," he said.

"Or fate," Lenithia replied with a smile.

Hallard and Mila exchanged puzzled glances.

"Let's focus on what we can do. We must show the Balor creature to the Great Council," said Lenithia.

Mila touched her master's shoulder, "Master, you have a meeting with the Great Council tonight. You could take the opportunity then; we must not delay," said Mila, who Hallard thought was trying hard to sound convincing.

"Mila, your obsession with the Balor Witches can be deceiving," Lenithia took a long breath. "I will discuss it with the Great Council tonight. However, I will need your help, lakeman."

Hallard looked at the Shabrani Witches, "I will do everything you command me. I owe you my life."

Mila let a giggle escape and said, "I told you, master, Demoria had good reasons to like this one."

BASON

The castle in Barral, the capital city of Borraral, appeared just as old and majestic as he remembered it. Bason had read in various books that the castle was one of the oldest in the world. Signs of rain and harsh weather were evident on every wall, roof, and window. He always wondered why his grandfather never renovated the castle. His thoughts then shifted to the city of Barral. Unlike the castle, most of its houses and buildings had been renovated. One other notable attraction in Borraral territory was the towering trees scattered across the land, reaching towards the sky as mountains do.

As Bason and his companions approached, the gates of the castle swung open to welcome them. The familiar musty scent emanating from within the castle hit him, similar to the smell of enclosed spaces devoid of fresh air.

"Prince Bason, Princess Amina awaits you in the Crown Room. Please follow me," one of the castle guards said with the utmost respect.

He nodded and followed behind the guard, matching his pace as they made their way through the corridors of the castle.

As they proceeded toward the Crown Room, they traversed the corridors of the castle. Memories flooded of his childhood days, when he would chase his siblings through these very halls, engaged in games and laughter. He couldn't help but notice the new pieces of art adorning the walls. "It seems aunt Amina has been spreading her wings throughout the castle," he said to himself.

Behind him, his two servants trailed, bearing the few belongings Bason had managed to gather. Walking alongside him was Caffia Titus, a messenger from Borraral, dispatched by his aunt. Ever since their escape from Velaska's prison, Bason had been keen on keeping a close watch on her until he could speak with his aunt personally.

The Crown Room was where the king convened with other members of the royal family and heard the requests of the public. In his younger days, Bason would occasionally sit beside his grandfather and listen to the concerns of the common folk.

Reflecting on those times, he remembered a particular instance that was imprinted in his memory.

"The taxes on fishing are downright excessive. We're barely making ends meet anymore. Some of us fishermen are even considering raising the fish selling price to the castle to compensate for these burdensome taxes. But we don't want to stir up any trouble, especially knowing how much the king enjoys fresh fish," said a robust man, whom Bason had dismissed at the time as just another commoner. Reflecting on it now, he realised that the man was likely the head of some sort of fishermen's guild.

King Hendrik Fitzroy typically tasked his counsellors with noting down petitions, which he would then study before giving a verdict within two or three days. However, this time, he deviated from his usual practice and posed a direct question: "Bason, you've heard this man's petition. What would you do?"

At that time, he was no more than twelve years old, with limited knowledge of taxes and government, his understanding shaped primarily by what his aunt Amina and his father had taught him.

He gazed at the fisherman and inquired, "Why can't you simply work double time? That way, you'd have enough money to cover the extra taxes."

The fisherman barely acknowledged him, instead he addressed his grandfather directly. "Your Kingship, he is merely a child. Please, hear my plea. If we don't address the tax issue, the other fishermen will..."

"Guards! Three lashes for disrespecting the prince of the Golden Nation," said young Bason firmly.

One of the guards obeyed Bason's command and administered the punishment. By the third lash, the fisherman was on the ground, tears streaming down his face as he begged for forgiveness. Even as a child, Bason had always been deeply unsettled by disrespect or disregard.

Following the incident, the King of Borraral ordered for the fisherman to be taken to the nursery within the castle. He also decided to adjourn all further meetings for the day.

"Bason, you mustn't be so impulsive with our loyal citizens. This is not the conduct befitting of a future king," admonished King Hendrik.

"I merely acted as my father would have. I've witnessed him handle such matters at court numerous times," said Bason.

His grandfather knelt down, gently ruffling Bason's thick blonde hair as he spoke with sincerity. "There's something important you must understand. You shouldn't aspire to be a king like your father. While he may rule over the largest nation in the Lower Lands, he lacks compassion and gratitude. Always remember, a king is nothing without the support of his citizens. A nation flourishes when its people are content and prosperous."

On that day, those words stirred something within him. He began treating his servants with respect, even going so far as to adopt two of them to be by his side. It was his way of giving back, or so he believed. Over time, he forgot the lesson learnt from his grandfather though. He knew sometimes he could be a real piece of work when it came to treating others with fairness.

"Prince, the King of Borraral is ready to receive you," announced one of the sentinels guarding the entrance to the Crown Room.

The heavy wooden doors swung open, unveiling an empty seat where his grandfather, the King of Borraral, should have been seated. As he and his companions entered, the doors closed behind them with a resounding thud. From behind his grandfather's vacant seat, his aunt Amina emerged. She was dressed in black robes, her grey hair tied back in a ponytail with a black ribbon.

"Bason, I see you've met Caffia. Isn't she wonderful?" Amina said with an amicable tone.

He glanced around the Crown Room, noticing the absence of anyone else from the royal court.

"Aunt, what's happening? Where is my grandfather?" he inquired.

Amina gripped the backrest of the king's chair tightly. "Sadly, your grandfather passed away three days ago," she informed him solemnly.

The sudden news left him speechless. King Hendrik had been a better father figure to him than his own. Despite not having seen his grandfather for some time, Bason regarded him as a strong man, not easily defeated by any illness.

"How?" was all he managed to utter. He noticed Recaro crying and being comforted by Valecio, who didn't easily succumb to emotions.

"I know what you're thinking, Bason, but your grandfather was ill; his lungs had been severely damaged for quite some time. The nurses said that he died due to a collapse in his lungs; they simply stopped working," Amina explained with a sorrowful tone.

He wasn't satisfied with the answers. "Where is his body? Why hasn't there been a ceremony for his death?" he pressed, his agitation was growing.

"Calm down, Bason. This is not the time for haste," Amina said with a steady voice. "His burial took place immediately after the nurses tended to his body. He rests behind the castle, in the graveyard next to other esteemed lords and kings."

Amina paused to catch some breath and continued, "Under my orders, his death is a secret to most of Borraral's citizens. Only a handful of trusted members of the court know of this sad news. I have my reasons for this. Please hear me out."

He was beyond reasoning. Exhausted from his travels without food or rest, his mind was clouded with emotion. He stormed towards Valecio, seizing a golden knife from his belt and directing it towards his aunt.

"As prince of the Golden Nation, I accuse you of conspiracy to take over Barral's castle. You will be... you will..." Bason struggled to finish his sentence, feeling an overwhelming pressure on his entire body that made it difficult to breathe. The last thing he heard was Recaro crying out his name, and his aunt standing before him, chanting something he could not understand.

Darkness enveloped his mind as memories flickered akin to bolts of lightning. First, memories of his grandfather from his childhood flashed before him. Then, the scenes shifted to memories of his siblings, recalling the fights they had as children. Amidst the haze, he heard a voice calling his name—it was his mother. Though her face was obscured, her voice remained familiar.

The memories shifted once again. Now, he found himself seated on the king's throne in Solaris Castle, in the Golden Nation, a heavy golden crown weighing down on his head. He tried to remove it, but it seemed fused to his flesh. As he stood from the throne, a group of witches in dark robes appeared before him, their eyes fixed on a colossal tree behind him. It was unlike any tree he had ever seen—made of flesh and blood. The tree's branches stretched toward the sky, forming a sort of road that extended endlessly, bearing countless crimson-coloured fruits. From one of the fruits emerged a woman dressed in white, with a fair complexion and blue hair, gracefully descending before him. He noticed she was much taller than him. She knelt before him and said, "I have found thee, Apocrypho."

He awoke to find himself in a familiar room, one he had stayed in during childhood visits. His clothing had been changed, and a pleasant aroma filled the air.

"Food!" he exclaimed eagerly.

Rising from the bed, he discovered a spread of food on a nearby table. Sweet bread, potatoes, pulled beef, and vegetables greeted him, accompanied by a jar of milk with honey, his favourite drink.

His hunger overtook him, and he devoured the meal in mere moments.

"Slow down, Bason. You will make yourself sick," said a familiar voice. It was his aunt Amina, standing beside his bed. *How long had she been there?* he wondered.

He resisted the impulse to accuse her of treason again. Instead, with a clear mind now, he opted to listen to her explanations first.

"Aunt, I realise now that you must have had your reasons for hiding my grandfather's passing. Please explain," he said.

His aunt nodded sympathetically. "I hoped you would understand, Bason. I've always tried to do what I believe is best for all of us," said Amina.

He felt a pang of guilt for his earlier outburst. "I'm sorry. I should never have threatened you without proof. I wasn't myself; the lack of sleep and food had taken its toll," he said.

"There's no need to apologise, Bason. I understand the circumstances. Valecio and Recaro explained what you have been endeavouring over the past few days," said Amina. Her calm demeanour reassured him.

He finished the milk and honey, then settled onto the bed. "So, you're a witch," he said plainly.

His aunt smiled and approached him, taking his hand in hers. "Yes, but there's much more to it than that. You must listen to what I have to say and understand why I've kept secrets from you," said Amina.

"Valecio, Recaro!" he called out, summoning his servants.

Both Valecio and Recaro entered the room promptly, ready to attend to his needs.

"Prepare my bath and clothes. I will meet my aunt properly," Bason instructed them.

With a smile, Amina bid him farewell and exited the room.

His servants brought hot water and soup. As he relaxed in the bath, Bason's thoughts drifted back to their journey to Borraral. He recalled the treacherous trap set by the Starr witch Velaska, who had imprisoned him within his own royal coach. Fortunately, Caffia had devised a daring plan for their escape; she presented a scroll given by his aunt Amina. Bason recognized the scroll as a spell, similar to the ones he had seen in the Heavenly Tower.

Caffia explained that the spell would create gravitational magic, causing everything around them to levitate in the air, slowly rising and falling in a mesmerising motion. Though unsure of its effectiveness, they hoped it would divert Velaska's attention away from them. Remarkably, when Caffia activated the spell, the couch, along with its contents—bed, chest, tables—began floating, and the sealed door unexpectedly opened, granting them freedom.

Acting swiftly, they gathered what essentials they could and fled in search of horses. As they made their escape, he observed that it wasn't just his couch affected by the spell; everything in the vicinity was floating, causing chaos among the soldiers who scrambled to retrieve their belongings. Though they didn't encounter Velaska herself, they surmised she was occupied attempting to dispel the gravitational spell.

Finding horses, they departed hastily, leaving behind the royal entourage and his little sister, Beatrice.

As he dried himself off, his thoughts lingered on the peculiar dream he had before. *What did that woman call me?* he wondered, struggling to recall the word. He tried but it eluded him.

Feeling refreshed, he stepped out of the bath, where Valecio assisted him in dressing while Recaro attended to his wavy hair. Opting for black linen clothes as a tribute to his late grandfather, he couldn't shake the strange sensation of not having had the chance to bid his grandfather farewell.

"It is time," he resolved with a made up mind.

Bason joined his aunt in the graveyard behind Barral's castle. Valecio and Recaro accompanied him walking a few steps behind him. He spotted the resting place of his grandfather—a tall, majestic tombstone befitting of a king. Having a close look, he realised there were no inscriptions on the headstone.

"Why aren't there any engravings on the headstone?" he inquired.

His aunt, kneeling before the tombstone with closed eyes, likely in prayer, responded, "I was hoping you could write something for him. I think he would've wanted that."

Helping her to her feet, he asked, "Are you telling me you knew I would leave Velaska and Beatrice on the road and come here alone?"

A smile played on his aunt's lips. "Walk with me," she beckoned, leading him away.

As they strolled back to the castle, the bright sun and brisk wind created a warm invigorating atmosphere. The clouds raced across the sky, while in the distance, a few towering trees stood majestic, though most had been cut down near the castle.

"Do you know the story of how the Golden Nation took over Echo?" his aunt inquired.

He recalled the story he had learned as a child. "Many years ago, my grandfather on my father's side, King Roland Artois, sought to stop the Dragani clan from bringing their god, Dragan, to the Lower Lands with the help of the king of Echo at the time. My grandfather frustrated their plans, put most of the Dragani Witches to the sword, and conquered Echo with the aid of the Starr Witches. The surviving Dragani Witches were prohibited from using magic, a decree known as the Third Cardinal Sin by the Great Conclave of witches."

Amina rolled her eyes. "Lies. The Dragani clan never attempted to bring their god to the Lower Lands. That part of the story is nothing but a machination created by the Starr Witches and their leader, Velaska."

He had heard those stories as well—that King Roland had fabricated an excuse to invade Echo, a topic forbidden to be discussed in the Golden Nation.

"Let's not get astray," Amina said abruptly. "You mentioned something intriguing—'with the help of the Starr Witches,'" she mused, rolling her eyes again. "They have wielded significant influence over the decisions of kings and queens in the Golden Nation, if you think about it," she added, gazing into the distance.

"Aunt, no more dancing around the subject. What is it you're trying to tell me?" he said impatiently.

Halting in her tracks, Amina turned to face him. "I am a Dragani Witch. When King Roland invaded Echo, he nearly wiped out my clan under orders from Velaska. At the time of the invasion, I wasn't in Echo. Years before the invasion, a Dragani witch made it to Barral, and it was then, by fate, that I was chosen to become a Dragani Witch. I learnt magic in the utmost secrecy; only my father and your mother knew about my abilities. When my master found out about the invasion in Echo, she fled, and I never saw her again. After that, I taught myself magic during my stays here in Barral, concealing it from the Starr Witches. That's why they never discovered my true nature."

Her revelations left him stunned. He had never imagined his aunt to be a witch, let alone successfully conceal her secret from everyone in the Golden Nation.

"Well, I'm sure my father will have one or two words to say about your witchcraft, Aunt. But frankly, I don't care," he said, resuming his walk as his aunt fell into step beside him. "What I'm most interested in is knowing what you're planning now."

He stopped abruptly, turning to face her. "By the letter you sent with Caffia, it's clear you don't trust Velaska and my father. You believe they're both scheming something. Am I right?" he pressed.

Amina placed a reassuring hand on his shoulder, prompting them both to pause and lock eyes. "As direct as always, you'll never change. So let me be just as direct," she replied with a smile. "I believe Velaska and your father are plotting against the Shabrani Witches. You're aware of their claims about the Shabrani Witches attempting to resurrect their god. But I think it's all a ruse. Velaska's ambition is to eradicate her biggest threat, the Shabrani clan, as they wiped out the Dragani clan in the past. And as for your father, he seeks to conquer the entire world, aiming to become the sole ruler of the Lower Lands."

He was taken aback by the accusations against his father and the revelation that Amina knew about the Shabrani Witches' plans to bring back their deity—a secret he believed was closely guarded by the Starr clan.

"Those are grave accusations, aunt. But do you have any proof?" Bason inquired, seeking evidence to support her claims.

Amina nodded. "I've been studying the Starr Witches for years..."

"You mean spying," he interjected.

A jiggle escaped Amina's lips. "Call it what you like, nephew. But believe me when I say that Velaska has manipulated your father with false promises and revelations from their enchanted Eye of Meteora. They convinced the king that he would become the greatest ruler, unifying all the nations in the Lower Lands, even Artoria and Celen, which have been at war for years. Your father has bought into these tales and has finally decided to take action. Sending such a large company to Borraral is a threat. If Borraral were to disapprove of your father's intentions, Velaska would order your royal entourage to put Borraral to the sword. It would signify yet another territory conquered by the Golden Nation," she explained.

He grappled with his aunt's revelations, finding them increasingly plausible, especially given his own distrust of Velaska. Her actions, imprisoning him within his own royal coach, only fuelled his doubts further.

"Let's entertain the notion that I believe you. If Velaska is indeed planning war upon the entire Lower Lands, what course of action do you propose? Keep in mind, Beatrice is with her at the moment; perhaps my little sister is already her prisoner," he said, weighing the implications.

Amina turned to face the horizon, contemplating their predicament. "Beatrice is now a Starr Witch; Velaska would never endanger one of their own. Instead, she'll likely poison Beatrice's mind as she has done with your father," she said, her gaze fixed on the distant skyline. "First, I propose to protect our own. We must evacuate this city. But I won't make that decision. It falls upon our new king," she said, meeting his eyes directly.

He recoiled at the suggestion, immediately rejecting it. "Me? I cannot be king. By tradition, you are now the Queen of Borraral until you have a son. Then, he would ascend to the throne," he said, attempting to convey his perspective.

Bason felt a wave of shock wash over him as his aunt grasped his hands firmly. "You're forgetting something, nephew," she said earnestly. "I am a witch. I cannot bear children. By tradition, if the queen is unable to conceive, the reign passes to the member of the royal family deemed most suitable by the Queen. And I choose you, my nephew, Bason. There is Borraral royal blood in your veins," she declared.

He released his aunt's hands; his mind was reeling with disbelief. "No, no, no. This is too sudden. I cannot become king. My father will never approve," he protested, still grappling with the idea.

Amina retrieved a small piece of parchment from her robes, unfolding it to reveal a strange glyph engraved upon its surface. *Witchcraft*, he thought.

"I knew you wouldn't readily accept the crown. That's why I am prepared to reveal a secret that was not mine to share until now," she explained. Pressing her thumb against the glyph, she said "This is a voice glyph. It can capture any speech and record it. Please, listen," Amina handed it to him.

As the voice emanated from the glyph, Bason's heart clenched. It was a voice he knew all too well, one that stirred emotions deep within him. Tears welled in his eyes as he realised he had heard this voice before— in his childhood.

"My dear sister. You must keep it a secret until the time comes when one of my children is in a position to face Velaska. Do not reveal your true self; remain in the shadows, seek help when in need, you know where. Velaska is exerting considerable effort to

manipulate Delray into opposing other nations. It may take years, but I fear the king will fall under her sway. If this occurs, he will no longer be the king we once knew; he will be Velaska's pawn. My children need this information to stand against their own father. If they fail to act, I fear he will put the Lower Lands in death and despair. Velaska must be stopped," the voice urged.

As the voice of his mother echoed through the air, its familiarity struck him deeply. Though a flood of questions clamour for attention in his mind, he chose to set them aside for the moment.

Turning his attention to Recaro and Valecio, who walked a short distance away, he couldn't help but muster a faint smile. "Hey you two, how does King Bason sound? It has a good ring to it, doesn't it?" he remarked.

HALLARD

He woke up to the sound of animals galloping. With no space available for him in the witches' encampment, they offered him shelter in the stables to spend the night. Hallard, being a man of battle, was used to the smell of horses and other animals. Besides, the abundance of hay made for a surprisingly comfortable bed. Lying on the hay bed, he recalled the events that occurred the night before.

Lenithia had introduced him to the Shabrani Great Council. They convened in a room within one of the towers in the Crimson Castle. Upon entering, the Shabrani Great Council welcomed him and invited him to a position in the centre of the room to be interrogated by them. He noticed that most of the members of the council were wearing black robes with hoods on, except for a couple, one of them being Lenithia. He felt less nervous after seeing her, knowing that Lenithia had devised a plan to deceive the Great Council into aiding him against the Balor Witches. Before the interrogation began, Lenithia informed the council that the Balor Witches had captured him and forced him to ingest a poisonous concoction known as phantasm brain poison.

Before the council meeting, Lenithia had explained to him that phantasm brain poisons were a specialty of Balor Witches. When consumed, it could compel the user to do anything the witches desired.

Lenithia also fabricated another lie, explaining that under the influence of the poison, Hallard's mission was to infiltrate the Shabrani clan, pretending he had a message from Demoria to Mila. Once inside, he was to activate a special weapon hidden in a bag given by the Balor Witches. However, Mila discovered he was under the influence of magic and helped him regain control. Once he returned to his senses, he had no recollection of what happened to him. Mila contacted her master Lenithia, who then brought the matter before the Great Council.

It was the perfect lie, with all the pieces fitting seamlessly together. Lenithia emphasised that manufacturing a lie would help sway the Great Council. Because of his discomfort with lying, a trait ingrained in him since childhood, he attempted to propose alternative plans. However, each suggestion was swiftly rejected by Lenithia and Mila. Eventually, he agreed to the witches' plan, realising that this matter transcended his personal principles. The only falsehood that truly troubled him was the fabrication about his beloved Demoria. They led the council to believe that she could have been killed by the Balor Witches—a revelation that greatly surprised the council members.

"Demoria is one of our most skilled witches. It's hard to believe she would succumb so easily. Are you certain you have no recollection of what befell her?" questioned one of the witches in the Great Council.

He turned to Lenithia, who regarded him with a serious expression. "I truly don't recall anything before the Balor Witches captured me. All I remember is that Demoria was with us at the Grey Skull. And then I arrived here with this glyph inscribed with Demoria's blood," he said, striving to sound convincing.

"We must hold onto the belief that Demoria is alive and persevering in her mission," Lenithia said firmly. "We will await further updates on her whereabouts and progress."

The Great Council also requested proof that he had indeed fallen victim to phantasm brain poison. Fortunately, luck was on his side, as he had been poisoned by the Balor Witches during his fight in the Blue Bell Mountains. Lenithia explained that while Demoria had eradicated the poison at the Grey Skull, she could still detect small residual traces within his body that were insignificant and posed no further threat.

"Demoria didn't remove all the poison from your body because she knew doing so could harm vital organs. Instead, she skilfully erased it until it reached a level that wouldn't pose any danger to you. She truly is an exceptional witch," said Lenithia, sounding proud of her disciple.

The Great Council asked him to remove his clothes and armour to be examined, a request he was not expecting. Although he didn't feel comfortable doing so, he had no choice but to comply. *These are strange circumstances after all*, he thought. Then, the Great Council extended their hands towards him. At first, he wasn't sure how they would examine him, but after a few moments he started to feel a warm energy flowing through his body. He felt a slight tickle running along his skin. It only took them a short time to conclude that there were residual traces of vega magic in his body, confirming the veracity of Lenithia's arguments. After that, he was allowed to put his clothes and armour back on again.

They also asked him to present the secret weapon given by the Balor Witches. He presented it to the Great Council, leaving the bag containing the Balor creature on the floor. They examined it for a considerable time. He heard them whispering between each other, which made him think that they remained puzzled. When they finished the examination, they agreed that it bore the mark of Balor Witches' craftsmanship. Lenithia suggested further examination, volunteering herself to lead the study. The council unanimously consented. Additionally, they announced that they required one more day to deliberate and reach a final decision on whether to aid Hallard against the Balor Witches or take no action.

"Neigh!" The sudden sound interrupted his thoughts about the night before.

Around the stable, some sleipnirs were nickering nearby, indicating their need for feeding. Hallard had encountered sleipnirs before, often brought to Lakefields by merchants from various regions. It was rumoured that the finest breed could be found in the Shabrani Witches clan.

"Hallard! You're awake, excellent!" exclaimed a familiar voice. It was Mila, who had just arrived at the stable. She was clad in crimson robes with a black ribbon cinched around her waist and wore black sandals on her feet. Her short hair remained the same as the day before.

"I had hoped to arrive before the stable's attendant. She's not particularly fond of visitors," said Mila.

She carried a plate of food and a jug of milk, along with some cold meat and potatoes, all intended for his morning meal. Hallard thanked her for the food and devoured it in no time; he didn't realise until then how hungry he was. Afterward, he donned his armour and slung his large sword onto his back. Ready to depart, he exited the stable alongside Mila.

"Quick, put this on. Let's avoid drawing attention in front of the other witches," urged Mila, handing him a large robe. He draped it over his armour, feeling a bit absurd but recognizing the wisdom in staying hidden among the public.

On his way out, he caught sight of the witch in charge of the stables. She met his eyes, showing an unfriendly expression on her face.

Turning his gaze to the sky, he saw that it was overcast, with clouds obscuring most of the sunlight. He couldn't help to see in the distance how large the volcano Dukkah was. As they walked, they passed by witches heading in various directions, and he also noticed several new tents that had not been there the previous day. Mila had informed him that witches could dismantle their tents and depart on missions, returning to set up camp wherever they pleased upon their return. However, certain areas near the Crimson Castle were reserved for witches of ranks three and four who were the most skilled witches among the Shabrani clan.

"Where are we headed?" he inquired of Mila.

"We're going to my tent. My master wishes to speak with you," Mila replied with a smile gracing her face.

As they approached the Crimson Castle, he learned that, as a rank three witch, Mila was permitted to reside nearby. He couldn't help but notice small clusters of witches whispering amongst themselves, their demeanour suggestive of secretive discussions. *Something seems amiss*, he thought. Some of the witches cast defiant glances in his direction, prompting him to wonder if they were indeed discussing him.

"Something transpired this morning, which has left us all a bit unsettled. I'll fill you in on the details once we reach my tent," Mila explained to him as they continued walking.

Upon stepping inside Mila's tent, he was immediately greeted by the familiar scent of the aromatic candles Mila favoured, which filled the air with their pleasant fragrance.

"Well, it seems the robe isn't exactly helping you blend into the camp," Mila said with a playful giggle.

He removed the robe from himself. "Does everyone know why I'm in the citadel?" he inquired.

"Some of them might be aware. However, they could also be gossiping about something entirely different," responded Mila.

Another witch entered the tent covered in black robes from head to toe, revealing herself to be Lenithia. He noticed her grey and black hair slightly untidy; she bore the weary facial expressions of someone who hadn't slept in days.

"Oh, I'm relieved you're here. Firstly, Hallard, thank you for your involvement in last night's Great Council meeting," said Lenithia. "They're not easily swayed, but I believe we've presented enough evidence of the Balor Witches' threat."

She walked towards a table beside Mila's bed, where a bottle of what appeared to be wine sat. Lenithia poured herself a glass of wine and took a sip. "Forgive me, but wine is the only thing keeping me awake," said Lenithia.

"Unfortunately, one of our Great Council members was assassinated last night, shortly after we concluded our meeting with you at the Crimson Castle," she said, pouring herself another glass of wine.

This revelation caught him off guard. He glanced at Mila, who remained unperturbed, suggesting she was already aware of the news.

"It's the first instance of such a tragedy within our citadel in a very long time. It's devastating news for the entire clan," said Mila, sounding tinged with sadness.

Lenithia then resumed speaking. "Early this morning, the council members convened to address this tragedy. Two matters were discussed: the urgent need for a replacement in the Great Council, and an accusation levelled against you and me, of colluding in the death of the Great Council member," Lenithia explained to him.

He didn't react immediately to the accusations as they left him speechless. *The accusations seem baseless and easily disprovable*, he meditated.

"That's absurd. I've been in the stables since last night. What evidence do they have?" he demanded.

Mila placed a comforting hand on his shoulder. "They have no evidence. This is an unprecedented event in the history of our clan. The elder witches are in a state of panic and are quick to place blame without knowing how to navigate the present situation. That's why they accused you—a visitor who arrived at the Crimson Castle just before the incident," said Mila, her voice laced with reassurance.

"There's no need to worry. I refuted the accusations immediately, and for the time being, you and I are cleared from further investigation," Lenithia assured him.

Lenithia continued talking while pacing around the tent with a cup of wine in hand. "However, there's more to this," she added gravely. "The witch who was killed was in favour of aiding you, Hallard."

He was taken aback by the revelation that a witch had already been supportive of him. With her sole advocate besides Lenithia now deceased, he couldn't shake the thought that someone had purposefully eliminated the witch.

Lenithia regarded him solemnly. "I hope you comprehend the gravity of our current situation. There's a witch within the Great Council who will stop at nothing to hinder our efforts in aiding you. They've gone as far as taking the life of one of our own. I fear this could mark the beginning of a civil war within our clan."

She's right, Hallard mused silently. *Until last night, only us and the Great Council were aware of our plan to confront the Balor Witches.* He contemplated deeply. *The true perpetrator must indeed be among the council itself.*

"Master, we must uncover the true culprit behind Melchora's death," said Mila firmly.

It was the first time he had heard that name, assuming Melchora was the witch from the Great Council who had been assassinated.

"I'm willing to assist in any way I can. But what about the accusations towards you and me made by the other witch? Couldn't she be the true assassin?" he inquired of Lenithia.

Lenithia finished her fifth cup of wine, setting the empty cup on a small side table.

"It's entirely plausible, but it seems too convenient. I doubt the true killer would incriminate themselves by making such accusations. The witch who accused us is named Merma, and she's the most esteemed historian within our clan," Lenithia explained with her arms crossed in thought.

"Master, the Great Council convenes again tonight. If we don't uncover the murderer before then, they may all vote against Hallard's request," said Mila, showing great concern.

Lenithia closed her eyes briefly. "You're correct. If we don't apprehend the killer by tonight, our efforts to oppose the Balor Witches will be frustrated."

He felt a wave of despair wash over him. *I've come too far to return to Lakefields empty-handed*, he contemplated with a heavy heart.

Suddenly, a powerful voice reverberated throughout the entire tent. "Mila, this is a new quest for you. You must find Melchora's assassin before tonight," the voice commanded, then fell silent. He noticed Lenithia was holding a small parchment with a red glyph on it. She extended it towards him, displaying it for his view.

"This is a voice glyph," said Lenithia. "This morning, the Flame of Eldoria has bestowed a new mission upon you, Mila."

He struggled to conceal his confusion at the mention of the Flame of Eldoria. *Flame of what?* he pondered inwardly. *I've never heard of it*, he thought to himself.

Lenithia continued to explain, noticing the confusion on his face. "The Flame of Eldoria is a potent relic within our clan. It has the ability to foresee the future and bestow quests upon us, the Shabrani Witches, that might bring prosperity to our clan. Thankfully, I was the only witness when it happened. I managed to capture the message within this parchment. Until this matter is resolved, I would rather not inform anyone else in the council about this new mission," she said firmly.

He couldn't help but think that such a powerful relic could potentially benefit not only the Shabrani clan but the entire world. However, he chose to keep his thoughts to himself during these precarious times.

"I didn't anticipate the Flame to issue orders so promptly regarding this matter," Mila remarked, sounding surprised. "Nevertheless, I will fulfil this new mission. I've..." She was interrupted by her master.

"I have already made preparations to apprehend the killer. Mila, go immediately to the catacombs. Raven and Tabitha are waiting there for you. They will provide further information about my plan. Take Hallard with you; he may be of assistance," Lenithia ordered firmly.

He couldn't help but wonder why Lenithia couldn't disclose the full plan at that moment. However, he restrained himself from asking further questions. He had learned that witches' schemes were calculated and often concealed until the opportune moment.

"Master, what will you do?" Mila inquired, echoing Hallard's own thoughts.

Lenithia approached Mila, taking her hands in a comforting gesture akin to a mother comforting her daughter. "I have other matters to attend to. The accusation made at the council may resurface, and it's best if I don't intervene directly. Besides..." she said, casting a glance at a dark corner of the tent, "as of now, I am being watched."

Mila's smirk transformed into a wide smile. "It's been too long since we've embarked on such a mission. I can't wait!" she exclaimed with enthusiasm.

He couldn't help but notice the sudden change in Mila's mood. It was almost as she was enjoying the moment.

"I have high expectations, my former apprentice," Lenithia said, sounding filled with confidence.

As Lenithia made her way out of the tent, she turned to him showing a sparkle of amusement in her eyes.

"You're in for a treat, lakeman. You'll witness Sinister Smile Mila in action," she declared before exiting the tent.

He didn't fully grasp Lenithia's last words. He then turned to Mila who was still smiling, clearly relishing the moment. *Perhaps*, he thought, *I'm beginning to understand.*

"Hallard, we need to leave immediately. My master's plans are always, to put it simply, meticulous," Mila urged.

Together, they exited the tent. This time, he didn't cloak himself with any large robes. Mila explained that the disguise was no longer effective, as he had become quite well-known throughout the Shabrani clan.

"You're almost as thick and big as a mountain. There's no point in trying to cover up a mountain, right?" said Mila sarcastically.

As they made their way towards the Crimson Castle, he saw an increasing number of witches whispering amongst themselves while casting glances in his direction. *I never imagined I would become the topic of discussion in this clan. It's a bizarre notion*, he reflected.

Upon reaching the entrance of the castle, the sentries halted them, demanding the reasons for their entry into the castle. Instead of responding, Mila snapped her fingers.

Suddenly, crimson chains materialised, wrapping around his wrists and ankles. Confused by what was happening, he attempted to speak, only to find that no sound emerged from his mouth. It felt as though something was blocking his voice—a gag of some sort.

"I am his custodian; we have business in the catacombs. He poses no danger, as you can see he's securely imprisoned with these chains. If he attempts to escape or act out, I'll activate the chains, and he'll incinerate to death in seconds," said Mila confidently, flashing a smile at the sentries.

The sentries then requested his longsword, which Mila promptly handed over. After surrendering the weapon, they were permitted to pass. Mila gestured for him to follow her, and they proceeded inside the castle.

Once inside, Hallard noticed a palpable shift in the atmosphere compared to the previous night. The castle seemed more crowded, with an increased presence of witches. Conversations were hushed, carried out in whispers. He observed others clutching parchments as they moved in and out of the castle, disappearing into unknown corridors.

He trailed behind Mila as she ventured down a dark corridor devoid of windows. The passage led to a narrow staircase that spiralled downward. They descended for what felt like a considerable amount of time, with only a few flickering candles illuminating their path. He took care not to trip in the dim light, though he found it challenging to walk with the chains on his ankles.

"Just a little farther," Mila reassured him with her voice echoing faintly in the stairwell.

They eventually ceased their descent and proceeded through another corridor illuminated by candelabras. He felt waves of hot air emanating from the passage, leading him to speculate that they were venturing toward the heart of the volcano Dukkah itself.

Mila then halted abruptly, her gaze fixed on something ahead. He strained to see what had captured her attention but discerned nothing except the continuing corridor and the intense heat emanating from it.

He observed Mila raise her hand and begin to make intricate

gestures with her fingers, as if unlocking something through unnatural means. Suddenly, a red barrier materialised in front of her, dissipating after a few seconds.

"I have unlocked the barrier that conceals the catacombs. You see, this place is sacred to us. Should anyone else attempt to enter and unveil our secrets, they will perish instantly upon crossing the invisible barrier," Mila explained.

Hallard grasped the situation. *What kind of secrets are the Shabrani Witches hiding here?* his mind was swirling with curiosity and intrigue.

He continued to follow Mila through the long corridor, noting that the intense heat had dissipated. *It seems the heat was emanating from the barrier*, he reflected, observing the surroundings with a newfound sense of curiosity.

Exiting the corridor, they entered a vast oval-shaped room illuminated by numerous fireplaces scattered throughout. Hallard observed the ancient nature of the chamber; its walls were grey and rusted, bearing the marks of age. At the centre of the room, chairs, tables, and witches congregated, engaged in fervent discussions.

As he surveyed the surroundings further, he noticed tall wooden shelves laden with countless books and unfamiliar objects. Looking upward, he initially mistook the flickering flames for stars, only to realise they were flames dancing on the ceiling. Upon closer inspection, the flames were engulfing metal cells hanging from the roof. He noticed strange human figures within.

"It's best not to dwell on them too much. They've met the ultimate punishment," said Mila with a stern tone.

Hallard chose to heed her advice and refrained from asking any questions.

"These are the catacombs. Beyond this point, aside from other uses, we witches learn fire magic. Imagine it as a training camp," Mila explained. "At the end of this large room, there are several other corridors leading to different areas. Now, we need to find those two," she said, setting their objective. By *those two*, he imagined

Mila was referring to the witches Lenithia asked them to find in the catacombs.

Another witch hurriedly approached from behind and covered Mila's eyes with her hands. The witch appeared younger than both Demoria and Mila, clad in a robe that appeared to be a combination of red and blue. Her black hair was tied back in a ponytail, and Hallard noticed that her eyes were completely covered by a piece of cloth or fabric.

"In darkness she dwells, yet visions she weaves,
No sight to behold, yet all secrets she retrieves.
No need for eyes in her world so tight,
Who is she, this enigma of the night?"

It appeared to him that the young witch presented Mila with a riddle to solve. Mila pondered for a moment before responding, "Hmm, a blind girl... you are Tabitha!" she concluded with certainty.

"You're far too clever for me," replied the young witch with her voice gentle and innocent, resembling that of a child.

"Tabitha, I've been searching for you, and..." Mila was interrupted by another witch who approached from one of the corridors.

"And me?" inquired the newcomer.

"Raven! Excellent!" exclaimed Mila, clearly pleased by the arrival of the witch.

Raven also appeared youthful. Compared to the witches Hallard had encountered thus far, Raven sported black pants and a white shirt with buttons. Her hair was tied in a ponytail, adorned with long braids. As she approached, Hallard noticed something unusual about her step—it seemed as if one leg was shorter than the other. Upon closer inspection, he observed that instead of a left leg, Raven had a wooden stick in its place. It dawned on him that she had lost her left leg.

"Allow me to introduce you to Hallard. He's a lakeman, but you've likely already heard of him. The gossip around the citadel this morning has mainly been about you, " said Mila, gesturing towards him.

"It seems I'm quite popular today among your clan. Greetings to you two. I am Hallard, son of Hollard Rikers, lord of Rivercrash," he introduced himself, noticing that he was once again able to speak. It appeared that Mila's magic on him was beginning to decline.

Tabitha stood with her mouth agape and her hands clasped together as if in prayer. "A real son of a lord. I've never met anyone of royalty. You will inherit Rivercrash castle someday, won't you?" she exclaimed, her expression conveying a level of happiness that surprised him.

Raven didn't even glance in his direction, maintaining her focus on Mila.

"Mila, we have orders from Master Lenithia. Let's discuss this in a private room," said Raven.

They all trailed after Raven as she slowly made her way towards one of the corridors on the opposite end of the large oval-shaped room. Hallard couldn't help but sympathise with her, realising the challenges she must face with only one functional leg.

Tabitha walked alongside him, with her gaze fixed on him with intense curiosity. Even though he couldn't see her eyes, her interest in him was palpable as they made their way through the corridor.

"You want to know what happened to Raven's leg? Well, she had an accident, just like me," Tabitha spoke softly, her voice akin to the gentle song of a bird.

"No, my lady, I would never inquire about such personal matters," he responded hastily, but it was too late. Tabitha removed the piece of cloth covering her eyes, revealing two scars in the place where her eyes should have been. The scars appeared old.

"It's okay. I don't mind sharing," said Tabitha. "This happened to me when I was a curious little girl many years ago. Initially, my blindness posed challenges, but I eventually learned to navigate the citadel with ease. However, I fear I may never leave the citadel, which means I'll never have the opportunity to meet new people or royalty like you," she said, offering a gentle smile.

They continued down the corridor, which branched off into various narrow passages. Eventually, they veered right, then left, until they reached their destination. Before them stood a rusty metal door that appeared deceptively easy to open at first glance. However, as he had learned recently, barriers were in place throughout this area.

His suspicions were confirmed when he observed Raven making gestures with her right hand in front of the door, akin to what Mila had done earlier. After a few moments, the rusty metal door swung open on its own accord.

"I can't imagine what sort of trap master Lenithia had set on this door for those who don't know the password. I can't help but feel pity for them," said Tabitha, smiling wryly.

Upon entering the room, he found himself in what appeared to be a witch laboratory. Though he had never been in one before, it matched his expectations. Shelves lined with empty flasks and books, alongside potions containing vibrant green and red liquids, greeted him. Several tables were scattered about, accompanied by a fireplace nearby.

"This is Lenithia's laboratory," said Mila.

As they entered further, Hallard detected a peculiar scent in the air—a familiar odour he had encountered on the battlefield: the smell of death. It seemed to emanate from the far-left corner of the laboratory, where a bed lay covered by a large cloth.

"What in the world is that smell? Is it a corpse?" Mila exclaimed aloud, sounding filled with disbelief. She approached the mysterious bed and lifted the cover, revealing the naked body of a dead woman. The body bore numerous wounds, with holes puncturing her chest and stomach, resembling knife stabbings. Additionally, burn marks disfigured her skin, scattered across her body.

Mila gasped. "This was Melchora," her gaze shifted to him.

"But why is she here?" she asked.

He found himself pondering the same question.

"Our master's plan begins here," said Tabitha.

The blind witch retrieved a small parchment from one of her pockets and unfolded it, revealing a glyph inscribed upon it. He recognized it as a voice glyph, likely containing a message. Tabitha pressed the glyph firmly with her thumb until it turned red, prompting a voice to emanate from the parchment.

"I've asked Raven to steal Melchora's body. Mila, you are the only one skilled enough to decipher the true killer through her dead body," the voice of Lenithia stated before falling silent.

He was perplexed, unsure of how Mila would accomplish such a task. "Mila, what is she talking about?" he inquired.

She didn't answer his question. Instead, Mila proceeded to walk towards the body. "It can be done," she said, smiling confidently.

Tabitha touched his arm to get his attention. "Master is referring to the use of forbidden spells. Fire necromancy can temporarily reanimate a corpse, but only for a few moments. Once reanimated, the dead will enter an uncontrollable state of anger. Subduing the resurrected would allow us to ask a few questions afterward just for a few moments," her gentle smile shifted to a serious expression. "There's another important detail. Historians and ancient texts mention that those who wield this spell would perish immediately due to the immense energy it consumes. No ordinary witch possesses such reserves." Tabitha then turned to Mila. "But she is not an ordinary witch. Mila possesses an enormous amount of energy within her. Master once told me that she holds the fire energy of ten Shabrani Witches within her."

He began to grasp why Mila had been assigned this mission.

Just as he was about to approach the dead body himself, he sensed a cold breeze behind him. Tabitha, who was still gripping his arm, suddenly released him and shoved him to the side. In that moment of being pushed, he glimpsed a strange shadow looming between Tabitha and himself. The shadow took the form of a woman with two piercing yellow eyes, shrouded in red smoke wielding curved knives clutched in each hand. Stumbling from Tabitha's push, he managed to evade the shadowy figure's attack. Had it not been for Tabitha's intervention, he would have been struck by the assailant.

Then, the attacker launched toward him with a menacing scream, revealing long, white fangs resembling those of a wolf. Panic surged through him—the creature was targeting him. Deprived of his longsword and hindered by the red chains still bound to his wrists and ankles, his movements were sluggish. As the creature advanced, the tips of its knives scraped against his armour, leaving scratches on the surface. Desperately, he attempted to defend himself, but the creature's speed and agility made it a formidable opponent. In the midst of the chaos, the red chains unexpectedly shattered; their fragments swirled around and ensnared the dark enemy by its wrists and ankles. Despite its struggle, the creature was immobilised by the tight bonds, ultimately collapsing to the ground unable to move.

He glanced around and noticed that Mila had cast a spell on the creature. "Sorry, Hallard. It caught me off guard; I couldn't react quickly enough. Are you hurt?"

He gestured with his hand to indicate that he wasn't hurt.

"Tabitha!" he heard Raven scream. The blind witch was on the ground, clearly in pain, with blood staining her robes around her stomach. It was evident that their enemy had cut her just before attacking him. Despite having only one good leg, Raven moved swiftly towards Tabitha.

He wanted to rush to Tabitha's aid, especially considering she had taken the attack meant for him. However, a sudden wave of intense heat struck him, causing him to collapse to the ground. The heat was emanating from their enemy, who was beginning to catch fire.

"It's a Fire Spectre, everyone! Take shelter now!" Mila screamed.

He wasn't sure where to take shelter; there were no sturdy

objects nearby he could use as a shield. Seeing Mila taking cover behind a metal table she had turned sideways, she extended a hand toward him, inviting him to join her. He sprinted towards her as fast as he could. However, just as he was about to reach her, another heatwave struck him from behind. This one was ten times stronger than the previous, pushing him with such force that he flew in the air, only to be caught by Mila, who was now making him float in the air with magic.

Mila released him as he landed on his feet. It was then that he realised he had a few burns in spots where his armour wasn't protecting him. "Ouch!" he exclaimed, expressing his pain.

"We have bigger problems, Hallard," said Mila, who was smiling at him. At that moment, he remembered Mila's nickname, *Sinister Smile*. *It seemed like she truly enjoys situations like this*, he reflected.

The creature had turned into a fire monster which appeared extremely menacing, its body composed of flames that emitted a loud burning noise and expelled traces of fire around it. *Fire Spectres*, he recalled their names. He had seen these creatures before at the Grey Skull; however, back then, they were his allies. Now, he would have to fight one of them. Recalling how formidable they were, he realised this wouldn't be an easy battle.

The spectre charged towards Mila and him. Glancing around, he couldn't spot any weapon within reach. The overwhelming heat emanating from the creature left him uncertain how to engage it bare-handed without getting burned. His gaze then shifted to Tabitha and Raven, who were in the opposite direction. Tabitha remained on the ground, covering the wound in her stomach in an attempt to stop the bleeding. Meanwhile, Raven was behind her, assisting Tabitha in removing her blindfold. Curiosity piqued, he wanted to ask what she was doing. To his surprise, instead of Tabitha's missing eyes, he saw eyes made of fire, gazing directly at the fire spectre. Suddenly, the creature halted its advance, and even its noisy flames seemed to quiet down.

"Tabitha is using fire vision. When Tabitha lost her eyes, she gained the ability to project visions onto live beings. She won't be able to hold the projection for much longer though," said Mila.

"Are you suggesting that the spectre is somehow hypnotised by Tabitha?" he asked.

Mila nodded, confirming his assumptions. "It won't last long, I'm afraid. Tabitha is injured. I need to act quickly," she said.

He turned around and noticed Mila moving towards the dead body of Melchora, which lay in a far corner of the laboratory.

"What are you planning to do?" he asked.

"Raven and I could defeat the Fire Spectre; however, there's a less dangerous option," she explained. "I could use fire necromancy on Melchora's dead body. Once her dead body's reanimated, it'll be so enraged that it will want to attack us immediately. Our goal would be to direct its aggression towards the Fire Spectre instead. With luck, they'll eliminate each other. If all goes according to plan, we won't need to engage either of them in combat."

Then, Mila closed her eyes and began moving her hands in a peculiar manner, almost as if she were sketching in the air above the dead body. He observed her also chanting something he couldn't comprehend.

Something struck him on his left shoulder, hurling him to the side with such force that he thought his arm had broken. It was the Fire Spectre which delivered the blow. He noticed it started behaving strangely.

"Mila, hurry up! Tabitha won't be able to hold it much longer!" Raven screamed from the other side of the room. He noticed Tabitha bleeding from her fiery eyes, realising she was reaching her limit. This explained the Fire Spectre's erratic behaviour; it was flailing and throwing punches aimlessly. It was drawing closer to Mila, who remained focused on chanting and casting a spell.

I need to act fast, he thought.

He surveyed his surroundings, noticing debris scattered around from the destroyed furniture. His left arm, injured and bleeding from the shoulder, rendered him unable to use it. With his right arm, he seized a piece of metal resembling a short sword, likely a fragment from a metal chair. Rushing towards the Fire Spectre, he began striking it with the piece of metal as if wielding a sword. "Come on, you beast!" he screamed at the monster, drawing its attention away from Mila.

His plan worked, it was now focused on him, who attempted to lead it away from Mila's location.

The Fire Spectre's flames abruptly intensified, and it delivered another powerful blow to his chest, sending him flying backward. Though the impact was forceful, it didn't inflict significant damage; it merely scorched his plate armour and possibly left a bruise underneath.

Another explosion erupted from where Mila had been casting her spell, leaving behind a peculiar mix of green and red smoke. Emerging from the smoke, Mila dashed toward him. "It's done. Now, let those two destroy each other," she said to him, pulling him towards where Tabitha and Raven lay on the ground.

From the green and red smoke emerged another creature, hovering in the air. It was Melchora's reanimated corpse, brought back to life through Mila's spell. He observed the wounds on her stomach and chest were filled with raging fire. Despite the dire circumstances, he found himself strangely grateful to witness such a remarkable event. *The dead raised once more*, he thought, *magic can indeed be quite useful.*

The Fire Spectre and the witch collided in combat. While the spectre launched punches, the witch countered with fireballs from a distance, deliberately avoiding the blows. However, the skirmish was short-lived. The spectre seized the witch by the leg, engulfing her in its fiery embrace, attempting to consume her entirely. Then, a massive explosion erupted, shrouding the laboratory in smoke once again. He realised the Fire Specter had self-destructed. The force of the blast demolished the remaining furniture. Fortunately, Raven and Mila reacted swiftly, pulling the metal entry door and using it as a shield, preventing all of them from sustaining significant damage.

From the smoke and ashes emerged the charred corpse of

Melchora, still standing despite missing its left arm and right hand. The body was riddled with holes, and its head was diagonally severed in half.

"It's our turn. Let's ask our question before it completely vanishes," said Tabitha, sounding determined despite being hurt.

Mila approached Melchora's dead body and inquired, "Melchora, who was responsible for your death?"

To his astonishment, the severed head of the dead witch turned towards Mila, and then emitted a chilling scream. It was a sound unlike any he had ever heard before, seeming to send shivers down his spine as if it were piercing his very nerves.

Melchora then raised her right arm without a hand, as if pointing towards something on the ground. Hallard approached the indicated spot, where a heap of debris lay—stones, wood, and metal. He began to clear away the rubble, determined to uncover whatever the witch was directing them to. At the bottom of the pile, he discovered something familiar: the same small creature he had seen before at the Grey Skull—the Balor creature he carried in a bag.

"Is that...?" Mila began, her voice trailing off in disbelief.

He stood up, taking a deep breath. "The creature that attacked us, which later transformed into the Fire Spectre," he continued talking slowly, "It was the Balor creature all along."

Raven, who had been assisting Tabitha in readjusting her blinds, stood up and approached his location. She reached out towards the creature but was halted by Mila.

"Do not touch it. It will try to steal your energy," Mila cautioned firmly. She then retrieved a small pouch from her robes, performing enchantments reminiscent of those she had seen Demoria use back in the Grey Skull. With a display of levitation magic, she enclosed the Balor creature inside the pouch.

"Hallard, you brought this to us. I'm returning it to you," said Mila, her voice still resonating with the shock from the revelation.

Clack! Clack! Clack! The sound of clapping echoed from the entrance of the laboratory.

"I've lived for a long time, but I've never witnessed a fight like this before," remarked a witch who entered the laboratory, followed by several others. Hallard counted four or five, but amidst the lingering smoke, there might have been more.

"Calcia, how long have you been observing us?" inquired Mila.

"Long enough to discern the true assassin of Melchora. To hear of these events is one thing, but to witness them firsthand is beyond belief, beyond anyone's imagination," replied Calcia. He couldn't make out her face clearly; she, akin to the other witches accompanying her, wore a hood that obscured her features.

"It's not enough. How did the creature transform into a shadow and kill Melchora? It had to be activated by someone," remarked another witch.

"Lenithia. She directed us here. She must have answers. We must interrogate her."

"We need to take action immediately. Lenithia may be implicated, but the Balor Witches have become our adversaries."

"And what of the lakeman? He brought the creature to us. Is he to blame?"

"We witnessed him sacrificing himself to protect one of our own," another witch chimed in.

"Is it decided, then?" Calcia asked.

"Yes, it is," came the collective response.

As the witches took turns speaking, he recognized some of the voices—they were all members of the Shabrani Great Council he met the previous night.

After their discussion, the Great Council departed from the laboratory.

"Mila, what's going on?" He asked, still feeling perplexed by the recent events.

Mila brushed dust off her robes and approached him, placing a hand on his chest. With the biggest smile he had seen from her yet, she replied, "We've won. The council has made its decision. We're going to war against the Balor Witches."

DEMORIA

The drum beats ceased, signalling the end of the attack. "Attacking another small village, quite the achievement for your kind," she said sarcastically to her captor.

The barbarian remained silent.

The muscular barbarian stood sentinel, armed with a spear and clad in metal armour, yet much of his muscular physique remained exposed. He had stood watch at the entrance of her tent since they made camp.

She harboured a mix of emotions towards the barbarians who had taken her in. On one hand, they had tended to the wound on her side inflicted by the mysterious man in Duskenwood. Using herbs and unfamiliar spices, they had diligently cleaned and treated the injury, for which she was grateful. Yet, on the other hand, she couldn't shake the feeling of being a prisoner. When she woke after fainting in Duskenwood, she found herself surrounded by barbarians. Her belongings were gone, including the arm she had fought so hard to obtain, which she assumed the barbarians had confiscated. This left her disappointed, knowing it was a crucial part of her mission.

Furthermore, she was kept separate from the rest of the barbarian clan, accompanied only by a silent barbarian who watched over her. Despite her attempts at conversation, he never responded, leaving her to wonder if he simply couldn't understand the common language.

Though her health had greatly improved, she remained unable to cast spells. Recalling the intense battle in Duskenwood, she acknowledged that she had pushed herself beyond her limits. Yet, as days passed since then, she expected her magical abilities to return. After all, it was not uncommon for a witch to temporarily lose her powers after such exhaustive exertion, but the prolonged absence of her magic puzzled her. *As soon as I regain my abilities, I will escape*, she resolved, her determination unwavering.

She found hope in the fact that they allowed her to keep Lucy, her sleipnir, by her side. Although she was unsure why the barbarians were so attentive to her, a Shabrani witch, she appreciated their provision of food and care. *Perhaps they intend to use me as bait in the future*, she speculated. *Only time would reveal their true intentions.*

About a day ago, they had trailed closely behind the rest of the barbarian clan and reached a small village on the far western edge of Lakefields. As the barbarians swiftly erected their camp in the morning, she marvelled at their efficiency, a hallmark trait of their clan well-known to most. Despite the speed with which the camp was assembled, she noted that a few tents remained half-built, lacking sturdy structures. She set up her own tent with the help of her guard, in a location close enough to hear the voices of the barbarians in the distance.

"I have to pee," she said to her guard. Since the guard couldn't understand her, she resorted to miming the action by crouching down. Her guard finally caught on and allowed her to relieve herself in a nearby bush, though still with shackles on her hands and under close watch.

On the way back to her tent, she heard the beat of drums echo through the air, signalling the start of the barbarian invasion against the small village. From a distance, she noticed most of the barbarians in their camp grabbing their axes and swords, then marching toward the village. She caught a glimpse of their battle-ready group: not particularly large, but heavily armed. After that, her guard confined her to her tent, locking her inside.

Later that night, she heard a lot of noise coming from the barbarian camp, leading her to believe the invasion had ended and the barbarians had returned. Amid the sounds, she could distinguish cries and laments, suggesting the barbarians had taken prisoners during their raid.

Sometime during the night, a female barbarian entered her tent. The newcomer appeared to be around twenty-five or thirty years old, drenched in blood from head to toe, and visibly agitated.

The female barbarian spoke in a native tongue, "¿Mayqen warmiqaq ch'inkanaq k'ankiypaq?"

"Kanmi rikurun," Demoria's guardian replied.

"Ñak'ariyki puntrawpi munani," the female barbarian seemed to affirm.

The guard nodded and exited the tent.

"What an interesting language. I've never heard of it before. Are you here to teach it to this poor wounded witch?" she asked, her tone carrying a hint of provocation.

Ignoring her remark, the barbarian seized a jar of river water left for Demoria earlier. Without hesitation, she emptied the contents over herself, attempting to cleanse her body of the blood.

"You appear to be healthier. We must talk," said the female barbarian.

Demoria was taken aback by her visitor's proficiency in the common language. She also detected a slight accent, one that she recognized.

"Your accent is from the south. Did you grow up in the Golden Nation?" she inquired.

The barbarian's gaze turned to one of fury, and she delivered a powerful slap across her face. The force of the blow sent Demoria sprawling to the ground, blood trickling from her mouth.

Then, something struck her—something she had forgotten until now. She had met the barbarian standing before her once before. It was in Duskenwood, after her battle with the mysterious man. This same female barbarian had taken her when she fainted. Demoria refrained from mentioning it, wanting to test her visitor first.

"Did I hit a nerve? Well, you'd better kill me or tell me why you took me as a prisoner," she said defiantly.

The barbarian screamed in fury, poised to launch an attack. Demoria scanned her surroundings frantically, but found nothing she could use as a weapon. She attempted to summon fire energy within her body, but to no avail—she remained powerless.

"¡Hatun!" exclaimed an older barbarian who had just entered the tent.

The female barbarian halted her attack, instead letting out a heavy sigh and stepping aside.

To Demoria, it appeared that the older barbarian was around sixty years old, judging by the weathered lines on his face, his short grey hair, and his long, messy grey beard. His attire consisted solely of leather garments, suggesting that he was not a warrior.

"Ñuqanchik munanchiktaña, ñak'ariykiyqa mana ch'inkanaq k'ankiypi, imata willayku?" He yelled at the female barbarian, his tone resembling that of a reprimand. "Diskulpa, nukanchik yanapanipi," he added.

"Apologies for my previous behaviour. My name is Jacqui. I am the second-in-command in the Runakuna clan," the female barbarian said apologetically to her. After that Jacqui exited the tent.

"I would also like to express my apologies. My name is Amaru, I am an elder among the barbarian clans," he said respectfully. Gesturing towards the entrance where Jacqui had just departed, he added, "She's usually quite polite. You must have said something she disliked."

"I asked if she was from the Golden Nation," Demoria shrugged. "Why haven't you killed me already? Are you planning to sell me? I have no use. I am just a woman," she said.

Amaru gave her a wry smile. "A Shabrani witch is no mere woman," he chuckled. "You see, a few of our scouts witnessed you fighting a man who could conjure magic with his left arm. In fact, one of those scouts was Jacqui. I thought you two would get along, but it seems I was wrong," he paused, giving her a look of pity. "Jacqui reported that you emerged victorious using fire magic. She also followed you until she found you near the border of Duskenwood and Lakefields, close to death. You know the rest—she took you in and brought you to us. Oh, and she also secured your belongings, including the arm you ripped from that man. It's heavily guarded within our clan."

The news startled her. She had been wondering what had become of the arm. Knowing its location provided some reassurance. *At least I still have a chance to retrieve it for the Shabrani clan if I play my cards right*, she thought.

"I see the news about the strange arm has distressed you. Don't worry; we plan to return it to you once we've finished using it for our purposes," he said, approaching her and locking eyes with her. "And this is where you will assist us," he added defiantly.

Now, this will be interesting, she thought, sitting on the bed she had been given.

"How can I assist?" she inquired politely. Though she had no intention of cooperating, she realised that by feigning interest, they might reveal their plans. *As long as I know what they're up to, I can figure out a way to retrieve the arm and escape from this place*, she reflected inwardly.

Amaru offered her a friendly smile before beginning to pace slowly around the tent. "First, allow me to share a story I heard in my youth," he said. "It's the tale of the only man in the Lower Lands who can wield magic."

A man that can wield magic? Is he talking about the mysterious man I fought in Duskenwood? she contemplated. He caught her full attention.

"We called him the Cursed Warrior. His presence was known among our people after the Age of Ashes, which, as you know, occurred more than five hundred years ago. He was spotted all across these lands—one day in the Glacier Crown, the next in Celen. As you're aware, such swift travel is impossible without powerful magic," Amaru narrated.

She interjected, "That's impossible, even with our magic. We witches can only teleport short distances, and it requires a significant amount of energy. We avoid using that spell unless absolutely necessary. However, I saw with my own eyes the Cursed Warrior, as you call him, using magic unlike anything I'd ever seen." She decided it was safe to share some of the information she had learned from her last battle to gain his confidence.

Amaru nodded in agreement. "Indeed. Our reports also suggest that this man indiscriminately targets specific individuals with no apparent connection between them. It appears to be either a random selection or he has some obscure motive for the killings." He paused to take a drink from a bottle he retrieved from his satchel.

The story intrigued her. *If what Amaru said was true, I could have been on the Cursed Warrior's death list. He seemed to have foreknowledge of my arrival in Duskenwood. The Cursed Warrior's power might rival that of the Flame of Eldoria*, she reflected.

"Anything you got for me?" The old man's face was uncomfortably close to hers.

I won't divulge any more valuable information to this man, she thought.

"You mentioned that your men followed me after my encounter with the Cursed Warrior. Did they stay to ascertain what happened to him? I left him with significant injuries," she asked.

"Hmm, you ask good questions," said Amaru, taking another sip from his bottle. She caught a whiff of the rancid liquid emanating from it and had to hold her breath to avoid coughing.

"Yes, they did. Initially, we sent five of our scouts to examine the area. One followed you, while the other four stayed behind. Of those who stayed, only one returned. He reported that your blue flames eventually consumed the Cursed Warrior, and he stopped screaming in pain. When they approached, hoping to capture him, they assumed he could no longer move due to the severe burns covering his body. But as they got closer, the Cursed Warrior still had enough strength to kill three of our scouts with his bare right arm. I'll spare you the details. All you need to know is that only one scout made it back. Afterward, we sent more scouts to find the Cursed Warrior's whereabouts, but he had vanished. We couldn't locate him."

The events intrigued her. Despite enduring her full wrath and being deprived of his left arm, the Cursed Warrior remained remarkably powerful. *I think I was lucky to emerge victorious from that fight*, she thought, glancing at the necklace adorned with the strange leaf that Hallard had given her.

"This is all very intriguing, but you still haven't told me how I can assist you," she pointed out.

"They say your kind is very direct. Rumour also has it you are fearless," said Amaru, observing her with a keen eye.

She smiled back confidently, ready to face whatever challenge lay ahead.

Amaru clasped his hands behind his back. "Our men informed us that after you tore off his arm, the Cursed Warrior could no longer wield magic. We believe the arm is the source of his power," said Amaru.

She had already deduced those details. During her battle with the Cursed Warrior, she distinctly felt the magical energy emanating solely from his left arm.

"And you want me to somehow use the arm to what? Create gold out of thin air for you? Bring back the dead?" she asked in a sarcastic tone.

"Hahaha, you are quite amusing," he chuckled, letting out a hearty laugh. "Before revealing our goal. Answer me something, what do you know about our kind?"

She rose to her feet and began to pace around the tent, circling Amaru. Peeking outside, she found the entrance completely blocked by her guardian. "It's common knowledge that barbarians can't be entirely eradicated. Your kind can appear anywhere with little notice.

Moreover, you all worship different gods, deities that don't align well with the usual deities in the Lower Lands," she explained.

Applause erupted in the room as Amaru clapped a few times. "Clever witch, clever witch," he exclaimed. "Though we barbarians belong to the same fundamental culture, we can be very different. Our methods vary from clan to clan; besides, there are clans I don't even know exist. Some of us dedicate ourselves to collaborating with other nations, while others act independently," he explained. Taking one final sip from his bottle, he realised it was empty and angrily threw it to the ground. "If the left arm from the Cursed Warrior can instantly teleport us anywhere in these lands, we want to use it to locate every single clan and unite us physically as one. It will be the greatest army ever known," Amaru proclaimed proudly.

"You could conquer any territory with such a formidable army," she said.

Amaru nodded in agreement. "Once we're finished with the cursed arm, as we should call it from now on, you can take it. We'll have no further use for it," he said.

She surveyed her surroundings, considering her options. While it seemed an opportune moment to attempt an escape, the conditions were far from ideal. Her magic had yet to return, and she couldn't spot any weapons she could use.

"And if I refuse?" she asked with a firm tone.

The old barbarian chuckled. "Now, why would you refuse? Haven't we treated you well so far? You know that could change at any moment," he remarked before turning and heading toward the tent's exit. "Have a think tonight. We'll talk again in the morning."

Before Amaru's departure, she decided to confront him about something that had been on her mind since she met Hallard and his company.

"What did the Balor Witches give you in exchange for assisting with the attack on the Lakemen in the Blue Bell Mountains?" she asked provocatively.

Amaru then turned around to face her, showing a smile playing on his lips. Without saying a word, he exited the room.

She lay on her bed, feeling a slight sting in her belly. Though her wound was healing well, she knew she needed more rest for it to fully recover. Her thoughts drifted back to her conversation with Amaru. *There's no way I can help them achieve what they want—it would mean betraying my clan*, she thought. But another idea formed in her mind. *However, if I can get hold of the cursed arm before they use it, I could harness its magic for my own purposes.*

She then heard noise outside. After a few moments, her guard returned with a metal bowl of food for her. As was the case every night, she was served burnt pieces of meat alongside stale bread and river water. She tried the meat, finding it flavourless and chewy. Unable to discern the type of animal, she suspected it was either horse or pork.

"If only you'd allow me to leave this tent and assist with cooking, you'd be enjoying delicious food instead of this disgusting meal," she said to her guard, who remained silent.

Before she could finish her meal, she received a visitor—none other than Jacqui, the female barbarian.

"We need your services now," Jacqui said with a rude tone.

Demoria stood up from her bed where she was eating. "You people think you can use me as you please. I won't help you," she said firmly.

The female barbarian growled. "If you help us, we will take you out of this tent for a tour."

She found the offer intriguing. "Why don't you tell me what it is you need from me, and then I'll decide if I can help you or not?" she asked peacefully.

Jacqui sighed. "Our scouts have discovered an unusual camp of witches south of here, near the border with Duskenwood. Five scouts were sent, but only two returned. The survivors, who returned with strange wounds, reported that the others had died from a poisonous, heavy cloud surrounding the area—most likely caused by magic," said Jacqui.

She wasn't aware of any witch camp in this part of the Lower Lands. However, the description of the heavy mist made her suspect it could be the Balor clan. While she had been prepared to refuse helping the barbarians, this might be the opportunity she had been waiting for. She could break free from the prison they had put her in, seize the cursed arm, and escape. She had to try.

She stood up and began walking towards the entrance. "What are you waiting for? Let's go," she urged Jacqui, eager to seize the opportunity.

The barbarian took her by the hands and securely fastened shackles around her wrists. These shackles had a long chain attached to them, allowing the captor to maintain control over the prisoner—in this case, Demoria. "For security," Jacqui grunted at her.

When my magic returns, I could melt this metal in the blink of an eye, Demoria thought to herself, finding a hint of amusement in the situation.

Outside the tent, she observed the agitation among the barbarians. Horses, men, and women dashed in all directions, their movements frantic. Jacqui led her forward, navigating through the chaos while occasionally being swept up by the rushing crowd.

"Hinata q'apaykuna! Wañuchisqa, uqhañiykuna!" Jacqui screamed to the multitude.

"What is happening?" she asked Jacqui, seeking clarification amidst the chaos.

She had expected Jacqui to ignore her, but to her surprise, the female barbarian was more talkative. "The rest of the clan knows about the witches' camp our scouts found. They're not too fond of your kind. The thought of being attacked by witches makes them nervous," Jacqui said, her tone far from friendly.

She realised that Jacqui meant the barbarians were afraid of the witches' powers—an insight she could use to her advantage in the future.

"I haven't thanked you yet for saving my life when you found me in Duskenwood," Demoria said, attempting to start a conversation with her captor. Though Jacqui hadn't been the friendliest, Demoria sensed she might be able to form a bond with her.

"I was just doing my job," Jacqui replied curtly. "But... yes, I do thank you for... thanking me," the female barbarian added awkwardly.

They walked in silence, passing through more barbarians and half-built tents. She noticed that some of the barbarians were already packing their belongings, perhaps preparing to move again. In the distance, she spotted a group of barbarians gathered together. There couldn't have been more than forty of them, but they looked menacing as they wielded small axes in both hands. Among them, she recognized Amaru.

"My friend, I'm glad you decided to join us," said Amaru with a smile. Demoria couldn't help but notice he was carrying something wrapped in leather pelts. Her eyes were drawn to it, curiosity stirring as she sensed a faint trace of magic emanating from within.

"Ah, I see you have noticed what I am carrying. It is safer with me here than with the rest of my clan," said Amaru.

Jacqui pulled the chains attached to her wrist shackles with strength, causing her to nearly lose her balance. "Are you sure we can take this witch with us? I don't trust her," Jacqui said to Amaru, pointing a finger at her. "We could leave this place and forget about the witches' camp."

Amaru shook his head, signalling a negative response. "That's not possible. Our reports indicate that the Lakemen army hasn't detected our presence in this part of their land. This is our chance to claim the entire territory, which means dealing with the witches' camp as well."

Jacqui grunted in response.

Two barbarians stepped in front of Demoria, and she noticed they had bandages on their faces and other parts of their bodies. She could sense magic emanating from them.

"These two are the survivors I mentioned earlier. They received these strange injuries that appeared to be normal wounds, but none of our medicine could heal them. The wounds remain open," said Jacqui, pointing at the afflicted barbarians.

She approached them and examined their injuries closely. "Curious," she said in an intriguing tone. "The wounds emanate magic, but I can't discern the type. This is unlike anything I've encountered before."

Much akin to the magic used by the Cursed Warrior, she felt an unknown energy emanating from the injured barbarians. *Since I've left Gorgon, I've encountered two new types of magic*, she thought to herself. *Why does it feel like something terrible is about to happen in the Lower Lands?* she wondered. She felt a foreboding sense of unease settling over her.

Jacqui and Amaru exchanged a glance.

A barbarian who smelled akin to horse shit approached. "Pasakuna riqsisqa," he said.

Amaru took the chains of her shackles from Jacqui's hand. "We've been told the horses are ready. This way," he said, gesturing toward their location and leading the way.

The barbarian group and Demoria walked toward the horses, where, as expected, a few were saddled and ready to ride. Demoria's sleipnir, Lucy, was among them, and she felt a sense of relief seeing her well-fed and healthy. She also found all her belongings attached to Lucy's saddle.

"You'll find everything there, except for this scroll. Mind telling me what the glyph on it means?" Amaru asked.

Demoria considered telling the truth but decided against it. Something told her it wasn't wise to reveal its meaning just yet.

"It's a spell to kill nosy barbarians," she replied with a sly smile.

Amaru laughed, placing the scroll with the rest of her belongings. Then they both mounted Lucy, and their journey began.

As they rode, she contemplated the scenery illuminated by the torches carried by the barbarians. The terrain appeared to be filled with grass, and she noticed a few rabbits and other rodents scurrying away, likely frightened by the noise of the galloping horses. Looking up at the sky, she couldn't see any stars or the moon. *The clouds are too heavy*, she thought to herself, noting the thick cloud cover.

"By the way, you never said your name," Amaru called out loudly over the sound of the horses' galloping.

She smiled in response. "I don't owe you that much, old man," she said. "Be thankful I am willing to help you, considering I still can't use my magic. But you already knew that, didn't you?"

Amaru laughed heartily. "Of course we knew. Otherwise, you would have roasted us at the first chance you had," he joked. Grabbing a chicken leg from his satchel, he began chewing on it.

"How is it that you can sense magic if you're not able to wield it?" Amaru asked, chewing on a piece of chicken.

Demoria decided it was safe to reveal this information, as it seemed unimportant. "It's actually quite easy for me to detect magic. One simply needs to access a different ability. It's said that even ordinary men and women can tap into it. Of course, that excludes your lot, since you're closer to animals than humans," she added with a jest.

Amaru laughed. "Haha, I like you. To be honest, when they brought you in, my people wanted to let you die. I opposed," he said between bites, casually spitting out the bones.

She wasn't surprised by his revelation. *Barbarians are not known for their hospitality*, she thought.

"I would hug you and thank you, but my hands are all tied up," she said sarcastically, gesturing to the shackles on her wrists.

They rode for some time until one of the barbarians leading the group signalled to stop. They all halted and dismounted. She struggled to use her hands properly due to the shackles, so Amaru helped her dismount. Two barbarians stayed behind to safeguard the horses while the rest continued on foot to the south. The barbarians still carried their torches, illuminating the path ahead.

She noticed that the ground beneath her feet felt more moist than usual, and the smell of dead trees contaminated the air. *We are near Duskenwood*, she thought, rolling her eyes at the familiar surroundings.

"Kay llaqtapi chayqa ch'alla chiri p'itiqan qhawaykachkan churaykachkan," said one of the barbarians, whom she recognized by the bandages on his body. He was the one who had reported the discovery of the witches' camp and returned injured.

Amaru turned to face her. "They said this is the place where the other scouts died," he explained while his right hand stroked his grey beard thoughtfully. "Although, I don't seem to see any heavy mist around."

"¿Ima k'iraypi kananpi?" Amaru asked, looking around.

"Imaynataqqaqaqa, qhali," the injured barbarian replied.

Amaru later explained to her that he had asked about the heavy mist, to which the barbarian swore that they were in the right place.

Sensing the air around her, she sensed something strange. "I sense some sort of spell around here, although very weak. It seems to have been dispelled very recently. It is harmless at this point."

"We must keep walking," said Jacqui, her tone tinged with impatience.

They all continued walking south for just a moment when they heard an explosion nearby. Following the explosion, a blue light became visible to the south from where they were standing. The blue light grew brighter and brighter, so much so that Demoria thought the moon itself had materialised on the ground. Then, she noticed the clouds above disappearing, revealing the bright moon. However, in front of it, she saw a small, strange dark object she didn't recall seeing before.

Suddenly, something odd happened. She could feel an unknown type of magic emanating from where the blue light was shining. Her entire body started to shake due to the powerful magic she felt. This is the third type of magic I have recently encountered that I don't know the roots of. Something is definitely changing in the world, she thought, her mind racing with questions.

"Tukuy llank'aykunaqmi," screamed Jacqui.

She saw that the group of barbarians had their weapons ready to attack.

The group of barbarians launched towards the blue light, running at full speed. Amaru and Demoria followed closely behind.

Concerned for her own safety, she urged Amaru, "You must tell your men not to attack. Whatever the blue light is, it is dangerous."

Amaru laughed. "Forgive me, but you should not underestimate the brute force of us barbarians," he said proudly.

As they approached the blue light, she saw it emanated from a small figure floating gracefully in the air, with long, flowing blue hair. Upon closer inspection, she realised the figure was a young girl. Beneath her lay several lifeless bodies—perhaps ten or fifteen in number. They appeared to be women in black robes. *Witches*, she thought. Nearby stood a man who appeared to be older, clad in dark robes and bound by shackles on his hands and feet.

She observed that the girl's gaze was fixed on something ahead. Obscured by the darkness of the night, she couldn't discern what it was. Disregarding the presence of the barbarian nearby, the girl extended her hand with a delicate motion, causing the older man near her to levitate. With a swift movement, she threw him forward, akin to the action of tossing a small stone into the distance.

The old man collided with something, tumbling to the ground in a motionless heap. The impact left a trail of blood on the surface of a structure hidden by the night. However, it became clearer as it started pulsing with a crimson colour. Now more visible, the structure revealed itself as a gigantic fist made of bones, its form reaching upward.

The ground around them began to tremble.

"Hatun!" Jacqui screamed at the barbarians. Demoria recalled from her earlier encounter with the barbarians that *hatun* meant *stop* in their native language.

"What's happening?" Amaru inquired.

"I don't know," she replied, "there's some strange magic surrounding us. It's not safe."

Moments later, the gigantic hand began to slowly open, triggering a larger earthquake. She and Amaru stumbled, falling to the ground. She noticed that the other barbarians were no longer paying attention to Jacqui's orders; instead, most of them charged forward with weapons in hand toward the girl who remained suspended in the air.

The girl pivoted to confront the attackers, her blue hair glowing even brighter than before. Suddenly, blue spheres materialised in the air near the barbarians. She sensed magic emanating from the spheres. They revealed themselves to be magical bombs, detonating with devastating force and instantly killing half of the barbarian group.

She watched as the remaining survivors, overcome by panic, attempted to flee from the scene. Yet, their efforts proved futile as they were ensnared by strange chains attached to their limbs, including Jacqui. *When had she trapped them with those chains?* The realisation struck her— the chains had materialised almost out of thin air. *The girl is a formidable witch*, she thought.

As the tremors subsided, she observed the gigantic hand fully open, revealing its palm adorned with a flashing red light in the shape of a large cross. Sensing air emanating from the cross, Her eyes widened in realisation. "It's not just a cross," she said, "it's an entrance."

"An entrance? What are you saying? Who is that girl?" asked Amaru who seemed to be in panic.

"She's a witch, that much is clear. She's unlocked something hidden here using that old man's blood, who..." She glanced around looking for the older man, only to find him nowhere in sight.

Amaru yanked her chain forcefully. "Get up! We need to go. This is too dangerous, and we are too important. We have a bigger role to play!" he shouted.

Summoning all her physical strength, she pulled herself up, standing defiantly. "The only role you'll play is to unchain me, hand over the cursed arm, and watch me leave freely," she said.

They grappled with each other, pushing and pulling. The wound on her belly stung, sending waves of pain through her body, but she fought to ignore it. Despite Amaru being an ageing barbarian, his strength remained formidable. Demoria struggled to overpower him.

"Ah! Ah!" she heard consecutive screams echoing from a distance. Amaru and she both halted their struggle, turning to locate the source of the screams. It was the remaining barbarians. The girl was hurling them one by one against the gigantic hand, which prevented them from passing through the cross-shaped entrance in its palm. Before they could make any progress, the hand squeezed them, killing them instantly.

By the time she could grasp what was happening, all the barbarians lay dead, except for Jacqui, who was suspended in the air with chains around her limbs. Blood and body parts littered the ground surrounding the area near the gigantic hand.

"Leave me be! Leave me be!" Jacqui screamed, crying in panic.

The girl paid no heed to Jacqui's cries. She seemed to be searching for something or someone.

"Where art thou, Blood Priest?" she called out aloud.

Still levitating, the girl floated closer, her eyes fixed on Amaru and Demoria, as if examining them closely.

"Hast thou seen an old man clad in dark robes around this area?" the girl asked.

Demoria, recognizing her current situation, realised she was no match for the girl before her. She decided to attempt an alliance, at least temporarily.

"Was he the one you threw to that gigantic hand? I can't see him anymore. Perhaps I can help you look for him if you break these shackles?" she suggested. Amaru looked at Demoria with a frightened expression.

The shackles on Demoria's wrists suddenly broke. Directing her gaze to Amaru the girl made a dismissive gesture with her hand. "I am no friend of thy kind, and especially not of those who prey upon vulnerable women," the girl said to Amaru with a menacing tone.

"She is not vulnerable, she is a witch just like you," Amaru said angrily.

With a swift movement of her hand, the girl caused Amaru's arms to contort unnaturally, snapping the bones within.

"Aargh!" Amaru screamed in agony, blood spilling from his mouth as tears streamed down his face.

"Thy kind is a pathetic imitation of the Primes, liars, thieves, and rapists. I shall make thee cry in pain until thou diest," the girl said, a blue light within her shone brighter and brighter.

Amaru's satchel, Demoria thought. *I must take it; the cursed arm is in there.*

Another tremor shook the entire area. She looked around, attempting to locate the source of the tremor. Suddenly, a powerful red light blinded her, overpowering even the intense blue light emitted from the girl. She shielded her eyes with her hand and attempted to peer through the brightness. As her vision adjusted, she noticed a multitude of shadows moving rapidly around her.

"No!" she heard the girl screaming amidst the chaos.

Then, the red light gradually dimmed, transforming into a warm, bright glow, akin to sunlight. Though still intense, the light was no longer blinding, allowing her to cautiously open her eyes. As she looked around, she realised she was alone. In front of her, the gigantic bony hand was now fully visible. The red cross in its palm, which she had assumed to be some sort of entrance, still pulsed with a faint red glow.

"Methinks this be thine own," said an unfamiliar but soft and calm voice.

She turned to locate the source of the voice. Floating in the air before her was a woman with fair skin and long blue hair, draped in thin white robes. A black crown rested on her head, and her eyes, as dark as the night, were fixed intently on her. It seemed to her that the woman was much larger than herself—her arms were longer, her face bigger, and her height much taller. *A Prime?* she wondered. Then, Demoria noticed Amaru's satchel in the woman's hand. The woman extended it to her. As she did, a memory flickered in Demoria's mind—she had seen this woman briefly near a lake in Duskenwood some time ago.

"Who are you?" Demoria inquired, feeling a sense of calm wash over her in the presence of such power. *Magic,* she thought.

The woman, still floating in the air, delicately grasped her chin, "I am as thou wert, a witch. I pertain to a clan from a bygone era that hath already yielded. My charge is to seek out souls such as thine, thou being an Apocryphos."

It took her a moment to decipher the woman's words, as they were spoken in an old-fashioned manner. "What do you mean, 'as thou wert'? I am a Shabrani Witch," she affirmed.

Then the woman gently touched Demoria's belly. "Nay, not so henceforth. Behold, thou art with child. The dark moon didst appear once more in the sky, clouding the vision of the Goddess of the Blue

Moon. Apocrypha hath taken root within thee, contrary to fate, fashioning a marvel for thee to merge with the tree of life and death, forging a path to access the Witches Road. Yet, as the fruit of the tree, thou art not fully ripe," the woman explained. She then began to float backward, distancing herself from Demoria and drawing closer to the gigantic bony hand.

"Wait, that's not possible. Witches can't procreate. What do you mean by 'Apocrypha'?" Demoria exclaimed, shocked and bewildered, having never heard that word before.

"I shall come unto thee when the fruit is ripe, and until that hour, prithee, yield not thy spirit unto death," the woman concluded.

Afterward, the woman radiated light brighter than the sun. Demoria was blinded for a few moments. When she opened her eyes, she looked up at the sky. The heavy clouds had dispersed, revealing the moon illuminating the night. As she gazed at it, she saw something—a dark, small sphere hovering in front of the moon. *Could that be the dark moon that woman mentioned?* she wondered.

She scanned her surroundings in every direction, but found only Jacqui lying on the ground, motionless—perhaps dead. She looked for Amaru, but he was nowhere to be seen. The gigantic hand and the girl had also vanished. It was as if nothing had occurred.

Suddenly, a noise came from the ground beside her. The Blood Priest crawled out from beneath the dirt and stones, covered in blood and smelling like a decaying horse. She had to cover her mouth to stifle a cough.

"Have you seen my wife and son?" he asked.

Demoria didn't reply. Instead, she collapsed to her knees, touching her belly delicately as tears streamed down her cheeks. For the first time in a very long time, she felt vulnerable and weak.

ELLA

She mustered the strength to open her eyes once more, though even that simple act seemed to drain what little energy she had left. As her eyelids parted, she realised her vision had fully healed, allowing her to gaze up at the sky. The bright moon and stars gleamed above, casting their ethereal light. In front of the moon, she noticed a small dark sphere. *I might be imagining things—perhaps my mind hasn't fully recovered yet*, she thought.

Her eyelids grew heavy, and before she realised, they shut.

After several days, she regained full consciousness. She could now open her eyes at will, and her limbs had mostly regenerated. However, her legs had ceased growing altogether.

"I always believed that with enough water and rest, we could regenerate any limb," remarked Fila as she carefully examined Ella's body. "It seems there is something different with you. Your legs simply won't grow."

Ella's vocal cords were still healing, so she chose to remain silent for the time being, a decision supported by Fila, who surprisingly proved to be a supportive sister. After the skirmish at the Grey Skull, Fila gathered what remained of Ella, and together they journeyed southwest. Along the way, they encountered a few friendly travellers who generously lent them a spare horse. Water was scarce in the arid landscape, dominated by sand and stones. Fortunately, they found an oasis in the middle of the desert, providing them with enough water to sustain themselves for days, a unique trait of their kind.

Once she regained enough energy to stay awake all day, Fila explained her plan. "We can't return to the Balor clan; we failed in our mission. They'll likely consider us failed experiments and cast us aside. The only place I can think of going is Artoria, my birthplace. Before joining the Balor clan, my magical skills were highly valued and praised," Fila explained.

She was an adult wielding magic before joining the Balor clan? Ella pondered. The revelation about Fila's origins intrigued her. Most witches she knew had found their way into a witch clan before they even realised their ability to wield magic, often through circumstance or accident, as if guided by fate. She hadn't known that there were women who could wield magic freely without being inducted into a witch clan.

"You still can't speak?" Fila asked calmly. "That's alright. I'll handle the talking. Come to think of it, you've never been much of a talker with me anyway."

And so, Fila spoke. She narrated her story of how she ended up in the Dark Forest. From birth, Fila displayed a remarkable proficiency in magic, particularly vega magic. By the age of sixteen, she had become well-known in Laminio, one of the three largest cities in Artoria. When news of her abilities reached the king and queen of Artoria, she was summoned to present herself before the royal family in Tartessos, the capital of Artoria.

Fila explained that she saw this as the opportunity she had been waiting for, longing for recognition on a grand scale. She believed the royal family would welcome her and make her a valuable asset in the court. However, her hopes were dashed when she discovered their true intentions: they planned to send her to war against Celen, intending to use her as a disposable weapon. Fila strongly refused to be a pawn in their schemes. Despite the royal family's attempts to coerce her compliance, she seized the first opportunity to escape Artoria and fled northeast.

"So, I journeyed to the Dark Forest," said Fila. "I was confident that the Balor Witches would welcome me once they witnessed my power. True enough, they accepted me and in no time, they invited me to join the Dark Thorns. The rest, as they say, is history," she concluded.

As a few more days passed, the scenery began to change. They were drawing closer to the border with the Rockshade Highlands and the Crucible. Lush grass and a brisk wind became part of the new environment.

"We must be nearing the Crucible," Fila said. "It's a treacherous land with many mountains and caves. Some who escaped the war between Artoria and Celen have sought refuge there, living miserably in dark caves and scavenging whatever the lions leave behind."

Ella, who had regained her ability to speak, felt uneasy about what Fila had implied. "We should be able to handle any attacks easily. Why are you worried?" she asked.

Fila pointed skyward, noting the intense brightness of the sun and the absence of rain for several days. She also observed that their satchel, once full of water, was now nearly empty.

"Do you understand now?" asked Fila, halting the horse and dismounting. "The closer we get to the Crucible, the scarcer water sources become. Just look at the grass; it's already getting drier."

She noticed the grass turning yellow.

"We could try heading closer to the ocean for some salty water," suggested Fila, pacing in circles. "But that would take us off course, and with those steep cliffs by the ocean, climbing would be out of the question for you."

"Unless..." Fila trailed off, her gaze shifting to the west. "They might be able to help us by providing enough water for our journey through the Crucible. It's been many years, though. I'm not sure if they're still there," said Fila with a mysterious tone.

She didn't quite grasp what Fila was hinting at, but she wanted to be helpful. "It's worth checking out if it's not too far off our path, I suppose," she said.

Fila nodded. "Yes, it's not far from here. There's a village to the west. The people there don't belong to any nation. They've gathered to help the less fortunate, many of whom are slaves who escaped the war in the south. I think it's worth a try. Let's go."

And so, they set off towards the west. The scenery transformed dramatically along the way. Instead of dry grass, lush greenery with small yellow flowers dotted the landscape. She, using her vega magic, sensed that nature was benevolent in that area. Even the sun seemed less harsh.

Suddenly, the horse halted and stumbled slightly. This caused Ella to lose her balance and fall to the ground. She saw Fila, still mounted, gripping the reins tightly to prevent a fall. Quickly dismounting, Fila steadied the horse before it collapsed to the ground entirely.

"Are you alright? That sounded like quite a fall," Fila inquired, sounding concerned.

She, still surprised by Fila's display of concern, replied, "Yes, I'm fine. It seems our horse has had enough, though."

Fila approached the exhausted animal, noting its heavy breathing. "It hasn't been fed in almost three days," said Fila, placing her hand on the horse's belly, causing prominent veins to bulge along the animal body. The horse attempted to kick and emitted distressed sounds while still on the ground. She realised that Fila was using vega magic to drain the last traces of life energy from the horse.

"I've absorbed the moisture and water from it," said Fila, who then approached her, lifting her as if she were a baby, and gently placing her near the dying horse. "Now it's your turn. You must do the same as I did; otherwise, you'll be the next to die."

Her Balor witch sister was right; she looked at her hands and noticed they were turning a pale yellow colour, a sign of dehydration.

"I... I've never done what you just did," she said, reaching out to touch the horse's body.

Fila rolled her eyes. "Really? I've seen you do the most powerful things. Never mind. Listen to me," said Fila, sounding a little irritated.

Fila then explained that she needed to transfer vega magic to the horse, sensing water elements inside its body. Each time she felt water, she had to absorb it using her magic. She didn't quite understand how to sense water elements; it wasn't a skill commonly practised by Balor Witches. In fact, no witch in the Lower Lands could do it.

"You already know how water elements feel; it's our primary source of life, after all. You don't have to manipulate water. Use your magic to trap the water element instead," Fila explained further.

While touching the horse's body, which had no more energy to move, she did as she was told, transferring vega magic into it. She closed her eyes, attempting to visualise water and recall how it felt in her own body.

"Focus," Fila urged.

Just as Fila had said, she began to understand what it meant to feel water. She could sense the same sensation she experienced when she drank water—a feeling she had encountered countless times without ever realising it had a distinct sensation.

She opened her eyes, observing the horse's body as it started to shrink until it was nothing but skin and bones. She had successfully extracted the remaining water from it. She was already starting to feel better.

"I deliberately took more water because I will have to carry you on my shoulders," said Fila, taking some ropes from her satchel. She proceeded to attach them back to back with her.

"You're even lighter than before," said Fila as she began walking towards their destination, with Ella securely attached to Fila's back.

"Thank you," she said softly.

Fila remained silent.

As they continued their journey, she noted most of the path was adorned with abundant green grass and dotted with yellow and white flowers reminiscent of joyful energy and calm serenity. Even the distant hills were cloaked in vibrant green colours. She felt as if she had entered an entirely different world.

"There it is," said Fila, turning around to let her glimpse ahead.

In the distance, she could see a cluster of houses. They appeared to be constructed from hides, wood, and bark. Not only that, she could hear sounds as well, almost as if they were music.

As they drew closer, the sounds grew louder, revealing themselves to be the harmonious voices of a choir singing in front of the village entrance. *This music somehow makes me feel at peace*, she thought.

The entrance stood as a grand arch adorned with yellow and white flowers, the same blooms they had passed on their journey. As she observed the choir members, she noticed their diverse origins; individuals from Celen, the Golden Nation, and Lakefields. It was uncommon to encounter such a mix of people in a village setting. They all wore robes and dresses in shades of white and yellow, paired with sandals on their feet.

As they drew nearer, she could discern the lyrics more clearly.

In this world of endless faces,
Strangers passing in the night,
Let's embrace their unknown graces,
And welcome them into our light.

We'll set a table for the weary,
Offering warmth and cheer,
In our hearts, there's room for all,
No need for doubt or fear.

Come gather 'round, let's break bread together,
In this place where hearts unite,
Where strangers become friends forever,
In the glow of our shared light.

With open arms, we'll find connection,
In the stories we each bring,
Every flaw, every imperfection,
Adds a thread to the tapestry we sing.

Let's build a bond that's unbroken,
Through every joy and tear,
As one we stand, our differences woven,

Into a community that's strong and clear.

Come gather 'round, let's break bread together,
In this place where hearts unite,
Where strangers become friends forever,
In the glow of our shared light.

Hand in hand, we'll journey on,
Through the highs and lows of life,
United by our common song,
As we banish darkness with our strife.

Come gather 'round, let's break bread together,
In this place where hearts unite,
Where strangers become friends forever,
In the glow of our shared light.

So, let's welcome strangers to our table,
And let love be our guiding role,
For in embracing every fable,
We create a world that's whole.

"Did they know we were coming?" she turned her head to ask Fila.

Fila seemed engrossed in listening to the words, or so she thought. *Perhaps, Fila knows this song. Fila did tell me that she met these people before*, she thought.

Fila, who had been in some sort of trance, snapped out of it. "It seems they somehow knew we were coming; otherwise, how would they arrange such a welcome party? And before you ask, no, I don't recognize these faces. When I came here, this place was a sad shelter with the ill and the hungry asking for mercy and help. These people in front of us seem to be well-fed and happy," Fila seemed surprised at how the village she once knew had transformed.

"Welcome, friends. We've been expecting you," said a man in a friendly tone.

Fila turned around so that Ella could see. A member of the choir had approached them—a mature man with short white hair. Ella noticed a strange glyph on the back of his hands; it didn't look like paint but rather as if it were carved into the skin.

Her Balor sister, never one to beat around the bush, didn't hesitate to ask, "You knew we were coming? Do you have witches in this village that can see the future?" Fila asked abruptly.

"Not a witch, but a prophet," the man replied, then extended both hands to them as a sign of welcome. "But please, we can discuss the details later. You must be tired from your travels. We have arranged one of the cottages for you two. Please, follow me," he said warmly, sounding very inviting.

Fila turned her head to look at her for some sort of response to what was happening. Unable to think clearly, she just shrugged in uncertainty. Fila then followed the man.

Before entering the village, the choir extended their hands in welcome. Ella noticed some had ornaments made of flowers on their hands. The choir placed flowers and necklaces made of shells on her and Fila's heads and shoulders. It seemed the objects were harmless, so she didn't refuse the gifts. Even Fila accepted the peculiar offerings.

Inside the village, she could see many other groups of people dressed in white and yellow engaging in various activities. Some were dancing, others were washing clothes, and many others were simply walking around. Most of the people she made eye contact with responded with a smile on their faces.

"This is definitely not the place I once knew," Fila said aloud.

"Oh, you're a returning visitor. That's strange; we rarely encounter someone who visits this village twice. What are your names?" the man asked.

"We'll share our names once you've answered our questions. For now, just know that I've been here before, though things have changed considerably," Fila said to the man.

"Oh, I see. All the changes you notice are because of the prophet," the man said.

There was silence until they all entered one of the cottages. The outside of the cottage was old, constructed of bark and wood. Inside, she observed a whimsical kitchen area, wooden drawers, and two beds. Fila gently placed her on one of the beds. Glancing around, she spotted a peculiar wooden chair with wheels.

"We've made this for you; we think you'll find it very useful," the man said to her with a smile.

She quickly understood the man's offer—a peculiar mechanism she hadn't seen before, but one she believed could be effective, especially since she had no legs to walk.

Before she could express gratitude for the gift, Fila abruptly intervened. Two green vines with spikes emerged from under Fila's robes, seizing the man by the neck and causing him pain.

"Stop!" she screamed at Fila.

As soon as the scream escaped her mouth, a wave materialised and struck Fila, forcing her to release the man. Fila turned toward her, furious. Ella questioned internally whether Fila had stopped because of her command or not.

"Please, don't fight. I'm the one to blame. I'll share the details you were expecting. I understand this is a strange situation for you," he said, sounding apologetic. Ella saw that blood trickled down the man's neck, but he appeared unworried by it.

They both listened to the man attentively.

He retrieved a scroll from his robes, carefully unfolding it to reveal a peculiar drawing divided into four sections. "The first image depicts a beautiful woman with blue hair. She arrived in this village many years ago, and her beauty and abilities rid us of sickness and hunger. As a result, we became a prosperous village. She also predicted how the weather would behave, giving us time to prepare for harsh conditions. We called her prophet."

The man began to cough, likely due to his injured neck, but he persisted with the story.

"The second image illustrates how our prophet departed from us. She ensured that we could sustain ourselves independently, assisting us in establishing a system that suited our needs. Glyphs were inscribed on everyone's hands; mine signifies that I am a priest. Furthermore, before her departure, our prophet entrusted us with three commandments: to always be hospitable to visitors, to refrain from engaging in conflicts, and to await patiently for our queen and obey her."

The final part of the story prompted Fila and her to exchange a glance. *Is this prophecy referring to one of us?* she thought.

The man continued speaking. "The third image depicts our queen. In her final form, she will come to us on one of the brightest days, following the appearance of the dark moon in the sky. Our queen will arrive with wounded legs, in need of the artefact we have crafted," he gestured toward the wheeled chair beside her bed. "She will remain with us, and we will obey and serve her."

The man looked at her and smiled. "You are our queen."

She experienced a surge of conflicting emotions throughout her entire body. Uncertain of how to interpret this news, her instincts whispered that this prophecy was merely a fabrication. Yet, the drawing shows a girl with the same conditions as her.

"You're a fraud, old man! That prophet you speak of is a charlatan. You've been deceived!" Fila screamed at the man.

Ignoring Fila's accusations, the man approached Ella and lifted her into his arms, placing her in the artefact created for her. "All you need to do is push the wheels with your hands; the chair will do the rest. The village has been prepared for it, so you'll find it easy to move around," he said gently.

She sensed vega energy surrounding the room, emanating from Fila. Her sister was preparing to attack the man once again. Before Fila could act, almost reflexively, Ella extended her right arm. She felt her vega energy swiftly leaving her body and connecting with Fila's neck. Suddenly, Fila's neck seemed to contract from the sides, snapping it. Fila collapsed to the ground.

"You must not fight. It is forbidden!" yelled the man, expressing concern after witnessing what had just transpired.

She paid no attention to the man, her gaze was fixed on her right arm. Astonished by the attack she had unleashed, she contemplated the newfound power coursing through her. While her magic typically conjured vines, poisons, and spikes from the ground, this new ability surpassed anything she had ever witnessed among the Balor Witches and the Dark Thorns.

"I could feel Fila's bones and bend them at will," she said quietly, a smile creeping onto her face.

In front of her, Fila's body began to stir. Her head moved as if attempting to readjust the bones in her neck.

"Out of everyone in the Dark Thorns, it had to be you? The weakest and most stupid," said Fila while still on the ground.

Ignoring her sister's insults, she asked, "What do you mean?"

"I overheard our former leader, Ceca, saying something interesting about the Dark Thorns bodies. She mentioned that our current state is not our final form. Someone in the past who underwent the same process as us managed to elevate her power to what she called Blossoming. Unfortunately, this witch perished after reaching this final form. Ceca mentioned that the witch also transformed into a large tree before unleashing a massive explosion of vega magic. After these events, she died. They found no trace of her except for green grass in the area where she exploded," Fila stood up and turned around to face her. "I witnessed the same events at the Grey Skull with you, Ella. The explosion destroyed all those fire demons, yet you survived. I should've disposed of your remains, but I thought if I was kind to you and healed you properly, I could use your powers to end the war in the south. Then Artoria would finally give me what I deserve!" Fila yelled. "There is no point in going south anymore, I can see you must be killed now. You are truly useless!"

Even though Fila's tale was hard to believe, part of her trusted the story. It seemed to offer an explanation for the newfound power she felt within herself. Furthermore, she wasn't surprised by Fila's true intentions; she was familiar with her behaviour and had been expecting her to reveal her true nature at any moment.

Feeling empowered by her newfound abilities, she exhaled a breath directed at Fila, which carried a paralysing poison. Fila's body stiffened, rendering her immobile as she collapsed to the floor once more.

Turning her attention to the man standing nearby, she inquired, "What is your name, noble priest?"

The man, poised to aid Fila, was stopped by her. "Do not concern yourself with my sister. I have paralyzed the Balor seed inside of her; she won't be able to move. I will speak with her once she regains composure. I ask again, what is your name?" she pressed.

"I am Gorm, Priest of the Blossomveil Village. I am at your service. Do you believe what I have told you, that you are our queen?" Gorm asked, kneeling before her.

She nodded and smiled at him in response.

"I don't think I have properly introduced myself. My name is Ella."

She gripped the wheels of her chair firmly and propelled herself towards the cottage's exit. "Let's go, Gorm. They await us," she said with a gentle smile.

As the day progressed, the villagers busied themselves with preparations for her coronation. She observed their diligence and satisfaction as they worked tirelessly. Some constructed structures from wood and bark, while others gathered flowers from nearby areas. Upon visiting the kitchen, she noticed that the villagers responsible for cooking bore different glyphs engraved on their hands. Gorm later explained that each villager was assigned a task upon deciding to stay in the village, whether it be collecting flowers, cooking, washing clothes, managing the library, building, or other duties.

As night fell, the preparations were complete. The entire village gathered in the central square. She was adorned in a stunning gown crafted from flowers and adorned with silver ornaments. Placed atop a tall platform adorned with peculiar totems crafted by the villagers, she looked out upon the happy faces of the villagers who were wearing white clothing.

Fireplaces dotted the village, casting a warm glow around the gathering. Gazing up at the sky, she admired the beauty of the moon, its radiance captivating her. Yet, she noticed a peculiar dark object in front of the moon. *There you are, the prophet mentioned the full moon's dark sister. I saw it the other night, I thought I had imagined it*, she thought. Dismissing it from her mind, she focused on the impending celebration, standing proudly alongside Gorm.

"It is time to commence the coronation ceremony," Gorm announced to the gathered crowd.

"Boom, boom!" echoed the beat of a drum played by someone in the audience. In an instant, the crowd formed circles and began to dance and sing.

In a garden fair, where blossoms sway,
A queen of flowers begins her reign tonight.
Petals crown her, radiant and bright,
Her rule brings hope, dispels the night.

Hail the queen of blooms, her power divine,
She'll vanquish darkness, let her light shine.
With grace and beauty, she'll lead the fight,
Bringing peace and prosperity, banishing plight.

From every bud, her loyal subjects rise,
With fragrant whispers, they harmonise.
Through thorns and thistles, she'll bravely tread,
With courage blooming, evil's dread.

Hail the queen of blooms, her power divine,
She'll vanquish darkness, let her light shine.
With grace and beauty, she'll lead the fight,
Bringing peace and prosperity, banishing plight.

As petals fall like tears of joy,
She'll reign supreme, no foe can destroy.

In her court of colours, love will thrive,
Under her rule, all hearts revive.

Hail the queen of blooms, her power divine,
She'll vanquish darkness, let her light shine.
With grace and beauty, she'll lead the fight,
Bringing peace and prosperity, banishing plight.

So let us sing, in gardens wide,
For the queen of flowers, our love won't hide.
With every bloom, her glory unfurled,
A reign of beauty, in a flower-filled world.

"Boom, boom," the drumbeats signalled the conclusion of the song.

From the audience, two girls stepped forward, bearing what appeared to be a crown fashioned from yellow and white flowers. As they approached the main stand, a shadow materialised between them. With alarming speed, the shadow seized one of the girls by the neck, wielding a knife threateningly to slice her neck. The shadow revealed itself to be Fila.

"How is it that you can move?" Ella asked.

"I told you before, not all of us rely on the Balor seed. I've found a way to redirect the Balor seed energy into my entire body, sister. Any other tricks up your sleeve?" said Fila.

The rest of the villagers watched the unfolding events with a mixture of shock and confusion. Just as she was about to intervene, Fila interjected menacingly, "Don't attempt anything, or this pretty little bird meets her end."

Though she dreaded the thought of harm happening to the girl, she resolved to stop Fila once and for all.

"Do not worry over the girl. We are at your service; she would sacrifice herself gladly for you," Gorm reassured her in a calming tone.

Ella noticed a reluctance among the other villagers to intervene.

Recalling their second commandment, she understood that they were forbidden from fighting.

Without hesitation, she commanded, "Stop!"

Fila's eyes widened, her body froze as if turned to stone.

"Little girl, stay away from her. She won't be able to harm you," she said to the trembling child.

Following her command, the girl retreated. She saw that tears welled in Fila's eyes.

"I wanted to test something similar to what I inadvertently did back in the cottage," she admitted. "You said that the Balor seed energy now lives in your entire body. All I've done is connect with that energy to control your body instead," she explained to Fila.

The girls ran towards her and placed the crown upon her head, starting a new reign with her as queen.

"My villagers, I hereby revoke the second commandment and establish a new decree. You are authorised to engage in combat, but only upon my direct command," she announced to the assembled crowd.

"Kill the witch!" she screamed.

As soon as she uttered those words, the villagers seized any available pointed object, from knives to stakes, and surged forward in unison toward Fila. They sliced, cut and impaled Fila's body. Because of the multitude, Ella could not see clearly, she only saw green blood being spilled around. In mere moments, they swiftly murdered Fila, bringing an end to the confrontation.

"Now, everyone, I command you to grab a piece of her flesh and eat it," she instructed with a plan in mind.

The villagers complied without hesitation. Even Gorm and the young girls followed as she instructed.

Relieved that Fila was finally out of the way, she allowed herself to immerse fully in the ceremony. The tall totems were set ablaze, and joyful songs filled the air. She savoured the moment, feeling a sense of contentment and happiness unlike any she had experienced before.

Ella suddenly recalled something she had nearly forgotten. Slipping her right hand into her robes, she retrieved something from within—ashes. "My dear Matena, we're finally free," she whispered at the ashes.

The following morning, she rose early, summoning the strength to transition from her bed to her wheelchair. Beside her bed, she discovered her new flower crown, which she carefully placed atop her head. Stepping outside, she found two girls patiently awaiting her wake, bearing provisions of food and water, along with a pristine white dress adorned with blue accents.

"For you, my queen," one of the girls spoke softly, her voice filled with reverence.

She allowed the girls to dress her, expressing her gratitude for their assistance. Though she had no need for the food, she indulged in it nonetheless. However, when it came to the water, she drank every last drop, appreciating its refreshing taste and the nourishment it provided.

"Where is Gorm? Take me to him," she commanded with a determined tone.

Outside, the scene appeared as if the events of the previous night had been erased. Every trace of the ceremony had been meticulously removed: the charred remnants of the totems, the scattered flowers, even the green blood stains from Fila were nowhere to be found.

As the girls led her towards a row of cottages, she couldn't shake the sense of a peculiar aura emanating from one of them.

"What's inside that cottage? I feel unsettled just by looking at it," she said.

"A visitor arrived a few days ago. He was severely injured, with burns covering his body, and he was missing his left arm. We took him in and tended to his wounds. He's been sleeping ever since; it seems he has no strength left to move," one of the girls explained.

She made a mental note to investigate the matter later; something about it didn't sit right with her. Continuing on their path toward Gorm's cottage, they encountered several villagers along the way, all of whom bowed in reverence as she passed.

Gorm greeted her at the door with an expectant expression. "My Queen, I was just preparing to come find you. How may I be of service?"

Entering Gorm's cottage, she glanced around quickly. It was a modest, unassuming space, with a single bed, scattered articles of clothing, and a desk adorned with parchment and ink.

"The scroll with the drawings you showed me yesterday—I wish to see it again," she said.

Gorm retrieved the scroll from his desk and passed it to her.

"This—the fourth section of the drawing—you never finished explaining it," she said, pointing to the specific part of the scroll.

Gorm smiled warmly at her. "The fourth drawing depicts a distant future, my queen. We seldom discuss it, as we struggle to comprehend its meaning. We were hoping that you might shed some light on it. Please, take this drawing with you. We can delve into it further at a later time," he said politely.

Examining the scroll again, she focused on the fourth drawing. It depicted a peculiar tree standing prominently, with one of its branches bearing a rounded object at its tip—something resembling a fruit. Upon closer inspection, it seemed that a human figure was enclosed within the fruit. Above the tree, a crimson trail stretched like a road. Beside the tree, she noticed numerous human figures, all clad in white, wielding knives and locked in combat with what could only be described as demons. Overlooking the scene was a woman adorned with a flower crown, her arms outstretched as if overseeing the events below.

"The flower crown in the drawing—it looks just like mine," she said, a wide smile spreading across her face.

THE EMPEROR OF CELEN

Every morning, without fail, the Emperor of Celen would have breakfast under the Sal Trees with his consort and children after praying to Amaterasu, the goddess of the Sun, for the gift of a new day. This tradition held firm, even in the midst of perilous times of war; it confirmed his commitment to maintaining a strong familial bond. However, this routine abruptly stopped after the arrival of devastating news. His eldest son, Riujin Saito, had been captured by Artorian forces in a skirmish on the border between the cities of Akiya and Arriaca. Riujin, who was supposed to act merely as an observer, had defied orders by engaging in the conflict. This unprecedented event marked the first instance of Celen's weakness in the century-long conflict against Artoria.

Artoria promptly demanded Celen's surrender in exchange for Riujin's release. As the emperor and his council deliberated their options, he found some solace in the incarceration of his general and leader of the Celen army, Ryota Hoshikawa, whom he blamed for the kidnapping of his son.

"You have failed the Empire of Celen! How did you allow such a thing! He is my son! My only heir," his voice boomed with disappointment and anger. "Guards, take this man to prison. Let him rot there for the rest of his days."

Ryota pleaded and wept, but the emperor's decision was final.

Immediately following Ryota's condemnation, he appointed Ryota's younger brother, Kaito Hoshikawa, as the new general of the Celen's army.

In response to the crisis, the emperor cancelled all other engagements and gatherings. Instead, he convened daily meetings with his entire council, dedicating hours to brainstorming ideas and strategies to rescue young Riujin. Amidst a flurry of proposals, Aiko Hagashi, Celen's chief diplomat, put forward a daring suggestion: to enlist the help of a group of rebels from Artoria whom she had knowledge of. These rebels, being native to Artoria, possessed the ability to find and infiltrate the location where Riujin was being held captive and effect his rescue. He personally endorsed this plan, and it was swiftly set into motion.

"Pay the Artoria rebels whatever sum they demand, Aiko," he instructed firmly. "If they can secure the return of my son, no price is too high."

A week had passed since the payment was made to the Artoria rebels for Riujin's retrieval, yet there had been no sign of progress.

During a council meeting, he turned to Aiko with a furrowed brow. "Why haven't we received any updates on your rebels, Aiko? Have they betrayed us?"

Aiko offered an explanation to him, stating that the rebels needed more time to infiltrate the Artorian army and locate Riujin safely. She requested patience from him and assured him that the results of her efforts would soon become evident. Reluctantly, he agreed to grant a few more days, though he emphasised that his patience was wearing thin.

As he prepared for another day with his council, the emperor took a moment to glance in the mirror. At sixty-three years old, he had always taken pride in his youthful appearance. However, in recent days, he couldn't help but notice the toll the situation with his son was taking on him. Dark circles under his eyes and newfound age marks now marred his once smooth complexion. He recognized them as signs of the mounting stress and anxiety he was experiencing.

Outside his dormitory, four guards stood ready to escort him to the council room. Beside them stood his personal protector, Rei Kazan, a skilled young female bushi warrior. Bushi warriors were trained separately from the rest of the Celen army. They were selected for their impressive skills with katanas and were appointed special jobs.

As they made their way along the walls of the Imperial Palace, he glimpsed a clear sky through the windows. Memories flooded back of mornings spent under the Sal Trees, indulging in delicious food with his beloved family. But those days were now a distant memory. With war raging at its peak, he knew he must devote every ounce of his being to the rescue of his son.

As the doors of the council room swung open, a large wooden table greeted him, adorned with six chairs—one for each council member, along with his own. He noticed that everyone was already seated, rising respectfully as he entered the room.

"The Emperor of Celen, Kazuma Saito," announced one of the guards, his voice resonating through the room.

The council members bowed reverently in acknowledgment of his presence, remaining standing until he had taken his seat. At his side stood Rei, firm in her vigilance.

As soon as everyone was seated, the doors of the council room opened once more, admitting a group of cooks bearing trays of food. Sushi, sashimi, tempura, nabe, sukiyaki, and sake adorned the table before them. The cooks deposited the dishes and silently withdrew.

Kazuma surveyed the array of food laid out before him, his thoughts drifting to his son, wondering if he was eating well wherever he was imprisoned. The realisation weighed heavily on him.

"My most valuable councillors. What news do we have today?" he asked, grabbing pieces of food and a glass full of sake. Everyone else waited for him to give the first bite to the food to start eating as well, which was the custom.

Haruki Kurogawa, second in command and Chancellor of Celen, began, "My Emperor, we have received news from various corners of the Lower Land. I defer to Aiko Hayashi to provide the details."

He turned his attention to Aiko, a middle-aged woman clad in traditional Celen attire adorned with green and yellow colours. Among the common folk, she was known as the "Queen of Gossips," rumoured to have informants scattered across every nation, or so it was said.

"Your Majesty, I will begin with a letter I received from the Crucible. According to my contacts, a crippled young girl arrived accompanied by a small army of villagers dressed in white garments adorned with yellow flowers. They brought ample provisions of food and water and distributed them to the needy in exchange for loyalty. Furthermore, reports indicate that this group is now marching southward, armed and singing songs of jubilation," said Aiko.

A sceptical murmur rippled through the council chamber as Yuto Tachibana, leader of commerce in Celen, voiced his doubts. "You're painting a picture of lunacy, Aiko. White clothes, yellow flowers, singing songs—it sounds more like fiction than fact," he remarked with a sceptical shake of his head.

Hana Arima, leader of commerce in Celen, interjected, "The news you bring is indeed peculiar, Aiko. The Crucible is known for drawing in eccentric characters, so we shouldn't dismiss this news lightly. Especially considering the recent demise of the Great Conclave of witches, it's conceivable that rogue witches will now act independently. They have a history of manipulating crowds, which fits the description of the crippled girl. We must remain vigilant of any potential threat this alleged army may pose to our lands."

Kazuma nodded in agreement with Hana's caution. "Let us dispatch a small company to the north. Instruct them to observe but not engage with this unusual group, and return with confirmation of their existence," he commanded. "Are there any other updates?" he inquired, turning his attention back to Aiko.

Aiko unfolded a second letter, showing a solemn expression. "We have received another message, this time from Lakefields, which I believe will be of interest to us all," she said. "King Larus Rikers has issued a warning, alerting us to the treachery of his brother and nephew, Holland and Hallard Rikers. He alleges that they have committed treason and may seek aid from other nations to usurp his throne."

General Kaito Hoshikawa scoffed. "The Lakefields folk are tearing each other apart—so why should we concern ourselves?" the general said sarcastically.

"We must not mock the misfortunes of others, Kaito," reproved Celen's Chancellor, Haruki Kurogawa. "It cannot be easy for King Larus to send such a message. Imagine if it were your own family plotting against you—how would you feel?"

Kaito brushed off Haruki's reprimand with a dismissive gesture.

He sighed, weary of the continuous stream of troubling news from foreign lands. "It is indeed regrettable news from Lakefields, but there is little we can do at present. Should Holland or Hallard Rikers seek our aid, we shall refuse them," he said firmly. "What other matters require our attention?" he inquired, turning to Aiko once again.

Aiko retrieved a third letter, this one bearing a seal. He recognized it as the seal of the King of the Golden Nation. "We have received a message from the Golden Nation. As it is sealed, Emperor, I shall leave it to you to open," she said, passing the letter into his hands.

As he broke the seal and unfolded the letter, he read its contents aloud to the council:

"Emperor Kazuma, the Shabrani Witches are attempting to bring their god back to the Lower Lands. The Golden Army is mobilising to Borraral to join forces, intending to march to the Shabrani Citadel in Gorgon in order to eradicate the Shabrani Witches entirely. I implore you to set aside your conflict with Artoria and instead lend your support to our cause. Send your entire army to Gorgon without delay. We anticipate your presence on the battlefield. Velaska has dispatched a delegation of Starr Witches to oversee the preparations, expected to arrive in Edo within a fortnight."

Yuto Tachibana, leader of economics, slammed his hand against the table in frustration. "This is unacceptable! The Golden King isn't asking for our assistance; he's demanding it. And to send Starr Witches into our territory after years of absence—it's an affront!" Yuto's anger was palpable.

Kazumi recognized Yuto's volatile temperament, though he often overlooked it. He silently wished for more composure, akin to that of Chancellor Haruki.

"The Golden Nation has aided us in the past, providing crucial resources to sustain our war effort against Artoria. It's only natural that they would seek something in return," Chancellor Haruki remarked calmly, attempting to diffuse the tension.

He sighed heavily, turning to Aiko with a glimmer of hope for an alternative perspective on the matter. "Do you have any insights from your contacts in the Golden Nation regarding this issue?" he inquired, eager for any additional information.

Aiko, who looked puzzled, shook her head. "Not on this matter, Emperor. It appears the Golden Nation has kept their plans tightly under wraps. The only news I've received from that region pertains to Echo territory—a powerful witch of unknown origin wreaking havoc and devastation, resulting in the deaths of many guards in the Castle of Whispers."

He dismissed the news as irrelevant in the current context. "Let us set aside the Golden Nation for now and revisit their request at a later time. Is there anything else requiring our attention?" he queried, addressing the council as a whole.

Chancellor Haruki carefully unfurled a series of scrolls, each depicting detailed observations of the sky. "Our meteorologists have made an intriguing discovery concerning the moon," he said, displaying a scroll adorned with diagrams and numerical notations that were beyond his full comprehension. Pointing to a small circle near the moon's portrait, Haruki explained, "This represents an object situated in front of the moon. Initially, it was minuscule and barely discernible to the naked eye, as depicted in this scroll from a week ago."

Haruki continued to display the subsequent scrolls, each one documenting the object's gradual enlargement. "Over the past few days, this object has grown significantly, now covering nearly ten percent of the moon's surface—resembling a second moon, a dark moon," Haruki elaborated.

"Emperor, we must investigate this phenomenon further," said leader of commerce, Hana Arima. "There may be historical records in our oldest scrolls that shed light on similar occurrences in the past."

Haruki nodded in agreement, presenting a weathered scroll that appeared ancient. "Indeed, I have already delved into our archives," said Haruki. "This scroll recounts a comparable phenomenon that occurred centuries ago, just before the onset of the Age of Ashes."

"Are you suggesting that we are on the brink of another Age of Ashes, as the Golden Nation claims?" General Kaito Hoshikawa's urgency pierced the tense atmosphere of the council chamber. "If that's the case, then the signs in the sky could indeed be linked to the Shabrani Witches' attempts to resurrect their god. Emperor, we cannot ignore this warning. Action must be taken," said Kaito, his tone resolute.

Kazuma's patience wore thin, and he rose to his feet, his voice ringing out in frustration. "I care not for these irrelevant speculations! My sole concern is the whereabouts of my son! Where is he?" he said, his demand echoing through the chamber, slicing through the tension as a blade.

Aiko rose from her seat and approached him. "Forgive me, Emperor," she pleaded, sinking to her knees before him. "There have been no updates from the rebels we enlisted. Based on my experience, I believe it would be prudent to wait one or two more days." Her voice carried a note of urgency and sincerity.

"Enough!" General Kaito Hoshikawa's voice thundered through the chamber, his eyes burning with intensity as they locked onto him. "Have you lost your senses? Failure to act will plunge us into a second Age of Ashes. If the old scrolls hold truth, our lands will become a hellish wasteland. Your son's capture must be set aside for now," said Kaito with anger.

"Rei," said Kazuma, his voice filled with authority.

In a swift motion, the bushi warrior, Rei, unsheathed her katana, moving as fluid as a prowling cat. With remarkable agility, she leapt onto the table and darted towards General Kaito with deadly intent. Anticipating Rei's attack, the general drew his own sword, bracing himself to deflect the imminent blow. The clash of metal rang out in the air, momentarily giving the impression that Kaito had successfully parried the strike. However, his sword shattered into pieces upon impact, leaving him defenceless against Rei's relentless assault. With a single, precise stroke, Rei's katana sliced through both metal and flesh effortlessly. The room was filled with the gruesome sight of Kaito losing his head to the merciless blow. Blood spilled in a crimson torrent across the council chamber.

Hana let out a piercing scream, her eyes wide with horror as she found herself covered in the splatter of Kaito's blood. Frozen in shock, she stared at the gruesome scene unfolding before her. Her hands were also trembling uncontrollably.

With deliberate steps, he approached the lifeless body of Kaito. His expression was steely as he raised the broken remnants of Kaito's sword. With a grim determination, he drove the broken blade into Kaito's body where his head should have been, a silent but chilling testament to his authority.

"I will make myself clear only once," he said, his voice laced with aggression as he turned to address the council. "I care not if the Lower Lands are consumed by flames. I care not if your loved ones suffer unspeakable fates. My son is, and always will be, my top priority. If anyone dares to challenge this decree, they will meet the same fate as this fool here. Understood?" His words hung heavy in the air, commanding obedience through fear and intimidation.

Everyone nodded, even Hana, who appeared to still be in a state of shock.

"Boom! Boom! Boom!" The door of the council room resonated like thunder.

"Who dares interrupt our council meeting?" he demanded. The guards in the Imperial Palace were well aware that the council meeting should not be interrupted.

The doors of the council room swung open wide.

"Rei," he said, signalling for the bushi warrior to be prepared to attack.

It was none other than his oldest daughter, Sakura Saito.

"Father, instruct Rei to cease threatening me with her katana. You all must hear what I have to say," said Sakura.

He disliked taking orders, especially from his daughter, whom he deemed not to be a proper lady. From a young age, Sakura showed more interest in swords and combat than in dolls and dance. Despite his scolding, Sakura never changed. At eighteen years old, Sakura's combat skills were relatively impressive, and she even commanded her own group of warriors known as the Shinobi. Though they were not permitted to participate in the war with Artoria, they dedicated their time to guard the cities in Celen.

"Father!" Sakura exclaimed loudly at the sight of Kaito's death. "Poor soul, the Hoshikawa family turned out to be a huge disappointment. Have you considered who will be the next General?" Sakura asked him.

He knew his daughter was eager to hold the title of General of the Celen army, hence her interest in the next appointment for general. However, he would never permit his own daughter to enter battle.

"That does not concern you, Sakura. What do you have to report? Speak quickly before I forget you are my daughter," he said with a menacing tone.

Sakura paced around the council room, casting her eyes over the other council members. "Father, a number of ships have been spotted in the distance. They are heading towards Hakata port. It could be an invasion, although our scouts cannot identify the ship models or the banners. They do not appear to belong to any nation in these lands," Sakura reported.

"Could they be from the Golden Nation?" asked Aiko, alluding to the Star Witches rumoured to arrive in Edo.

Sakura regarded Aiko with disdain. "As I said, the banners do not belong to any nation. Are you deaf?"

Aiko disregarded Sakura and addressed him directly. "The Star Witches could be employing a disguise."

"Why would they do that?" Sakura retorted sarcastically. "Besides, the scouts reported that the ships are double the size of normal vessels. If you ask me, the Daidarabotchi are returning to

Edo. We should prepare for battle."

The Daidarabotchi were legendary giants from tales passed down through generations. These stories, often recounted by elderly women to children, described these beings as colossal entities with the ability to shape the landscape with their immense strength. Despite their enormous size, they were depicted as benevolent and occasionally even helpful to humans.

Sakura can't possibly take those stories seriously, he thought.

"Haha!" Aiko chuckled. "Sakura and her vivid imagination are running wild today," she laughed.

Sakura then drew her katana, causing Aiko to startle and step back.

From the other side of the table, Rei approached with her katana in hand, advancing menacingly toward Sakura.

"Enough!" he screamed, feeling weary of the meaningless bickering. "This meeting ends now. We shall go to Hakata port and see what all the fuss is about."

Everyone nodded, stood up, and prepared to depart.

"Guards, clean up this mess immediately," he instructed the guards outside the council room, gesturing toward Kaito's lifeless body.

As the emperor and the others exited the Imperial Palace and boarded different carriages for the port, he gazed upon the marvellous city of Edo. Often confined within the walls of the palace, he sometimes forgot the prosperity that surrounded it. From the enchanting trees adorned with pink flowers to the bustling businesses and markets established by its citizens, Edo had flourished into one of the greatest cities in the known lands.

Despite the ongoing war that had drained resources for over a hundred years, the emperor and other leaders had managed to keep the nation of Celen and its citizens content. *The support from the Golden Nation has been crucial in maintaining the balance in the conflict with Artoria*, he reflected. Yet, beneath the surface, he couldn't shake the nagging question: *What were the true intentions of the Golden Nation in sending Starr Witches to Celen? It can't be anything good.*

His thoughts drifted to the war with Artoria—a conflict that his great-grandfather Tokugawa Saito had started more than a hundred years ago. It was said that the war began when Artoria attempted to conquer Celen land, specifically trying to take over the city of Akiya. On the other hand, he had heard that the people of Artoria believed the opposite: that Celen had tried to conquer Artoria by taking over the city of Arriaca. Religious beliefs also contributed to the conflict. Artoria encouraged its population to believe in Betatun, the god of War, and Ataecina, the goddess of the Underworld, while Celen's religion opposed them, portraying them as negative entities. Celen's deities were Tsukuyomi, the god of the Moon, and Amaterasu, the goddess of the Sun. In the past, his father Hideki Saito had tried to establish peace terms with Artoria, but they were not well received. Even during his own reign, he attempted to make peace with Artoria, but to no avail. *Blood seemed to be the only way*, he thought.

The port of Edo, Hakata, lay relatively close to the Imperial Palace. By the time they arrived at the port, the sun hung high in the sky, beginning its descent. As the door of his carriage opened, the wind carried the scent of dead fish and saltwater. He observed that only a handful of citizens had gathered to receive him, which struck him as odd. In times past, hundreds would turn out to welcome him.

Rei and the rest of his guards walked beside him. While behind him, his daughter Sakura and the rest of the council followed closely.

He noticed someone approaching to walk beside him—Haruki Kurogawa, his trusted advisor and chancellor. Haruki was known for his diligence, holding his role in higher esteem than his own life, for which Kazuma was grateful.

"Emperor, pardon the interruption, but we must discuss the next candidate for General of the Celen Army," Haruki said urgently. "The commanders will need to meet him sooner rather than later, I'm afraid. Many decisions must be made."

He acknowledged that he needed to select the next general, a responsibility he did not need reminding of. However, Haruki's urgency was warranted; the ongoing war with Artoria demanded daily meetings and swift decision-making. There had to be a general at all times.

"Isn't there a third Hoshigawa brother? Talk to him immediately to take the role of the next General," he ordered, recognizing the need for swift action.

Haruki appeared to still have other concerns.

"What is it?" he inquired, noting the lingering worry in Haruki's expression.

"The matter of Kaito's death, what should we say?" Haruki asked nervously.

Kazuma halted his steps to face Haruki directly. As he paused, the rest of the company also came to a standstill. "He died for insubordination, that is what you must say," he said firmly. With that, Haruki departed from his presence.

They continued walking until he caught sight of a multitude of hundreds of people, all blocking the entry to the port.

"What is happening?" he inquired.

"Emperor, it appears that the unidentified ships have arrived at our shores. The citizens of Edo have gathered to witness their arrival," reported one of the guards.

He was left astounded. "How is this possible? Why wasn't anyone able to intercept them before they reached our shores?" he exclaimed angrily to the guard.

"I commanded them to allow the ships to pass," said his daughter, Sakura.

He glared at Sakura with anger. "You did what?!" he screamed at her, losing his patience.

"If they were our enemies, they would have attacked our fishing boats. Trust me, Father, whoever is on board, they are not our enemies," Sakura reassured him.

Fuelled by anger and impatience, he raised his hand, poised to slap his daughter, when suddenly the people of Edo lining the shore began to shout, "A monster! No, a siren! Wait, she's a woman!"

He turned to face the crowd, noticing that they were all pointing at something in the distance.

Setting aside his anger towards his daughter, he began to stride toward the crowd, with his council and guards following closely behind.

"Clear the way!" the guards shouted, pushing through the crowd to create a path for him to walk unhindered. It took some time for the guards to make space, but eventually, he was able to move through the multitude, with his council following behind. As the citizens realised his presence, they began to welcome him. *A bit late for that*, he thought to himself. Nonetheless, he acknowledged his citizens with a salute, demonstrating grace as was customary.

As the shore came into view, he glimpsed them: ten colossal blue battleships. They were crafted in a peculiar manner, showing signs of struggle with slight evident damage. On top of one of the battleships, there was a figure moving. He strained his eyes. Gradually, the figure came into focus, and he discerned a woman wearing a robe. Her long blue hair whipped wildly in the strong wind.

"Who is that? Has anyone inspected the interiors of these monstrosities?" he inquired.

Sakura approached and knelt before him. "Father, no one has boarded the ships. Following my instructions, I commanded that upon the ships' arrival at our shores, we wait for your orders," she said respectfully.

"Very well. Bring the cannons to the port immediately and destroy those battleships. There's no time to waste on this matter; we must focus on more pressing concerns," he said, referring to the urgent need to rescue his son.

"Father, you must be joking. We should explore those battleships and discover who that woman is. There could be wonders awaiting us. The Daidarabotchi..."

He interrupted her, "I am tired of your tales, you foolish girl," he reprimanded his daughter.

"Emperor, it would be unwise to act hastily. We must ensure that these ships are not connected to the Golden Nation and their message to us. The mysterious woman could be part of the Starr clan delegation," leader of diplomacy, Aiko, said to him with a timid voice.

Then, a bright blue light emanated from one of the battleships, precisely from where the mysterious woman had been standing. After a few seconds, the light vanished, and so did the mysterious woman.

What was that? he thought to himself.

"Sakura, take your men and board those battleships. Be quick about it," he ordered his daughter, who promptly ran down to the shore with a group of her own men. After witnessing the bright blue light, he decided against blowing up the battleships. He was now almost certain that the mysterious woman was a witch.

It took some time for Sakura to board one of the colossal battleships. In the meantime, he ordered the guards to bring chairs and umbrellas to provide shade as they waited. They also brought food and sake to keep everyone in the council comfortable during the wait.

"Pardon me, Emperor, but I have been called for an emergency. I'll be back soon," said Aiko. As the leader of diplomacy in Celen, he understood that Aiko had to handle problems throughout the day. He didn't inquire further and allowed her to leave.

After a while, one of Sakura's men returned and addressed him, "Emperor, lady Sakura sent me. She requests your presence inside the battleships."

What nonsense, he thought.

He then stood up and reprimanded the messenger, "I will decide whether I go or not. Now, tell me what you have seen inside the ship?" he asked firmly.

"Giants, Emperor. There are sleeping giants in blue armour—at least fifty of them," the messenger said, clearly excited about the news.

He was shocked by what he was hearing. He decided it was best to see for himself. Leaving the rest of the council on shore, he took Rei and some guards with him. On his way to the ship, he asked the messenger sent by his daughter, "What about that mysterious woman?"

"We could not find her, Emperor," replied the messenger.

He didn't inquire further. *Strange things are happening today*, he thought to himself.

He boarded a small boat which took him to the side of the colossal blue battleship where his men had already set up stairs for him to climb onto the gigantic vessel. Despite his age, he didn't struggle ascending the stairs. In his youth, he had been an active warrior, and even now, he occasionally participated in combat classes with his subordinates. He recalled his father's advice: *In times of war, even the emperor should be prepared to fight. Always stay in shape; you never know when you will need to wield your own sword.*

Inside the battleship, he could see parts of the damaged structure, with pieces of blue wood scattered about, evidence of a previous battle. And then, he saw the proof he needed to believe in the existence of giants: a chair as large as an adult man. *Impossible! They are real*, he meditated, stunned by the sight.

"This way, Emperor," said the messenger, leading the way.

They walked down a long corridor and descended a set of stairs. The stairs were double the size of normal stairs, and he had some trouble descending, requiring assistance. They entered a dimly illuminated room, lit only by fire torches held by Sakura's men. He spotted his daughter inside the chamber.

"Father, look over there," she pointed to the back of the room.

The room was larger than he had anticipated. At the back of the room, there were three levels accessible via stairs. On each level, he saw the massive humanoid figures of the giants. They were, as the messenger had said, sleeping next to each other. Clad in blue armour and helmets, it was impossible to tell whether they were male or female.

"Incredible, they are truly Daidarabotchi from the tales," he said, still surprised by the discovery.

"Father, it seems they won't wake up. They could be under a spell," said Sakura, voicing her concern.

While his daughter may have been interested in learning more about the giants, he saw these events as an opportunity to shift the tide of the war with Artoria and retrieve his son. "We must find a way to awaken them and harness these giants for our advantage in the war," he said.

"Emperor Kazuma!" Suddenly, someone screamed his name. He noticed it was a member of Haruki's team, identifiable by the clothes he was wearing.

"What is it?" he asked, annoyed by the interruption.

"Master Haruki sent me. It's Renjiro, the youngest of the Hoshikawa brothers. He has sparked a revolution following the death of his brother. Master said Renjiro has seized the Imperial Palace and rallied all the commanders to his cause," said the messenger, breathing heavily, likely having run as fast as he could to deliver the news.

Next to him, Rei drew her katana.

A civil war, he thought, his expression displaying anger and concern. Then, he looked at his daughter, "Find a way to wake the giants, now!" he ordered urgently.

ELIOT

Three days had passed since Marli entered a cave hidden within the ruins of an ancient city atop the Glacier Crown. He learned that she needed to undergo some sort of a test before meeting the translators they were seeking. He didn't have a chance to say goodbye to Marli, as he had been unconscious for some time. When he finally woke up, he was startled to find two men dressed entirely in black robes, with only their faces visible, marked by strange white glyphs. They informed him of Marli's whereabouts, telling him they would wait for her to return from the cave—or until she failed the test which would mean her death.

"How will you know if she fails the test?" he asked his companions.

"Your friend carries a torch with a special blue flame," one of the men explained, gesturing toward the firepit in front of them. "This firepit is ignited by the same special wood used to make the torch, and the flames are connected. If the firepit goes out, it means the torch your friend is carrying has also extinguished, signalling her demise."

Eliot couldn't help but wonder what would happen to him if Marli died inside the cave. *Would these men help me return to the Frostwild Towns?* he thought.

He quickly realised that his companions were not inclined to talk much. Eliot was naturally curious and outspoken, but despite asking many questions, his companions often remained silent.

"Who are you? Why do you have those glyphs on your faces? Are you the translators Marli is looking for?" He asked many questions, but they remained unanswered.

He also noticed that his companions didn't eat. He set out to hunt with his bow and arrows and was surprised to find wild rabbits and deer scattered around. He brought back a few rabbits and cooked them over the firepit. When he tried to share the food with his companions, they refused to eat.

"Our bodies are not to eat for another seven days," one of his companions finally said after his persistent offering.

Water wasn't difficult to find either. Nearby, Eliot discovered a frozen lake. Having been born and raised in a land of ice and snow, he knew exactly how to extract water from the icy surface. Using his knife, he carved out chunks of ice from the lake and carried them back to the firepit, where he melted them into drinkable water.

"Here, have some water," he offered to his companions after pouring the water he had melted into a satchel he carried at his belt.

Both his companions looked at him with sour expressions, and he thought they would refuse again. To his surprise, they accepted the water.

"You are a kind boy, but you shouldn't be. We are not your guards, nor are we here for you. Our only purpose is to wait for your friend's outcome. You just happened to be here as well. You owe us nothing," said one of his companions.

Despite the harsh words, he was glad they were finally talking to him.

"I gathered as much. Sharing is part of my nature. Back in my village, I tried to help everyone I could, whether they were foe or friend. Some think I'm a nuisance, others believe I'm making a difference. But in reality, I just follow what my head and heart tell me to do," he said with a hearty smile.

Both men looked at each other in silence. A howl from a nearby wolf caught the attention of his companions.

He tried to catch their attention again. "My name is Eliot Frig, by the way. What are your names?" he asked.

There was no response.

Suddenly the fire from the firepit started flickering and dancing in an abnormal way.

"Oh no, Marli. What's happening?" he asked, his voice filled with worry for his friend.

"Your friend is having some sort of trouble; perhaps the torch she carries is about to expire," said one of his companions, showing no emotion.

Eliot clenched his hands tightly while watching the flickering fire. He wanted to believe Marli would succeed in her mission. He recalled the time he met the Dragani witch. Marli had been a friend to his mother before her passing. Many days, he would see Marli at his house, enjoying a cup of tea and chatting with his mother. As he grew up, he learned that Marli and two other witches had fled from Echo long ago after the Golden Nation nearly wiped out their clan. They had found a new home in the Frostwild Towns. One of the witches, known as Ma'am, was very old and wise. Eliot disliked her for the most part because she was always reprimanding him, but he still listened intently whenever she told stories from her past.

On the other hand, Marli always treated him well. Even when he was stubborn with his questions, she knew how to be kind to him. After his mother died from a mysterious illness, Marli took care of him—feeding him, dressing him, and comforting him during the sleepless nights. Her presence made the loss of his mother much easier to bear, and he was always grateful for it.

Eventually, Eliot learned that the three Dragani Witches had come to the Frostwild Towns not only to seek refuge but also to find a translator they believed was hidden in the Glacier Crown. One of the witches had travelled to the Glacier Crown but never returned, leading them to believe she had died. After some time, the Ma'am instructed Marli to travel to the Glacier Crown to follow the path of the missing witch and find the translators. Upon hearing this, Eliot didn't hesitate and volunteered to accompany Marli. The Ma'am didn't object; in fact, she supported his decision, thinking it would be beneficial for Marli to have a squire. Although Marli initially resisted travelling with him, he had a way of getting what he wanted.

The fire continued to flicker and dance for a while before it began to wane and slowly extinguish.

"No!" he screamed.

"It looks like your friend won't make it. You should start considering your next move, boy," said one of his companions.

Eliot paid him no mind, remaining focused on the firepit. Tears began to stream down his face as he watched the fire slowly diminishing.

"Eliot Frig, was it? You could join our order; I think you'd be a valuable addition," said one of his companions.

"Your order?" he asked.

"Our order, known as The Order of Eon, has existed for a very long time. Our ancestors established it even before the War of Ashes. Our mission is to eliminate anyone or anything that attempts to start another War of Ashes without our permission," said one of them.

"I am Barr, and he is Lumien. We don't use family names; we left them behind when we joined the order. From what I can see, there is no place for you in this world. If you try to return to your village, you'll only get lost in the snowstorm and die. So, what do you say, Eliot? Will you join us?" said Barr.

Eliot was intrigued by their order. *How could the old witch have never mentioned them in her stories?* he wondered.

"The old witch spoke of the Great Conclave, a group of witches who oversee the clans to prevent another War of Ashes. How is your order different from theirs?" he asked.

"Haha!" Lumien laughed. "The witch clans cannot be trusted. They are deceitful and treacherous. Our order is perfect, and only men and women of the highest calibre may join, with the blessing of our great leader, who was born even before the War of Ashes. Besides, the Great Conclave is no more; only we can prevent another War of Ashes," said Lumien.

The news that the Great Conclave no longer existed took him by surprise.

"The War of Ashes ended six hundred years ago. No man can live that long," he said.

"Our leader is no ordinary man; he wields powerful magic. If you come with us and seek to join our order, you'll have the chance to meet him," said Lumien.

Suddenly, the fire in the firepit erupted, growing into a towering blaze.

"Impossible", exclaimed Barr.

"What is happening?" he asked with curiosity.

"Your friend has done the impossible, she has passed the test," said Barr in a serious tone.

Eliot screamed with joy. He quickly grabbed the leather bag with the manuscripts and his belongings while his companions extinguished the fire. Before departing, he saw a few wolves watching them from a distance, almost as if they were keeping guard.

"Pay them no mind; those wolves aren't dangerous. You need to watch out for the big ones, though," said Lumien. He dismissed Lumien's comment about the wolves; his excitement about Marli was greater.

They then descended a narrow, snowy path until they reached the ruins of an ancient, abandoned city. The ruins were larger than he had imagined. They walked past half-destroyed stone houses buried in snow and ice. He noticed the houses were unusually large. Along the way, he spotted wild rabbits, reindeer, and owls. As they approached the other side of the ruins, the wind grew stronger. Despite his fur-lined clothes made of wolf and bear, he could still feel the cold biting at his skin.

"Keep walking, boy. If you're going to join us, you'll need to get used to the cold weather," said Barr.

I haven't decided to join you yet, he thought. While staying with Marli seemed appealing, he knew he would eventually need to follow his own path. The idea of joining an order with such an important mission resonated with his principles and nature. He thought that becoming a member of Barr's order might be his next step.

In the distance, he saw a tall tower, ruined by the harsh weather and covered with snow. The tower was situated on a hill, and beneath it, a small cave was visible. The entrance to the cave was partially blocked by stones and ice, with only a narrow opening left through which one could pass. This opening was so small and dark that it could easily be missed if not seen up close.

"We must wait here," said Lumien.

They stopped at the entrance of the cave. As Eliot looked around at the ruins, he could hardly believe that people had once built a city in such harsh weather.

"What a terrible place to build a city," he commented.

"The inhabitants of this city probably didn't mind the snow and cold wind. It is said the Primes could withstand weather like this," said Barr.

He recalled stories about the Primes from the Ma'am. The old witch had told him that they were the ancestors of humanity who vanished completely right after the War of Ashes. There was little information about their current whereabouts, but it was said they could be as tall as Borraral trees and possess the strength of polar bears.

"What is this cave?" he asked.

Barr and Lumien exchanged glances and nodded. It seemed that Eliot had earned their confidence.

"We call it Skadi's Rest Cavern. We believe the Primes used to practise magic and rituals inside this cave. Even now, magic lingers strongly in this cold place," said Lumien.

Eliot was intrigued by the idea of the Primes practising magic. The old witch had never mentioned this; he had always thought only witches could perform such practices.

"The Primes surely had women. Were they the ones practising magic?" he asked.

"We believe that before the War of Ashes, witches weren't the only ones who could wield magic. Men could also work with the elements. Something happened before and during the War of Ashes that caused men to lose the power to wield magic," explained Barr.

The information from Barr and Lumien captured his full attention.

While he was contemplating his next question, he heard footsteps coming from inside the cave. A figure emerged from the darkness, fully covered from head to toe in an old black cloth. As the figure stepped into the light and removed the cloth, he was surprised to see Marli's familiar face. However, she looked much older, with her hair having changed from the black colour he remembered to a dull grey.

"Water!" Marli murmured. And then, she collapsed to the ground.

He quickly ran towards her, clutching his leather satchel full of water. He gently lifted Marli's head with his arm and pressed the satchel to her lips. Her eyes suddenly opened, and she began drinking the water rapidly.

"Thank you," said Marli with a smile, her eyes distant, as if she were lost in thought.

"Marli! What happened to you? We've been waiting for you to come out of the cave," Eliot said.

At the mention of the word "cave," Marli's eyes widened with fear. She glanced toward the entrance and began to back away, her face clearly marked by terror. Eliot realised that whatever she had encountered inside had left a profound and disturbing effect on her. *Maybe it was best not to mention it again*, he thought.

"Dragani witch, we congratulate you. No one has ever left Skadi's Rest Cavern alive—until now," Barr said.

Marli shot him a look of pure anger.

"Look at what that cursed place has done to me. I feel as though I've aged a hundred years," she said, pointing to her face and hair. Wrinkles had formed around her eyes and cheeks, signs of ageing. Just days ago, she had appeared as a young witch in her twenties. Eliot was stunned by how much she had changed in such a short time.

"No matter your physical form, it's what you've learned and endured that truly matters," Lumien said.

Suddenly, Marli's eyes blazed with fury. She raised her arms toward Barr and Lumien, chanting words Eliot couldn't understand. Barr and Lumien were lifted off the ground, their hands clutching their throats as they struggled to breathe. Eliot realised Marli was casting a spell on them.

"Stop, Marli! Stop! You mustn't use spells. The Great Conclave might find out and take your head," he pleaded, grabbing her by the waist, trying to break her focus.

"In that cursed cave, I learned things—about the past and the present. If what I've seen is true, the members of the Great Conclave have been assassinated by wolves with long fangs. There's no one left to stop us Dragani Witches from using powerful magic," she said, her determination only intensifying her spell.

"That's not the point. You could kill innocent people. That's not what your magic is meant for," Eliot urged, desperate to reason with her.

Abruptly, Marli stopped her spell. Barr and Lumien collapsed to their knees, gasping and coughing.

"I'm sorry. I haven't been myself lately. You don't understand— I've seen true terror these past few days," Marli said, her voice softening with apology.

"You are excused," Barr said between coughs. "We are only here to guide you through this painful process. Don't worry about us—we can be replaced at any time."

Eliot was taken aback by their dedication to their order.

Suddenly, Marli turned to look at him. It was, in fact, the first time she had met his eyes directly since she left Skadi's Rest Cavern. Her gaze penetrated his, as though she was searching for something deeper.

"Who are you, boy?" Marli asked.

He shook his head in disbelief. *How could she not recognize me?* he thought.

"It's me, Eliot. Don't you recognize me?" he said gently.

Without warning, Marli grabbed a knife from her belt and slashed at his throat. If not for Barr pulling him aside, he would have been dead. Only a few drops of blood dripped from his neck. He realised the blade had barely grazed the surface of his skin.

"Marli, why?" he screamed, tears streaming down his face.

"You! YOU! You are one of them, one of the Apocryphos. The Third is within your soul, boy. Haven't you noticed it? Something inside you dictating your every move? But how could you? You're just an annoying little brat. Open your eyes! The Third who lives within you is defying fate. You must die—your kind will only bring calamity to the Lower Lands!" Marli shouted aggressively.

He struggled to believe what was happening before his eyes. His dearest friend, the one who cared for him more than anyone in the Lower Lands, wanted to kill him. He refused to accept this bitter reality. Summoning all his courage, he ran toward Marli, hoping to hug her, hoping she would forget about killing him. Barr stopped him, grabbing his arm.

"If the Dragani witch is right, then you must die," said Barr, drawing his own knife.

Before Eliot could react, something landed between him and Barr. At first, all he saw was black and white fur, then he realised it was a massive wolf—its size rivalled a bear. He recalled Lumien had mentioned something about big wolves.

The wolf turned to face Eliot, Barr's arm in its jaws—the same arm that had been holding the knife. Barr's screams filled the air, blood gushing from the stump of his right arm.

The wolf spat Barr's arm to the ground and began to vibrate in a peculiar way. In a few moments, the wolf was gone, replaced by a woman draped in a wolf pelt, with large fangs attached to her wrists. He assumed the fangs were her chosen weapons.

"Run north, to the nearest forest. Take this with you," the mysterious woman said, handing him the bag of manuscripts he and Marli had brought to Glacier Crown, hoping to find a translator.

He wanted to ask questions, but Marli had started chanting something unintelligible in the distance. Suddenly, large ice blocks from the ground began levitating, forming sharp arrows. *Gravital magic—the specialty of the Dragani Witches*, he remembered. The Ma'am had told him that Dragani Witches could manipulate gravity around objects and even people.

"We can exert gravitational pressure on objects and reshape them at will. It is an ancient ability we were once allowed to wield freely. After the fall of our Great Council and the near extinction of our kind, the Great Conclave forbade us from practising such magic. They call it the Third Cardinal Sin. I still don't understand why we were punished—aren't the First and Second Cardinal Sins far worse?" the Ma'am had said.

Two ice arrows shot forward, piercing the mysterious woman's right shoulder and left leg.

"Argh!" she screamed in pain.

Eliot wanted to help, but she pushed him away. "You must go now! There are others like me in the forest—they will protect you. The Order must not get hold of these manuscripts. Guard them with your life!" she urged.

She began to vibrate again, transforming back into the enormous wolf. As Eliot ran north toward the nearby forest, the last thing he saw was the wolf charging Marli with a ferocious growl.

The snowstorm intensified, and the forest soon vanished from his sight. Walking became difficult as the snow deepened, slowing him down. He trudged aimlessly for a few moments, then felt the ground give way beneath him—he had slipped off the edge of a cliff. He screamed as he plunged into a freezing lake below. The cold was so intense, he could feel it in his bones, but he knew he had to swim up fast. After what seemed an eternity, he broke the surface, gasping for air.

"A cave!" he exclaimed.

It seemed he had entered a cave. He looked up, but all he could see was darkness.

Then he remembered the manuscripts. Thankfully, the bag was still attached to him, though it was soaked. He swam to the shore, careful not to let the manuscripts get wetter. Once on solid ground, he opened the bag—most of the manuscripts were drenched.

"No, no, no..." he muttered in panic, fearing they were ruined.

As he examined them one by one, he saw the ink dissolving into faint remnants. Panic gripped him, but something told him to try drying the manuscripts near a fire. *Something inside you dictating your every move?* Marli's words echoed in his mind.

He gathered stones and wood from an old tree, likely fallen into the cave long ago, and used his childhood skills to start a fire. He placed the manuscripts near the flames and stripped off his wet clothes to dry himself, hoping not to catch a cold.

For a while, he watched the manuscripts dry, though most of the writing seemed lost. He was on the verge of cursing his fate when something extraordinary happened—the dissolved ink began to move, reshaping itself into letters again.

"Magic!" he gasped. The manuscripts must have been enchanted—perhaps by Marli, in case of disaster.

"Now I just need to find a way out of this cave," he thought.

Suddenly, he heard a scream from above. Something fell into the lake with a splash. Fearful, Eliot hid behind a large ice-covered rock. He watched as a figure emerged from the water—smaller than the large wolf he had seen earlier, but still a wolf. The figure vibrated and transformed into a young woman with wolf pelts draped over her back and fangs on her wrists.

"Come out. I followed the elder and saw you fall. You've got something important, don't you?" the young woman called.

For a moment, Eliot hesitated—he wasn't sure he could trust her. But something inside him urged him to trust her. *Maybe there is something inside me, just like Marli said*, he thought.

"My name is Eliot. What's yours?" he asked as he stepped out from behind the rock.

The young woman smiled. "There you are. My name is Arine. I'm here to protect you."

Eliot looked her over. She was skinny, not at all threatening, except for the fangs on her wrists. She seemed about his age. He felt a little underwhelmed by his protector.

"Oh, don't look at me like that, boy. I'm as dangerous as any Alpha wolf. Now, follow me!" she commanded.

And so, he did. What other choice did he have?

MAPS

See the Apocrypha maps in full colour and high definition at
https://henrydoes.com/books/apocrypha/maps

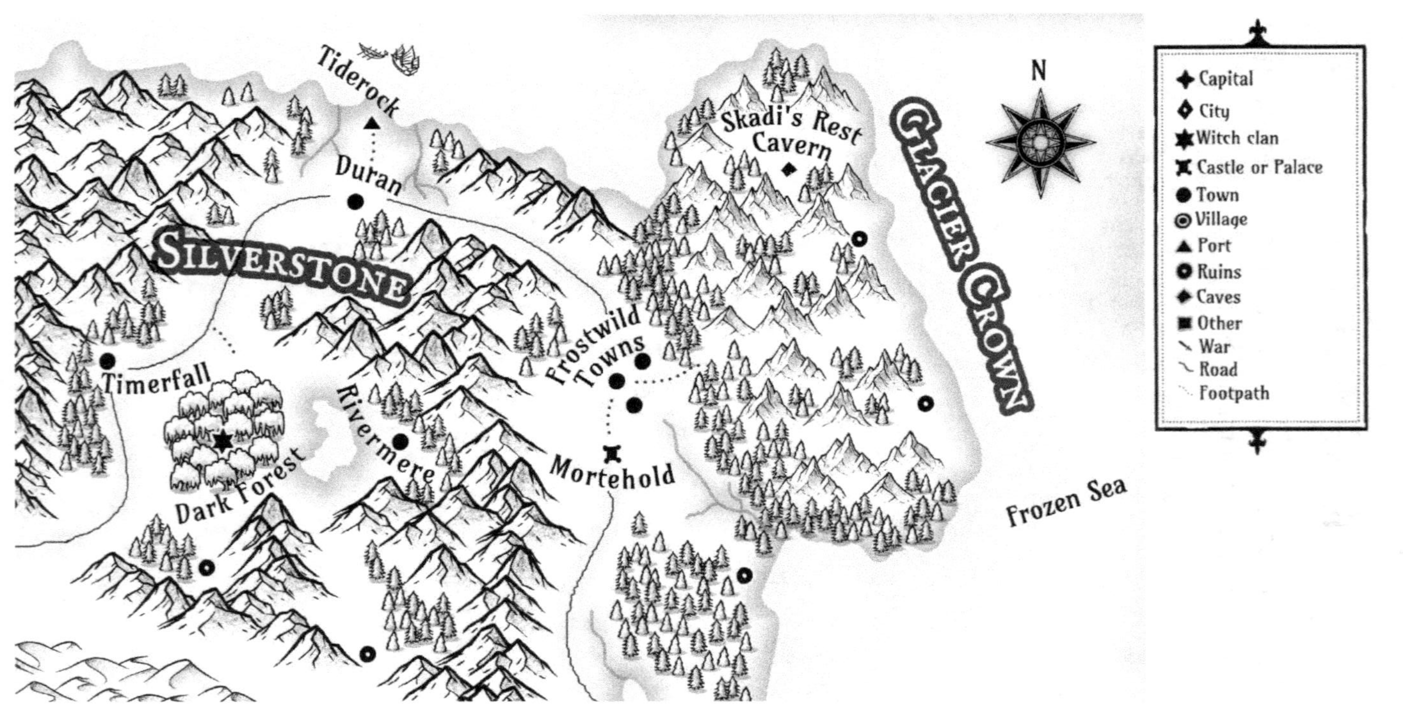
N
Tiderock
Skadi's Rest Cavern
GLACIER CROWN
Duran
SILVERSTONE
Frostwild Towns
Timerfall
Rivermere
Mortehold
Dark Forest
Frozen Sea
Capital
City
Witch clan
Castle or Palace
Town
Village
Port
Ruins
Caves
Other
War
Road
Footpath

Capital
City
Witch clan
Castle or Palace
Town
Village
Port
Ruins
Caves
Other
War
Road
Footpath
Sea of Casda
Cascade
Rivercrash
The Passing
Blue Bell Mountains
Rivermouth
Springres
LAKEFIELDS
River West Villages
Branchwater
N

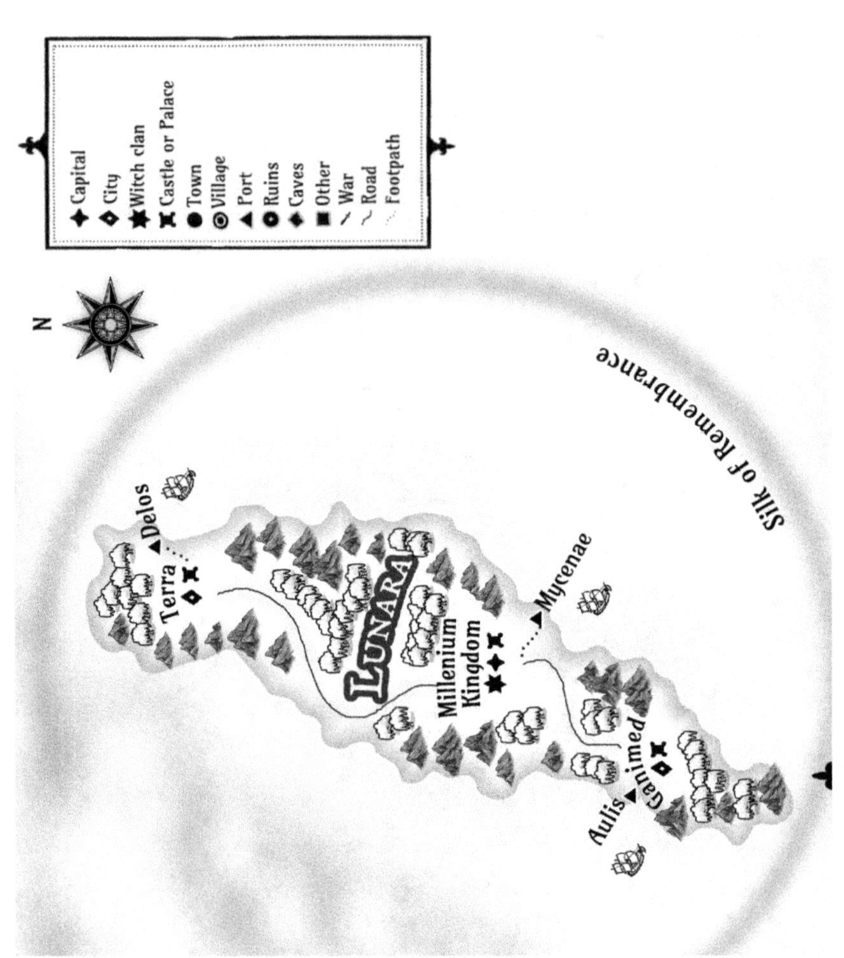

Capital
City
Witch clan
Castle or Palace
Town
Village
Port
Ruins
Caves
Other
War
Road
Footpath
N
Silk of Remembrance
Delos
Terra
Lunara
Mycenae
Millenium Kingdom
Ganimed
Aulis

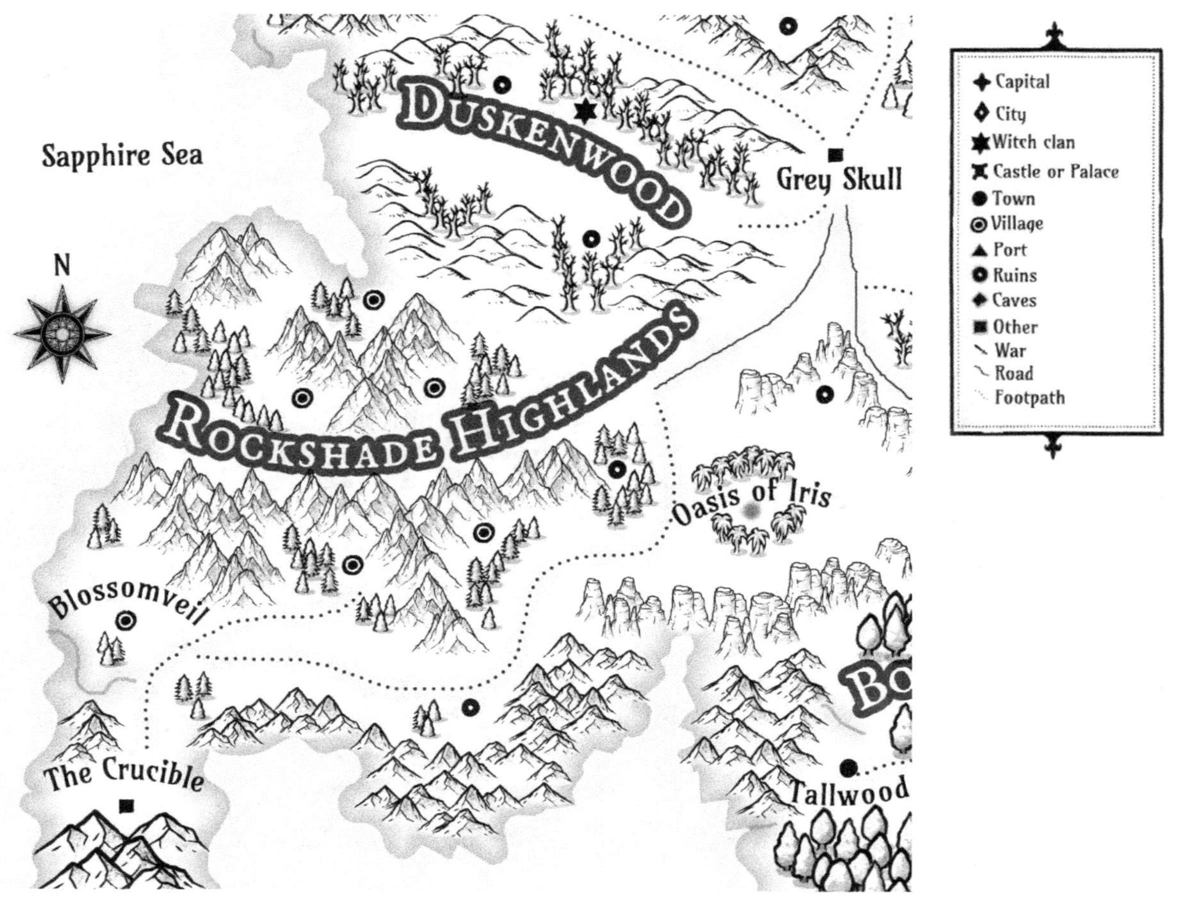

Sapphire Sea
N
DUSKENWOOD
Grey Skull
ROCKSHADE HIGHLANDS
Oasis of Iris
Blossomveil
The Crucible
Bo
Tallwood
Capital
City
Witch clan
Castle or Palace
Town
Village
Port
Ruins
Caves
Other
War
Road
Footpath

Capital
City
Witch clan
Castle or Palace
Town
Village
Port
Ruins
Caves
Other
War
Road
Footpath
GORGON
SILENT DUNES
GOLDEN NATION
BORRARAL
Azure Sea
N
Grey Skull
Oasis of Set
Oasis of Kal
Volcano Dukkah
Shabrani Citdel
Oasis of Iris
Oasis of Ram
Echo
Driftport
Dazzglen
The Junction
Goldentide
Tallwood
Barral
Sunreach
Treerise
Goldspire
Solaris
Windfall
Sylvanport
Grimwater docks
Mater

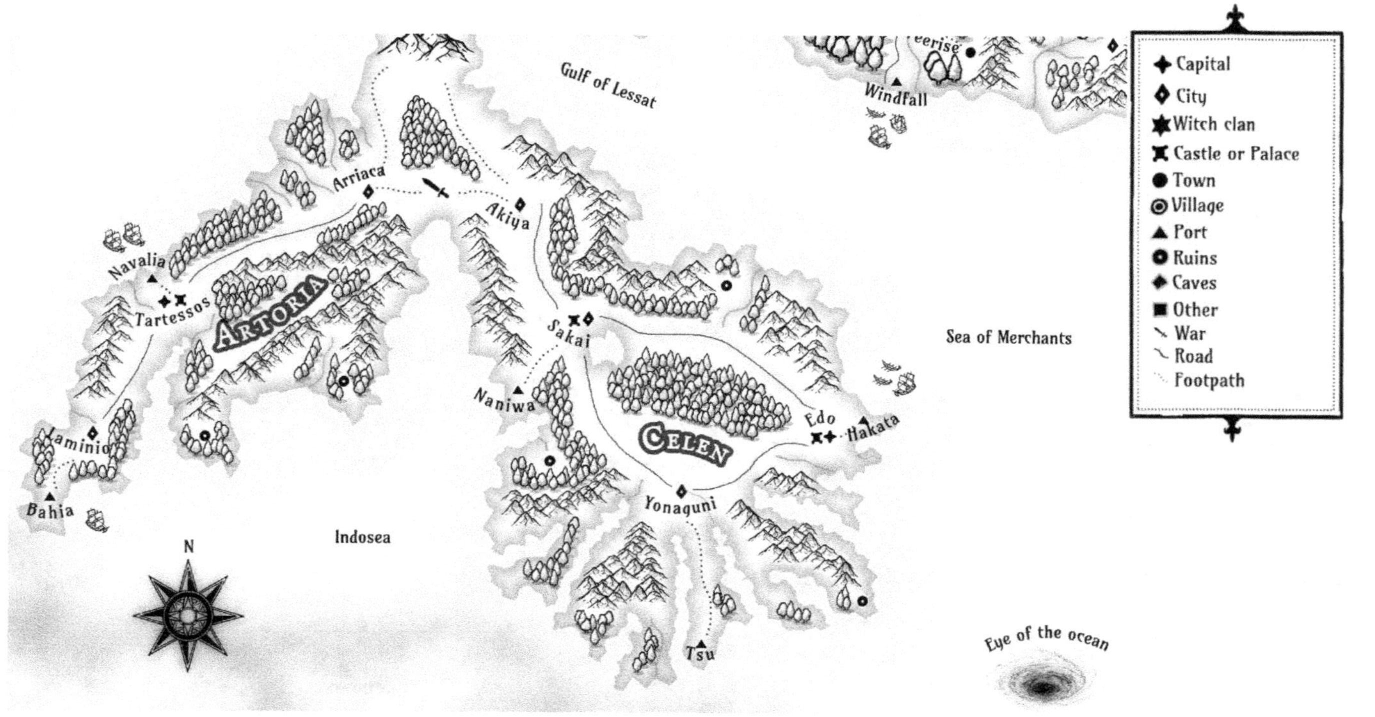

Capital
City
Witch clan
Castle or Palace
Town
Village
Port
Ruins
Caves
Other
War
Road
Footpath
Eerise
Windfall
Gulf of Lessat
Sea of Merchants
Arriaca
Akiya
Navalia
Tartessos
ARTORIA
Sakai
Naniwa
CELEN
Edo
Hakata
Laminio
Bahia
Yonaguni
Tsu
Indosea
Eye of the ocean
N

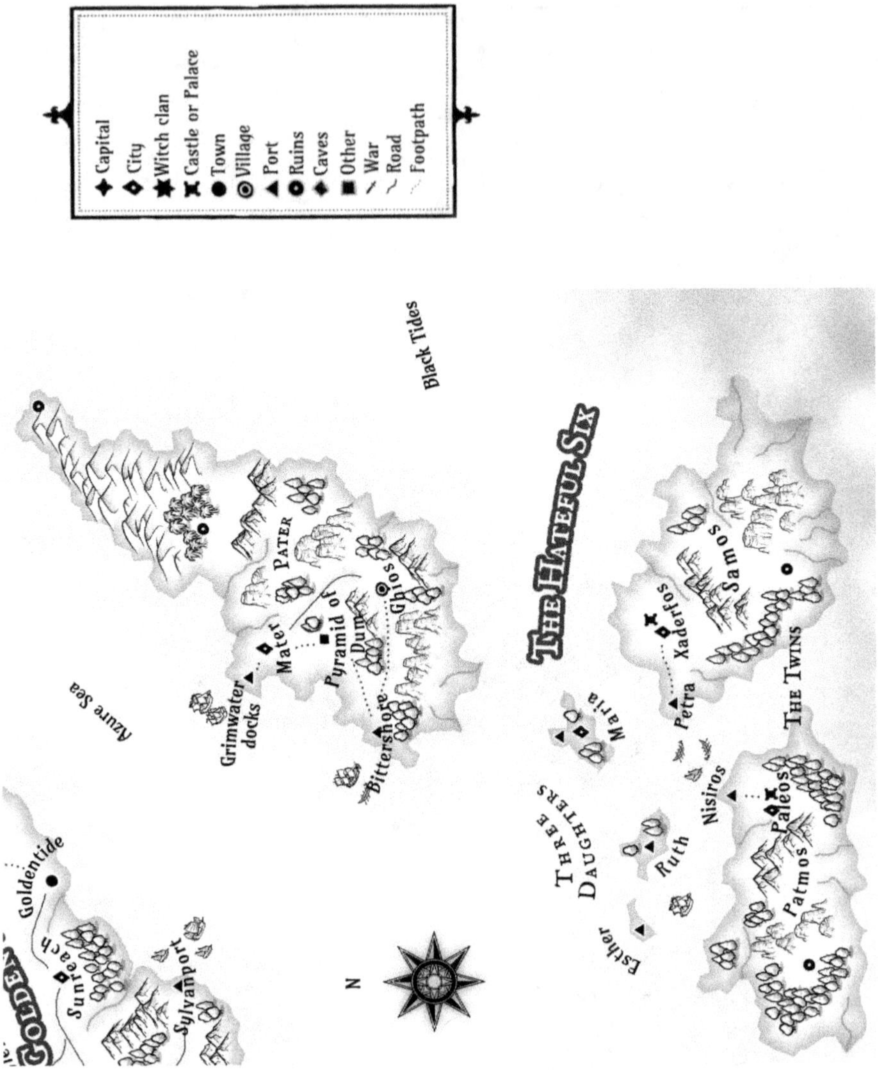

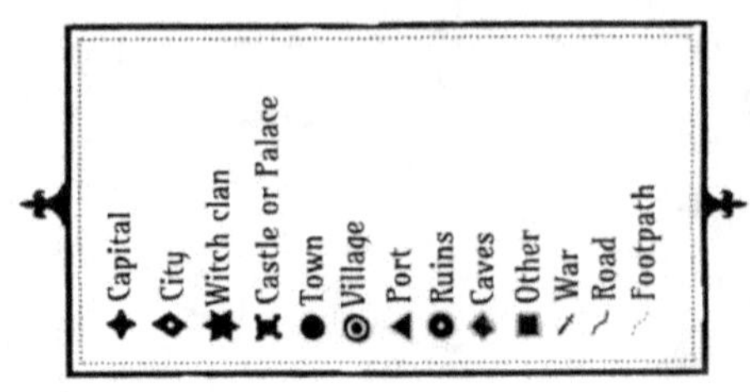

Capital
City
Witch clan
Castle or Palace
Town
Village
Port
Ruins
Caves
Other
War
Road
Footpath

Black Tides
THE HATEFUL SIX
Azure Sea
PATER
Mater
Grimwater docks
Pyramid of Dum
Ghios
Bittershore
Goldentide
GOLDEN
Sunreach
Sylvanport
Samos
Xaderfos
Petra
Marla
THREE DAUGHTERS
Ruth
Esther
Nisiros
Paleos
Patmos
THE TWINS
N

AUTHOR BIO

Henry A. Salas, also known as "Henry Does," is an emerging author with a passion for crafting dark fantasy horror tales that delve into the eerie and unknown. Drawing inspiration from classic horror literature, mythology, and the shadowy recesses of the human mind, Henry builds immersive worlds brimming with ancient curses, forbidden magic, and haunting creatures.

Currently, he has published his debut novel, *Apocrypha Act I*, aiming to captivate readers with a gripping narrative that delves into themes of fear, power, and the thin line between reality and nightmare.

When not writing, Henry enjoys exploring abandoned places, reading gothic fiction, and indulging in a good horror film.